*"I would like to dedicate this novel
to my husband, Ken, the love of my life,
and to my loving family"*

❖

Thanks also to my editor, Roy Robins, without whom I would not have been able to complete my novels.

A resounding Thank You to Toby Meyer for providing such stunning artwork for the covers of both of my books, and for being the first friend to read my novels and love them!

Sincere thanks to Nigel Dickson, who assisted me in uploading my novels to Amazon and with the design of the books.
His computer-savvy, knowledge, and patience were invaluable.

And finally, a heartfelt Thank You to my readers, each and every one of you. If one of the places or spaces described in my novel feels very different, or even at odds with, your personal experience of it, feel free to preserve your own experience of that place or space.

This novel is just that, a novel. Names, characters, business, events, and incidents are the products of my imagination.
Any resemblance to actual persons, living or dead, or actual events, is purely coincidental.

ISBN 978-1-7392966-3-6

Chapter 1

The word duplicitous has many meanings, and Fritzi would be described by all who knew her as a deceitful, double-dealing, underhanded rogue. Yet, if asked, Fritzi would describe herself as just, open-minded, and, above all, loyal to those she loved.

There are many ways to break an egg, and Fritzi had outrun all of her options. Growing up on the wrong side of the Berlin Wall had taught Fritzi never to take anything for granted or at face value, or to trust anyone, especially not the authorities. Always deemed as different, with few friends, she realised her lifestyle would never be acceptable if she remained behind the Iron Curtain.

Then a miracle: the barrier between boredom and freedom came tumbling down, setting Fritzi free from the claustrophobic world she had found herself locked up in. It wasn't hard to surmise that things were different in the West. Even East Berlin featured Western adverts on their TV. Most East Germans did not believe the commercials showing luxury household goods or the free abundance of foods were a reality; all but a few deemed it Western propaganda, but a young creative mind like Fritzi's wanted to believe it was true.

Another sign that things were extremely different in West Berlin was the Africans studying at the free East Berlin universities who had open passage across Check Point Charlie and into West Berlin. Greta, Fritzi's older sister, had taken up with a man from Cameroon, studying in East Berlin, who would bring back from West Berlin untold luxuries that were impossible to buy even on the black market. Life had to be better over the wall in the West, where perfumes, jeans, costume jewellery, and hair products (all items a young person would love to own) were easy to buy.

Fritzi's father had been a Stasi officer, so their family was privileged compared to most who lived through the communist era. Of course, her dictator of a father, who she hated, was now persona non grata in wider society. He had insisted that she complete her schooling; but with only two years to go and the excitement of the two Berlins becoming one entering her life, it was the perfect opportunity for Fritzi to disappear into another world, far away from her parents' authority and the stigma of being the daughter of a Stasi agent.

Being attached in any way to the old Soviet Union was almost as bad as being related to a Nazi collaborator. West Berlin was an aphrodisiac. The freedom to be who she chose released in her a desire to succeed at any cost. No one knew her real age, and it was easy with makeup to appear older than her fifteen years.

Thus, Fryderyka became Fritzi. She found her height and athletic, narrow frame an asset, and she soon took up with a modelling agency. This lifestyle introduced her to people from all walks of life travelling the world. Changing her persona for the camera lens was a lesson in itself: it enabled her to transform into anyone to suit any given situation. Being a chameleon and taking on a character others desired became her second nature.

Sauntering into an art gallery in Moscow on one of her modelling assignments, she met Yvetta Rubicov, the daughter of an oligarch (one of the richest in Russia) with a business empire reaching into many different countries.

The two women were complete opposites: Yvetta was petite, feisty, and, it seemed, very much in charge of her own world of art, managing two galleries that bore her family's name. It was a world Fritzi knew very little about but was willing to learn. She found that she was a fast learner, too.

Soon after that first meeting, they became almost inseparable. Yvetta travelled extensively to major art shows in London, Miami, New York, and Berlin, while Fritzi's modelling jobs took her to many of these places, too. They made Berlin their special love nest – yet it wasn't enough for Yvetta, who wanted Fritzi to be exclusively hers, and to move to Moscow to live with her.

It took a year for Fritzi to reorganise her life. Something about caring for Yvetta induced feelings of inexplicably defensive and possessive safeguarding in her. Yvetta never reacted well to the photographic modelling assignments that took Fritzi away from Moscow for weeks at a time. Before each assignment, the atmosphere between the two women would build to boiling point. Yvetta's petite frame had a strength of its own when she sunk into despair; no object was too heavy to be launched across the room, often missing Fritzi by inches, fracturing whatever lay beyond into umpteen pieces. By the time Fritzi packed her bags to leave, Yvetta had descended into dark moods verging on listless depression.

Fritzi felt deeply for Yvetta, who touched a tender spot foreign to Fritzi's heretofore single-minded, pragmatic German character. She soon realised that this feeling was more than mere tenderness; it was love. As she grew in love, so too did she begin to appreciate art, working in the galleries when not modelling, under Yvetta's tutelage. Yvetta suggested she end her modelling career and join her in the art business.

Fritzi took a special interest in artefacts, their history, and especially their value on the open market. On an assignment in Italy with Yvetta, she met many art dealers: most were aboveboard, but some (especially from Eastern Europe) were not. These people had initially approached Yvetta, who showed little interest. But it was Fritzi, a very different person to her partner, who got drawn in.

It started small-time, until she became proficient in dealing and handling the rare stolen artefacts from around the world. Later, her specialty became Russian artefacts. Her modelling assignments became fewer as she gained expertise in a new, more lucrative field: selling precious artefacts on the black market.

Unaware of her partner's new profession, which ran alongside her own business, Yvetta fell under Fritzi's charismatic spell, drawing whomever she set her sights on into her powerful orb, much to her family's chagrin. Fritzi soon realised the Rubicov family held and controlled the purse strings; even though Yvetta had free rein, the galleries were hers only in name.

From a young age, Yvetta had been tough – often impossible – to deal with. Her rages in the family home towards Anna, her mother, were one sign of her disturbed behaviour. No one quite knew how to handle her, although Alexi, her father, and Sasha, her younger brother, came closest. Her other brother, Mika, the oldest of the three children, was the bloodhound and trouble-shooter in all areas concerning their family and business empire.

Anna was divorced from Alexi, who now lived in London with Valentina, his wife of many years. Alexi's main interests were the Rubicov's European businesses, including the London Rubicov Restaurant. Sasha ran the Moscow Rubicov Restaurant, and was learning the ropes from Anna, the idea being that he would eventually oversee their Russian enterprises.

Anna had always managed the Russian side, including members of the extended Rubicov family, who were all employed by the companies in one way or another. During the communist era the family had a small capitalist enterprise running fruit stalls, largely ignored by the authorities, with small payoffs to the police. Once the Iron Curtain collapsed, the family empire grew. Sasha and his sister were sent to British schools from a young age, and American universities. Older than his siblings by several years, Mika was born during the communist era, and studied law and business at a foreign school in St Peterburg.

Yvetta never forgave her mother for abandoning her to an overseas boarding school at a tender age. The Rubicovs tolerated Fritzi for Yvetta's sake, putting up with the two women's friendship and business collaboration. But they didn't trust her. She wasn't Russian, for one thing; outsiders weren't family. Still, no one could deny her stabilising influence on Yvetta's behaviour. Yvetta's tantrums (especially towards Anna, but to everyone's relief) had become less frequent in the family home.

Fritzi became embroiled in smuggling artefacts, setting both herself and Yvetta on a dangerous path of no return. There were other criminal aspects as well. Yvetta's decision to fake a burglary in her family's Moscow home had been an insane idea, but Fritzi would have done anything Yvetta asked. Yvetta was deeply jealous of Anna's closeness to Sasha's young British fiancée, Safi, who now lived in their family home.

In order to reap revenge on her mother, Yvetta persuaded Fritzi to loot their priceless family artefacts: selling them to the black market, and enabling them to escape to Berlin together. From that point on, the Rubicovs knew Fritzi was bad news: a terrible influence on their daughter, and worse still, a criminal intent on bringing down the family.

The Rubicovs wrenched Yvetta away from her, an act Fritzi would not easily – or perhaps ever – forgive. They locked Yvetta up in various hidden sanatoriums, in America and Europe. Alexi had given Fritzi a choice: disappear out of their lives – or end up in a Russian prison.

But Fritzi had remained one step ahead of the family, rescuing the love of her life from every institution they locked her away in. Their happiness was short-lived, however, due to the long-reaching clutches of Yvetta's family, especially Sasha and Mika, who were like the KGB of the old days, resilient, resourceful, always managing to track them down. But Fritzi was able to outsmart the family over and over. After all, she was from East Germany; she knew the KGB, knew how to think like the KGB, think better than them, even.

The smuggling syndicate she worked for provided many opportunities for Fritzi to sabotage the Rubicov businesses, including having Sasha kidnapped. But in the end, Fritzi saved Sasha from certain death, all in an attempt to free Yvetta once more – this time from a Moscow sanatorium.

That episode had turned out better than expected, and resulted in over a year of happiness and peace for Yvetta and Fritzi in Namibia. Still, the Rubicovs' reach remained far and wide: the family tracked the couple down with the help of Interpol. It was at that point that Fritzi's life with Yvetta came to an abrupt end. She had been set up by the Art Fraud police, and Interpol made sure she was thrown into a Russian gulag.

Even in prison she managed to curry favour with the guards. Here, as everywhere, money spoke volumes, allowing her certain freedoms. And with the help of her criminal contacts, she soon disappeared into the ether. After a considerable amount of time had passed, she returned to the United States to track down Yvetta – only to find that the love of her life had moved on without her.

Fritzi's lowest moment came when she realised that Yvetta had begun a new life, one without her in it. Yvetta had found another person to love, a fact that Fritzi could not accept. She had to win Yvetta back. But in the end, in spite of her careful planning and disguises, all Fritzi managed to do was injure Sasha by accidentally shooting him, alienating Yvetta even further – and perhaps for ever.

Chapter 2

Fritzi spent time in an ashram, contemplating her past, but found that her emotional life was still in turmoil. She was a person of action, not prone to airy-fairy spiritual games. Circumstances had placed her on another continent, far from where she wished to be living, and in another existence, very different from the one she had left behind.

Always the pragmatist, failure never entered her thoughts. She lived in the moment and plotted for the future, never looking behind her. She reinvented herself to suit whatever situation she happened to find herself in. Time was supposed to heal a broken heart, but learning to let go was not part of her character.

Instead, Fritzi spent her time plotting: her revenge would be subterfuge, she decided. She would hurt the Rubicov oligarchs where it would cause them the most amount of damage: their reputation in the West.

She wanted to live in Australia, but it was a technologically sophisticated country with strict visa laws: entering Down Under with false documents would be taking a risk. So she travelled through southern and northern India, where she was able to lose herself in a hot, humid melting pot. She eventually reached Nepal and merged into a yogi lifestyle, living in the ashram for two months, trying to let go of all negative thoughts and replace them with positive energy.

Boredom set in and she moved on up through South East Asia, settling for a few weeks on one of Thailand's many beautiful beaches. From there she flew to Bali, closer to her desired destination, where she met many Australians, including one Darius Mattista from Sydney, who managed to lighten the loneliness and the void consuming her.

Her heart still ached for Yvetta, who had been the only one to truly fill the void in Fritzi's soul. Losing Yvetta was akin to losing a limb. Yvetta had not only been her lover; she had awakened a longing in Fritzi to protect her at any cost; she alleviated the childhood trauma that was buried deep within.

Darius was an Aussie with an Italian heritage. He had money, was good-looking, and seemed to be crazy about her. Having a little fun was what she needed. Fritzi created another new identity, reverting back to a shortened form of her Christian name. She called herself Freddie, preferring the ambiguity and confusion it caused. Not unlike others before him, Darius found Freddie's aloofness alluring. After all, she was a stunning woman, more handsome than beautiful.

She had transformed her boyish looks into those of a femme fatale. Her masculine name was yet another ruse; she was all woman now. Freddie had thick tousled blonde hair down to her waist. With her lithe, tall physique, she had men falling over themselves to befriend her.

A German-speaking Swiss couple in her yoga class was taken with Freddie and her nomad lifestyle. They were an aristocratic bohemian couple who chose to spend three months every winter chilling out in their Bali villa. They invited Fritzi to crash with them any time she pleased. Paying for their hospitality with private yoga classes (a discipline she had been encouraged to take up during her modelling years), Freddie accepted their kind offer and moved in with her newfound friends.

Known to all as Freddie, she involved herself with teaching expats yoga at one of the expensive, private retreats. Soon word spread around the island, and she became the go-to yoga teacher, giving private lessons to many retired islanders.

Bali was the perfect place to meet Australians: they visited the island in droves every summer season. Still set on living Down Under one day, Freddie wanted to familiarise herself with the people and their culture. For this reason, Darius caught her eye immediately. He was quieter and more refined than most of the Australians she met, and his dress sense was more European in style. Tall and lanky, he inhabited his body and clothes with ease. Freddie found it refreshing to have someone her own height, with whom she could stand shoulder to shoulder.

He had joined an advanced class, and it was here that Freddie noticed him, early one morning. Other than a few encouraging words and compliments, she didn't have a chance to speak with him after class. Apart from her handful of regular clients, people were mostly transient on the island, so she was pleasantly surprised to notice Darius back for several mornings in a row.

Her interest now piqued, she enquired whether he was staying on the island for an extended amount of time. Over coffee (a born-and-bred Sydney boy, Darius loved his coffee) at a nearby beachside café, he told her that he was. And so their friendship grew over coffees at the café that quickly turned into lunches at restaurants that stretched into dinners – and, eventually, Freddie succumbed to his charms, finding herself caught up in his tussled sheets one morning after a romantic dinner the night before.

Darius, she learnt, was on an extended break: he had sold one of his start-ups to a Hong Kong tech company for an undisclosed sum, and wanted only to chill for a while. He had recently extricated himself from an especially exhausting long-term relationship. Bali, he hoped, would give him the headspace he required before returning to work.

As was her manner, Freddie made sure she kept her cards very close to her chest. Even Yvetta, who had Freddie's heart, had never been privy to her clandestine business dealings. Having invented a new persona for herself, she had no intention of complicating her life.

Her new biography went like this: she was born close to Germany, in Alsace, but had lived all over Europe, her father having been in the diplomatic corps. Life had not quite worked out as she had hoped. She had taken time off from her career after losing her long-term partner from a sudden illness. She had decided to travel, hoping it would help her come to terms with the loss. The story was close enough to the truth. Yvetta had disappeared from her life for ever. Besides, it was important she keep her personal details vague.

Every person she met in Bali seemed to have a vague history, so her own backstory did not sound strange or out of place. Everyone was moving on with their lives, or reinventing themselves, starting over again.

Darius turned out to be a good listener, never probing for more details than she was prepared to provide. They discussed her travels through India and Nepal to Thailand, ending up in Bali, where, she informed him, she was happy to put down roots for a while.

The Swiss couple had flown back to Switzerland, where they lived for most of the year. They were happy for Freddie to remain in the villa for as long as she wished. And she was in no hurry to uproot and leave behind a paradise like Bali. For the first time in thirty years, Freddie found she was content with her life. She had enough money to live comfortably and with little stress. She had become the persona she inhabited: Freddie, the indefatigable adventurer, the seasoned traveller. She had always drifted between the sexes, feeling comfortable playing either role if it meant getting what she desired. She tried on and discarded identities, accents, mannerisms, and mores like clothes at a boutique store.

For years she had been the dominant, masculine partner to Yvetta's feisty, petite femininity. But that was then, this was now. Freddie was happy for her new beau to hang around for as long as his interest lasted. The fake passport she had obtained through underground connections had not caused any problems, but she still felt insecure about entering Australia. She was in no doubt that she remained on Interpol's list. If the authorities chose to investigate her papers, she would be exposed.

With the help of her Russian contacts, she managed to walk out of an open Siberian prison. From there she found her way into Scandinavia. After that, she flew into Central America, working her way close to the Mexican border with the United States. America was another country in which she was no longer welcome, having resided in their prison system for six unhappy months, accused of dealing in stolen art. America liked to advertise itself as the freest country in the world, but its prison system was anything but. Being in prison in America was hell. Being in prison anywhere was hell – she wasn't about to go back.

Travelling with the migrant smugglers, she had crossed over into Texas, and worked her way up to New York City. Using many disguised and contacts she had tracked Yvetta down. It came as a punch in the gut to observe the woman she loved from afar, happy with another lover. Not wanting to frighten Yvetta by revealing herself, she remained undercover.

Ultimately, Fritzi's hare-brained plan to grab Yvetta failed miserably. She thought she had come to rescue Yvetta, but it turned out Yvetta did not want to be rescued. To escape capture, she accidentally shot Sasha, leaving her exposed and vulnerable to the law. She had spent her time in the States as a fugitive, but the law was bound to catch up with her: her cover had been blown, they would now be searching for her. She had little choice but to make the crossing back into Mexico.

Downhearted, licking her wounds and trying to come to terms with losing Yvetta, feeling a failure perhaps for the first time in her life, she lay low for a while, until she had the strength to start afresh. One thing Fritzi excelled at was picking herself up, dusting herself off, and becoming a different person entirely. A fantastic mimic, a kind of human chameleon, her repertoire was almost infinite.

Planning a new course of action would have to wait. Her safety and freedom had become her first priority. A new passport with another false identity was her only option. She was tired of being on the run. Now she was in Bali, closer to Australia, where she believed she would begin again…

Beautiful Bali, a gem far removed from her previous life, seemed idyllic, but eventually she would need to leave. Taking up with Darius had been exhilarating at first. Like everyone, she needed some fun and affection, but a serious relationship would be a mistake she could not afford. She would soon have to distance herself from Darius.

Moving on again was an option – but to where? New Zealand, perhaps. Once safely in that country, she might enter Australia as a citizen. Australia presented new opportunities; after all, it was still considered a young country and vast. There she could reinvent herself, allowing her to enter the States to complete unfinished business and settle old scores. This time she would destroy the Rubicov business empire. She would sabotage them from within.

Yvetta had remained the centre of her universe. Nothing tarnished her in Fritzi's eyes. Without Yvetta she felt empty and worthless. Yvetta had made her feel human, and able to give love unselfishly. From almost the moment the two first met, all those years ago, she had always been in love with Yvetta – and nothing had changed for Fritzi.

Until she was able to hold Yvetta close once more, nothing would suffice or make Fritzi feel complete. Even if it meant winning her back by ingenious planning and underhanded stealth. Well, Fritzi was a master at these things, too.

Chapter 3

Freddie sat on the enclosed veranda staring out to sea. The servants were still employed during the owners' absence, and they tended to her every need. She had grown fond of the couple living on the property. They were pious Hindus, and she found little offerings of flowers and fruit to the gods on a daily basis. Concrete bowls around the veranda would be filled with water and petals. In the bathrooms sweet-smelling oils burnt throughout the day, leaving a pungent smell of cloves following wherever one went.

The house was filled with shabby-chic distressed off-white furniture covered in shades of white linen. Soft voile drapes hung from the windows billowing in the breeze. The whole place had an ethereal feel, and the only sharp colours were the abundant pink-and-mauve natural creepers which grew wildly around the property. The creepers would find their way indoors, stuffed into large earthenware urns that lined the passages. The floors were natural dark teak, which combined wonderfully with the pale shades in the rest of the house. Freddie's suite was a profusion of faded florals and mixed textures which she had grown to love. The bathroom was a cavernous spa in shades of travertine marble. It was a home filled with beauty and would be difficult to say goodbye to, as would the island of Bali itself.

Darius was away on one of his trips to Australia, which worked out perfectly, giving Freddie time to reflect on their relationship – which was progressing altogether too quickly, she had begun to think.

She had a lot on her mind. Relying solely on a pay-as-you-go mobile phone meant suffering through frequent signal difficulties, but it was worth it. The alternative was so much worse. She did not want anyone tracking her down through her phone. As someone who had hacked, wiretapped, and clandestinely kept track of others, she knew how easy it was to penetrate systems and be privy to private lives. The laptop she used was now set up under her new assumed identity, and she stayed off the dark web, where she used to receive messages in code from her contacts in Eastern Europe. That life was hopefully behind her now; the less chance there was of being reactivated, the safer she felt.

Once embroiled in the underworld, it was hard to extricate oneself. She had been under suspicion, she was sure, by her contacts on the dark web, where she received her orders for her clandestine jobs in stolen artefacts, and was suspected of giving the authorities an inside view of the organisation's operations, which was multi-layered, even she herself never knew where or who her orders were from.

Fritzi had managed to shift the blame when questioned by a source unknown to her onto someone who had, fortunately, been wiped out during a skirmish with the Russian forces – but one could never be too careful. The syndicate had fingers in every pie, eyes everywhere, and contacts far and wide. Fritzi feared her underworld contacts more than the police agencies and intelligence services. She felt safer being on an Interpol list than at risk of being taken out by the underworld she worked for. She counted herself lucky to have been dropped as one of their couriers, having become too hot to activate. Now she was free to start a new life, and on her own terms.

The Balinese were gentle people and the expats helpful with information. Fritzi knew it would be almost impossible to remain in Bali for an extended time without a multiple-entry visa or a work visa or a 'K,' as they were called.

When Fritzi first arrived she hung out in the cafés and bars to find out what was needed for an extended stay. Her problems would become evident if the Balinese wanted documentation apart from her passport. Darius, in the country on a business visa, had to leave every sixty days.

Thus Fritzi had an ulterior motive in befriending her Swiss hosts, needing their sponsorship to remain for an indefinite period. Putu and Ilush, who lived on the property, were most informative and explained they owned the deeds to the property. Without the name of a Balinese national on the deed, foreigners were not allowed to buy land or homes in Bali. It worked out for everyone: the Balinese had a home on the property, and the owners were able to buy the villa.

The laws were complicated, but with sponsorship and money the couple told Fritzi she was sure to succeed. In her original calculations, she had not factored in such complications. She had opened a savings account with her new identity, and had funds wired into the account from an offshore bank, where she had kept funds for years under a surreptitious business. Not wanting the long arm of the law to investigate her livelihood, she had spread her money into many different accounts. She needed to find out whether it was a viable option to remain in Bali longer, and decided to seek expert advice. Being a digital nomad in Bali seemed a workable option, and she was happy to extend her stay. It turned out that even here, if you had money to spare, you could bend the law to your advantage. Money made everything easier, and opened many doors.

After discussion with an immigration lawyer, Fritzi got around many of the constraints by opening a virtual business and applying for whatever was suggested with as little documented paperwork as possible. This allowed her to stay on long enough to satisfy her needs before she was ready to move on. She was not done with Bali yet – not even close. Her yoga teaching continued at the expat Australian Retreat with little trouble.

Johan and Brigit were adamant she should stay on. They were happy someone was using the house rather than have it standing empty. She offered to pay rent, but it was declined. Instead, she left money in a kitty for Put and Illi, her nicknames for the couple, to use for whatever they wanted besides the household bills, which she paid while residing at the villa.

The problem of her extended visa settled, she decided it was time to go backpacking round Bali on her own. She left no notification of where she had gone with Put and Illi, in case Darius enquired after her whereabouts. Hoping Darius, who knew she had visa issues, would think she had left the Island would make life less complicated.

With these thoughts in her mind, Fritzi reversed the jeep she was using out of the drive, and headed towards the interior of Bali to visit the sights. Leaving Jimbaran behind with its beautiful beaches, she headed away from Kuta, the main town towards Eastern Bali. Here, the rice paddies sloped endlessly down stepped terraces, dominated by a volcano called Mother Mountain looming in the background.

Not minding where she bedded down at night, she had her gear slung in the back of the jeep so leaving the tourist route did not matter. What mattered was to relax and have some time away from being suspicious of every stranger or every question relating to her life. She did not want to be always on her guard or eternally suspect, she just wanted to be.

The process for applying for a visa unnerved her and had put her on edge. She wanted to remain unfound her past was fast catching up with her and, from those who knew her before, she needed distance with no knowledge of her where a bouts, that was what she needed and wanted for as long as she could make it last, she hoped for a new beginning, a fresh start.

As night fell she stopped and camped under the stars, protected by palms and endlessly green fields and valleys. The sound of the rivers coursing down the green slopes lulled her into a restful sleep.

Waking to a rumbling stomach, she made her way into a nearby coastal town, to find it a hip resort filled with diving enthusiasts. After a few words with a waiter and some surfer guys with long hair, she was back in her jeep, heading for Tulamben, a sea side town to spend some time scuba diving.

When she was fifteen she had looked older than her years, could easily get into clubs and bars, drink, smoke, experience things and people and places she would not otherwise be allowed to. For better and worse, she had something of a head-start. Beginning her new life as a model was the first of many deceptions, to survive out of communist East Berlin, in the West on her own. Now, at thirty-two heading towards forty, she felt and looked like a student bumming around on a gap year. It was a good cover: amongst so many other partying gap-year students, airily spending their parents' money, no one would give her a second thought.

She had spent almost six years strutting the catwalks, and five years in the underworld smuggling artefacts. Not to mention the two years spent in the American and Russian prison systems. If it had not been for her contacts, she may have languished at the criminal justice system's leisure for many years, rotting away, watching what was left of her youth evaporate.

Now here she was, free as a bird once again, feeling young and carefree, flirting like a teenager with all and sundry, with the wind in her hair and the clear blue ocean cooling her body as she fell backwards into the sea off a diving boat to watch the magnificent creatures down below in the turquoise depths.

She felt truly free, her month spent lazing on the Thai beaches had never felt as exhilarating. Being physically active, diving off boats until sundown was the most carefree she had felt in her life. Her body ached at the end of each day, but for the first time she could recall she felt young, with no responsibilities or imminent worries to drag her down. Still, something inside her made her scope out any room she found herself in. Old habits die hard. She always felt safer once she had satisfied her angst. She had never liked unwelcome surprises.

At night she would join the surfers and scuba divers for dinner, then retire to the hostel she had booked into close to the beach. Some of the scuba divers were moving on to go white river rafting and invited Fritzi to join them. Thinking it a great idea she packed up her jeep and took three of them with her. Together they had found lodgings. Everyone travelled lightly, some opted for plastic Ziplocs with only essentials in. In a few areas of the river the experience was knuckle-biting as they hit the rapids; in others, the lush rain forests along the route were breath-taking. The rain season was just coming to an end, but the rivers were high due to unexpected rainfall.

Back in the jeep, alone again, Fritzi headed up the Island to see more of the sights. The temples were something she wanted to experience. The quietness and serenity of the Hindus and Buddhists had always held a mysterious interest to her. European religions, on the other hand, had never held any interest for Fritzi. During the communist era no religion was practiced and she had not grown up with any indoctrination of that kind. So, she headed towards Ubud to find the beauty and peace that she hoped the temples would bring to her troubled soul.

Fritzi spent days at a time just driving and stopping wherever her heart desired or her tired body needed to rest in a proper bed for a night or two. Eventually, she headed back to the villa, wondering what she would find when she arrived.

Chapter 4

Fritzi had gone walkabout and Darius had no idea how long she would be away for. Over the five weeks that he had grown to know her mostly, intimately, Darius had gathered that she was pretty much a law unto herself, fiercely independent with a suspicious vagueness about any questions to do with her personal life or her past.

When he drove up to the villa, the day after his return from Australia, Putu and Ilush were not forthcoming about where she might have gone. He decided this would be an ideal opportunity to delve into Fritzi's background. There was something disturbingly vague about her he felt needed some looking into before he became more besotted and involved with her, especially if she returned with him to Australia, which he was hoping she would.

While in Sydney he had been able to sort out his own complicated love life, his visa in Bali only allowed him a limited stay, before re-entering Bali, so his trips back to Sydney were packed with his personal life, being his own boss enabled him to take long breaks to recharge his batteries. After six years together, his relationship with his ex-girlfriend had ended on an acrimonious note. Wei had returned to Hong Kong, but during their time together they had set up various business interests which now needed to be dealt with legally.

After the heartache and politics of their protracted breakup, Darius never imagined he would become interested in anyone romantically, at least not anytime soon. But he had to admit that Fritzi had bowled him over; he was completely infatuated with her. Her beauty and sophisticated poise and obvious vulnerability were captivating. Yet underneath this façade lay a rigid toughness easily overlooked. Darius had observed this trait in Fritzi over a time. She was not scared of hard work or doing what was needed to survive on her own, but he had noted her dismissive tone when confronted with too many questions and her suspicious nature when entering a room full of people. She seemed to hang around the perimeter until comfortable.

He had also noticed her lack of interest in others, giving those she found uninteresting short shift. Fritzi moved on when situations did not suit her agenda, and Darius was not at all sure whether he fitted into her agenda or not. He hoped after her travels through Bali she had come to a decision about what she intended to do afterwards. She had not indicated her intentions and he felt she was keeping her cards close to her chest when it came to revealing any future plans.

He wasn't confident of his chances, but when she returned he was going to make a serious play for her. The question was how to play it. Should he be full-on in his pursuit, or would she be more attracted to a laidback Aussie attitude, allowing her to do the pursuing while he played it cool. First he had to wait for her to return, hoping she would then contact him. At the villa, Putu had informed him that Fritzi had left her cell phone behind, so there was no way he could contact her while she was away.

Through his software company he had many contacts in the tech world. It wasn't the right thing to do, but if he was going to allow himself to fall in love he needed to know who Fritzi was before he found it hard to extricate himself from another costly affair of the heart.

Two weeks in Bali and still no Fritzi. No one had heard from her. He continued with yoga, hoping she would resume her classes once she was back from her trip.

After another yoga class he found a busy café, making his way to a small table against the wall. He ordered a latte and checked his phone. Amongst the list of missed calls there was a number he did not immediately recognise. Dialling the number, he realised it was from one of his computer contacts. Darius walked out of the café to talk, leaving his coffee and kit bag behind. The contact was quick with his findings, the search with the information Darius had given them had come up blank. They were able to flag no one of that description or name. Darius, the contact said, had to give them more to go on.

Going back into the café, Darius noticed his table was occupied, but he could only see the back of the occupier from the door. As he got closer, he stopped, wondering whether it was Freddie. Her hair was pulled through the back of a cap, which shaded most of the top half of her face, and large sunglasses were shielding her eyes. Closer still, he noticed her once-pale skin was now a dark golden colour. Still not sure, Darius pulled out his chair, sat down, and peeked playfully at her in a questioning manner, realising it was Freddie after all. He felt his heart skip a beat.

They sat starring at one another for a moment, until the waitress came over. Fritzi ordered a smoothie. When the waitress departed, she eventually spoke: 'Hello Darius, you've missed me, yes?'

Before he could reply the waitress had returned with her drink. Thrown off balance by this direct question and her Germanic-accented manner that reminded him of Marlene Dietrich, he was lost for an answer and found himself laughing at her theatrics. Fritzi didn't react, instead removing the straw from her smoothie and holding it to her lips provocatively, not taking her eyes off him for a second. Then she dipped the straw back into the smoothie. Before he knew it she had lifted the straw and blown a tiny amount of the liquid straight into his face. 'We spend rest of day making love, yes.' But this time it wasn't a question.

Completely gobsmacked at this new, aggressive, but sexy role-reversal, he found himself nodding in agreement. Not a word had left his lips yet.

While she excused herself, he went to the bar to pay. Once outside he saw Fritzi waiting for him in her jeep. She patted the seat next to her and he hopped in. She put the car into reverse and they headed out towards the villa. Darius found it impossible to speak. Fritzi had put on loud rock music. The noisy jeep and the sharp bends in the road ahead kept him hanging on for dear life. Darius wasn't sure he liked this new dominant Freddie, but all he could think of was the phrase 'make love all day.'

On her return to the villa, she had found out through Illi that Darius had been around several times looking for her. One of the girls who worked with Fritzi at the yoga retreat had told her that Darius had been into her class every day since his return. He had enquired whether Fritzi was returning to take the class.

Fritzi decided her best course of action was to let him see that she was a force to be reckoned with. He might run for his life, and in the meantime, she would enjoy her role as a dominatrix, and hopefully the sex.

She led Darius to her room. First, she locked the door, then she pushed him up against it, and slowly undressed him. She then led him to the shower, shedding her dungaree shorts easily, wearing nothing underneath. Darius found he became putty in her hands. She soaped him down and slid her body against his, but never allowed him to touch her with his hands.

Once the suds had been washed off, she led him to the bed. Throwing a huge bath towel over the covers, she pushed him down and straddled him. She flipped him over easily onto his stomach, tying his hands to the bedposts. Darius felt her massaging his body with oil and was beginning to get into the swing of things when he felt a searing pain as he was entered from behind. Thrashing at the constraints on his wrists he yelled for her to stop, but Fritzi was enjoying her role as being dominant once more.

Satisfied and highly excited, Fritzi turned Darius over. Noticing he had a hard-on she mounted him. As his face contorted into a climax, she untied his hands and allowed him to hang onto her.

Darius lay motionless; for a while he wasn't sure what had actually happened. Fritzi was now spread out on the bed, her long tanned body relaxed and her fingers lightly touching his cheek. She had hidden the dildo under the pillow to confuse Darius even more. Perhaps he would never really be sure, although he had to admit that whatever had occurred had been painful yet pleasurable at the same time.

Regaining his equilibrium, he turned on his side and looked at Fritzi in a questioning way, something he had found himself doing since the moment she had arrived at his table at the café. Who was this new person?

Fritzi put her finger to her mouth, indicating for him not to ask questions. She kissed him lightly on the lips, threw on a long caftan, and unlocked the door, softly closing it behind her. 'I will be back with a feast,' she said.

Less than an hour later, she pushed open the door with her foot while holding a huge tray aloft, crammed with fruit, bread, cheese, and a bottle of cooled white wine and two wine glasses. She found Darius fast asleep. Pouring some ice-cold wine into a glass, she sprinkled some onto Darius. Waking up with a start, he leaned up on one elbow to survey the feast on the tray. They both tucked in, and neither spoke until they were satisfied.

This time Darius was the first to speak, and Fritzi became the Freddie he had left behind once more. They enjoyed a wonderful evening together watching old movies. He slept the night and when he woke at dawn the birds were singing their morning chorus, and the light was creeping in through the shutters. Freddie woke, pulling him close, making love gently, the way he remembered.

They left for her yoga class together in Fritzi's jeep, singing along to the radio. Darius thought he had never felt quite as happy with anyone before. He wasn't sure he wanted to know who she really was. Perhaps this was meant to be nothing more than a holiday romance. If only he wasn't quite as nuts about her as he was…

Chapter 5

Two months with Darius had passed in sheer bliss. Fritzi's thoughts about ending the relationship had conveniently slipped away. She never repeated the dominatrix episode and it was never spoken of. Darius, she felt, preferred to pretend it had never happened. His sixty days were up and he had to leave the country. This time he invited Fritzi to accompany him to Australia, but she found an excuse not to travel. Making light of it, she said, 'Some space won't hurt, give us a little time to reflect.'

Back in Australia, Darius did find time to reflect on their relationship. Fritzi was an enigma for sure, but she still bothered him, and not in a good way. He prided his strong instincts to smell out trouble, and Freddie, as he knew her, was without a doubt hiding something. Several weeks ago, finding himself alone in Freddie's bedroom, he had taken the opportunity to search through her drawers, finding only her passport, which he photographed and passed on to his contacts in Australia, hoping they would be able to uncover information on Fritzi before he returned to Bali.

He hadn't heard back from anyone, so he called to find if any information had been uncovered. His contacts were certain both the passport and the name were fake. The name had revealed absolutely nothing, apart from wired accounts from various offshore countries which had been flagged in electronic searches through the banking world.

The name 'Frieda Gisele Crantz' had matched with various people, but none with a significant criminal history. Many of the 'Frieda Gisele Crantzes' that showed up on the database were significantly older than his Freddie, or deceased. Only one matched Freddie's description from the photograph, and everything they tried to find with this photo match had been blocked. This usually occurred, Darius was informed, when there was already a search in process, which meant other, more significant agencies or organisations were looking for this person, or she had been given a new identity.

His curiosity about Freddie now piqued, he wasn't sure what to do with this information, Darius contacted a former employee who had worked for his company. Bruce, a balding, muscular, rugby-league bruiser of a guy, had been in the police force and was now a private eye. Not someone anyone in his or her right mind would tussle with, even in jest. Seated opposite Bruce in an airless Sydney downtown poorly lit old Irish bar, downing a few pints of Foster's, Darius asked for his opinion about the findings passed down to him by his security team.

'Hackers, you mean, right, Dasso boy?' Bruce said, pushing his considerable weight forward on the protruding foam stuffing of the chewed-up leather barstool. Though Darius had been his employer not so long ago, you would not think it from the way Bruce addressed him. More like an old friend or drinking buddy. Typical Aussie-speak, straight to the point.

'How would you interpret this info?' Darius asked.

But Bruce merely answered the question with a question.

'You involved with this Sheila?' Bruce inquired. 'Where is she now?'

'Bali.'

'Right,' Bruce said again, 'good place to hide, I suppose. Lax laws, lax authorities down there.' His tone lowered as he said, 'Never forgotten how many of our own were killed over there in the Bali bombing.'

'So you think she's hiding from something?'

'No, never said that,' Bruce said, 'but it has a smell, for sure. I'd be careful, unless you want to get dragged into something you might regret after the heat of the moment has passed.'

'I want some more info. Can you do some digging for me? Private job, you understand.'

'Dasso boy, I'd do anything for a quid.'

Darius gave him all the information he had, and promised to pass on more once back in Bali. Bruce asked what he knew about Freddie's former life – anything he had on her could be useful.

'Well, the passport says she was born near the French- German border. She speaks several languages fluently: Russian, German, French, and English.'

'That's a lot,' Bruce said.

'She's got a lot of talents,' Darius said, 'and I've got a lot of questions.'

'A lot of talents,' Bruce repeated dully.

'No doubt some hidden ones I don't yet know about,' Darius said.

'But you'll find out, presumably, in time.'

'Maybe. Maybe not. She says her folks were in the diplomatic corps, but she's not very forthcoming. She clams up if asked too many personal questions. I have noticed she scopes out any crowded room before she feels relaxed enough to engage. She is tall, very athletic, and made money on the catwalks as a model for a good number of years. That's about as much as I know right now.'

'Is she travelling on her own?'

'Yes. She says she lost a long-term partner to illness and is trying to come to terms with the loss.'

'Fair enough.'

'Can you find out the partner's name, it might help?'

'Anything else?'

'Will let you know, cheers,' Darius said, standing up and clapping Bruce on the back. If he was going to return to Bali, he wanted to tie up all loose ends before leaving Sydney.

He made his way back to his penthouse apartment on Bondi Beach with a spectacular view of the white sandy beaches. Dawn surfing was the best therapy before early morning meetings or when home from travelling. He wouldn't want to live anywhere else in the world. Lin had hankered after a house on Rose Bay. They had bought a waterfront property together, one of the many assets their lawyers were now haggling over, but to Darius it didn't have a patch on living on Bondi Beach, where he surfed, drank coffee at the many outdoor cafés, and chilled with his mates most days for brunches or dinners.

He and Freddie were both licking their wounds, it appeared. That was one of the things they had in common. Who knew what other secrets they shared, Freddie was alluringly secretive, and it had awakened his keen sense of curiosity. His relationship with Lin was great while it lasted, and it had lasted a long time, but Lin wasn't an easy girl to deal with.

At first their common interests helped bind them together, even when other, smaller difficulties arose – petty arguments or temper tantrums from Lin. Even then they were strong, or strong-ish, or strong enough. Sort of. But after he sold one of his many start-ups, she continued to work night and day on her own tech business, which did not suit Darius. He wanted to enjoy his life chilling out, but Lin wasn't built that way. With Lin it was all work and no play. She was focused – to a fault. She returned to Hong Kong to be with her family and continue her gruelling schedule of work.

Freddie was way ahead of anyone else he had met so far; he had never met anyone quite like her.

Darius had spent many sleepless nights wondering what or how she had overpowered him sexually. At first it had unnerved him so much he couldn't bring himself to think about it. But now, in Sydney, he couldn't think of anything else. He tried to relive the experience, with a curious, anticipatory mixture of pleasure and pain, but each time he got close to imagining the sensation of being penetrated by Fritzi the image that came to mind was too alarming and he blanked it out. The most frightening thought, he was slowly starting to admit, was that he had enjoyed the sensation. It had taken him to heights he had never before felt. He had never thought of himself as a prude, but had always accepted that he was a straight guy, with ordinary tastes, and now he wasn't so sure. He was reconsidering everything. Even Freddie. Even – especially – himself.

One night, alone in his penthouse with time on his hands, he lay on his bed and switched on the 42' flatscreen facing his bed. Scrolling to the adult channel he flipped through some of the movies, hoping to find on the screen some iteration of what had happened to him. Besides feeling slightly inadequate in the downstairs department, after noticing the impossibly virile studs servicing some pretty trashy girls, there was only one scene when the girl strapped on a dildo and started to screw the guy.

Darius was fascinated but shocked at the same time – a pleasant and stirring combination. The stud in question was obviously not gay – he had just serviced three girls in a very raunchy scene – yet here he was enjoying this, as he thought of anal sex, gay sex. The movie didn't turn him on, but it did pique his curiosity and he wanted to know more. Obviously, there was something missing in his sex education. The following morning, after scrolling through his cell phone, he called a sex therapist and made an appointment.

Finding the therapist's offices in an exclusive downtown building, he settled down in the plush waiting room after signing in at the sleek and modern-looking reception desk. Paging through a magazine about deep-sea diving, he had second thoughts about this appointment. What was he doing here? Like a deep-sea diver, he felt entirely out of his depth. Underwater, in a way. Not sinking, exactly, but something close. Was he being an idiot? Should he just leave before it was too late? As he put down the magazine and began to contemplate a brisk and efficient getaway, the receptionist came over to take him through to the therapist's rooms.

Sitting across from him was a shoulder length auburn haired quite attractive in a motherly way, rounded, middle aged woman, not someone he felt comfortable talking to about sex. It was like speaking to his mother, for god's sake.

Dr Singer took down some details about his health and sex life, and then sat staring at him. For a long moment he sat wondering: what was meant to happen next? The questions were, to say the least, embarrassing; he had never thought about his sex habits quite as clinically or his preferences, which as far as he was concerned were pretty average, normal stuff, not exactly Kama Sutra or erotic; he, preferred the good old missionary position.

Was he supposed to drop his drawers for her to examine him? Anyway, what did she mean by asking him whether he liked it from the back, sideways or sitting up, his mind was spinning. She wasn't a proper doctor; she was a PhD, a therapist specialising in sex, as far as he knew. That would be the bloody day! All he wanted to do was to have a chat with a professional in a stress-free environment, be reassured that his experience and desires were not abnormal, that he was, in fact, a healthy heterosexual male. Not have her play stupid mind games with him, asking about foreplay and eroticism, aesthetic sexual desire etc. he was beginning to feel like a boring old fart. Then he realised her mouth was moving. What did she just say? He reminded himself that he was paying for this – whatever this was.

Clearing his throat he said, 'Sorry, sorry what did you just say?'

He imagined she would give him a severe look – her demeanour, even her posture, suggested severity, but instead she smiled a knowing smile. That made it worse, somehow. Shit, he wanted to get the hell out of here. He felt trapped and he was sweating, something he never did. He should have walked off in the waiting room, when the instinct overtook him. That was his problem, he either overanalysed his instincts and impulses, or ignored them altogether. His relationship with Freddie was a case in point. He hadn't reckoned with his true feelings until she had left the island – and him. And now here he was, for some reason he couldn't comprehend, in a sex therapist's office, waiting for instructions he couldn't even make out.

'Mr Mattista,' she said in a surprisingly gentle voice, 'relax. Whatever it is you want to speak about, please feel free. I assure you, nothing you can say will shock me.' Her previously severe face softened into something resembling a smile. 'Why don't we start at the beginning, as if you were telling me a story?'

He sat for a few moments, not knowing how or where to begin. Then he heard the gentle voice again.

'Is it about penis malfunction, perhaps?'

He felt like he was in some sort of awful dream. This suggestion was the icing on the cake. Did he look like someone who had penis malfunction? This had been a huge mistake. He should cut his losses and leave. Before she made another absurd, insulting assumption about him. He owed her no excuses or apologies – nothing. He had paid for the session upfront.

Leaning forward now, her voice slightly less gentle, less slow and soft. 'Perhaps you can enlighten me as to why you are here.'

Okay, let's get this over with. 'I am not sure you can help me,' he began, 'but this is what recently happened to me, and I am not at all sure what or how I should feel about it.'

As he ended his description of being penetrated by Freddie, about the sensation and how it hurt then felt pleasurable, he said, 'that is what is bothering the hell out of me: am I gay?'

'Not at all, Mr Mattista, but I can understand why you have gone down that route.' She relaxed again, and he relaxed slightly himself. Then a frown creased her face – a note of severity again. 'If you were on your stomach with your hands tied, how do you know what was happening behind you? Was there a mirror?'

'Nope,' Darius said, finding it difficult now to thread his words together, not previously a problem for someone who had, on occasion, been described as garrulous, at least after a few drinks. 'After this happened, we had ordinary sex. I was too shocked to mention what I thought I had felt before. As time passed, and nothing like that ever happened again, I began to think I had imagined it.'

'Have you mentioned it to her since?'

'No, I haven't. Since being back in Sydney, away from her, the whole thing has been a recurrent nightmare.' He looked at her closely, made a snap judgement, decided to trust her. 'I decided to watch some porn movies and realised what she had done to me,' he said slowly. 'I was shocked at how I felt about the sensation. I decided to seek advice,' he concluded, bringing them to the present moment. Now it really was just the two of them in the office, strangers until a few moments ago but now on quite intimate (if one-sided) terms, and a silence growing between them. A silence Dr Singer broke.

'I can see why you are feeling confused, but I can assure you that what you felt was a completely natural sensation. Contrary to belief, men have a G-spot, too, like women. The male G-spot or P-spot, as in "prostate." It is located behind the testicles, and can make one's orgasm much more powerful. I think that is what you experienced, and because it's on the inside and not easy to reach, that is probably what you felt. Am I right?'

Darius was now fully engaged, relieved that he wasn't secretly gay. Perhaps it had been the right idea to come here after all. He hadn't been an idiot, just normal. After all, what constituted abnormal in the bedroom, and who exactly, in this secret sanctuary, got to determine the rules? One never knew what, exactly, one's neighbours were getting up to behind closed doors. All one knew were one's own guilt, one's own self-doubt, one's own fears. The indelible stain of shame, made that much worse by being kept a secret.

Now he felt relieved and refreshed. He had simply needed someone to talk to, and Dr Singer had been that someone: reassuring, rational, practical. Not severe at all. Perhaps all of his snap judgements, like his fears, were off the mark. Perhaps he was wrong about Freddie, too. Perhaps she wasn't incriminated in anything – perhaps the shadow of doubt fell on him for being too suspicious, too wary, too quick to judge. He felt ashamed of himself for being so cynical – and yet he was cynical still. His cynicism gnawed at him, but it had also served him well.

'Your sex partner took you by surprise,' Dr Singer continued. 'Men are often not open to this sexual act, and it can come as a shock if not discussed beforehand. This method is called "pegging," and the strap-on harness is called by some, a "Lovehoney."'

Though their chairs had not moved, he felt as though he had floated closer to her. She no longer appeared so removed. Indeed, in this light, she was not at all unattractive. Sharing something with someone, making yourself momentarily vulnerable, made you intimate with the other person, if only for a moment. No wonder so many people fell for their doctors, priests, psychologists.

'I see you are relieved to find your enjoyment was a normal reaction to having your erogenous zone massaged.'

Darius smiled and visibly relaxed back in his seat. 'I must be very ignorant. I did not have a clue about any of this.'

'Well, many men do not know about the erogenous area in their anus. Anything to do with that part of the anatomy can be off-putting for them from a physiological aspect. I am going to give you some reading material, and if you want to visit me again, please do.'

With considerable lightness, Darius realised the appointment was over. Feeling unusually grateful, he gave Dr Singer a soft hug. 'Sorry,' he said, 'but I am so relieved I just wanted to share that with someone.'

'It's quite alright,' she said, motherly once more. 'Off you go and enjoy your sex life to the full.'

That night Darius had what one could only call a right old piss-up with his friends. The weather was perfect out, the hot humid summer was coming to an end, and the nights were still warm but not as humid and much cooler after dark.

It was almost three by the time he hit his pillow. Happy with his life and lifestyle here, he wondered why he was bothering to return to Bali. Freddie wasn't who she seemed to be and, rightfully suspicious or overly cautious, he did not have an appetite for intrigue or further complications in his life. He drifted off to sleep peacefully for the first time in ages. He would review his decision in the morning, but he suspected he had already made up his mind. No Bali – or Freddie, for that matter.

Darius woke to his cell phone buzzing and his head pounding. It wasn't yet nine in the morning and the sun was streaming in through the bedroom window. Shaking his head to clear the fog of last night's many beers, he answered.

'Dasso, it's Bruce, mate. I've been digging and I suggest you bail on this Sheila, mate.' Darius sat up in bed, pressed the phone to his ear. 'It's been hard yakka getting anything on this Sheila of yours, but if it's the person I think she might be, it's not good news.'

He made his way to the kitchen with the cell under his chin, telling Bruce to hold on while he splashed some cold water onto his face. He still felt pretty groggy from last night. Cool air met his hot face. He felt a little better.

Sitting down on the couch in the lounge, he put the cell onto speaker, so he could jot down anything interesting.

'Okay, shoot,' he said, trying to sound sprightly but not quite succeeding. 'I'm ready. Let me have it.'

'Better to meet, mate. Same place.'

'No, come to Bondi. I'll text you a place to meet for coffee – and I'm sure you could do with some brekkie at this hour.'

Pulling on some shorts and a T-shirt, he jogged down the beachfront to the restaurant off Bondi Beach he had suggested to Bruce.

While waiting he downed a few strong coffees and read the morning papers. Jogging had refreshed his last decision before falling asleep: he remained doubtful about returning to Bali, or taking up where he left off with Freddie. Bruce may very well be right that it was time to bail, but he still wanted the information. It could still prove to be useful. He was nothing if not eternally curious, which was one reason why he had been so successful with his information technology start-ups. That curiosity was capable of getting him into trouble from time to time, too.

Bruce sauntered in wearing a sleeveless flak jacket, a felt outback hat, khaki shorts, and well-worn lace-up boots. He was the quintessential Aussie Crocodile Dundee kind of bloke. Taking a seat opposite Darius, they ordered and waited for the breakfast to arrive before beginning their discussion. Glancing at Darius, Bruce said with a laugh, in a knowing tone, 'Rough night?'

'You could say that,' Darius replied, but his voice wasn't tired and the hangover was gone. If anything, he felt unusually alert.

Munching away, Bruce spoke between bites and gulps of coffee. 'Now I had a bit of luck. I could be barking up the wrong tree, of course. This German Sheila could have nothing to do with the person my Interpol friend was able to dig up for me. But I doubt it, because sans the long hair in the photo you gave me, the computer found a match. This chick has a record as long as my two arms. She is a real piece of work, and a very accomplished one at that. Expert at disguises and turning into anything she wants, man or woman. Very clever, speaks more than four languages. Has been locked up first in the States for dealing in stolen artefacts, then in Siberia, and would you believe it, managed to escape from a Russian Gulag. She has pulled off more escapades than I can mention, but her one and only weakness is her love for – now get this, are you sitting tight? – a Russian Sheila called Yvetta Rubicov, daughter of a very rich, now deceased oligarch.'

'Hold on a minute,' Darius said. 'This can't be the same person. Freddie definitely isn't a lesbian, I can vouch for that one.'

'I mentioned that, but my Interpol friend assured me she plays both ways. In fact, any way it suits her to play it. Now, are you ready for her early history?'

Darius wasn't sure he was, but, if this person was his Freddie, the story thus far was pretty amazing. He had known there was something tough about her. She had grit, something unusual, something he couldn't easily explain. He had seen flashes of something akin to unsentimental determination in her manner.

'Okay, shoot,' Darius said again.

'Born behind the Iron Curtain, father was in the Stasi, like the KGB or CIA, pretty vile in those days. Hard bastards. No one had a private life; everyone spied on everyone. She hated her father, escaped his clutches the minute the two Germanys united. She did become a model – that part, at least, was true. But even then, she lied about her age. She was only fifteen when she joined a modelling agency. She hit the big time, too: Paris, Milan, New York. Then she met this Russian chick. From a big-time family. I mean really, really rich. Billions, Dasso. She joined the Russian chick in Moscow, gave up her career, and got involved with a major smuggling ring in stolen artefacts.

'The story goes on and on. The last my informer knew of Freddie, as you call her – it's actually Fritzi, by the way, not Freddie – she ended up in New York to abduct the love of her life, this very same Russian Sheila. Ended up shooting the Russian's brother, after which she disappeared into thin air. Until now, that is.

'The syndicate Freddie is involved with has many contacts, and she probably has more than one passport. They have helped her escape on many occasions. She even entered the States illegally with smugglers, crossing over the Mexican border into Texas. She is one determined woman. I don't know, maybe you like determined women, but this one is bad news. Very bad. Apparently, she pulled off more than one escape with her Russian girlfriend, after the girlfriend's parents locked her away to get mental help and to escape from Fritzi's clutches. So, mate, if this is your woman, I think it's a lucky escape. You had the right instinct to have her investigated, and just as well – and just in time. Back out now, before things get very, very bad.'

Darius sat back dumbfounded, visions of this beautiful creature entering his mind. Freddie. Or was it Fritzi? Who was she really? Was anything she had told him about herself even true? It was hard to imagine she had had such an incredible life and was only twenty-eight. But then maybe her age was a lie, too. She had lived through more than he could ever live in two lifetimes. Something to admire, really, even though she had chosen a path most would never dream of going down. He wondered why she had joined a smuggling syndicate when her modelling career was so successful?

He had so many questions, and now he supposed he would never learn the answers. There were Freddie's lies – and then there was the truth behind the lies. The shading, the contours, the mask over the true face and the face itself. The makeup, the mannerisms, the fake names and identity documents. She had told him the love of her life had died. Now he knew she hadn't died, but to Freddie she had died all of the same, because she'd lost her. Love could be cruel sometimes. Bruce had mentioned that she had helped her Russian girlfriend escape more than once from sanatoriums the girlfriend's parents had locked her away in – something to be admired, really. That was real sacrifice for real love. Putting your life and livelihood at risk for the sake of your lover. He bet she was still on the same mission, biding her time. Perhaps nothing had changed.

Freddie clearly really loved this Russian girl, whoever she was. He felt sad for Fritzi rather than mad at her for her duplicitous nature. She wasn't a good person, but perhaps, deep down, she didn't have a bad heart. And she had not done anything malicious to him.

Darius would not return to Bali. He had made up his mind before meeting Bruce. Their conversation had changed nothing, rather cemented his plans. But there was one more thing he felt he needed to see to, and it wasn't something he could ask Bruce to do.

Chapter 6

Fritzi was sitting in the lounge at the airport, backpack over one shoulder, sipping champagne, waiting for her flight to Auckland. She had passed through the passport checks and security without any problems.

Now here she was with a new identity, drinking bubbly as if to celebrate. But celebrate what? She was getting out, backing off, leaving another country and another life behind. She had left the femme fatale behind in Bali. New Zealand would welcome a new Fritzi, one called

Freya Brant, from Zurich, Switzerland. Freya looked Swiss, whatever Swiss looked like. Her hair was short once more, and instead of honey-blonde it was now auburn, cut to just below her ears in a severe bob. Her eyes were green rather than blue, an easy alteration with contacts. She was so used to wearing them that, on occasion, she had forgotten what colour her own eyes were, and often surprised herself when brown eyes stared back at her once her contacts had been removed.

Relaxing in a café close to her yoga class, a stranger in her yoga gear with her mat slung over her shoulder in a sling, slipped into the seat opposite her, a pretty petite woman. Fritzi did not mind: after all, the café was pretty full this time of the day. The woman leaned close to Fritzi and spoke softly in French. At first Fritzi wasn't sure what was said or whether it was even said to her. Perhaps the other woman was chatting on her phone.

But just as suddenly Fritzi's eyes widened as she realised, she had just been given a message, one she could not ignore. No one would have noticed her or even remembered she had shared her table. She was there one moment and gone the next. Fritzi felt the hair stand up on her neck. A familiar shiver crept up her spine. She had been rumbled – how she had no idea, but she had been given forewarning. It would be foolish beyond belief to ignore such stark advice.

The woman had quietly leaned forward and said, 'It's time to leave Bali and time is not your friend.' Then she vanished before Fritzi had a chance to reply. But Fritzi had gotten the message.

Fritzi returned to the villa, packed only the necessary, retrieved her numerous identities from the safe, and left without further ceremony. Pulling the jeep over to the side of the road, she took out a mirror, stood it on the dashboard, donned a short bobbed auburn wig and green contact lenses, touched up her makeup to suit her new look, and continued with confidence through airport security.

Her next test would be to enter New Zealand. The best time would be the last flight into Auckland when airport security and the officers at passport control were tired and ready to go home. She had a stop-off in Singapore, where she would wait for the last connecting flight into Auckland.

Once on the flight she gave herself permission to relax, recap, double back on her mental tracks, figure out how she had been tracked down. If she could be so easily tracked down, she could not afford to relax her guard again. She had to understand how and why she had gone wrong. She couldn't afford to repeat the mistake. Who had come to understand that she was in danger, and how had they come to this understanding? Who had uncovered her rouse? Darius flashed through her mind. After all, he had slept in a room in which she had – perhaps stupidly – kept some of her papers. Or was it Brigit and Johan? Or someone else altogether. Perhaps it was a random sighting. It was a comforting thought that she had a friend out there somewhere. She didn't have many of those. If she ever found this friend, she would repay the favour tenfold.

New Zealand was a small country and not that easy to get lost in, so she had to be as inconspicuous as possible. The people weren't flashy, they were down to earth, straight-talkers. They were mad about rugby and sheep, and Fritzi didn't know much about either. Backpacking with the tourist crowd would give her a good idea where to put down roots for a while, until she figured out whether going to Australia was a safe option.

Fritzi visited a tourist office the following morning, and with a travel itinerary in hand, she proceeded to spend the day sightseeing in Auckland. That evening she took a flight to South Island, where she would slowly find her way around on various stop-offs from Christchurch.

Her sleep was disturbed by piercing screams. Someone was running down the passages banging on doors and the ground seemed to be shaking and moving. Everything attached to the walls began crashing down around her. Flying out of bed she grabbed her belongings (not needing the wig, having dyed her hair brunette the night before, in the shower).

Finding mayhem around her everyone screaming, as they all made their way out of the building, pierced her already heightened senses as, she made her way outdoors, the beautiful cathedral and plaza in front of the hotel in ruins. The whole structure had crumbled, leaving boulders of concrete everywhere. The ground was undulating in waves and had opened into gaping holes. It was like a scene from a horror movie. People were crying out for help, others were obviously beyond help.

Without a second thought, Fritzi ran to assist those in need. The emergency services had not yet arrived, the whole city was still in the throes of the earthquake. Everywhere she looked the earth seemed to be splitting open and buildings were crumbling to the ground. Eventually she managed to help the person, a young man, covered in dust and grit, closest to her to safety, away from the cavernous holes opening up around them. They huddled together, holding onto one another until the sounds of cracking and hissing began to recede and the ground had stopped moving under their feet.

For a while there was total quiet. Nothing moved, no sound could be heard. Not even a bird stirred across the sky. The silence was unnerving. Fritzi considered herself tough, she had been through a lifetime of misadventures, starting from the age of fifteen. Now here she was shivering and shaking, clinging to the man she had managed to drag out of a hole before he disappeared into a gaping fissure in the road.

He was covered in dust from head to toe with blood caked to his face. His hands had been cut to shreds as he clung on for dear life.

The silence hung in the air around them. Neither was brave enough to move, the aftershocks could be worse. Her lungs felt like they were bursting from lack of oxygen. Either she had forgotten to breathe or the atmosphere was so thick with dust and debris her lungs were clogged. Turning round to see how her companion was doing, she found he had passed out from shock or some other injury she had not been aware of. Now that the quake had reached its finale and deafening crescendo, help had to be on hand somewhere. The damage was horrendous. Even sitting in this bolthole, one could see the disaster zone surrounding them, and probably far worse out there.

Fritzi gingerly untangled herself from the figure lying against her and managed to move out into an open space to survey her surroundings further. The street resembled a war zone after the final battle. Lifting her rucksack off her back she found the bottle of water she never travelled without. Taking a few gulps, sputtering water all over her face, she finally felt her mouth less dry and her tongue able to move once more. Ferreting for a T-shirt she poured water onto it and dabbed some onto the man's dry lips, eyes and face.

As she was assessing his hands, he opened his eyes. The vagueness behind his stare made clear his state of shock. Fritzi decided it was safer to leave him where he was and look for help, and perhaps be of assistance. She did not have any injuries she was immediately aware of. Once on her feet, she climbed over concrete boulders, trying to avoid the gaping holes cars were protruding from. A number of people had been hit by flying debris; some appeared to be dead, others were bleeding profusely. Some were beyond help, but she tried to administer water to those who were still alive.

She tore up her clothes to make tourniquets to stop blood flow from gashes. Working her way around the bodies until she became aware of others working alongside her. No one spoke. Some cried helplessly as they found loved ones or people they knew, cradling them in their arms. Through it all, Fritzi felt helpless, but continued assisting until exhausted, allowing the emergency services to guide, with their arms around her shoulders, to a safe shelter. With great difficulty, barely able to speak or move now, she managed to tell them about the man needing help, and they went off to find him.

Sitting in the shelter people slowly began to recall their experiences to one another. Homes had been lost, many people would never be found, but everyone felt lucky to be alive. The Dunkirk spirit kicked in and she knew that the city would eventually be rebuilt with pride. Once all foreign aid had arrived from far and wide, as she knew it would, they would then evacuate all tourists; until then she could perhaps help in some small way.

Fritzi did whatever was needed, ending up at a field hospital, having sustained a head injury she hadn't been aware of. Seen to by a French doctor she learnt the medical team needed interpreters. The time spent helping had gone by in a flash, she later realised; she had not given a thought to herself for one moment. Once emergency services found she was multilingual, they recruited her to help with tourists who did not speak English well.

She was given responsibilities for jobs she had never before done, translating for whoever the emergency services crew needed to communicate with, and delivering supplies to various stations in the field hospital. On one such mission a hand reached out to grab her. Looking at the man in the makeshift hospital bed, Fritzi realised it was the person she had sheltered with during the earthquake. Relieved to notice he had recovered apart from a leg injury, still partially covered in dust it was hard to distinguish his features properly but she noted he was tall and probably attractive once cleaned up. His eyes were red but his vision was clear. His sincere expression of gratitude caught her by surprise; there was no reason for her to be on guard now.

'Hi,' he said in a voice so soft she had to strain to hear. 'Can you stay and chat for a moment?'

'Of course,' Fritzi said. 'How are you? I tried to revive you but you passed out and I went in search of help.'

'I broke my leg in a few places, nothing serious, but I wanted to thank you, you saved my life.' Grabbing her hand, he brought it to his heart and looked at Fritzi with tears brimming in his eyes. 'If you ever need anything, here is my card. Please, anything I can ever do for you, just ask.' Feeling a flush of embarrassment (not a familiar feeling for Fritzi), she quickly moved on to complete her task. As she left, she noticed his eyes following her out of the field tent.

The following day all tourists were given an option of flying home or onto another destination. With the current upheaval, it was the ideal opportunity to take advantage of an offer to fly into Australia as a tourist escaping from the earthquake. She was sure her passage through security would go smoothly, since she would be viewed as one of the many injured and evacuated tourists from an earthquake zone.

Boarding the flight, she was astonished to be designated a seat in first class.

'I would love to,' Fritzi exclaimed to the flight attendant. With Yvetta she had flown on private jets, or first-class. Flying economy class wasn't quite the same, although she was used to it now, and it was certainly the best way to travel if one did not want to be obtrusive or draw attention to oneself. Still, she couldn't help herself but ask, 'But how come?' A smile briefly creased the neat face of the flight attendant. 'The son of the prime minister had requested you be given five-star passage into Australia, as a thank you for saving his life in a selfless act of bravery.' Still smiling, she added, 'Besides all the other selfless tasks you carried out during and after the quake.'

She placed her hand on Fritzi's for a moment in gratitude. Stunned, unable to decide whether this was a good or bad thing in her situation, Fritzi sat back, trying to work things out anew. She took a snap decision to enjoy the short flight to Sydney, until some damage control was needed. There was nothing she could do about the situation now. To object to her first-class status would simply bring unwanted attention on herself. The situation had changed and she would just have to change accordingly. But she excelled at attuning herself to the moment, to shape shifting and adjusting.

Three hours later, she disembarked with the other tourists and Aussies. They were given a special passage through security and bussed into Sydney. The tourists were put up at a hotel in the centre for the night, all expenses paid. Having been injured in the line of duty, selflessly saving the Aussie prime minister's son on a short work break to New Zealand, Fritzi was given an escort through all passport checks. Far from being suspected of being a criminal at the airport, Fritzi was apparently something of a local hero. As such, normal restrictions did not seem to apply to her, she was delighted to find. Still, she couldn't afford to let her guard down, not even for a moment.

Settling down in her suite overlooking the Sydney Opera house, she pinched herself to make sure she wasn't dreaming. Nothing like this had ever happened to her before. Not only had she been escorted as a minor celebrity through immigration, she was where she wanted to be in Australia, and home-free for the moment. She would have to deal with the fallout in the morning. She just hoped her newfound celebrity did not bring renewed scrutiny. This was her fear. It would be easy for even a photograph in the newspaper and an initially appreciative news story to backfire badly on her.

The world was, after all, a small place, and even confidential information could be easily attained if you wanted it badly enough. What Fritzi badly wanted right now was to blend into the crowd, to become invisible even, not to stick out. Still, all of this gratitude was enormously flattering, and she felt light on her feet, as though in a daze or a dream. It didn't feel quite real.

Sunglasses and cap pulled low over her face, with running gear on and backpack slung over her shoulder, she evaded the press outside, who were waiting to interview the tourists. She knew they would want an exclusive interview with her; after all, it wasn't every day one saved the son of a prime minister. The last thing Fritzi needed was to have her photo splashed all over the newspapers.

As she jogged along the pier to the ferry terminal, she marvelled at the sight of the stunning architecture looming over the harbour. The Opera House was even more spectacular during the day, and she couldn't wait to experience its wonderful acoustics. Hopping onto the ferry, she enjoyed the view from the water, watching the crowds disembarking into the city, and the land slowly rolling further and further away. The ticket lady had suggested she try one of the boutique hotels on Bondi Beach, but first she wanted to enjoy being a tourist in Sydney, and being on the water was obviously one of the best ways to view such a gorgeous city, she reflected as they passed under the bridge moving out into to open water.

Tired and in need of a shower, she made her way to a small hotel hidden off a side street close to Bondi Beach. Wearing a soft towelling gown and her hair wrapped up in a towel, she opened the shutters to survey her surroundings. The beachfront with promenade could only just be viewed from her balcony, but she wasn't fussy. Far from it, she felt enormously grateful, watching the waves gently rolling onto the sand.

It was the perfect spot to familiarise herself with the city before she decided to move on, perhaps taking a trip into the interior for what they called a 'walkabout.' She may even go bush and travel without a fixed address, just wander in the outback as the aboriginals did for months on end.

Relaxing for the first time since her feet hit the ground in New Zealand, she was able to reflect on the events of the last few days. She decided that her usual antennae for smelling out trouble was not as efficient as they had once been. She suspected that they had been compromised by her dalliance with Darius, she had allowed herself to be lulled into a sense of false security, sex had a way of dulling those senses. She had not wanted to move on from Bali, but circumstances had dictated her sudden departure. New Zealand had presented her with a situation not of her own making. Now she found herself in Australia, her passport stamped for a year, after which she hoped she would have mastered the finer points of Australian immigration requirements to remain for an indefinite period.

As far back as she could remember, her life was spent in some kind of subterfuge, evasion, bluff, or pretence, whatever the occasion required from her, as she was growing up behind the Iron Curtain. Subterfuge and roleplay had been so deeply ingrained into her character that she had continued to live by those same set of rules, set down for her so long ago. Reflection or introspection, she discovered, never came naturally to her. Her decisions were made depending on her needs at any given time during her life; pragmatism ruled.

The earthquake had shifted some personal paradigm. It brought about a deeper understanding of who she really was when all her layers of duplicity were peeled away, and she liked what it revealed. Her narcissistic need to protect herself at all costs had vanished. She had applied what little knowledge she had in a dire situation not to protect herself but to help others, in spite of being in mortal danger. Never before had she put others (not even Yvetta, if she was honest) before her own needs. Her services to Yvetta had not exactly been altruistic. It helped Fritzi to help Yvetta, and to keep her close. Yvetta filled a deep-seated need reaching way back into her childhood, she needed her in some way she hadn't figured out yet.

Flopping onto the cushions piled up behind her, she lay for some time staring at the ceiling, her mind in a fog. She felt numbed but somehow simultaneously excited and alive. Was this what they called a religious experience? With this in mind, she fell into a deep sleep.

She woke feeling slightly disorientated, still in the towelling robe, her hair still damp, on her pillow. She rose from the bed, feeling a little less ethereal, and also a little less secure about her earlier decisions. The ground had shifted underneath her. She was experiencing her very own earthquake, and her usual, steady equilibrium felt a little off-kilter for once. She was second-guessing everything – especially herself.

Having no one with whom to discuss the many thoughts in her head, she dressed and made her way to one of the many outdoor cafés along the beach. Here she could enjoy the fresh air, a swim, and a hearty breakfast. Food always helped.

Padding her way up the beach after a refreshing swim, she sat on the warm concrete, watching the other swimmers. People were on early morning runs, and mothers with toddlers, babies, and pets were being walked along the pier before the heat of the day became unbearable. Washing the sea salt off her body under a beach shower, she made her way to one of the many cafés, for breakfast. Her stomach felt hollow from hunger.

Chapter 7

Darius wondered where Fritzi had gone. He hoped she had heeded his warning. The French girl he had recruited to deliver the message had been pretty convinced that the message had got through to Fritzi. Fritzi probably thought Darius had returned to Bali to find her gone. It was a pity but it couldn't be helped. He imagined she would have been disappointed to find he had not returned. Still, it had worked out for the best.

Drinking his morning coffee at his local café, reading about the devastating earthquake in New Zealand, he marvelled at the selfless tourist who had saved the prime minister's son. The funny thing was she had seemed to vanish into thin air. Something about the story niggled at the back of his mind, but he let it go.

Looking up from his paper as his breakfast arrived, he watched a girl take a table in the shade under the awnings. She reminded him of Freddie: she had a similar build and easy relaxed manner of walking, she carried her casual beach wrap slung around her hips with a little more than style it was hard not to notice her. He went back to his breakfast and paper, but after a few bites he returned his gaze to the girl.

Something about her drew him to her. He wanted to watch her more closely, and he did. Slyly, between mouthfuls of coffee, spoonful's of Greek yoghurt, and shifting pages of print, he studied her. She did not appear to see him, or return his gaze. But on closer inspection he was convinced it was Freddie or was it Fritzi. Her hair had changed colour and it was piled up on her head, huge black sunglasses were covering most of her face, yet something in her manner, the way she scoped her surroundings casually, always on guard, was very familiar. He watched her flag down a waitress. A few seconds later (the service here was always excellent), the waitress returned with the morning's newspaper, the one that Darius was reading.

After thanking the waitress, the girl, too, began scanning the front page. The more he looked at her, the more sure he was. He saw her head buried in the paper. The likeness was almost uncanny.

Trying to put the scenario together of what might have happened after his warning, he smiled at the brilliance of it and the sheer luck of her situation, if it had been her who rescued the son of the Australian prime minister, he knew he was grabbing at straws, but the more her re read the article and, the description of the girl who saved the Australian prime minister's son, it made sense, especially her, disappearance, after arriving in Sydney. If so, she would enter Australia with little difficulty and, knowing Freddie, she would take full advantage of the situation she found herself in. Once here she would conveniently disappear before the tabloids had time to interview her. The last thing she would want, he thought, was her photo splashed all over the papers, and, she would feel safe in Sydney, confident that Darius had returned to Bali, as arranged.

Luckily, she could not see him from her vantage point, for a family of five were blocking her view of his table. Darius moved his seat further out of her eyeline. Her breakfast had arrived, so he had time to decide what his next move would be. He had no intention of putting her in harm's way, in any way. He had a healthy respect for this girl, who had lived a life he could only imagine. She was a contradiction in terms, an oxymoron, a Sheila (as Bruce would call her), a dinkum bad angel.

Now convinced it was Freddie, Darius had to decide how he was going to play this. If he confronted her, he may have to tell her he knew her secret – but he felt it wasn't to his advantage for her to know, not yet, at least. He wanted her to feel secure. She was adept at vanishing, and he had to decide whether he wanted her back in his life, seeing

Freddie made his heart flutter in his chest, he realised his curiosity about her and, his feelings seeing her again in the flesh, were hard to ignore.

Fritzi had finished her breakfast and was still paging through the paper. Indeed, he hadn't seen her read anything so intently, and in such a focused manner. He watched as she called for the bill, thanking the waitress once again. Having paid his own bill, he was free to follow her from a distance, his best option.

Cap pulled low over his face and sunglasses still on, for cover he chatted to a mother pushing a baby. As they reached some steps leading up to the road, he lifted the pushchair for her and stood a few feet behind Fritzi her walk was unmistakable, head held high her strides long her hips moved as if on a catwalk, she was he thought maddeningly attractive, as they crossed the road. Staying a good distance behind, he walked past as she entered a trendy boutique hotel. Now he knew where she was staying, literally ten minutes from his apartment.

Darius had the written report from Bruce in his safe; once indoors he settled down in his study with the report. After deciding not to return to Bali, he hadn't bothered to study the report in depth. Now he read every detail intently. After reading the report through several times, he sat back reflecting on what he had learnt. She had not killed anyone. Sasha, the guy she had shot, her girlfriend's brother, had been injured but had survived. On a previous occasion, she had saved his life from the people who kidnapped him in Russia. The circumstances about the kidnapping were very vague; he wasn't sure whether Freddie (whose real name, he learnt, was Fritzi) had organised for Sasha to be abducted, but how could she have done so if she was in a jail somewhere in the States at the time? Something did not compute. Perhaps one day he would hear the real story from her – if, indeed, that was the real story. Most of her years had been spent trying to free Yvetta from one institution or another, while working for the syndicate.

Her escape from the Russian jail was pretty spectacular. As he re-read the report once more, his decision was made. Fritzi, to his mind, was not a bad person, perhaps a misguided one. He felt sure that her heart was pure. She had dealt in illegal artefacts, but had served her time in jail. Her still being on Interpol's list of undesirables seemed a ridiculous waste of time and money, although of course he was not privy to all of Interpol's information, or reasoning. Obviously, since she had escaped from a Russian jail, they were still keeping an eye on her. Darius ever the optimist, wondered whether a deal could be struck, through the right parties. He wanted to help Fritzi now. He thought she deserved a break. She was still young and had her whole life ahead of her. He also had to admit to himself that his reasons were not entirely altruistic; he was completely infatuated with her.

The question was how would he could go about achieving this mission he was embarking on, not only to clear her name with the authorities, but to convince her to trust him. Darius had been at school and uni with Jared, the Prime Minister's son, not that he was back then, but he was a good bloke at school, and Darius had been told his personality had not changed in the intervening years. A chat about what had happened to him in New Zealand could be the way to go, that's if it had been Fritzi who saved his life? There was no time like the present. Darius tried Jared's number, hoping he would pick up. 'Hi, Jared here,' a familiar if faint, slightly pained, voice said.

'Jared, it's Darius Mattista. How are you, mate? I couldn't believe what happened when I read the papers. That girl really saved your life?'

'I know,' Jared said in his warm, affectionate but urbane voice that hadn't changed at all over the years. Still, echoes of the physical pain he was in could be heard in his voice from time to time. A softening and lowering of his cadence, a kind of wince between the words. Still, it quickly became apparent that his trademark, boyish humour had not left him. Even between the obvious physical pain ran a healthy streak of mischief and joviality. 'She was quite a stunner, too. I managed to run into her at the field hospital the next day, but I got the impression she wasn't keen on being a hero. It certainly seems that way, because none of the papers can track her down.'

'This might be an odd question, but can you describe her to me? I think I might know who she is.'

'How so?'

'From the paper's vague description, she sounds a bit like someone I met in Bali.'

'Well, as I said, she was a looker, for sure. Tall, with long auburn hair and green eyes. She was helping the medics out. There was a serious shortage of personnel. She's apparently multilingual, so they used her for interpreting where needed. I tried to show my appreciation, asking the airlines and the ground staff to give her five-star treatment. My dad would like to thank her personally. You know, maybe give her some award for the fantastic, selfless work she did during the quake. I know the New Zealand government wanted to know her name to thank her, but she seems to have gone walkabout.'

Darius had his suspicions confirmed. It was definitely Freddie who had saved Jared's life, and probably the lives of others as well.

'Listen, mate,' Darius said, 'do you think we could have a chat about this? There is something I'd like to share with you. Maybe we could do some major payback where this Sheila is concerned. I think she might be in a spot of bother.'

'You mean with the law?' 'Not directly,' Darius said after a moment, 'but if you're willing, I think we can help her.'

'Absolutely,' Jared said. 'I'm a bit housebound at the moment with this leg and a few other injuries. Could you drop round?'

Darius knew he was taking one hell of a chance, but after reading through the Interpol report he was hoped that she had served her time. Her escaping a Russian gulag, could be, problematic, but Jared was the expert in that field.

Backing his car out of the garage, he made his way to Rose Island with the report. He would feel out Jared on the matter before allowing him to see the report; after all, Jared was a human rights lawyer.

On arrival at Jared's home, he was greeted by a posse of plain-clothed security men, who opened the door for him and ushered him in. He was obviously expected. The house was a canal-front property, modern and sleek, with views of the water. Darius was shown through to Jared's suite of rooms, where he found his old schoolmate resting on his bed. But he hadn't expected his friend to look like this.

'You look done-in,' Darius said, struggling to keep the shock from his voice. Jared, was a boyish good-looking guy and a sports fanatic, he remembered from their school and college days, now looked haggard, aged even – and in obvious pain, bruised and battered and, by his fragile demeanour obviously still in shock. I had no idea you were so badly injured, are you sure you are up to this?'

'Mate, if it wasn't for that girl, I would be a goner for sure.' Jared's voice, though tired, was obviously excited while recalling these details. Perhaps Darius wasn't the only one who had feelings for Freddie or Fritzi or whatever her name now was, Darius thought. 'I'm getting better steadily,' he said with a smile, but his thoughts had clearly returned to Freddie, and Darius could see that Jared wasn't able to think about much else. 'But that girl, she took her own life into her hands, pulling me out of that hole in the ground.'

Jared sounded shocked still, as though he couldn't believe it himself. Darius reflected that Jared must have told this tale a hundred times by now – to the media, to family, to friends – and still wasn't tired of it. Not even close. He would have this story, these images, in his head for the rest of his life.

'The aftershock was still pretty violent at the time. I was literally hanging on by my fingernails,' he made a fist with his right hand and flicked his fingers back for emphasis. Not for the first time, Darius noted how pale his hand, his skin, was. As he was watching the hand it stretched out again, touched Darius on the arm, pulled his hand tight just above his wrist in an almost intimate grasp that was, nonetheless, surprisingly strong. Darius recalled again how Jared had excelled at sports at school, 'when she grabbed my arm and pulled me out with her arm locked round mine, using every bit of strength she had, lying flat on the ground.'

To Darius's relief, he released his grip. But the story continued, in the same soft but sturdy, enthralled voice.

'Then she half-carried me to shelter from flying rocks. It's a pretty amazing story. She didn't only save my life, I heard from others at the field hospital that she worked tirelessly on her own before the emergency services arrived. She hadn't even noticed her own injuries to the head from flying debris.' The voice became low again, straining in its sincerity. I would do anything for her if it was at all possible.'

Darius had no problem believing this. He thought a moment before speaking, weighing up the situation as best he could in his mind. It was too complex, too much was at stake, to come to any snap decisions, so he decided to trust his gut and speak his mind. He needed someone to talk to, and Jared had always been, if not exactly a close friend, a trustworthy and warm acquaintance.

'Jared, I'm going to take you into my confidence here,' Darius said, already thinking twice about it as the words came out of his mouth. But it was too late. Too much of his life had been planned, strategic, overanalysed, thought through – to a fault. And for too much of his life he had felt lonely in his calculated safeness, hermetically sealed off from true emotions, from wider, and wilder, society. He longed to set himself free. Perhaps Fritzi was the person to do it. She was nothing if not free – even when imprisoned, he reflected. It was time to trust his instincts, to surrender himself to the moment, to make a bet. But still that old guardedness reared its head, that crooked finger came out of nowhere and wagged at him. Beware! it said. Trust no one, it said. Not even yourself.

He wanted to tell that finger to go to hell. So many of his old decisions had been just plain wrong. Lin, for example. Where had his guardedness and caution been when it came to Lin? 'It's taking a hell of a chance, to be honest: not for me, you understand, but from her perspective.'

Jared's lips pursed, as if to say, 'Whose perspective?'

Darius pushed on. 'If it goes pear-shaped, she'll be the one to pay. The thing is, I got into a relationship of sorts with her in Bali, and something about her wasn't quite kosher. She was just a little,' he looked for the right word, 'off. She used to scope out any crowded room before she would relax, and she kept her cards very close to her chest. She was always fiercely independent, but I used to wonder why. For what? So I did a bit of digging when I returned to Sydney. At first, my people couldn't find a thing. But then I employed a private eye to check out a passport photo I found and some banking details.

The thing is, the private eye had a friend at Interpol and he asked him to do a check. The result of that check is what I have in this folder. I am more than 99.9% sure it's about our girl.

Jared, if you feel the way I do after reading through that report, you have to admit it's a bloody amazing story for someone so young to have lived through such intrigue and danger. I must admit she made some dubious choices – why, I am not at all sure, because as you will see she had a very successful career up until that point.'

Jared sat up slightly in bed. His face relaxed, so that he looked, for a moment, younger and more content, like the Jared Darius remembered from school. The Jared so quick to kick a goal or score a try. Or to help one of his many friends. He had a lot of friends, and he had a lot of connections through his wealthy family, but he was never boastful or superior or arrogant in any way. On the contrary, he was always one of the boys – perhaps even to a fault. At uni he had had a reputation as a playboy, someone living the high life, and, like so many young men, directionless for a time, but, by all accounts, he had soon afterwards settled down and worked hard both at law school and, later, as an accomplished lawyer, as valuable a member of society in his own right as his father was. But he didn't want the kind of high-status job that his father had worked so tirelessly for – he wanted, mostly, to do good. And, still, glimpses of the schoolboy and the playboy, to have fun. 'Can you stay for a while or do you want to leave this with me?' he said.

'I'd prefer to stay, if you don't mind,' Darius said, 'and we can discuss what you think.'

Jared seemed relieved to have his company. Recuperating in this big house, surrounded by security guards, couldn't be too much fun, Darius reflected. 'Fine,' and his voice was cheerful once again, 'I will have the housekeeper make you some lunch while I go through this.' But he had already switched to lawyer mode, suddenly distant and serious, almost dismissive as he removed reading glasses from a side table and slipped them on, already lost in concentration, no longer in this room but somewhere else entirely, far away.

Darius was shown onto the patio overlooking the ocean while he waited for lunch. One of the most beautiful views in this beautiful city. Still, the view didn't exactly calm him. He was nervous and couldn't help feeling as if he had betrayed Fritzi in some way. He checked his cell for messages and spent some time working through his texts and emails. Lunch was a naked hamburger folded in romaine lettuce with diced dill cucumber and relish with a side of chips – he couldn't ask for more, and it was cooked to perfection. As he finished his iced Kombucha the housekeeper led him back to Jared's suite of rooms. He found Jared sitting at a glass desk in front of open sliding doors, leading out onto furnished decking. He noticed an infinity pool beyond the decking, leading down to a manicured lawn. The house was pretty spectacular.

'Jesus,' Jared said by way of a greeting, 'we are dealing with quite an operator here. She doesn't play for small stakes. I can see why she gave up modelling; dealing in stolen rare cultural artefacts is a very lucrative business, much more reliably lucrative than working as a midlevel model. Seems like she made quite a name for herself as a crook, too. And, all the other stuff she got up to, wow, wow, wow!' Despite his exclamations, he was smiling. But there was colour in his face now and he looked altogether healthier than he had just half an hour before. 'Never mind the fact that I have given this person with a criminal record as long as my arm free passage into our country! Darius, my friend, are you sure this is the same person who we are both involved with, but in very different ways, of course?'

He looked at Jared for a long time. The Interpol document was pretty comprehensive, much more detailed than what Bruce had detailed when he first laid eyes on it, in the café over breakfast.

They were both in a quandary, Jared from a legal standpoint. Darius realised that he hadn't taken Jared's situation as the prime minister's son into consideration – after all, this whole thing was very much unravelling in real time, and he hadn't thought that far ahead. Jared was in a fix if Darius opened up this can of worms. If the papers got hold of this information, it would be embarrassing and a disaster for the government.

The opposition party would have a field day and Fritzi would be thrown to the wolves.

'Sorry, mate,' Darius said, 'I should never have involved you. Really stupid of me.'

'Well,' Jared said slowly, removing his glasses, 'this is how I see this mess I have unwittingly got myself into: it might have come out in the wash sooner or later. So, don't feel badly. This way we might be able to exercise some damage control for all of us, including Fritzi. You know what they say: never do anyone a favour because it will come back to bite you on the arse – and that applies for her good deeds as well. I think Fritzi might regret her selflessness; it has brought unwanted attention to her. Now it seems to me we have a few options.' There were four options, and Jared marked each one off with the fingers on his right hand, the same hand he had grasped Darius's wrist with earlier that afternoon.

'Option one: allow her to melt into the outback with her false identity. If lucky, she might get away with it.

'Option two: gain her confidence, and let her know her secret life is safe with the two of us – and gently persuade her to leave the country.

'Option three: let me sit on this for a bit longer to see whether there is a possible solution. Obviously, this one takes time, and time is maybe not on our side right now.

'Option four: one good deed can be ignored, but putting your life on the line for others in such a dramatic and dangerous way deserves recognition, even if not publicly.' He tapped the folder on the glass table. 'Reading this, I think she has made bad choices, no question. But the real question is, at only twenty-eight, having served her time, shouldn't she be given another chance?'

Darius wiped his brow, went over the options on his own fingers, tried to think straight and to keep all of the options in the front of his mind. It wasn't easy. He was stressed and he could tell from Jared's voice that he was tired again. He no doubt wanted to head back to bed to recuperate.

Darius wasn't unaware that he had considerably disrupted Jared's recovery. He felt guilty, amongst other things. Still, against all odds, he had to keep his head straight. As a software developer and former workaholic, this wasn't too difficult. He was generally good with numbers – just not these numbers. Number one to three didn't sound much like options, but number four was what he had in mind and he voiced his thought hesitantly, not sure how Jared and him could make this a possible solution. Sure, Jared had a lot of powerful contacts on his side, but that wasn't always a good thing. He also, no doubt, had powerful enemies. This could very easily backfire.

'Well, I am going to leave you to sleep on that one,' Jared said, pushing his chair out and gesturing again at the folder, 'because I am in total agreement with you. I am prepared to stick my neck out to help this Sheila, but I am whacked right now, so let's go through this one more time. Is tomorrow okay for you?'

Darius shook his head. 'It's not a bad idea to sleep on it, but time is not on our side. The only issue is how do we contact her without sending her into flight mode, which is her pattern. Her default position, if you will. I must tell you when I received this information initially, I decided on the spot that I was going to help Fritzi. So, I sent an emissary to warn her: I imagine that is why she ended up in New Zealand in the first place. She is, after all, a master at deception, so it was easy, with a new passport, for her to change her identity once more.

'Yes, I can see your dilemma,' Jared said, 'but right now my head is aching and I need sleep. Darius, I am going to leave that side of things to you, unless I get a eureka moment, you won't hear from me until tomorrow.'

Chapter 8

Fritzi returned to her hotel after another great morning's swim. She was beginning to enjoy the Bondi Beach life. Coming here, now, was the right choice, she felt. And there was more opportunity here for upward mobility than there was in Bali – but more risk, too. Up at dawn, before the heat was unbearable, fitting in effortlessly with the rest of the residents, who were jogging, powerwalking and dog-walking. Everyone seemed to be outdoors before sun up, and that suited Fritzi just fine.

She had chatted to people about going into the interior, but was advised to stay put until the heat wave abated. There was no real rush: she had managed to slip under the radar before the media were able to splash her photo all over the newspapers. The article printed in all the papers had not given any personal details, and the story thankfully had now died down. She might move on to Melbourne, and then travel onto Tasmania, where she'd read about the modern art museum carved out of rock, called Mona.

Preoccupied with her options, she entered the hotel to collect her room key. Noting the receptionist's uneasy manner, Fritzi spun round to find two burly, plain-clothed men with earpieces standing in the lobby. Uncertain and suddenly scared, she stood rooted to the spot. She breathed, reminded herself that whatever was going on might have nothing to do with her. But her instinct, every fibre in her being, said otherwise. The expression on the girl's face said a lot, and none of it was good. Best option was to be cool, nonchalant. One of the gorillas stepped forward and whispered something in her ear. He obviously did not want to create a fuss. It was a whisper, all right, but every word echoed through her body, a shiver that became a vibration that became something else entirely. Fear. Breathe.

'Ah, yes,' she said evenly and quietly, but in an admirably easy, untroubled manner. Always cool, always calm, especially under pressure. She may only be twenty-eight, but she was an expert, a professional. She had seen and experienced more than most people had at twice her age.'

'I understand, but as you can see I have just returned from the beach and would like to change.' She managed a most agreeable smile. As expected, the gorilla did not, or could not, smile back. His was a face unburdened by emotion, and unaccustomed to it. A pale, thickset, heavy face. Purely professional. If he was interested in women, or ever had the inclination or desire to flirt, it did not show now. A grimace, not even that. A mask of indifference.

'Could you give me half an hour, and I will meet you back here in the lobby,' Fritzi continued.

The agents had been given strict instructions not to give her any opportunity to slip away. They had been briefed on her history, too. They knew that if she gave them the slip, they would never see her again.

Instead, they stuck to her like glue, travelled up in the lift with her, entering her suite to wait while she changed. Now she was thinking fast, reminding herself to breathe all the time. Slipping on clothes without a second glance, taking her time, almost unconsciously, figuring out a way out of this. But what was it? She could delay – but for how long? And to what end? There was no handy window to crawl out of. No magic door to another dimension, one without police or security personnel. There was no way out of this predicament but to go along with them. One thing she was good at was thinking on her feet.

Before she knew it, the road stretching ahead of her, the sun still bright out, she was sitting in the back of a dark-windowed black saloon car. One of the gorillas had informed her she would be attending a meeting. What she really wanted to know was how they had managed to track her down. Obviously, someone was onto her – who she had no idea.

The door was held open for her and she was led into a sleek, spectacular modern house built into the cliffs cantilevered over the ocean. Her welcome party appeared to be a party of two: the prime minister's son, who still looked pretty beat-up from his ordeal, and – Darius! But how? Fritzi was rarely in shock – but she was in shock now. She tried to speak, but no words came out. That was unusual, too. Better to find out first what was going on, before she possibly incriminated herself. In this most beautiful house, in a breath-taking location, she felt suffocated, trapped.

She wanted to run, but she couldn't speak, couldn't move. Was this where it would end for her? Where Fritzi would finally run out of road? She loved surprises – when she was the one to provide them. But she detested being taken by surprise. She needed to feel in charge of all situations, at any given time. And right now, she had no control. She felt like she was spinning in all directions, disoriented, dizzy even.

Both came over to welcome her. There was an ease between them; it appeared that they were familiar with one another. The prime minister's son, with a sly, almost shy, smile, spoke first. 'Sorry for the subterfuge,' he said, 'but what we have to share with you might be to your benefit. And after you so selflessly put your life on the line, both Darius and I believe you deserve a break.'

Now, she finally managed to speak. Her normally clear, confident voice came out jumbled now. 'Sorry, but I am not altogether sure what you are referring to.' She turned to the other man.

'And Darius, how on earth did you know where to find me?'

Darius smiled and said, 'May we call you Fritzi? That might give you some idea why you are here.' That was the moment when her heart felt as though it would give in, when the room began to spin.

She stared at Darius, his words not quite registering at first. Then she sank down in an armchair as her knees began to buckle; she could feel her whole body going into meltdown. This was her worst nightmare, her jig was up, and she had nowhere to run now.

Shocked at her reaction, Jared poured her a vodka and told her to drink it down. Well, she didn't need to be asked twice. She downed that vodka as if it was water. Jared poured her another.

'Now look,' Jared said, 'we aren't here to judge you, Fritzi. We have a comprehensive report about your life from Interpol.

She could feel the vodka hitting her brain as it burnt down her throat and into her empty stomach. After the second vodka, she began to feel less threatened being faced down by these two men. Surely, she was smarter than both of them put together? She was still shocked at being tracked down and exposed in this way – but they did not seem to be at all malicious in their intent. That perhaps gave her an opening, an advantage. Her brain was working overtime, going one way and then another; in the end she indicated that they should fill her in. 'I honestly do not know which way to turn. What do you both want from me?'

Again, Jared was the first to speak. 'First, we want you to go through this document from Interpol with a fine-tooth comb. You will be staying here while we figure out the best course of action to take.' They could tell she was in flight mode, not quite figuring out yet how to read this situation she now found herself in.

'I am a human rights lawyer,' Jared said softly. 'That may make it easier for you to understand why it's necessary for us to work on a solution for your future together. I am sure you do not want to spend the rest of your life on the run.'

Visibly shaking, reeling from the vodka, she was barely holding it together. She noticed a platter of food on the glass table. Food would probably help her think with more clarity.

Jared indicated that she should eat something. She did not need another invitation; grabbing a plate, she filled it with bread, fruit, and downed some strong coffee. She hadn't realised how hungry she was. She refilled her plate with cold meats and smoked fish, juice and more coffee. Hopefully now she could think more clearly – clearly enough to think her way out of this situation, whatever this situation was. That was the thing – she didn't know. And she hated not knowing. But they didn't seem to want to betray her, nor did either of them have a reason to. They watched her carefully as she ate hungrily, noting her colour slowly returning. When she was done, Jared said, 'I suggest further discussion should be behind closed doors, in my study.'

Darius, taking a seat a distance from Fritzi, explained how he had employed a private eye to learn more about her.

'Why?' Fritzi asked.

'Well,' said Darius, who had expected this question, 'I was a little suspicious of your cover story. Also, your lack of trust in others. The way you scoped out any crowded room when entering, and your guarded attitude when asked anything personal. If we were going to continue our relationship, I wanted to know what I was dealing with.'

'Oh,' she said, lost for words again. When she had met Darius, her inner voice had told her not to embark on a relationship. A fling was fine, of course, but anything longer and deeper than that opened up a world of complication – and danger. She should have taken heed. It was dangerous to let one's guard down, and intimacy with a lover was the worst of all: they were bound to pick up inconsistencies, others did not notice.

Jared and Darius exchanged glances, then Jared passed her the Interpol document. She glanced over it and passed it back in a disinterested, almost flippant, manner. 'It's my life. Why do I need to go over my own life?'

'Perhaps it's not comprehensive enough,' Jared said firmly. 'I want to know every detail of your life, all the way back to your childhood.'

'But why?' Fritzi protested. Her previous tone of indifference had been replaced by one of urgency, even anger. Her eyes flashed.

'It all helps to build up a picture,' Jared said, his voice softer now, 'you understand? We are going to spend many hours together. Luckily, I have the time off to recuperate. So, it's the ideal opportunity, and to save time and to keep you safe, it's best you remain here with me.'

Fritzi's eyes turned to Darius. 'Tell me, Darius, did you pass any information about me onto Interpol that I should know about?'

Darius didn't flinch. 'I found your passport,' he said, 'took a copy of it and of some minor banking details. My guy did the rest. Actually, he had an old mate still working for the agency. Unfortunately for you, Interpol were able to find you on their database, with all the details of your arrests.'

'So now they know where I am?' she asked.

'If they do,' Darius said, 'they will look in Bali – but luckily you are not there.'

'How did you know I was in Sydney, Darius?'

'Another fluke. You did not know I have an apartment on Bondi Beach. If you had known that, you would have known that I would have run into you at some stage. I noticed you yesterday at my regular breakfast place. Freddie – or should I say Fritzi? – your body language is pretty familiar to me. Your hair colour might have changed, but I noticed you walk in, and, on further examination, was convinced it was you – even with the large sunglasses and your hair up. I then followed you to your hotel, and watched you walk in. After that, I decided the best course of action to help you was to confide in my friend Jared, whose life you saved.'

'Oh,' she said again. As she realised how easy it had been to track her down, she felt less and less confident. She was still uncertain – about so much. She felt unusually vulnerable – and she hated that feeling. She was not sure how this was going to pan out. She wanted to trust them, but it seemed foolish to do so. Perhaps she had been too trusting already. She had always thought she was cynical and untrusting, but obviously she wasn't untrusting enough. she had no choice but to be willing and compliant. But with each revelation, she became more and more angry at her own lack of care.

Her carefree attitude had endangered and ensnared her. She thought she was an expert, a model criminal, but she was anything but. She was being exposed now not only as a criminal, but, much worse, as an amateur. If she was going to expose her true self to Darius, she would do it on her own time and in her own space. Not here and now. Not like this. Not with someone else calling all the shots, she felt strangely powerless.

She could feel her legs flex, her body at the ready. She was still in, flight mode – but there was nowhere to run to now. It was going to be a sharp learning curve to change her behaviour and to trust these two with her wellbeing, no matter how well-intentioned they appeared. Yvetta aside, she had learnt to leave other people out of the equation of her life, to trust almost no one, to shape her own fate. Darius had said he began to be suspicious when he saw her scan a room. So her own suspect nature had helped to do her in. Maybe she had scanned the wrong rooms, or not been clandestine enough in her activity. She had played the game all wrong. Now she had to unlearn everything, concede defeat, declare her old ruse a fraud, become someone else entirely once more.

She looked over at Darius, who now seemed so distant.

'I want to ask you, Darius, did you send a messenger to Bali to warn me to leave?'

Darius was trying not to show his feelings, he felt conflicted Freddie still made his heart flutter, she was an enigma but an extremely attractive one, someone who he felt protective towards, even though Fritzi gave the impression of being a hard-nosed professional operator he had noted, and, felt her vulnerability and, her need for love.

'Well, yes, as a matter of fact, I did, and I am pleased you heeded my warning straight away. I am sorry, Fritzi – or should I still call you Freddie? But you must be able to see this situation you find yourself in as an opportunity – a kind of blessing, even. If you play this right, it could set you free to live the rest of your life without having to lie or go on the run.'

No one had ever done something like that for her – no one legit, anyway – she owed him big-time. Or did she? Time would tell, but one thing she knew for sure was that their relationship was well and truly over. Darius had been frightened off, and she was pleased. He may have thought he was protecting her, but she could tell he was visibly shaken, not quite as keen to be with her now. He had taken it upon himself to have her investigated for his own curiosity and guarded instincts about her, now she saw a Darius who had withdrawn his boyish crush, he no longer appeared to see her as a lover, or, even someone he may have wanted in his life, did she really feel relieved, she was conflicted herself, her usually controlled emotions unreliable right now.

'We have a lot of work to get through, you understand, Fritzi?' Darius said. 'We know your true identity. But it is entirely up to you whether you want to go ahead with this option we have put before you. Of course, we cannot force you, but frankly I do not see any other course of action – unless you prefer to remain on the run. In that case, you need to leave Australia straight away.'

Everyone imagined Fritzi's own interests came first. Situations often presented her with dire options. Yet her cunning had saved her from life-threatening situations –more than once. And not only her, but Yvetta, her partner, the love of her life, too. It was a relationship that sustained both of them – or so Fritzi had thought. Yvetta needing her had always been Fritzi's strength. Now Yvetta had moved on with her life. She no longer needed Fritzi, and as a result, Fritzi felt her life lacked purpose, that her soul and her energy had been sapped, if not entirely destroyed.

She felt lost, and she had lost herself in Bali and Bondi Beach, and would have continued to lose herself if she had not been so rudely interrupted. She had tried to mourn Yvetta's loss, but she hadn't truly come to terms with it, even now. As these thoughts raced around her mind, the fight to carry on diminished, leaving her feeling beaten – an unusual and frightening sensation for her – depleted of energy. With few options, she no longer had reason to continue. Getting back to (and winning over once more) Yvetta had been her raison d' etre, and now that was off the table, too.

She was faced with a new reality and the possibility of a clean slate – and why was that so terrifying? The prospect of another shot at life to her, who had re-invented herself so many times, should have been exhilarating, but right now it daunted and depressed her. She felt unusually exhausted and worn-out. Darius noticed her fatigued state, her odd enervated posture, and was disturbed by it. This wasn't the Fritzi he knew, although, of course, he had not known Fritzi at all. Who knew, he thought now, who she really was. Did she even know herself? Possibly not.

She did not immediately respond. Jared and Darius remained quiet now. She was struggling with her options, or lack thereof, and they gave her the space to think everything through. From somewhere, she could hear the ticking of invisible clocks.

'Yes,' Fritzi said slowly, finally, almost painfully, after a long pause, 'my answer is okay. You must understand, I have never entrusted my freedoms to anyone – not since I was fifteen years old, and first became independent. I am my own person, and always have been. It's going to be a steep learning curve.'

'No one is asking you to be someone else,' Jared said quickly. But Darius was thinking, your own person – don't you mean your own people? She was, indeed, fiercely independent – or maybe just fierce. But fierce people could be tamed, too – or at least learn to live a better life. Perhaps she could be herself, whatever or whoever that self was, but a better version of that self. After all, everyone deserved another chance.

'Good,' Jared said, 'let's get you settled, and we can begin tomorrow. For now, you can familiarise yourself with the house, because it's best you remain here until we figure out what's safe.'

'Not such a hardship,' Darius said, 'it's a beautiful property, and if you like I can visit.'

Fritzi shook her head vaguely, in a state of disbelief. This was kindness she hadn't before experienced, but it was hard to show her appreciation feeling this exhausted.

'I know you mean well,' Fritzi said, 'and I do appreciate it, but right now I'm done in. Would you mind if I rested a while? I might feel differently after I've slept.'

She was shown to a spare room opening onto a garden and infinity pool that looked out on the bay and Sydney beyond. Her small suite was compact and beautiful, yet she had little interest in her surroundings. Crawling into the double bed, she lay staring up at the ceiling. For once, her mind blank, the shock of being hunted down like a fugitive with no options numbing her brain, and her body felt fatigued exhaustion.

Chapter 9

Jared had been keeping a low profile. His cases were either being put on hold by the courts, or partners would take over in his absence. They all specialised in different areas of the law. His father, though a politician, had never interfered with his youngest child's more liberal views, even those that clashed with the conservative policies of his government. His sister was married with three kids, leaving him space to enjoy his freedom as a single man, and to live his life as he pleased. Coming from a supportive, loving family, Jared had strong feelings about protecting those less fortunate. He was looking forward to hearing Fritzi's story, and hoped it would enable him and Darius to set her free from her present predicament. She was obviously a very troubled soul.

Jared's bedroom suite was on the entrance level; since the accident he had not been able to have his morning swim on the lower level, where Fritzi was sleeping. He had been encouraged to seek physiological help. Apparently, the aftershock of staring death in the face could overwhelm one emotionally. So, he started to meet with his shrink for a chat on a weekly basis, as advised by his doctor. Leaving early in the morning, he therefore asked his housekeeper to see to Fritzi's needs.

By nine o'clock, deemed ready to face the world, he spent the morning going through his cases at the office, catching up on office gossip with his secretary, and meeting his colleagues for lunch in the conference room for a chat. Apart from his broken leg, his injuries had more or less healed. Everyone in the office shared their sympathies about what had happened. It was, after all, an amazing, dismaying story.

Jared had been on business in Christchurch when the earthquake struck. He was on his way to their offices when the pavement he was walking on suddenly cracked open under his feet, nearly swallowing him in the process. Repeating the story gave many an insight to what had happened, both to him and to Christchurch, and he took the opportunity to retell how his life was miraculously saved by a woman's selfless heroism. Many questions were asked about the woman in question, but Jared kept her identity a mystery, and the details of the story deliberately sketchy, not ready to share her story, or to expose her to the world. He knew how much was at stake for her – and for him. She had gambled her life for him, but he wasn't quite ready to gamble with her life, at least not like that.

The housekeeper was waiting for him when he walked through the front door, and he immediately knew something was wrong. Her usually calm exterior was uncharacteristically agitated, her face even more lined than usual and her mouth hanging open, as if about to ask a question but unsure about her words.

'What's wrong, Maggie?' he asked.

'Mr Jared,' Maggie said, in her accent that was still heavy despite her many years in Sydney. 'I am so sorry, but the lady downstairs has vanished. I went down with a tray at 10 this morning and knocked on the door. When I got no reply, I opened the door. The bed was made. It looked untouched. I don't think she even slept there. Where could she have gone? I looked all over the house. There is not a sign of her anywhere. The security man did not see her leaving, either. It's very strange, sir.'

Jared was as shocked as Maggie was. He remembered what it said in the Interpol report: 'must be watched at all times, likely to flee at any moment. Highly resourceful – and highly intelligent.' Had they made a mistake trusting Fritzi? Could she turn their kindness against them? Perhaps they, too, were in danger now. He decided to stay calm. After what happened in Christchurch, he couldn't stomach any more heightened drama. Neither his heart nor his head could take it. Living a high-drama life was all well and good, but it took its toll on the body. After a while, even the most seasoned adventurer craved only for a cup of tea, a warm bath, and a good sleep. In other words, a life free – at least for a moment – from adventure. Blessed quiet. Even boredom could feel like a treat after too much excitement. Not that Jared's life, from childhood onwards, had ever been close to boring. If anything, it was the opposite.

He spoke calmly now, in a clear voice. 'Well, let's go look again,' he said with a false note of confidence. Maggie looked at him sternly; she didn't believe his tone, either. Her round, open face was never good at concealing her emotions. That was one thing he valued most about her – her unflagging honesty, even in matters he would rather not hear about. He had a filial urge to protect her from certain things. Sometimes he wondered to himself who, exactly, was charged with looking after whom. Still, they had a terrific relationship that had spanned now over several decades, since Jared was a boy. She knew him – and knew when he was anxious, and now was one of those times.

'Maybe she slept outdoors,' he said hollowly, not even believing the suggestion himself. 'It was very muggy last night. The temperatures have been up this year.' Temperatures up in Sydney. Earthquakes in Christchurch. A strange girl in his house – or, rather, not in his house. The world was upside-down.

They checked Fritzi's room again, searched for her beaten-up backpacker's rucksack, but found nothing. Then searched the terraced lawns down to the marina, where Jared's boat was moored.

'Fritzi, are you there?' Jared called. He hadn't realised how worked-up he would get over this girl he barely knew. Really, knew just two things about her. She had saved his life. And she was trouble. Big, big trouble. 'Please answer, we are all very worried about you. Just let us know you are okay. If you are on the boat just shout yes. I really don't mind,' he lied, 'as long as you are fine.'

They waited a few moments, but nothing. He looked at Maggie and she looked at him. They both looked at the boat, then at each other again. Then down at the ground, at nothing. Hoping to see Fritzi, or even a glimpse of Fritzi. Some sort of memento. Anything, at this point, would do. Did she not have the grace to at least write a farewell note? he wondered. He shook his head, about to give up, when a head popped out of the boat. It was Fritzi, thank God. She appeared to be okay, but looked dishevelled, her hair hanging lankly and obviously messy. Her movements, her posture, were sluggish and slow, too. It was as though she was still asleep, not quite awake or alive. Her demeanour was of someone in a funk of depression.

Maggie immediately went into mother mode, which was, it often appeared, her default mode in any occasion. Certainly, after all these years, he was susceptible to it himself. All adults, he felt deep down, enjoyed being babied from time to time, having responsibility taken away from them and replaced only by warmth and light, promises of safety, promises of love. 'Oh, my dear girl,' she said softly, 'please come up to the house with us. I have some homemade bread and a hearty vegetable soup.' But Fritzi did not, perhaps could not, move. 'Please, dear, come give us your hand, let us help you out of that muggy boat, it's so much cooler indoors.'

Fritzi stared in astonishment. No one had ever spoken to her in such a kindly and motherly manner. She couldn't recall either of her parents being so gentle in their Germanic fashion. In fact, her father was a tyrant in private (and in his professional life as well), a bully, who prided himself on being able to break men (and, it turned out, women) down.

Her own mother was too busy enabling her husband's tyranny to care for her children. An old-fashioned woman – and an unsentimental one. Loyal to her husband – to a fault. Largely indifferent to her children and their needs. Sometimes cold, sometimes cruel, but always emotionally absent. In any case, the business of motherhood did not appear to appeal to her. And so Fritzi grew up in a house empty of love.

Tears welled in her eyes. That was another shock – when did she last cry? She couldn't remember. For that matter, when had she last felt safe, secure in her true self? Ever alert, her guard always up, she was tired of trusting no one. She had trusted her old traits – but where had they ever got her? Nowhere. Here. Trapped. Perhaps it was time for a change. Eventually, very slowly, she stirred. Still barely moving, she stretched out her hand to be hoisted off the boat and followed them indoors.

Sitting at the sleek metal kitchen table she picked at the bread and hardly touched the soup. Jared watched, concerned for her wellbeing, but relieved that she was at least in his sight again.

'Fritzi, please eat some more. You need some strength. We can start whenever you are ready, if that's what you want.'

She looked up forlornly. 'I have always had Yvetta to fight for. Now I have nothing anymore. I feel lost, completely lost. Yes,' she said hollowly, 'I have lost myself.' And then, as if to herself alone, her voice low now, 'Who am I now?'

Maggie felt her heart ache for this girl. In her firm but kind voice she said, 'Kind, du must dich delbst kamphen.'

Fritzi's head shot up.

'You are German?' she asked, surprised.

Again, Fritzi thought, she had misjudged someone. Perhaps she was losing her touch. Now she had to reassess everything.

'I am a German Jew, yes,' Maggie said, 'but my German is not so good. My parents spoke at home only.' For some reason – she did not know why – Fritzi got up from her chair and went over to Maggie, putting her head on her breast. Jared understood. Everyone knew that there was something profoundly motherly about the old woman. Just having her around caused a kind of calmness in his house, and in his heart. Maggie held her close, stroking her hair, patting her back as if to comfort her. Fritzi's body shook as she sobbed uncontrollably.

Maggie's eyes met Jared's. He indicated she should keep holding Fritzi until she calmed. But who knew how long that would be? It seemed to Maggie the girl was breaking down, sob after sob, and how tightly she held onto her, as if for dear life. Eventually, they led her downstairs. Maggie turned on the shower and, as a mother does to her young child, helped her get ready for bed. Tucking Fritzi in tight, making sure she felt secure and safe she sat on an armchair beside the bed until she saw Fritzi breathing evenly, close to sleep, she hoped. Then she quietly left the room and shut the door, making sure not to rattle the handle.

Upstairs, she went into Jared's study and sat down heavily, shaking her head sadly. 'Mr Jared, I do not know what happened to that beautiful woman, but she needs help.'

'I know, Maggie,' he said, pleased to have someone to talk to about this most pressing and complicated subject, 'and that's what we are going to try and do – help her. You know, she saved my life in New Zealand, and the lives of many others, too.'

'Mine Got, I read about that. This is the same girl?' Her amazement was evident, but now she surprised him by following it up with an expression of renewed concern. 'But they never found her to interview. Now I can understand why; she is not well.'

'I agree with you,' he said softly. 'We will wait and see how she copes in the next few days. I forgot you spoke German. Your parents were second generation. So your grandparents came after the war?'

'Correct. I have worked for many ex-prime ministers in the past, but your father wanted me to take on this job. It's not as demanding, you understand, and I wasn't ready to retire.'

'But you don't need to work, Maggie.'

Lifting her shoulders in a resigned manner, she said, 'And what would I do? No children, no grandchildren no husband to care for any longer.'

'Well, I am pleased you are here,' Jared said. And then, after a moment, his voice softer still, 'You do understand that everything that happens here in this house is in strictest confidence.'

Smiling, suddenly looking much younger, Maggie said, 'Well, it has been like that since I started in this job long before I came here.'

'Yes, sorry, of course,' Jared continued, 'but we absolutely do not want the media to get hold of Fritzi's story or to learn that she is here. If that happened, it would literally ruin her life.'

'I understand,' Maggie said, 'and we will nurture her so she gets a spring back in her step once more. She is too young and beautiful to be so unhappy.'

Jared smiled. 'So right,' he said. 'Thanks Maggie.'

Maggie took this as her cue. On soft feet she left the room and at the door turned.

'Good night, see you in the morning.'

'By the way,' Jared said, 'what did you say to Fritzi in German?'

'You have yourself to fight for.'

The following morning, Maggie found she did not need to go down with a tray: Fritzi was up and waiting for her in the kitchen, sitting at the sleek table with a mug of coffee in her hand.

'Good morning, dear,' Maggie said. 'Goodness, it's just gone seven and you are already dressed. Are you going somewhere today?'

'No. Maggie, do you mind if we talk? I wanted to catch you before Jared was up. I need to apologize for my dreadful, weak behaviour yesterday.'

With a fresh cup of coffee for them both, Maggie sat down at the table with Fritzi. 'What for?' Maggie said. 'You are human, like the rest of us.' She looked closer at Fritzi. 'Being strong all the time is exhausting, yes?' Fritzi met her gaze head on, then turned her head away, shook it, and sighed.

'Oh, I don't know,' she said softly. 'I have always known how to fight, but now I am so weak, crying all the time.' She touched just below her left eye, for emphasis. Then, her tone suddenly stronger, self-rebuking, 'Ach, this is nonsense.'

'Give it time,' Maggie said, standing up from the table but not yet moving from her spot, still tightly facing Fritzi, 'you will see, it will pass and you will know what to do. You are in the right place, and safe, so take advantage of Mr Jared's help – he was very grateful for yours. Give him the opportunity to say thank you for saving his life.'

For half an hour, she watched Maggie as she went about preparing breakfast, organising the other staff, ordering the necessary groceries, making lists for household chores, drycleaners, deliveries. The gardeners were due and needed to be sorted; the security duty were changing over. Maggie did all of this in her unbreakable, unflappable manner, in a brisk and practised way, a model of efficiency and economy. Maggie had been doing this job for a very long time, and was clearly very good at it. Fritzi realised Maggie was an integral part of Jared's household. Without her, this well-oiled system would surely break down. Perhaps Jared, who just days ago had been in significant physical pain, would break down, too. Nothing would function smoothly without her.

At thirty-two years old Jared had not married, and under normal circumstances was out of the house and at his office by 8.30, and often not home until well after midnight. It was Maggie who kept his home life organised, who functioned as his housekeeper, secretary, personal assistant, mother, confidante, and – Fritzi suspected – occasional shoulder to cry on. Maggie was calm, orderly and organised. Doing a dozen things at once didn't faze her: answering calls, preparing meals, writing lists, delegating – Maggie took it all in her stride.

Watching a life that had such purpose and order, yet seemed blissfully uncomplicated (and uncorrupted), pure even, felt like a tonic to Fritzi. Fritzi suddenly, wonderfully, felt so safe, almost happy, just sitting there surrounded by domesticity. Like a child idling their afternoon away, in sunlight and safety, without a care in the world, while her mother stood beside her, working in the kitchen. It had been a long time since she was reminded of her mother, but Maggie's no-nonsense, straightforward nature made her feel safe – it was a strange feeling, but a nice one, nonetheless. Ever attentive, with seemingly a hundred eyes and ears, Maggie watched Fritzi watching her. Softly she suggested, Fritzi wished her mother's no-nonsense approach was as warm as Maggie's, sadly she only remembered narrow minded coldness, mixed with an ever present fear of the state's interference in their already controlled lives.

'Why don't you go and have a swim? It's still cool enough, and the exercise would do you good, clear the cobwebs.' She gave Fritzi a concerned look. 'Nothing better for the mind and body.'

As always, Maggie had a point. Indeed, Fritzi's body felt heavy, lethargic, sitting and watching all that activity going on around her was about as much as she could manage right now, but she nevertheless took Maggie's advice. Despite (or because of) her soft tone and caring cadences, it was difficult to say no to Maggie. Fritzi found herself wanting the older woman's approval. It felt good to get out of the kitchen and explore the environs a little, and this house was, indeed, expansive and magnificent.

The ocean view was best of all, but the swimming pool, the house's own interior ocean, was impressively large – and deep. The water was surprisingly cold, but refreshing. Swimming lengths until exhausted, feeling now like a new person, revived and refreshed, she lay on the warm concrete beside the pool, allowing it to dry her body. It was not yet ten, but the heat was already unbearable, and she made her way indoors for a shower. Pulling on a pair of ragged denim shorts and a top, she went in search of Jared.

Maggie informed her that he had left for a doctor's appointment. Jared was hoping his cast could be reduced to just below his knee. Not knowing how to fill her time, still exploring the many rooms of this seemingly endless but nonetheless compact and stylish house, she found her way to Jared's library, which was a small room partitioned off from the upper level by sliding oak doors. Spending a few hours here wouldn't be a hardship, she thought.

Among the hundreds of volumes of legal tomes and modern novels, he had a comprehensive collection of classics. Ignoring the Russian classics (many of which she was altogether too familiar with, from her years with the literate-to-a-fault Yvetta), she went for English literature. Jane Austen took her fancy and she had always loved Dickens (who had, she recalled Yvetta telling her excitedly, albeit in a characteristically know-it-all manner, inspired Tolstoy, the god of Russian – and, really, all – novelists). She found many titles of interest, and soon had a small but sturdy stack beside her on the table. The late-morning sun was enervating, but not unpleasant. This space, this light, the books and their bright pages, became comfortable, familiar, her own. Still, there was only so much time you could spend engaged in yesteryear before you longed to return to the modern, and that which was altogether easier to read.

Cocooned inside this room, with a view of a shimmering blue ocean far below, she settled into a comfortable linen chaise longue, to page through some fashion magazines she had found in a magazine rack next to the chair. She herself had had a front cover once, and had been featured often inside, her pictures taken by the best fashion photographers. That was a life time ago, yet reflecting back on years past, she wondered what her life would be like if she had not veered from such a successful modelling career. Had she been crazy to do so? Or merely sensible?

She would never know for sure, but considering how her life had turned out, the answer was almost certainly crazy. Many of the girls who had worked with her in her first few years on the job had gone on to do television work and endorse products such as perfumes and skin creams. She, too, could have been seen around the world – instead of trying hard to be seen by no one, to mask her true identity. Feted in the big cities in the world, instead of running from one anonymous island in Southeast Asia to another. But now here she was in big-city Sydney, in the middle of – well, she wasn't yet sure she exactly what.

Confined to the house, she felt like she was in a luxurious prison, but a prison nonetheless. The layout was more Waldorf Astoria than Alcatraz, true, but she did not feel entirely comfortable, not yet, at least. She was too wary, too suspicious, to make herself entirely at home. Too cynical and battle-hardened to trust anyone absolutely. It went against her nature, years of posture, deceit, and defensiveness. Years of the hustle, the scam, the con. The long game had the word long in it for a reason. Decades of deceit, wasted years; a good portion of her life now. Gone. Ruined.

And what had she learnt? A great deal. And also, nothing. How different things would have been if she had stayed in another lane, played another game, continued working as a model. Sure, there were lots of other models – beautiful girls were everywhere, if you went to the right places, at least – but she was special, had been told that by more than a few photographs and agents, women and men. Men, there were always men, wherever the models happened to be. You had to beat them off with a stick, and she suspected that some of them might have enjoyed that, too. Closing her eyes, she tried hard not to feel dejected about the choices she had made. Yet here she was with nothing to show for her years with Yvetta, for her life choices, alone but for the generosity of others - generosity she felt that she did not deserve.

She tried to be positive – her nature was nothing if not optimistic, or at least it had been up until very recently – was she becoming more cynical with age? Well, she was still relatively young, and in a new country, she had heaps of experience in the fashion world and Sydney wasn't a backwater. She wondered if she could find her way back into the industry in some capacity; it was a thought she would hold onto. There was plenty to still be optimistic about, no matter how often her thoughts veered towards darkness and self-doubt, previously unfamiliar emotions.

Jared returned with fresh pastries from a nearby cake store and went in search of his troubled resident. He was able to drive now that his leg was flexible from the knee down. Relieved at having movement once more, feeling lighter, swifter, and more robust, less like an invalid and more like a human being, as though a weight had been lifted from him, he was in a buoyant mood.

Before arriving home, he had met Darius for lunch at a restaurant close to his doctor's offices. Since his initial meeting with Fritzi at Jared's home, Darius had kept a low profile. Jared filled him in on Fritzi's state of mind during the course of the day and her meltdown.

'Well, it seems Fritzi has lost her fighting spirit,' Jared said. 'According to Maggie, Fritzi has confided that she no longer knows who she is, and feels as if she has lost her reason for being. Her anchor, so to speak, has disappeared with her lover, Yvetta, I believe.'

Shocked at the sudden change in her personality, Darius said, 'I get what you're saying. I guess she was holding onto her pride and hope for the future, until we came along and exposed her past, bringing her situation into sharp focus. Now she has nowhere left to run.'

They discussed moving forward at a gentler pace.

Thankful for Maggie's kindness during her crisis of self-doubt, they hoped the housekeeper's homely, organised, and motherly presence would continue to be beneficial. Jared suggested Darius join them for lunch on Sunday. A more social, relaxed day out on the boat could work wonders for her depressed state of mind, he said. Darius suggested they pull up at a restaurant up the coast, where they would be inconspicuous and Fritzi would feel safe. It was low-key and no one would bother with them, and the crab was delicious.

Finding Fritzi in the library, sleeping, with the magazine open on her lap, he quietly pulled the door closed and retired to his office to work. Now that his doctor had given him the all-clear to return to work, he had masses of preparation to do. He had to attend to calls he had neglected from clients; it was time he got back to his life.

Absorbed on his phone, Jared became aware of a soft knocking on his door.

'Come in,' he said, surprised. Fritzi popped her head around the door, but held back, waiting for an invitation to enter. 'Hi,' she said softly, almost shyly, 'are you ready for tea? I brought some great pastries back, and Maggie left us a tray all prepared. Can I prepare the tea and bring it through? Where would you like to have it?' And then, as if realising she had asked one too many questions, she stepped back with the same shy reticence with which she had entered.

'Great,' he said slowly, looking at her carefully, as if for the first time, reassessing her now, in light of everything he knew about her – and everything that he didn't, 'thanks. Let's sit in my TV room: the sofas are comfy there, and it's more relaxed and has a great view of the garden sloping down to the pool. I use the room mostly to watch sports, but you are welcome to use it to watch movies whenever.'

She poured tea from a proper teapot, something no one ever used any longer, with the pastries already arranged – impeccably, by Maggie – on a decorative art-deco plate on a tray with china cups and saucers. Indeed, Maggie had done all the hard work – all Fritzi had to do was pour the boiling water into the pot. There was an awkward silence while they both ate and sipped their tea. Fritzi felt it was time to clear the air, but she was having trouble finding the right words. For once, she was awkward, stumbling, feeling oddly defenceless, weirdly (but not unpleasantly) timid, waiting for an appropriate moment. She waited another minute, before realising an appropriate moment would not independently arrive. She would have to go ahead and speak. She looked at the floor, the gleaming tiles, then at her hands, then back at Jared. It was not lost on her how handsome he was. But what about his friend Darius?

Suddenly Darius was in her mind. Darius was handsome, too – beautiful, too – and they had a history, however brief, a connection. It seemed wherever she went, however she felt, whatever position she took, life could not help but be complicated – sometimes deliciously so. Jared met her gaze and smiled, prompting her to speak, or trying to read her mind. He nodded reassuringly, as though in answer to an unspoken question, and she had to remind herself that she had, as yet, said nothing at all. That had to change.

'Jared,' she said finally, 'I am not good at saying thank you.' He saw where she was going with this, and it seemed to surprise him. His mouth opened but she put her hand up before he could intervene. She pushed on, the words hurried so that they sounded, even to her, unfamiliar. 'I am at a loss. Really,' she added, as if he was in any doubt. But at that moment, no one could doubt her sincerity, least of all herself.

'Never before in my life have, I received such hospitality,' she paused, waveringly, 'without returning the favour. It has left me quite at a loss, really,' emphasising really, a Germanic tic of hers. Now her voice became flatter, almost dour, 'Usually, I know what people want from me, and I either deliver or I reject their offer.'

Had she been so soured by life that she had to be cynical about everything? She wanted only to be a free spirit, pure if not entirely unsullied, unregulated if not entirely lawless, independent, without the anchors society and family so often imposed. Perhaps that was possible after all. Or maybe not…

'This situation I find myself in is quite unprecedented, and I have no way of knowing how to behave. It has left me with few options. I understand my circumstances only too well, I am sincerely grateful to you, as I've tried to express in my clumsy way, but should you be involving yourself with my problems? You are a busy man with a life of your own. Why should you do this for me?' He opened his mouth again to speak, but she continued, her tone harsher still. 'I am not finished.' She sounded almost angry. 'Yes, I helped you out of a very sticky patch, but it was my choice to put my own life on the line to help you. And, under the circumstances, what else could one do?

'All the same, you and Darius know my past – not a very good one, by all accounts, and I do not want to embroil anyone in my problems any longer. Fritzi leant forward in her seat the plush armchair now to comfortable for her mindset, I learnt my lesson with the Rubicov family: once I am set on a course, I lose all self-control, and I will do anything – and I mean anything – to get what I want. As you've read, I have done some pretty nasty things. She looked at the thick knotted rug under her feet, then up at Jared unflinchingly, caught his eye with a direct stare, many people would say, 'Lock her up and throw away the key'. Honestly, on reflection – which I have never had either the time nor the inclination to do – I believe they are right.'

She felt a cool breeze and felt relieved, it felt like a whisper of encouragement blowing back her self-respect, to take back control of her life. I do not deserve this, really. I am not worth the trouble; it would be better if you pretended you never met me.' Now she felt light-headed, able to hold her head up again, she wasn't used to feeling beholden to anyone for her life, who's future was it anyway, she needed to take back control, but for the first-time doubt about who she had been up until now was eating its way into her soul.

'Tell me, Fritzi,' Jared said, 'have you ever wondered why you have been so protective towards Yvetta? By all accounts, she is from a very rich family and behaved in quite a brutal fashion towards her own parents, who, from what I have read, gave her every opportunity in life. Why have you, at every turn, put your own safety on the line to try and save her from herself?'

Fritzi sat for some time digesting Jared's direct intervention to a situation she had never questioned, only ever felt compelled to act on, whatever the outcome might be.

'Ja, this is a very interesting question,' Fritzi replied, not sure how to answer, considering his statement still. She leaned forward pensively, posturing subconsciously, then dropped the façade when she realised what she was doing. It was time, finally, to get real. To face up to her past, once and for all. It was only by being brutally honest that she could heal, change, move forward and improve. And, in spite of her instincts, she desperately wanted to change. 'You know, I am not sure, but perhaps it has to do with my childhood. Who knows the answers to these things – to what makes us behave the way we do. We just do, I suppose. You must have asked your clients these, questions, many times and come up with no answer?'

'Some yes and others not,' he replied. 'You are right, in a way, but with you, Fritzi, there is a pattern. Let me tell you, I have dealt with many cases that often seemed a lost cause, because the person was beyond saving or understanding. Where you are concerned, this is not the case; you show benevolence and care without wanting anything in return, when protecting a loved one, or like myself someone in need of help. You wanted to help free Yvetta from every institution at any cost, with no thought to your own safety. Why?'

She sat in thought, jumbled flashes of her childhood kept penetrating her mind. Something she had suppressed since childhood sprang to mind. She shuddered, trying to stop the thought in its tracks, not wanting to delve further: the consequences had been horrendous and too horrifying even then; it had changed her for ever.

'I can tell there is something, perhaps,' Jared said.

'It happened when I was fourteen years old,' she said slowly, cautiously, not sure whether she should proceed, not quite able to believe she had come this far. What was she thinking – or not thinking? Was she making a mistake? 'It's a story I have never shared with anyone. And, yes, I believe it had a profound effect on me, influencing many of my decisions.'

'Do you think you are able to tell it now?' he said softly, tenderly, his speech slow, to match her own. She could trust him, she thought suddenly – or at least give it a shot. Why not? She hadn't trusted many people up till now, and where had that gotten her? Here. There must be a reason for that, for this, for him. Which is perhaps the reason she should take a different tack.

'I will try,' she said, more to herself than to him. 'Maybe it's time, yes?'

He nodded, comforting her with his mere presence, the warmth of his body beside her, his aura of quiet understanding, but knew better than to interrupt her by speaking. It was her turn to speak now, and no one – or nothing – could get in her way. She had waited a long time for this moment, to tell this story, and now was the time.

'Erica was my best friend through school,' she continued, breathing deeply, trying to gather more strength, not thinking, relying on memory and sensation alone, the strong currents of the past pulling her backwards and forwards at once, 'we did everything together. She was a very spirited girl – maybe today one would say she was on the spectrum, because she always said what came into her mind. When we were little, it didn't matter so much – but when we were teenagers and became aware of politics, it mattered a great deal, especially in East Berlin. Erica would not adhere to the ideology of the GDR, as it was known then, the German Democratic Republic, part of the Eastern Bloc. Controlled by the Soviet Union.

'We would be brainwashed at school – in fact, everywhere. We had to chant and swear allegiance to the communist ideal. But Erika refused to chant, to pledge allegiance, to believe – in anything authoritarian, really. She was utterly, almost blissfully, independent. That was the way she was, and no one or nothing could change that. She told them how she felt. No matter how young she was, and she was never any threat to anyone, her refusal to be brainwashed and her outspoken manner was a threat. And, on top of that, her family were supposed to have been Jewish, or had Jewish roots, known troublemakers, theatre types, authors, degenerates. It's true that Erika's father was a musician, a very famous violinist, whose career had been thwarted by the Iron Curtain.

'The state tried various punishments, took away her freedoms – or at least the few freedoms any of us had – not allowing her to travel to other Eastern Bloc countries. Her father must have known that, sooner or later, she would be punished in a more deliberate way, because he tried to get her out of East Berlin into the West, some succeeded, there were tunnels people used to escape through to West Berlin, and with help from the West, some made it through if properly planned, Sadly, they were caught.

'Erica was taken away – no one knew where. My father was a Stasi officer. I begged him to tell me where they had taken Erica, she had been in our home many times, but he would never tell me. Maybe he didn't know, although I find that difficult to believe. He knew everything – everything bad, anyway. All he said was that she was a bad influence and deserved what was coming to her. I knew my mother did not agree, so I asked her if she knew where Erica was. My mother was a good German hausfrau, you understand, what my father said was law in our house, even if she felt differently, she never contradicted my father, that I was aware of, for her to confide this information to me was her way of showing how she felt, I believe.

She told me my father had seen to it that Erica was taken to an institution for the mentally disabled. He wanted to be rid of her – and for her to be out of my life. I was only fourteen, you understand, but even then, I realised what a terrible man my father was to do such a thing. I found out the name of the institution, and one Sunday I took my bicycle and cycled out to this place. Pretending to be a relative of one of the inmates, I tried to ingratiate myself with some of the people standing out on the lawns, shuffling back and forth or biding their time, doing nothing really. They were really ordinary people, just locked up for the state's convenience.

'One of the inmates smuggled me in with him. He took me through to a section no one was supposed to enter – no one who wasn't sanctioned to be there by the state, at least. He put an inmate's tunic on me and we were allowed through by a guard the inmate helping me said was new and, wouldn't know all the rules. I followed him down a long corridor to a door that had a small peephole in it. Through the peephole I saw a padded cell, horrendous and inhuman. I saw someone tied to a gurney, they seemed alive but dead. The inmate who was helping me, told me this is what they had done to Erica. I was totally confused, not knowing what he meant.

'People were moaning and screaming all over the place. It was like being in hell, Dante's inferno comes to mind. Then I followed him into a small room off the main passage and discovered that he was right. Erica, my lovely, vibrant best friend, had been turned into a vegetable. She had been given a lobotomy. Fritzi having for the first time voiced something hidden so deep inside her brain and heart, felt desolate her former fight for control completely gone, she felt beaten down by her past revelation, and, had no fight left in her now. The beauty of the scene below a mirage, her comfortable surroundings uncomfortable in the ugly truth of Erica's childhood, stolen by evil people and her father was responsible, how could she live a comfortable life after knowing that?'

Jared sat uncomfortably, feeling Fritzi's pain, years old but still fresh. Passed on to him, that pain was his now, and he felt it burn. Through this whole tirade Fritzi had not stopped to take a breath. It was, without a doubt, one of the most inhumane crimes he had been told of in a long, long time (and, through his job, he heard recounted much that was illegal and inhumane) and he felt physically ill at the thought of a fourteen year old girl having a part of her brain removed to shut her up – to say nothing of the fact that Fritzi, another fourteen year old finding her friend had been made a vegetable by her father's intervention. How does such a young brain process such evil, and in her own father?

Jared got up out of his seat, and sat next to Fritzi. He took her hand in his and held it for a long time. 'I am so very sorry,' he said softly. He could not think of anything else to say. It seemed she felt the same way, for she sat silently, motionless, with her head hanging drained of all emotion and energy. Repeating this part of her life, so deeply hidden until now, had exhausted her. Jared had to find the breath, the words, to speak again.

'Would you like to continue,' he said after a long moment, 'or perhaps sleep for a while?'

He had not expected Fritzi to respond to quickly, or with such a clear voice.

'No, I must continue,' she said, with surprising firmness. And then, in a much softer voice, 'if you don't mind. I should have exorcised these demons a long time ago.'

'May I ask,' Jared said, leaning forward, 'what did you do after leaving the institution?'

'I never wanted to see my father again,' Fritzi said. 'I wanted him to die. I felt such utter contempt and hate for him, for my whole family – even my mother, for standing by him.

I rode to my grandparents' place and hung out there for a while. I didn't want to leave. I was hanging onto excuses, hanging onto time, making every minute count. I was frightened, suffering from shock, and appeared ill, so they put me up for a week – which was exactly what I wanted. I guess my act paid off – only it wasn't an act at all. Luckily for me, things had started to happen: there were rumours. It was very close to my fifteenth birthday and school holidays, so after I left my grandparents' home, I went straight to my older sister and her Cameroonian boyfriend. East Berlin had a free university and, many from Africa came to study. Many girls went with African men hoping they would if married with a family be able to leave with them. My father had disowned my sister, but my mother kept in touch. They loved having me over and allowed me to stay. It wasn't a secret that I did not get on with my dad. And just before school began, the Berlin Wall came down; and the rest, as they say, is history.'

'So, what happened then?'

'I went across with everyone else. it was mayhem you can just imagine what freedom, even the guards were free, everyone rejoiced and for a time, things were chaotic enough for me to disappear into the night with everyone else who partied all night. Bars and restaurants and cafés remained open into the early hours. Berlin was like a giant free-for-all. The first night of the German reunification everyone was so happy. Amongst all this chaos I tried to find my friends, who had escaped to West Berlin. I knew their address, though, and some kind kids gave me a lift there. Then, finally, I knew I was safe.' She smiled, almost in spite of herself. All of these years later, she thought, she still wasn't safe. Or was she? 'From there I slowly found my feet, started to model, ventured out in the world, and the rest is history.'

'Did you ever see your father after that?' Jared asked cautiously.

'No,' Fritzi said flatly. 'I saw my mother and told her I never wanted to see my father again. Sadly, she understood. She wasn't surprised. After I told her I had found out about Erica, she knew it would be the end. My mother, you understand, was frightened, too: not only of the new Germany but of her future, she would never leave my father, he whoever he was to me or my sister, was her husband, and her life. She knew that our lives were no longer under their control, she just gave in to the inevitable, that our family would never be the same again. They retired all the Stasi after reunification. Many of them went on to do very well, I believe – probably my father, too, but I wish he had gone to jail. He deserved to be punished for what he had done. I only wonder at the things he did that I don't know about – terrible things…' her voice trailed off. 'It's better not to know,' she said finally. 'I can only hope my father had a conscience, and that it kept him up at night. But I doubt it somehow. Obviously, I'm not innocent myself – I have my own past, my own crimes. Everyone deserves forgiveness, even my father, perhaps.'

'Yes,' Jared said, 'I agree, everyone deserves a second chance. And that goes for you, too.'

She smiled, but it was a tired smile. 'I am exhausted,' she said softly. 'I think I will just grab a sandwich and go to bed. Can I get you anything?'

Jared shook his head. 'I have a sounder insight into your past now. We will discuss everything else at a later stage. Goodnight, Fritzi. Try and sleep well. We are going out on the boat tomorrow with Darius. It should be a great day.'

With the cool breeze blowing off the water as they sailed down towards the Hawksbury River System – and, if time allowed, on to Broken Bay – the steaming hot day became more bearable. There were so many places to visit and inlets with restaurants and marinas to pull up along. Fritzi sat alone on the front of the boat, enjoying the scene as it passed alongside and around her.

She felt lighter somehow; her talk with Jared had opened a dam she had been holding a finger in for far too many years. Her clothes today reflected her light mood, a white silk floaty halter neck top, cut off white jeans slung low on her hips, a khaki baseball cap and rimless gold mirror sunglasses added a touch of glamour she had, had little use for recently.

Darius, who had for some time been quietly sitting and observing Jared and Fritzi's body language and (mostly unspoken) interactions, knew something had changed. She appeared relaxed with Jared, who appeared to treat her differently, too, in an altogether more comfortable manner, less distant and formal, and with polite deference. Darius wondered what – if anything – had happened between them. As the two men chatted about where to go and where to stop for lunch, Fritzi safely out of earshot, the conversation turned to their guest. Smiling, looking for an opening in the conversation, Darius said, with a warmth that was not entirely authentic, 'Fritzi seems happy today. So do you, for that matter.'

Darius looked at him keenly, much as (Darius imagined) he looked at his clients in his law office. 'I cannot divulge what was said by Fritzi when I managed to get her to open up yesterday, Darius,' Jared said, but what I can tell you is that that girl has gone up tenfold in my estimation.'

Darius's smile did not leave his face, but it became considerably colder. 'I understand that whatever she said was told to you in the strictest confidence, but it's obvious she is happier than when we last spoke, lighter of spirit – so whatever she imparted about her life must have been a weighty load.'

Since they were on a boat, on the open water, it was perhaps appropriate that Darius was now attempting something of a fishing expedition. Always attentive, empathic by both nature and profession, Jared smiled, and his smile was at least authentic, and shook his head.

'One day, when this is all over,' Jared said slowly, 'you'll know.'

When, Darius thought darkly, shouldn't that be if? Or perhaps Darius, by nature and experience, wasn't quite as optimistic or buoyant as his old classmate. After all, their lives had gone in different directions, though both had been successful in their own right. And, of course, Darius hadn't been blessed at by birth by a wealth and infinitely connected father. Still, old envy and resentment was long gone now. Now, in spite of himself, he felt envious for an altogether different reason – one now perched peacefully on the other end of the boat, her long legs dangling over the edge, almost – but not quite – touching the water. He still had deep feelings for her, he knew. And she must know, too, he suddenly thought, and possibly Jared knew, too. And what on earth had happened between them, at his oceanside villa, yesterday?

He didn't want to think about it. But think about it he did. Now he felt anxious for entirely different reasons – a little angry, and edgy, too. He tried to shake it all off, enjoy the boat ride, the day, the warm, almost sultry, air. He was overheated, he suddenly thought. Calm down. He looked at Jared again, as though if he examined him closer, he would detect a clue of some kind, Jared looked the part skippering his boat, in his casual blue jeans and white shirt rolled up to his elbows, while Darius chose to wear white and blue suede sockless loafers, ever the Italian in his taste.

Still smiling, Jared said, 'Perhaps she will choose to include you in our conversations. I do not know.' Was that patronising? Darius wondered. For all of his talk of inclusion, the words felt oddly exclusive – and empty. He felt alone all of a sudden, and not for the first time. As though life was imperceptibly moving on ahead of him. Or perhaps that was the movement of the boat. Or the hot and lazy morning still slowly unfurling. 'No one could have suffered through her experiences without repercussions,' Jared said confidently, his tone changing now, becoming less airy and more empathic and familiar, more like the old Jared of rugby and roughhousing days, before legal tomes and heavyweight human-rights conferences had claimed him. 'But on the bright side she has managed to remain stable, even when the shit hit the fan. The thing is,' and his voice became softer now, as though suddenly remembering that Fritzi was, in fact, close by, 'what kept her sane was her love of this Russian woman.'

'Yvetta Rubicov,' Darius said, perhaps a little too quickly.

Jared nodded again. 'I believe if she had not been caught, rumbled, by the authorities, she would have concentrated all of her energies on trying to see this Yvetta again – no matter what it took.' He stopped suddenly, gazed at Fritzi, felt secure in knowing she was some distance away, and said, softer still, 'and perhaps that's what she may still do.'

'It seems that this Yvetta has brought Fritzi nothing but grief,' Darius said, 'if that report Bruce gave me is anything to go on. I hope she gets over that part of her life to begin a new one – without all of that cloak-and-dagger stuff she was into. I looked Fritzi up on Google – her real name, I mean – and came up with a whole lot of stuff on our girl. She was a seriously beautiful model. Even did a cover for one of the major fashion magazines.'

Jared wasn't surprised to hear this. He had done the same Google search, and viewed the same results. Those photographs were in his mind still. He smiled at the thought of them. 'Had she stuck to it, she could have been up there with those top models who have made amazing amounts of money.'

Darius looked at Fritzi again. She had not moved. He watched her lower her bare foot so that it sliced through the water for a moment. Her expression did not change. She looked idyllic, at peace. She could be dreaming, he thought. But her eyes were open and her face was affectless, almost blank. She was very much awake. He thought he better join her up front, be more sociable, not leave her alone with her thoughts so much – God alone knew what those thoughts were. From all he had read about her many escapes, she was more than capable of jumping overboard and swimming away – to another country, another identity. Never to be seen again.

The idea of it stung him all of a sudden. She had already left him once – and that had hurt more than it should. And he had found her somehow, by good fortune, or dumb luck, or something altogether more profound. Twice was too much to bear. They did not want her to feel under constant discussion, paranoid or unnecessarily wary. It could make her more anxious, which would increase their anxiety in turn, make everything more difficult. The idea was to have a pressure-free day, one of relaxation and enjoyment, free of suspicion and second thoughts, carefree. They could even throw caution to the wind – to a point, at least. Although Darius suspected that Fritzi had, over the years, thrown altogether too much caution to altogether too many winds. Now it was time for steadier weather.

Holding two glasses of freshly poured champagne, he made his way unsteadily towards her and nearly fell into her lap with the drinks as the boat hit a swell; the traffic on the water was quite busy. He interrupted a startled-looking Fritzi, who had been deep in thought, obviously enjoying the fresh air and the scenery with its rocks and alcoves and overhanging lush greenery. Handing her the glass, they both had a giggle at his clumsiness. He apologised for taking her out of her reverie, but she smiled and gestured to her glass, making clear that she was happy still. Suddenly, after hours of quiet, she was as bubbly as the champagne.

Making eye contact and shifting slightly so that they were sitting close, she chatted away, asking question upon question, before enquiring about the area they were heading towards. But his answer was interrupted by Jared's voice, calling for them to join him up front. For a cynical moment, Darius wondered if Jared was purposelessly interrupting his time alone with Fritzi. Perhaps Jared was jealous, too. He watched Jared watching Fritzi. There was a glint in Jared's eye now, a possessive look, Darius thought darkly. Or was he just projecting? Jared invited Fritzi to steer the boat under his guidance, but it quickly became apparent that Fritzi did not need guidance at all. She appeared to be a dab hand at steering. Watching her they both noticed how relaxed she was. Poised, cool, carefree, her long slim body a straight line, she seemed in her natural habitat behind the wheel.

There was no doubt she was a stunner, every bit as much as now as she had been years ago on those magazine covers. Looking at her now, Darius recalled vividly those covers, and imagined that this moment, this image of Fritzi, was a cover of its own. He froze the moment visually, tried to make it last. What had changed, he wondered, between now and then, her modelling years and today, or, for that matter, the timid Fritzi of yesterday and the confident, carefree Fritzi of today. He remembered what the Interpol document had said: her multiple identities, as fluid as endless as the ocean, and her ease at playing different parts and assuming different roles.

'A masterclass in acting,' the document had read in one especially damning sentence. 'An Oscar-calibre performance.' Well, she may not have won any Oscars, but she had certainly won him over, he could no longer deny that. Framed by the light, the heat shimmering off the ocean in invisible but perceptible waves, her long limbs were bronzed by the sun, and the wind whipped at her lustrous hair. She was so elegant, so artful, so natural behind now, steering, leading, in complete control. Darius looked from Fritzi to Jared, who was staring at her, too. Both Jared and Darius were transfixed.

Again, Darius felt resentment towards Jared, but something else as well: an indisputable connection. Understanding, sympathy even. The ocean, the champagne, the warm air, Fritzi – all these elements combined to make him feel inebriated, almost dizzy. A man like him, otherwise so rational, in a moment like this, could do something irrational. Could do something dangerous. He was second-guessing – everything. He should not have left her in Bali. But, wait, wasn't it she who left him? He could no longer now remember. His mind was a sea within the large sea; Fritzi a blur of the real and imagined, Google images and snatches of an Interpol file and remembered conversation and now, here, whatever this was. He stared below, at the ocean, trying to steady himself, snap himself out of whatever reverie afflicted him now.

Strange, he thought. Ever since I met her, this Freddie/Fritzi, I've felt strange. Unlike myself. Maybe I like being someone else. Like Fritzi with her many masks, changing identities as often as some people change their underwear. Judging by her tight clothing, it did not appear that she was wearing much (or any) underwear that day. He wondered if Jared noticed this, too. Again, he wondered what, exactly, had taken place between them yesterday, after he left. He turned his gaze again to Fritzi, but somehow his eyes fell, again, on Jared.

As they continued to watch Fritzi enjoying the day out, seemingly oblivious to everything and everyone around her, to the complexity and severity of her own predicament, almost blissful – even innocent – in her attitude, something became clear to both men at the same time and they acknowledged it fleetingly as they made eye contact.

'I guess we both feel something for her,' Jared said softly, standing beside Darius now. Darius was surprised, for it was as if he, not Jared, had suddenly spoken his mind. 'But I think right now it would be best to remain uninvolved – for me, anyhow. Since Fritzi is my client, it would be highly unprofessional – not to mention awkward. I won't even mention it again.' He touched Darius gently on the shoulder; his soft voice was strained. 'But you, Darius, can continue what you had.' Was Jared giving Darius his blessing – or telling him, in an opaque and complicated manner, to back off? Right now, Darius wasn't sure.

'I suppose I could,' Darius replied, 'but after I had her investigated, I felt the whole episode got too hot for me to handle. I've had drama in my life.' He was thinking now of Lin. 'More than enough, in fact. Right, now I want as little drama in my life as possible. But you are right: I still have feelings for her, too.'

There was nothing more to be said. As if acknowledging this, Jared stepped forward and took over the steering from Fritzi as they pulled up along a jetty, The plan was to moor the boat while they got off to see the sights and to find a place for lunch, to be grounded again for a while.

Fritzi was in her element. With her long, cool stride, as though a boat still cruising along fluid, almost invisible, waterways, she forged ahead, stopping at the market stalls, trying on various items – various identities, Darius thought, cynically but enchanted with the performance, nonetheless. Her manner was carefree, almost childlike and, her expression unencumbered by her dark past. After buying sunglasses and a hat, she moved onto a stall selling sun dresses. She purchased several dresses, modelling some for their – or perhaps, more accurately, for her – enjoyment, and holding others up for them to approve. Suddenly it was as though they were both judges and spectators in some sport, they were not previously aware of.

As they moved along the stalls, Darius feeling ever lighter and more relaxed, enjoying the moment, his jealousy in the past, Fritzi bought two Panama hats, one for each of them. Thinking they would object to wearing them, she was delighted when they put them on immediately. Smiling broadly and giving the thumbs up, she moved on. She really does live moment to moment, Darius thought, weirdly impressed. She makes the most out of life – her life, on her terms. He wondered, not for the first time, how other people fit into this.

By now, Fritzi was some distance from him, far along the row of stalls. And yet there she was, unmistakable and yet somehow anonymous, but still striking, beautiful. She made his heart pulse hard. He smiled, realising again how intoxicated he was by her. He had underestimated his feelings for her – and for a reason. To keep his sanity – to say nothing of his humility – in check. To keep himself safe. But now it was too late for all of that. Way too late. Events had overtaken him, destiny had interceded (or was he merely attempting to excuse the mistakes he was, almost certainly, about to make?) and whatever happened next was clearly beyond his control. Finding a linen, stall she stopped to browse. Not having brought much with her, she indulged in further items to add to her meagre wardrobe.

She shopped as easily as she smiled and breathed. Darius thought again of Lin, but this time with a considerable pang of anguished unpleasantness. Lin had been a shopaholic of note, but only when she wasn't spending her own money, of course. But Fritzi was very different in every way, he reflected, and he could not help but smile again, not least at the fact that Lin was finally in the rear-view mirror. At least Fritzi was right here – only she wasn't, becoming smaller and smaller as she disappeared down the line of stalls.

His heart pulsed again as he realised, she may escape into the crowd and be gone. Him and Jared had made a mistake, become too at ease, too relaxed, too infatuated perhaps. Jared seemed to have the same thought because his body tensed and he moved fast. They caught up to her, she looked at them, smiling, beguiling. It was as if she was only now remembering they had accompanied her and she was happy all over again to see them.

Playing cool but clearly flustered, Jared teased, 'If you carry on like this, we are going to need a suitcase.' He smiled, wiped sweat from his brow. 'Only joking,' he said quickly, seeming – at least to Darius – unusually off his game, 'it's great to watch you having some retail therapy. Everything you showed us so far looks great, and thanks for the hat.'

Darius, standing some distance away from them but in earshot still, wondered if Jared wasn't trying too hard. He could not recall his old friend ever really infatuated by a girl, although Jared had certainly had his fair share of women – being handsome and coming from a wealthy family meant that women were never in short supply. On the contrary, they probably banged down his door trying to get to him, Darius thought, and felt the old envy return. But now Fritzi was looking at him and he waved his thanks, waiting for them to walk up to him. Or did he have to join them? No, he felt that – for once – he needed some measure of control. 'All these stalls specialize,' Fritzi said, and the coy and affectionate curiosity that Darius remembered from their long days and sultry nights in Bali had returned to her voice, 'and the quality and uniqueness makes it worth buying.' She held the clothes up to them, and the bright light struck the fabric. 'I am sure I won't find these in the Sydney stores.'

Jared asked, 'Do you want to continue shopping or stop for lunch?'

'You know,' she said, still smiling, looking at neither of them in particular and yet, somehow, both of them intimately at once, 'I haven't shopped for so long, I am having a wonderful time.' Her voice became higher, sweeter, more singsong, imploring and impossible to resist. The heat, the warm air, the brightness of her gaze seemed to increase as well. 'Would you mind if I continued? I could meet you at a bar or the restaurant.' Was this a good idea, though? Darius wondered. But before he had a chance to figure out how to respond, Jared nodded and said, 'Sure, just don't get too far, please. We will watch you from the restaurant.'

'I won't be long,' she said hurriedly, and already she seemed to have moved on from them, 'just one or two more things I wouldn't mind getting that I saw back there.'

Fritzi made her way to a stall that sold leather sandals in a Roman style; she had loved a pair that laced up the leg. Jared and Darius, unspeaking, sipping still water from an ostentatiously curved and overpriced bottle, watched her from the restaurant. They were interested only in her. If she did make a break for it, they would have time to stop her. But neither of them voiced their concerns. It was a kind of test, Darius thought. Fritzi evidently passed, because after a couple of minutes they saw her making her way over to the restaurant Jared had pointed out to her, still smiling but now wearing her new Roman sandals laced to her knee.

Clearly the two men were not the only ones who found her remarkable. Most in the restaurant turned to watch her as she made her way over to the table. Darius felt oddly special – lucky in a way, and proud. Jared was no doubt used to being something of a celebrity, but all of this was new to him. Here Fritzi was, wearing a newly purchased wide-brimmed straw hat, black sunglasses, and, of course, her new leather sandals laced to her knees, showing off her long limbs to perfection, in her new linen mini strappy dress. She felt great knowing she could have walked straight out of Vogue – and, judging from the faces of Jared and Darius, they felt great, too.

Jared and Darius whistled softly as she moved in beside them.

Darius, whistled softly, 'Wow, that's quite a transformation.'

Fritzi was happier than they had both seen her, since her depressed state a few days ago. 'I feel great,' she said in a low, almost teasing, voice.' Neither men spoke, which seemed an endorsement of the perfection of the clothes – and, indeed, of the wearer. Their fresh lobster and oysters arrived with abundant beer to wash it all down, conversation stopped as they indulged in the delicious fresh food.

Back on the boat she regaled them with stories of her modelling career, and how she had loved travelling at short notice to far-flung places to do shoots, always flying first-class, of course. She said (to Darius's interest but also annoyance) that most of the people she had met in time, and all of the photographers (even the gay male ones) came on to the models.

Luckily for her, she said – to Darius's considerable relief – she had a protector on location with her at all times. As Fritzi had been only fifteen, one of the agencies was savvy enough to send a minder when she travelled, and she had been grateful to them (indeed, she was grateful still today). Warm, happy, and relaxed in her new purchases, Fritzi wanted only to talk. She told them that the attention she received wasn't always of a sexual or transactional nature, and it was possible to make true friends in the business. For example, in Paris a very famous tiny in stature but powerful in personality Algerian designer had taken a shine to her, and instead of bunking down with the other girls (which almost always resulted in cliques and catty behaviour – and sometimes worse), she had moved into his apartment. He became the father she never had.

He lived with his long-term middle aged, balding French business partner Andre, and Fritzi accompanied them wherever they were invited to. The clothes he cut and designed were figure-hugging, unapologetically showing off a woman's form and her curves. He was a master at his craft and she was his muse for many years. He was also an uncommonly kind human being. Sadly, he died of Aids. His death was, another reason she was happy to leave the fashion industry: for her, nothing would be the same again without him.

They tied up the boat at the jetty and climbed the steps to Jared's home. Once indoors, Fritzi, feeling light-headed from the wine and wonderful day, offered to show off her new clothes for them – if they wanted a private runway show, that was. But really, she didn't even need to ask. Yes, they wanted it – badly.

Neither wanting to dull her mood or high spirits, feeling suddenly tipsy themselves from the heat and the excitement of the day, the two men settled down at the dining room table where the glass bridge would make a perfect ramp for Fritzi to strut her stuff on.

Wearing a tight-fitting yellow halter-neck catsuit, high-heeled sandals, and her hair tied in a high ponytail, they watched as Fritzi strutted like a thoroughbred racehorse towards them, turning just before she reached the end of the walkway, her hips moving from side to side in the lowcut catsuit as she walked away. Both men were transfixed, blown away by the transformation before them. Here was a highly professional model, right in front of them. She had been in both of their homes (well, in Darius's rented apartment in Bali) and was now in both of their hearts and lives, that was for sure. Neither had ever been to a fashion show, but there was no mistaking that Fritzi was one of the best. She knew how to use her body – and then some.

Stunned into silence, they waited for her to reappear before them again in a stunning new outfit, the silence and sudden distance grown elastic and infuriating – but instead she came running up barefoot in her ragged old shorts and tank top, hair all over the place. Back to the old Fritzi.

'God, that was captivating, powerful stuff, do all the girls walk that way?' asked Darius.

She laughed, her voice and body relaxed once again. 'Yes, more or less. We are taught to walk that way; it's all about showing off the clothes. Models are interchangeable, the outfits are the star of the show.' But, looking at Fritzi now, Darius found this difficult to believe.

'The haute couture shows are legends on their own,' she said excitedly, sounding suddenly much younger. 'Fashion designers like John Galliano, Karl Lagerfeld, Valentino, and the enfant terrible Jean Paul Gaultier not to mention Alexander McQueen, produce shows that are highly staged and themed. They use the runway like artists, wielding their artistic power. Some of these shows are ridiculously over-the-top, especially the McQueen and, Galliano shows. To be on their runway is super exhilarating,' she said, and from her voice there was no doubt how exhilarating it was, 'even if you are out there for such a short time. The high you feel out there in that moment is an adrenalin rush. I have felt nothing like that moment, since.'

'Well,' Darius said, feeling, in spite of the excitement, the spontaneous show now over, the first flush of fatigue hit him quite unexpectedly, 'you gave up a lot by cutting your career short at the height of your success.'

'Maybe, Darius,' Fritzi said, 'but perhaps that is the right time to quit. It's sad to get old in that profession. It's all about being super skinny and very young.'

Darius was bushed. It had been a long day. As much as he was hesitant to leave the two of them alone together again, what choice did he have? It wasn't like his hanging around here indefinitely was going to serve any purpose. 'I'm going to say goodnight,' he said. 'If you want me along at any of your sessions with Jared, I am happy to be there for you to lean on.' He paused, the words were coming out clumsily. Lean on? Fritzi appeared to be stronger than both him and Jared put together. Did he mean 'lean on' or 'sleep with'? Or both? He was no longer sure.

'When things become tough emotionally,' he mumbled, feeling foolish all of a sudden. He had been in the sun too long, he thought. He wasn't thinking straight.

She stared at Darius, seemed to take in the sun-strain, the sensitive face, the past heartache and sudden exhaustion. It was hard to believe he had been her lover not that long ago. Now here he was behaving like a brother; she wasn't at all sure she liked the feeling.

'Okay, maybe,' she said, suddenly unsure she wanted him to go, 'can I think about it?' She looked to Jared now, as though weighing the moment against the two men, and not for the first time. 'If Jared thinks it's a good idea, I will. That's kind, thank you.' Darius wasn't sure he liked Jared being included in her decision, but at this point one thing was clear: they were all in this together, for better and worse.

For his part, Jared wasn't sure what Darius had in mind by offering to be there when they went over her past. He doubted it would happen that way: Fritzi needed to feel secure divulging her innermost feelings, and doing it in front of an ex-lover wasn't a great idea. As he saw Darius to the door he wondered about this friend he had hardly seen in over two decades, and was now seeing all the time.

They parted knowing without a doubt that they both wanted Fritzi. She had managed somehow during the day out on the boat to pull them both into her orbit.

Chapter 10

Darius arrived home to an empty apartment. Although he prized himself on being self-sufficient, the emptiness was not at that moment something he relished. Being in Fritzi's company had a way of unsettling him. Only days before, on Bondi Beach with the surf, sand, and a Bondi lifestyle coveted by many, he had felt the luckiest man alive. Yet walking into an empty flat, with no one to greet him, not even a dog, made him feel suddenly lonely.

He reminded himself that a person's, reality and desires shifted, adapted, and evolved over time; his certainly had. Darius when with Lin, had been work-obsessed for a long time, until he taught himself to free himself of this obsession and enjoy all life had to offer again. Unlike Lin, Darius had moved on. Certainly, he had worked hard and achieved success, now he wanted to sit back, relax, and enjoy the benefits of knowing he could do just that without financial hardship. Bali had been his idea of chilling out away from Sydney and his work-intensive lifestyle, believing it would enforce a slower pace of life.

Then Fritzi walked into his life and his desire for a relaxed lifestyle had once again changed. She had somehow managed to destabilize his normally organised mind into one of tumult and turmoil. One moment he was in heaven, enjoying a fantastic sex life with a beautiful woman on an idyllic Island, and then just as suddenly everything changed. Freddie became Fritzi, and he found out stuff he'd rather not have known about. Indeed, he wouldn't even have investigated Fritzi if it hadn't been for his cautious nature. It was that very nature which had set him on a road of no return – the Interpol folder, the Google searches, and still the hunger to learn the truth, to uncover, to investigate, to know more. Once Bruce had supplied him with that Interpol report, the decision to leave Bali and Fritzi had been made easy for him.

Now he was back on Bondi Beach, enjoying his home and his lifestyle. Much had changed – and yet, in a way, nothing changed at all. He had run away from commitment and possible trouble, only it had found him, it had tracked him down. Here he was once again back in her orbit, feeling her magic, her vulnerability, and her incredible beauty creeping under his skin, so much so that he had walked through his door after leaving her company dissatisfied with his existence, feeling the absence of her presence in his life. He rarely felt this empty – and he didn't like feeling this way.

He fell onto his sofa, staring out of his floor-to-ceiling windows at the street lights sparkling on the white surf as it rolled onto the beach in the darkness. His mind and his being were full of Fritzi. Every pore in his body was aching for her. He wanted only to be back in bed with her, with her doing things to him only she knew how to do.

Jared was a professional man with integrity, but he was also a man, and Fritzi was living under his roof day and night. Things could happen, and Darius was sure they would. The thought was, painful; he closed his eyes and clenched his fists. Everything was suddenly so complicated. He had come back to Sydney for a second chance at life, a simpler life. But it seemed complication followed him everywhere, endlessly. The harder you tried to avoid it, no matter where and how long you hid, complexity sniffed you out and pinned you down.

On the one hand, he felt Fritzi was in the right place, as safe as possible, shielded from the scrutiny, the klieg lights and hard glare, of the media. Not that any of them were free from that scrutiny – not yet, not even close. He knew how relentless, how unscrupulous the media was, even the more genteel, non-tabloid Aussie press. If they got wind of her staying with the prime minister's son, it would be the perfect story of media madness, a veritable hurricane of hype that would almost certainly go international. You couldn't blame the media for pursuing the story, either – it was a story they could not ignore. A once-in-a-decade sort of story, something estimable and amazing. When he closed his eyes, he could see the headlines: 'Prime Minister's Son in Love with Girl Who Saved His Life'.

Something like that would spell disaster for Fritzi – to say nothing of Darius himself, and especially Jared. He couldn't bear the thought of Fritzi on the run once more. How things had changed – and so fast, too. Just a few days ago he thought he never wanted to see her again, now he felt sure he couldn't live without her. He was going to have to play a clever game if he wanted her back in his life, one that did not endanger both of their lives. He opened his eyes and felt a fresh weight press against his head.

Darius suddenly wondered whether Fritzi had any idea what had happened to Yvetta or her family since her skirmish with them in New

York. He doubted it somehow. He closed his eyes again. He was ready for bed. He was all out of ideas, and felt oddly out of hope as well. A good night's sleep would bring fresh ideas. He had always found this to be the case: when something wasn't quite right and no solution was immediately in sight, after a good kip the solution always came to him.

He had his ritual dawn swim, breakfast on the beach and, read the papers as usual. He was reading words, articles, but he may as well have been sleeping still. He was concentrating on nothing. His mind constantly worked on how to move forward with the Fritzi problem. A good night's kip still hadn't given him a clear idea of what to do. Still, he had something, finally, or rather a fragment of something. An idea was forming, but he needed a bit more information before he flew halfway around the world to investigate for himself.

'Bruce here,' the familiar voice on the other end said.

'G' day, mate,' Darius said. 'I need you to do some more investigating for me.'

Bruce did a good approximation of a semi-frustrated, semi-affectionate sigh. 'You still dating that Sheila, mate? I told you she's trouble.'

'I've got no idea where she's gone,' Darius lied, 'but I would like to find out more about that Russian family she was involved with – especially Yvetta Rubicov, her former partner. I would be grateful to have some kind of profile on her and the family.'

'Shouldn't be too hard,' Bruce said, his merry old self once more. 'After all, the Rubicov family are oligarchs. There must be info out there on them.'

'Great. Get back to me when you have something. I am flying over to New York this week.'

'Business or pleasure?' Bruce asked.

'Bit of both.'

'Give me twenty-four hours and I'll get back to you.'

Darius hung up the phone and opened his laptop. Sitting around wasn't his thing; being decisive was. He hadn't got this far in his professional life being timid, half-hearted, or haphazard. Professional life, romantic life, you had to go at life full-bore in every aspect.

On a travel website he found flights to New York and looked for a hotel. Preferring the smaller boutique hotels, he reserved a room at The Pierre, close to Central Park and 5th Avenue.

So as to have a better idea what he would find when in New York, concerning the Rubicov's and a deeper understanding of Fritzi's relationship with Yvetta. He checked in with some business associates and friends living in the Big Apple, who he met at Harvard business school when studying for his MBA, and cultivating a network to grow his business.

Now all he needed was some documentation to take with to study on the flight, giving him some information to work with.

Two days later he settled in business class on a Qantas flight to the Big Apple. He had called Jared and spoken briefly to Fritzi to enquire how she was, informing them he'd be away on business in the States for several days, and that he would still be contactable on his phone.

He knew Jared was quite capable of managing things in his absence, without his input, but all the same he needed to remain connected. After all, he had a vested interest in what happened to Fritzi, which, he admitted to himself, was personal, including his unscheduled and spontaneous visit to New York City. Once they were comfortably up in the air, and dinner (surprisingly tasty) was over, he set up his laptop and opened the file Bruce had dropped off.

A Google search had given him some idea about what Yvetta Rubicov's business was. He had no idea how Yvetta was connected to some of the other players in this very sordid story, besides her parents and siblings, what was her connection to Sasha's girlfriend for instance, it appeared to affect both Fritzi and Yvetta in some negative way, that Fritzi had gotten so involved with. Some background snooping would give him ammunition – in the event, that is, that he would somehow be lucky enough to come into contact with, one of the Rubicov's and pry further into Fritzi's influence. This was the unspoken purpose of Darius' sudden trip. Darius never liked to leave a stone unturned; as far as he was concerned, the more he knew, the less of an unwelcome surprise would lie in store if he ever became involved with Fritzi again. And he hoped to be able to fill in some blanks for Jared about the Rubicov's if, needed.

Settling back in his seat, with his feet up, he switched on the side light, opened the folder, and began to read Bruce's information about the extended Rubicov family. He hoped the dossier would enlighten his understanding of how all the pieces of Fritzi's life, including her criminal history, fit together.

By the time he closed the folder, the lights in the cabin had come on and breakfast was being served. Lying back in his seat he closed his eyes and, for the first time during the flight, near the very end, began to relax. He felt that wonderful, floating feeling of being up in the air, of escaping your problems, if only for a moment, of a new adventure, of getting away.

His mind filled with information about the fabulous, fascinating, and quite complicated lives of the Rubicov family he had just learnt about. There was only one thing left to do and that was to meet as many of the Rubicov family members as he could, without alerting them to his motives. It might be a tricky balancing act, but he had every intention of pulling it off – and, at that moment, in mid-air, his eyes closed and his feet up, he felt oddly confident.

Sadly, Yvetta's brother Sasha Rubicov had passed away. Darius had a healthy respect for Sasha's widow, the English girl Saffron: she had had a rough time, and much of it had been caused by Fritzi and Yvetta. Safi's marriage into the Rubicov family had obviously catalysed Yvetta's anger and jealousy, he thought, and set the stage for the dissolution of the Rubicov family. As he understood it, Yvetta had used Fritzi not only against her hated sister-in-law, Saffron, but also against her mother, Anna. In fact, Fritzi and Yvetta did not come off well in anything he had read about them. The two women were ultimately a wicked duo when working together as a team, or so it appeared to Darius. Once set in motion by her lover, Fritzi had continued, and intensified, her feud with the Rubicov family. Darius was shaken by what he had read in Bruce's file; it was even more damming than the original document from Interpol. He opened his eyes, suddenly awake and alert – and worried, too. The moment of optimism was over, he realised with a start.

He found his feelings for Fritzi conflicted. It was becoming clear to him now that there were two different Fritzis: The Fritzi of his own experience, the Fritzi in his life and in his bed, and then the other Fritzi, the Fritzi he had only read about, the Fritzi featured in the document and in Interpol's database, and in jails in more than one continent. Or perhaps there was a Freddie, and there was a Fritzi, and the two personas were irreconcilable. Indeed, these two, entirely different, conflicting personalities were difficult to reconcile with each other, or with his own experience of tender, sensitive Fritzi.

Was Interpol mistaken – or was he? Or was he, despite his considerable experience, hopelessly naïve? Perhaps he was a chump, a mark, a fool. It wasn't just him, though, he reflected – for better and worse, Jared felt this way, too. When in Fritzi's company, it was impossible not to fall under her spell. She was obviously a master at manipulation and she was highly duplicitous. If one took her own past into consideration, her abusive father and tough, loveless, joyless Eastern

European background, it was almost impossible not to feel for her plight. Her youth totally controlled by the State, her father's cold Stasi background and her eventual escape to a free world, but not from her childhood experiences. Yet reading in Bruce's comprehensive, detailed document how Fritzi had connived with the help of her criminal contacts in the underworld to work against the Rubicov family, to upend and ultimately destroy the family, made one wonder what kind of person she really was. The document certainly made for sobering reading material. Too sobering for his liking, he thought grimly, and, flagging down the flight attendant, ordered a double whiskey. 'On the rocks,' he said, although he might as well have said, 'Up in the air.'

He wondered whether he should pass the folder on to Jared now or at a later date. Jared's opinion of Fritzi was likely to be tested, too, Darius thought. Perhaps he would have second thoughts about her. That may not be a bad thing, actually. As long as they continued to work to save Fritzi – that was crucial, for all of their purposes. Still, it was important that Jared had all the relevant information in his possession before attempting to go ahead with building a defence in her favour and submitting it to the Australian immigration authorities. Darius looked at the map on the screen. They'd be landing at JFK in a couple of hours. He decided the best course of action was to acquire more personal information on Fritzi, and on the Rubicov family as well. He decided that after he returned to Sydney, he'd have a conference with Jared to discuss how to move forward. But for now, he needed to switch his brain off and get some shuteye if he wanted to hit the ground running on his arrival in New York.

Now here he was on a completely different mission, one he had no idea how to set in motion. The best thing, he decided, was to go about it methodically. First things first: he had to wake up and shake off the lethargy, sluggishness, and fatigue of the flight. Then he had to think on his feet, something he was normally pretty good at. But everything was different now. And, in this enormous city, where was he to start with his plan?

The galleries the Rubicovs owned were publicly accessible spaces. He figured he could enquire about the owners under the pretext of buying art. Most Americans were helpful (though New Yorkers perhaps less so than elsewhere in this enormous country). But he had experience with New Yorkers, too, and people were all the same at the end of the day, with similar instincts, responses, and principles. He felt confident that once he made contact, with people in, or near, the Rubicov's circle, he would gain some sort of access.

The 5th Avenue hotel was not in his preferred area but it was conveniently close to Madison Ave, and the Rubicov gallery; he usually liked the rougher, arty Lower East Side of Manhattan, and had stayed at the Bowery and the Ludlow and the Soho Grand in the past. Katz's Deli had always been one of the main attractions; he just loved the salt beef sangers. He hoped he would get down there to indulge, not to mention visit the Aussie bars he had got drunk in on previous visits.

Darius hadn't given his past much thought. His life had been a pretty ordinary one, and certainly, by most people's standards, privileged. His parents were hardworking restaurateurs, who owned a string of pasta places all over Sydney and Melbourne. As the family restaurant became many restaurants, and the business thrived, so did the family finances. They sent him to the best private schools. and he had gone on to a top university. His dad had passed on and his mom, a typical Italian grandma now, kept herself busy with all his nieces and nephews. Even though she already had eight grandchildren, she was still always nagging him about marriage and kids. They were a family of four brothers, and Darius was the youngest and the only one not to join the family business. He adored his mother, as did everyone in the family. She never criticised, just poured love into each and every one of them. Darius never missed a week without visiting her when he was home, and when he was away, he'd try and call her as often as possible. The time difference between New York City and Sydney made calling difficult, but he knew his mom would want to know that he had arrived safely, and he sent off some texts to his family.

Oddly, from the comfort and distance of his hotel room in Manhattan, he was thinking now about his mother. His mother had never said a negative word to him about Lin, but he felt she never approved of his Chinese girlfriend. Lin wasn't homely enough for his mom, who wanted someone who would look after her son. He knew without a doubt she wouldn't approve of Fritzi, either. Secretly, he wanted to please his mother, but so far had not met the right girl. Was Fritzi the wrong girl?

On paper, certainly, she was wrong – very wrong. His brothers were married to Italian girls and he knew there was no chance he would be doing that; he had never been attracted to Italian girls, just too close to home. Whatever girl he brought into the family was going to have a tough time to begin with, and him being the youngest son and, not in the pasta business didn't help either. All the same, Darius would do anything for his family, and he knew the feeling was mutual: they were a close bunch.

Apart from being at university with Jared, he didn't know much about his past. They were never close. They hadn't been besties, but they ran with the same crowd and mixed with the same people at certain celebrations. Things had tightened up for Jared once his dad became prime minister. The formerly hard-partying playboy, now esteemed professional, Jared had sensibly opted for a low profile, staying out of the press and keeping his head down when taking on controversial cases. If the media got wind of certain facts, Fritzi would no doubt be a catalyst, and sparks would fly. He knew Jared would try and do a deal for Fritzi if he had a good enough case, especially since Fritzi had been hailed as a hero for saving not only his life but the lives of others, and at her own personal risk.

But first he had to do some serious research, preferably on the ground in Manhattan. His priority was for the three of them to be safe. He wanted neither himself nor Jared to fall foul of any major problems, and he could already foresee more than a few up ahead. Not only personal problems, but professional problems, too. Not so much for him, who could retire comfortably on the money he had earned from selling his start-ups, but for Jared, who had a thriving and socially valuable career as a lawyer for the downtrodden and the dispossessed. Now, with the sudden distance between himself and the problem with Fritzi in Sydney, he felt conflicted about what they had taken on. And he felt responsible, too, and would feel more so if, anything untoward happened.

Darius realised he was going out on a limb, but that was his way. He couldn't help being the person he was, to the great annoyance of certain others. Once he got his teeth into a project, he couldn't stop, and he knew he wasn't the only one with this problem. Fritzi had become a personal project for both him and Jared. He contacted his mates in Manhattan and arranged to meet them for the next few evenings. During the day he decided to visit his old hangouts and go on a serious walkabout round Manhattan.

He started with lunch at Katz's Deli, which he had been looking forward to with relish ever since he planned his trip to the city. It had been a long time since he had enjoyed a salt beef sanger as much. he went for all the trimmings, the pickles and coleslaw. He could now envision his afternoon activities ahead of him: the gym would be seeing him later on today to work off all those calories. He enjoyed this part of town; the atmosphere was very different to Uptown, where he was heading. He took in all the new stores and restaurants; the area was becoming gentrified, very different from when he was last here, in 2008.

Quite a few galleries had moved into the area, which was a signal that the usual inhabitants, who had made the East Side what it was, would be moving out as everything around them became upscale and landlords started charging more. There were still rent controlled buildings but the old Jewish quarter was now a Museum and, the Bowery now an upscale, boutique hotel area. The Chinese were always a presence but less visible and China town was buzzing. The younger professionals had moved in making it a hip area to visit. As he walked along the pavements, he stopped to marvel at all the small specialty stores. Another great thing about Manhattan, in addition to the delicious ethnic food.

Heading back towards his hotel, he walked along Madison Avenue, coming to a stop in front of a prestigious gallery. Peering inside, he decided to take in the exhibition; the Russian theme and iconographic pieces captured his interest. All things Russian suddenly seemed significant to him. Enormous TV screens in the entrance showed simultaneous exhibitions in a sister gallery in Moscow and St, Petersburg. Intrigued, he picked up a leaflet from the reception desk, a sleek, vast, and most impressive marble counter. As in most galleries the girls at the front desk were used to people idly walking in and out; for this reason, they paid scant attention to visitors, unless they enquired directly about the art. The leaflet had the name of the gallery printed in Russian and English. Darius could not believe his good fortune. Perhaps it was fate. He had walked straight into the Rubicov Gallery.

What a surprise – or was it? On further inspection of the leaflet, he saw the address of a second Rubicov gallery, with details of that gallery's contemporary collection. The director of the gallery he was presently in was listed as 'Saffron Rubicov,' while the second gallery listed 'Yvetta Rubicov' as its director and owner. Passing through to the next section of the gallery, he found a second exhibition by an artist called Dax: three enormous works, taking up one wall each; fascinating baroque canvases of naked ladies, fruit, animals, and tattoos. Darius found the paintings rich in colour and depth, and bold in subject. They certainly held his attention.

'I see you find these paintings of interest,' a voice said. For a moment, lost in thought and still staring at the wall, he wasn't sure whether he was being addressed. Turning around he starred into the eyes of a very beautiful woman, her thick brunette hair was shoulder length, but it was her delicate features and elegance that captured his attention

'They are fascinating,' he said quickly, regathering himself, 'verging on porn, but much too elegant to be simply pornographic.' He felt shy all of a sudden, especially in front of this beautiful woman. 'I find them so alluring, they draw you in.'

She smiled a bright, perfect smile. Again, he admired her beauty; she, too, drew him in. 'My feelings exactly,' she said smoothly, and he detected a transatlantic accent, with a British inflection at times. 'Well, you can, if you wish, have a meal surrounded by these ladies at the Rubicov restaurant in Tribeca. The paintings were originally done as a commission for that restaurant, but the artist had these, three left over. And now we have them here,' she said happily. 'Two have been sold, and the third is under offer.'

'You are English,' he said, suddenly unsure of himself, feeling out of his depth once again, shy and oddly aroused by the artwork around him.

'Yes,' she replied, 'and you are, if I'm not mistaken, Australian.' Darius put out his had to introduce himself. 'Nice to meet you, Darius,' she replied, with the same confident aura of efficiency, professional, and animated, almost youthful, warmth. 'I am Safi Rubicov, the owner of this gallery'

He couldn't help staring at this woman, and he enjoyed looking at her almost as much as at Dax's artwork. She was stunningly pretty. He knew so much about her life, but couldn't get his head around how attractive she was. The document had not prepared him for her deep and mesmerising beauty.

'I wonder,' Darius said, still feeling awkward, struggling to find his words, 'could you let me have the price of this painting?' He gestured to the wall in front of him, which featured his favourite of Dax's three exhibited works.

'And, also the address and telephone number of the restaurant. I may just stop off for a meal, during my visit here.'

Safi smiled winningly – difficult to think that she could look more beautiful than she had even a moment before, but, somehow she accomplished that feat, too. Indeed, there seemed no limit to what she could do – she appeared enormously accomplished, self-assured, but sensitive and charming, too.

'Absolutely,' she said sweetly. 'You aren't here long then. If you have the time, perhaps you would like to visit our other gallery; it has a more eclectic collection of art.'

Darius left the gallery, smiling broadly, still lost in Safi's beauty (which made him momentarily forget Fritzi, and, indeed, his reason for being in New York), wondering whether his luck would hold out. He wanted another opportunity to ingratiate himself with these important players in Fritzi's past, to find out more information, first-hand.

What he really wanted, right now, was to see Safi again. Perhaps a face-to-face meeting should be his next step. But how honest should he be? And, if it was not advisable to be wholly honest, what ruse should he equip himself with? What, he wondered, would, Fritzi do in this situation?

Safi had disappeared into her office so he did not have a chance to speak with her again. But he did have the price of Dax's artwork, and he was definitely going to put in a counter offer of $140,000, $10 thousand more than the asking price, to keep the dialogue open, and his ruse intact. Even if the bid was successful and, he had to ship the enormous canvas to Sydney, it was a work he could live with, and would be a conversation-starter for ever, and a memory of his time here. Who knows, it may even turn out to be a shrewd investment.

His own apartment had mostly Aboriginal paintings on the walls and, Lin had taken him to a small Island off Hong Kong, where he had fallen for an antique costume. He took the costume back with him to Australia, where he had it boxed and framed. It now hung in his entrance, greeting all who stepped inside his abode, and the start of a hundred conversations, questions, flirtations. He felt that Dax's enormous, impressive, and eye-catching work might not look out of place in his bedroom suite, which could do with a baroque, sexy facelift.

He spent that evening at the Rubicov restaurant, with his mate James and his girlfriend Nicole, neither of whom he had seen in years. But he was distracted still, thinking about Fritzi and how she was getting on with Jared (had it really been wise to leave them for an extended period of time? for Darius' sanity, at least, coming here seemed a wise decision – or did it?), about the enchanting Safi, and even about the artwork that was now so firmly fixed in his mind.

He now wanted to see the other Dax paintings, too. Or was this just an excuse, on his part, to get even closer to Safi? To what degree, he wondered, was it still about Fritzi. That was his problem, it was difficult for him to be pinned down to anything or anyone, for long. It was the same with his business. He was hyper-focused – to a fault – but only for so long. And then he would get bored, sell his company, start with something else. In this way, he thought, perhaps he and Fritzi weren't so different after all. Still, he was more strongly drawn to Fritzi than to any other woman in a long time.

On entering the restaurant, he wasn't disappointed: the most alluring of Dax work, with a pug and tattooed beauty eating from a bowl of glistening red apples perched on an armchair, with a tiled floor to rival the Uffizi gallery in Florence, hung in full view over the reception area. It was a very welcoming sight and, made him feel right at home. They had a few drinks at the circular bar and moved onto their table.

As Darius passed the staircase that led to the restaurant's upper level, he was greeted with another Dax painting hanging on the landing, this time a bulldog was the chosen pet and, seated at the feet of a luscious female figure sporting a tattoo on her shoulder. He had to admit these were powerful, sensuous works of art and, suited the Red walls also covered with modern works of art with medieval wooden circular light fittings that hung low over white clothed tables, filled with burning candles. The restaurant was pure theatre a baroque contemporary Russian feel brilliantly, offset by Dax naked ladies. Seeing them in this setting, especially after imbibing a few strong vodka-based cocktails, Darius no longer needed any persuading: he definitely wanted that painting. He also badly wanted to see Safi again, to talk to her, to find out more. He felt intoxicated, and in over his head, and it was an exciting feel, to relinquish control to a larger situation or sensation, much as he had lost control to Freddie all of those weeks ago.

He would call the gallery in the morning and set up a meeting with Safi to make an offer. He hoped he could persuade them to let him buy it. Money certainly would not be a problem. At this point, his owning the painting was about more than just a monetary purchase.

The next morning, awake and alert despite the night's vodkas and excitement, his feelings had not lessened. Sitting in Safi's chic and expansive office, drinking a much needed, coffee, Darius felt unusually empowered. He decided he was going to ask some pertinent questions.

'Tell, me' he said suavely, shifting forward in the soundless, expensive leather chair, in amiable, disarming, business-meeting mode, 'how does an English lady like yourself end up owning a Russian gallery?'

She smiled but something was different now. It wasn't her usual wide and winning smile. He could detect the sadness in her eyes now. He waited for her to speak – words usually came so easily to her – but instead she surprised him with a sigh. 'It's a very long story,' she said softly. And that appeared to be all.

'How about the short version?' he said, trying to keep his voice level, amiable but disinterested. She turned away from him, pretended to look at some papers on her desk. When she looked up again, she said, 'I married into the Rubicov family, although my husband Sasha sadly passed away.'

'I am truly sorry for your loss,' Darius said, perhaps a little too hurriedly, trying to sound surprised. Safi looked at Darius, acknowledging his wishes. He could tell she had no intention of saying anything further. She was a friendly girl, to a point – but some things were private, and he was very much a stranger to her. The subject was closed. So where could he go from here? Thinking, quickly he said, 'You might call me a nosy Aussie, but Russians have always fascinated me. Such a rich cultural history, and since the Wall came down, they have spread their money and their influence far and wide.'

She nodded and said, still softly, her words flatter now, almost an afterthought, 'Yes, that's true. Many Russians have reluctantly left to make their lives in a safer environment.'

'Is that what happened to the Rubicov family?' he asked.

'Yes,' she said, but her voice was still flat, and now there appeared to be a note of wariness, perhaps even suspicion. He pushed his chair back. He was asking too many questions too fast, impatient as usual, but at the expense of the entire purpose of his trip, tripping himself up, coming on too strong. Time to be more passive, but more cunning, too; let her lead. 'I suppose you could say that.'

'And where have these Russian emigres gone to? America, I suppose.'

'Many are right here, in New York City,' she said. 'But the Russian diaspora is wide. Many are in London. You'll find them in Sydney, too.' Her tone, this turn of the conversation, back to Australia, full circle, as it were, seemed to signify something: the topic of Russia was over; it was back to business. 'Now, Darius, I have not yet managed to contact the client who put the painting on hold.'

She was eyeing him keenly again, as though trying to determine whether his interest in the painting was real, or whether he had just staged a meeting to talk about Russia in general and the Rubicov family in particular. Being part of a famous family, more than one hustler and chancer had approached her under false pretences over the years, and her years of being naïve were long gone, over even before Sasha was imprisoned by terrorists, leaving her alone and anxious at a very young age for years, around the time she realised, too late, as it happened, that the man she married wasn't deeply involved in criminal activity, but a pawn in one Fritzi's many elaborate plans.

She was not immune to the fact that she was attractive to men – she had been keenly aware of this from a fairly young age – or that not all men were scrupulously honest, especially not in their pursuit of women. All was fair, some said, in love – or, at least, lust – and war. or that, being part of the Rubicov family, she was in a position of power, no matter how powerless she often felt. And, in New York City at least, striving to be part of a higher social class – the highest social class – could often seem like a kind of warfare.

'Apparently, he is away in Europe. Would you mind waiting?' He found it very difficult to say no to her, of course. 'As soon as we hear, I will let you know.'

Darius reluctantly agreed. 'By the way,' he said, 'I am on my way to your other gallery today.' Perhaps he was coming on too strong again, but he desperately wanted to please her.

'Oh, really,' she said warmly. Perhaps he had misjudged her, perhaps she had not been suspicious after all, because she smiled and said, 'that's a coincidence, so am I. I have a meeting there. Would you accept a lift? My driver is about to take me.'

Darius immediately accepted, of course. His luck was certainly holding out. Who knew where this could end. He hoped he would get the opportunity to meet Yvetta, possibly through Safi.

Moments later he was sitting next to Safi in the back of a black limousine, sailing through the sleek streets of midday Manhattan. Here, things were suddenly more intimate between them. Out of the office, she appeared more relaxed, too, smiling often, and rarely looking out of the black tinted windows. Instead, they chatted away about Manhattan and how it was forever changing. He gazed at her, forgetting often where he was, in a transitional state himself. When he did look out at it, the city appeared sleek and entrancing, like Safi herself. He could tell Safi was entirely at home in New York: chic, brisk, at times business-like, but fast-moving, urbane, and not without considerable charm.

'I wondered whether you have thought of showing Aboriginal art in your galleries?' he asked. It was a long shot, but if they were at all interested, he could perhaps persuade Yvetta to visit Sydney, a dangerous thought, but wildly exciting from his perspective, playful, yet crazy to even consider. He had good friends who could set up meetings for her with some of the best artists in Australia. Safi looked at him closely, warmly, a different look than the casual-but-professional one she had given him in the gallery. He could tell her interest was piqued, 'Actually, I have visited Sydney,' she said smoothly. 'My brother lives in Australia.'

'What a small world,' he said. 'Where about?'

'He used to live in Sydney, but is now in Melbourne.'

Darius couldn't stop gazing at her. 'What does he do for a living?'

'He is in computers.'

'That's interesting – so am I. We might have run into one another at some stage. You must give me his details'

She smiled. 'Absolutely I will. In fact, it's time we visited again.' We, Darius wondered with a pang, who is we? He recalled reading that Safi's husband, Sasha Rubicov, who Fritzi had shot, had later died. 'I would actually love that. You have put the idea into my mind.'

The car pulled alongside a huge double door, which opened to reveal tables and chairs leading into the gallery, where people were enjoying drinks and light snacks. Inside the cavernous space, which housed fully grown trees and a glass bridge linking some of the floors, Darius was looking around with interest when he felt a light touch on his arm. Standing alongside Safi was a petite, dark-haired woman who, on first glance, he felt certain was Yvetta. He extended his hand to introduce himself, not wanting to appear too familiar. Still, it was difficult not to be familiar; having read so much about this family, he felt he knew them personally.

'So nice to meet you,' the petite woman said, in an unmistakeably, but elegantly, Russian accent. She offered a smile that would have been shy if it wasn't so perfectly polished and all-consuming. She seemed to be taking him in fully, and perhaps she liked what she saw, for she added, 'Why don't I give you a personal tour after my sister-in-law and I have finished our business. Do have something to eat. We have another restaurant on the first floor. I will come and find you.'

Darius said goodbye to Safi, thanking her for the lift, and made his way to the restaurant. He had no idea how he was going to draw either of them out on the Fritzi matter, but at some stage he knew he had to broach something that might lead to a discussion about Fritzi. But he was getting ahead of himself: he hadn't expected to get so far so soon, before having even settled on a strategy. But here he was, as usual, in over his head, and thinking on his feet. Yvetta was everything Fritzi had described. Compared to Fritzi's elegant, lanky frame, Yvetta was tiny. She was also quite stunning, in a very Russian way, charming and flirtatious. He sat nursing a cup of coffee, a slice of healthy, gluten-free pie squash, and a side of arugula salad. In fact, he felt great, refreshed, almost saintly after his salt beef indulgence the previous day, and his generally unhealthy diet since arriving in New York.

The restaurant was full – it was obviously the place to lunch – and there was a buzz about the place he liked. He could hear the familiar New York tones all around him. It was fun to be back in this frenetic atmosphere, everyone absorbed in conversation.

As he drained his coffee cup Yvetta joined him at the table. She asked for a refill for him (she was sipping a green smoothie from the juice bar), and sat down.

'That looks healthy,' Darius said, gesturing to the smoothie. 'Let me guess, cucumber and some ginger concoction.' Yvetta laughed, but it was a nervous laugh. Indeed, her aura was one of nervous energy, much more highly strung than Safi, he thought.

'Safi tells me you are interested in purchasing the Dax,' Yvetta said. 'You know, he is married to her cousin.'

'I had no idea,' Darius said, surprised again, and thinking how small the world was – even here in New York City.

'Yes,' she continued, 'Dax and her cousin have an architectural design company. They were employed to do the restaurant. In fact, that is how Sasha met my brother Sasha, who became her husband.'

'Really,' he said, 'how interesting. That must have been quite some time ago now.?'

'Oh, yes,' she said, lifting up her smoothie again, 'a lot of water under the bridge, as they say.' For a moment, Darius couldn't think of anything to say. His coffee arrived just then, and he felt grateful to the waitress for the welcome interruption. He waited for the waitress to leave, then, stirring his coffee, making eye contact with Yvetta again, he said, 'Is Safi's cousin British as well?'

'Sort of,' Yvetta said slowly, as though finding the right words. 'Daniel was born here, but his dad was British.'

Now Darius was surprised anew. 'So, Dax is a woman,' he said. 'Funny, I was under the impression that a man had painted the ladies; they are so alluring.'

Yvetta gave that highly strung laugh again. 'No, no, Dax is a man, not a woman.'

Now Darius felt awkward, unknowing, uncool, conservative even, as though he was always two steps behind, old-fashioned in ultra-progressive, urbane Manhattan.

'Okay,' he said quickly, 'I get the picture. They haven't yet made same-sex marriage lawful in Australia. We need to catch up with you Yanks.'

'Well,' she said, in a sensitive, reassuring tone, as though to tell him that his confusion about the matter was entirely forgivable, 'some States here haven't made it law, either.' She surprised him again, this time with a smile. 'But thankfully, both of the two D's, as we call them, got the opportunity to marry. And I myself am about to marry my long-term partner.'

Not knowing quite how to answer, he said, 'Congratulations are in order then. Perhaps I'll invite myself to your wedding. Only joking, but I have never been to a same-sex marriage. I would love to experience one.'

'Well,' she said smoothly, 'let's see if we can interest you in buying some art. If we do some healthy business, I might very well invite you. It can't be a bad thing to have an Aussie at our wedding.'

'Ha, good on ya. You got me there, mate, as we say in Aussie-speak.'

Smiling, she said, 'You ready for a tour?'

Her pride in her profession and the gallery were immediately clear to him. He had to admit that she had an amazing gallery, which she had established herself, through years of passion, dedication, and painstaking work. Oh, and family money, of course – lots and lots of it. It was not only a gallery that housed art, but it was also innovative in its approach to the public. Thus, the gallery had been transformed into a space where anyone could wander into off the street, and feel stimulated by the artwork and the environment, by the many worlds outside of this one. The space felt inclusive, and not at all intimidating. The foyer was often on loan to small groups of musicians or poets – anyone who had an artistic contribution to make. The gallery often featured interactive artwork during the school breaks. Always, Yvetta stressed, she and her small staff tried to make the gallery space a work in progress, a site of adventure, improvement, and constant change.

He had to keep reminding himself of the Yvetta he had read about in the Interpol document, the Yvetta who had conspired with Fritzi to destroy her family – the very family she appeared so proudly a part of now. The document had stressed that Yvetta was especially adversarial towards Safi, to the point where she had assaulted her, tried to strangle her at a family gathering in Miami long ago, if he got his sums right probably a good fifteen or more years ago, in an act that some said was attempted murder. He therefore found it baffling that she now had what appeared a close relationship with her sister-in-law.

'Well, thank you for the tour,' he said, trying to conceal his confusion. He had realised quite quickly that he was out of his depth. He had come here with a plan, but was no longer sure what that plan was. Or, really, why he had even ventured to Manhattan in the first place. To get away from Fritzi – yet again? Or to get even closer to her? 'You have a very innovative gallery. You should visit Hobart in Tasmania; we have the Mona, an underground gallery, it's quite awesome, but I can honestly say there is nothing similar to your gallery in Sydney – or, really, anywhere else I've travelled. The NGV in Melbourne has amazing curators, it's innovative in aspects too, but I enjoyed my visit here immensely.'

She smiled, gratified, and for the first time in a while he felt he had a handle on the situation again. Leaning forward, his demeanour more confident now, he said, 'Have you ever considered hosting an exhibition of Aboriginal art and artefacts? It would be awesome for the kids, teach them about the indigenous peoples from our part of the world. And, indeed, in my experience, most Americans are fairly ignorant about Australia.'

'Most Americans are fairly ignorant about all countries outside of America,' she said softly. Then, cocking her head sideways, she gave him a cheeky smile, 'But I like the idea very much. We can discuss it, perhaps as an idea for the future.'

He felt a small thrill, and, buoyed by it, said, 'I wondered if you and your partner would consider meeting me for a drink one evening? I am staying at The Pierre Hotel.' 'Another good idea,' she said. 'I will get back to you.'

Darius took an Uber back to his hotel. But in the hotel lounge, ready to head up to his room, he instead sat down in an armchair. He wanted to think. Things were moving a lot faster than he had imagined they would, and he was at the risk of being left behind. He hadn't been in Manhattan very long and he had already met Safi and Yvetta. He needed a plan to draw them out. Both were beautiful, interesting, complicated woman. Darius could be shrewd and canny, sure, but so could they. One woman he admired greatly, the other he had to find a way to understand.

He found both women enormously attractive, albeit in different ways. Yvetta, of course, was gay. But he had other questions about her. How had she turned from a mad viper into such an amiable and pleasant human being? Or was the latter nothing more than an act? In fact, the same could be said about Fritzi: she had spent most of her adult life trying to destroy a family, but had somehow become someone who would put her own life on the line. How? Why? Perhaps the answers were beyond his understanding, but he was going to delve deeper and try to find out, nonetheless. Of course, everyone (even criminals) changed their ways, but the sheer level of change here was monumental and astonishing. Someone, he hoped, would be able to explain how her behaviour had changed between then and now. He wondered if it were true about certain people meeting, and if the circumstances were toxic, they could drive each other to do evil things? Yvetta and Fritzi it seemed to him were vulnerable from the start, emotionally scarred from past experiences. Fritzi, after all, had grown up under an oppressive East German regime, Yvetta, on the other hand, must have been born at least five years after Perestroika, when the reformation of the economic and political system in Russia changed, yet she had spent a large part of her life in mental institutions. Something just did not add up, why was she so screwed up?

He jumped in the shower, deciding to put his delving into the Rubicov's lives on hold, he needed to get his head space freed up from Fritzi's past. This evening he had an arrangement with Jacques, an old friend he had not seen in a long time. They had met through mutual friends, and the Frenchman was a delightful raconteur. Darius actually enjoyed spending time in his company, which wasn't true of most of the people he came into contact with.

In spite of the fact that Jacques was in his late seventies, with his shock of silver hair and elegant height, he still managed to turn heads. Ladies – all ladies, it appeared – loved him. At least that was what Darius observed as the two men made their way to the table in the rear of the restaurant, close to a sleek stone fountain quietly burbling.

'I have to be honest, Jacques,' Darius said once both men had been comfortably seated, 'I have ulterior motives for inviting you to dinner this evening.'

'This is Manhattan,' Jacques said with his characteristically mischievous, nicotine-stained voice, 'the capital of ulterior motives. Ulterior motives are to be expected,' and he opened up his hands, which, unlike his face, were surprisingly aged and creased, 'even admired.'

Darius smiled, realising at once how much he had missed his old friend's company and quirks. Jacques always made him feel immediately at home, no matter where in the world they happened to be at the time.

And the older man was enormously entertaining – and enormously well-informed besides.

'Besides wanting to see you, of course,' Darius continued, paging through the menu without looking at it, 'and to pass on my mother's greetings – she still raves about you and your charm.'

The mention of Darius's mother seemed to lighten up Jacques even further, and now both men were smiling.

'Ah, your dear Italian mama. What a lovely lady she is. Give her my very best, please.'

They ordered a bottle of expensive red wine that Jacques recommended, and both indulged in a rare steak, triple-fried chips, and, a bowl of creamed spinach to share. Spinach, Darius thought, that was something healthy, at least – but the creamed part, not so much. Still, in for a penny, in for a pound – or a dollar, in this case – and he was determined to have a good time in the city that never slept.

'Now that's done,' Jacques said slyly, wiping his mouth on his napkin (he performed even this small movement with a sly elegance and gentility), 'why don't you tell me what's going on and why you are back in New York?' The voice was as friendly as always, but it was firmer now. The unmistakable undertone, no matter how amiable, was: let's get down to business. It was time for the ulterior motives part of the meal.

Darius tried to tell Jacques a shortened version of Freddie's story, using only her nom de plume. By the time their food arrived, Jacques, one of the quicker minds Darius had encountered, had got the gist of why he had been invited.

'Well,' Jacques said, 'blow me down with a feather, as the British say: I actually have a very close friend who this story may interest.'

'How so?' Darius asked. 'He is a very well-known art dealer and has worked with Russians on many occasions.'

Jacques paused to slice and swallow a piece of steak. He chewed slowly, thoughtfully. 'In fact, he is very close to a Russian family here called Rubicov, who own art galleries in New York – and, I think, in Moscow as well.'

'Well, that is a coincidence,' said Darius, who had been flattered by good fortune this trip. 'I can't believe my good fortune. Only yesterday I walked into that gallery you mentioned, on Madison Avenue, and met with a Safi Rubicov. I later met Yvetta at the other Rubicov gallery. They are both very beautiful, charming women.'

'What,' Jacques said, sounding unusually impatient, 'in particular, did you want to ask me about this whole saga?'

'Well,' Darius said slowly, trying to craft his words to be as efficient and economical as possible, and not to waste any more of the older man's time, 'you are a doctor of philosophy and no doubt understand human nature much better than I do.'

In fact, Darius thought, much of the time I don't understand humans at all well – and perhaps, for that matter, they don't understand me. Lin had either not understood him at all, or understood him all too well and decided she wanted nothing to do with him.

'I can't get my head around how these two women could have contrived and carried out abhorrent criminal acts,' Darius continued, speaking faster now, the words overtaking him, yet here they are today, both moving forward with their lives in what appears to me a very normal, nonviolent way.'

'But both women,' Jacques said, 'are only showing you the side of themselves they want you to see, no? There are perhaps other, possibly less flattering, sides. Which is to say, you don't have all of the information at your disposal.'

'True,' Darius said, thinking he wanted all of the information. He felt especially impatient now. He was hardly listening to Jacques. 'So, you are saying that they may not be as normal or non-violent as they appear?'

'I am not saying anything,' Jacques said. 'I am still very much listening to what you are telling me. Then, perhaps, I will offer my opinion – if it's prudent to do so.'

'Let's call my friend Freddie,' Darius said. 'For now, it's safer. She saved a close friend of mine's life – and the lives of more than a few others. In doing so, she put her own life in danger without a thought for her own safety. The other antagonist seems to have reconciled with those she harmed and plotted against quite viciously. How is this possible?' His confusion was evident in his voice.

'Ah, isn't human nature complex,' Jacques said gently. 'To be honest, the question you ask is a tough one. My mind tells me that both women had some sort of epiphany, or catalyst – a significant emotional event to make them change and transform their psyches, their personalities and trajectories. And, of course, life intervenes: some people find religion, others find love, if they are lucky. But the question is: if one scratches the surface, is the old behaviour, the original traits, still there, just lying dormant?'

Darius shifted in his seat, tried to absorb all of this. 'Yes, maybe you are right,' he said slowly, 'but I feel there is another element in play here.'

He stopped suddenly, as though trying to untangle his own words. Jacques, too, appeared confused.

'Right now,' Darius continued, 'this other element is not evident to me, but in time it might reveal itself – but hopefully not after my friend and I have helped her gain, entry into Australia as a citizen.' They walked outside – it was surprisingly bright, even warm; a beautiful Manhattan day – and Jacques gave Darius a hug.

'It's always stimulating to see you, dear Darius,' the older man said, and slipped into his hand a slip of paper. 'Here is the phone number of my friend. Do call him. He is another charming Frenchman, by the way.'

The next morning, waking early (as was his habit in Sydney; his old rituals and routines clearly reasserting themselves, even in this new country) to find the weather still clear and beautiful, and his own body feeling wonderfully refreshed, he called the contact Jacques had given him. Less than two hours later he found himself sitting in very plush offices on Madison Midtown Manhattan, in a sleekly furnished area filled with art and, the odd occasional French armchair, covered in what could only be described plush French brocade fabric, waiting to meet a Mr DuPont. The attractive brunette at his front desk introduced herself as Gina, DuPont's secretary, offered him a cup of coffee and a thick folder of Dax's work to page through. DuPont obviously thought Darius would be looking for more of the artist's work to buy, Safi had probably asked DuPont to contact his client who had reserved the work he was after.

He was shown into an office with floor-to-ceiling windows and furnished in a white minimalist style., Tall, slim, smiling, long-faced, silver-haired DuPont strode to meet him from behind a French antique desk, the only ornate object in an otherwise contemporary room. Jacques was spot-on in his description about his friend – he was, indeed, 'another charming Frenchman.' More so even than Jacques, DuPont oozed Gallic charm – and urbane intelligence, too, sporting a paisley Cravat rather than a tie and red braces under a slim tailored jacket. Darius made it clear he had not come to enquire about buying art, but was nonetheless, hoping to purchase a Dax from the Rubicov gallery. Darius had, in fact, come on a fishing expedition, one he hoped DuPont could help him with. Hoping to be illuminated on the frustratingly complex issue of Fritzi, and to hear another perspective in order to – finally – establish his own, Darius decided to tell his story once more.

DuPont sat for a long time staring out of his window. Something had changed. His face was no longer quite so handsome, or his manner so charming. He bore a grave expression now, and his once buoyant tone was now flat and low. He had listened without interruption to this Australian's story about a woman he hated and feared. As far as DuPont was concerned, this woman was a charlatan, a devious, duplicitous heretic, a sociopath who had proven herself (more than once) to be a danger to others. She respected no one's boundaries, apart from her own.

He had to decide what to tell this young man – he could speak forever about Fritzi (for his knowledge of her was sadly encyclopaedic), but he wanted to spend as little time as possible discussing her, and spoiling his day and his mood. Discussion of Fritzi always brought with it dark thoughts, and life was too short for any of it. Besides, much of this information was private, and he was nothing if not diplomatic. Darius was a friend of a friend's, certainly, but there remained such a thing as too much information. DuPont hadn't got so far in Manhattan high society or the art world by being indiscreet. Still, he owed this Australian some sort of answer – and some sort of honesty, too. He had the responsibility to save him a great deal of pain in his life – and possibly even much worse. He could not, in good conscience, let this manner go. He sighed, tried out a smile but could not accomplish even this, his usually gentle face was suddenly so heavy with distaste. Instead, he settled on a headshake.

'Fritzi,' he said slowly, as though it had been a long time since he had uttered that, 'I fear to even say this name.' He was revealing too much of himself to this young stranger, but it could not be helped. It was in the young man's best interest – and DuPont's own interest, too, perhaps. After all, this Australian, with his obvious money, could, out of his own misplaced virtue, prop Fritzi up and put her in a position to return to Manhattan – and, therefore, to DuPont's life. This was a horrible thought. I do not fear many people, or, for that matter, hate anyone but this woman. But I do hate her – and for good reason. She tried to destroy the life of someone very close to me, and probably would have destroyed my own life, if it came to that, and without a second thought.' He gazed at Darius intently, making sure to convey the seriousness of his words. 'No, she is not a hero – never. She is a charlatan, a heretic, a fake, and, above all, a criminal!

In fact, this woman you describe to me, this Fritzi,' again, he said the name as though spitting out a poisonous substance, 'cannot be the same person that I knew. Not at all.' He shook his head again. 'Your woman sounds positively charming compared to the snake I know.'

Darius had not expected this reaction, the full fury of it. In fact, he was shocked into silence By the Frenchman's violent response. He waited for DuPont's words to settle, for the mood to lift, but that did not appear to happen. He shifted uncomfortably in the elegant chair, not quite sure how to move forward now. He was usually quick on his feet, but not now. He felt like the air had been knocked out of him. All he could do was stare at DuPont. Perhaps the older man would elaborate. After all, he had told Darius that he hated Fritzi (he had made no bones about that), but not, exactly, why. Perhaps the Frenchman could not bring himself to revisit the reason, or perhaps it was something so sordid and secret that it could never be discussed.

Suddenly, for some reason, Darius recalled the night that Fritzi had pegged him, and his reaction to that moment. They sat for some time, neither spoke until the phone on his desk finally broke the silence, thankfully shifting the stupor that had descended on them both. DuPont seemed to be interrupted from his outpouring of venom for Fritzi, returning to the present moment, to a calmer demeanour.

'I apologise for my outburst,' DuPont said, after the telephone was abruptly silenced. 'I do not blame you at all. How very rude of me.' He smiled apologetically, brushed imaginary crumbs off his elegant striped shirt. His face was more relaxed now. 'Please allow me to take you to lunch,' he said sweetly. And then, his voice a little tighter, 'We can discuss this further over a good glass of French wine, oui? I certainly need it if we are to regurgitate something I'd rather not think about again.'

They made their way across the road to a small French restaurant DuPont obviously ate in often, since everyone there seemed to know him and he was warmly welcomed, and in his native French. The waiter (tall, elegant, but in his early twenties, so he looked almost like a younger version of DuPont) showed him to a table that was reserved only for his use. Finishing his second glass of wine (the man consumed a hell of a lot of wine, Darius began to think), he appeared to gain his composure and returned to being the charming Frenchman Darius had originally assumed he was.

'Mon dieu, what a shock you gave me – not intentionally, of course.' He smiled again. 'Really, Darius, my friend, you have no idea what any of us were put through by that woman. She tried to set me up with a fake – not only here in the States, but also in London at a Sotheby's auction. She absolutely tried to ruin my reputation with my clients and in the art community, which is a fragile business at the best of times. One sniff of dubious dealings and, poof, your reputation is in shreds. It's not an exaggeration to say that she tried to destroy me. Thank goodness, I'm pleased to say, she failed. Otherwise, I would not be here today. You must promise me, my dear friend, not ever to mention her name to Safi or Yvetta. Please, I beg you, they do not need to know that she is alive. I fear for them, I truly do.'

Darius shook his head in agreement, promising DuPont he would honour his wishes, and asked him to continue.

'Here in the States, we caught her red-handed, and she went to jail for a few months. It should have been a lot longer, but that woman has her contacts everywhere and she managed a release before her sentence was over.' He sounded exasperated, but also oddly impressed. Again, Darius realised that Fritzi was almost impossibly complicated, and she made other people's lives complicated as well.

Even the ever-articulate DuPont seemed at a loss for words when it came to describing Fritzi. Instead, he smiled sadly and said, 'Well, we all thought that would be the end of her – but no, not at all. I guess she outsmarted us – and everyone else as well. She came like a bad penny to haunt us once more. This time, my beautiful, dear friend Safi suffered a fate worse than death, all because Fritzi wanted to kidnap Yvetta. This has been an obsession, you know, with Fritzi. She shot Sasha, Safi's husband and, they both spent many months on his rehabilitation, and, then just as they regained their lives back, Sasha died of an embolism, a nightmare for Safi after all their suffering, you cannot imagine.'

Darius nodded – this he did, indeed, know. But Darius was thinking about something else. My beautiful, dear friend Safi… The way he had said those words, almost enchanted, his voice and body softening, the opposite of his tone when describing the dreaded Fritzi. He wondered if the old man didn't have feelings for the beautiful Safi, too.

'That is a saga on its own, how many times Fritzi has helped Yvetta escape out of institutions her family put her in, partly so that she would be free from Fritzi's influence, and partly because Fritzi had such a devastating, effect on Yvetta's mental health. She kidnapped Yvetta and tried to control her. I'm not absolving Yvetta – she isn't innocent in any of this, but Fritzi corrupted her absolutely, and was a terrible influence. Now that she is finally free of Fritzi she is, at last, flourishing as both a gallery owner and a human being. It's no coincidence that, the entire time she was with Fritzi, she accomplished very little of value; she spent all of her time on evil schemes and planning revenge for imagined slights. Trying to destroy others, but always destroying her own life and livelihood as well as her relationship to her family.

'Her and Fritzi together were quite evil. I know the Rubicov family: they are not perfect – no one is – but there is much good about them. The same couldn't be said of Fritzi and Yvetta when they were together. When Fritzi was put into a Russian jail she managed to escape once more, but not before she had Safi's husband, Sasha Rubicov, kidnapped. No one heard one word from him for over a year, if not more. Everyone – even Safi – thought he was dead. Fritzi's game had far-reaching implications. Sasha's father, Alexi, died from a broken heart. Sasha did not even get to go to his own father's funeral, which was something that bothered Sasha for the rest of his life. Can you imagine what Safi must have suffered, not knowing if her husband was even alive.'

Safi. DuPont's voice had softened again, and he had the same stricken expression on his face when mentioning her name. Darius suspected again that he had feelings for the British woman who was young enough to be his daughter. 'No one knew where he was or what had happened to him. Except Fritzi, of course, who orchestrated everything. Nothing good ever comes from being around Fritzi – nothing. I can tell you that for a fact,' the Frenchman warned.

'Then, just when we thought this nightmare was over and Fritzi would finally be locked up for good, Fritzi disappeared again.' He paused and something akin to confusion flashed across his face. 'I might be getting my details confused in terms of her reappearances in our lives, but it has been going on for years, and each time she reappears something terrible happens to one of us, and every time she appears it's for Yvetta. But now Yvetta doesn't want to see her again. She has finally come to her senses. She is happy with her partner and knows how much she has to lose – everything – if she invites Fritzi back into her life. Maybe this will prevent Fritzi from trying to enter her life again. Maybe. I doubt it though. Fritzi is nothing but resilient – and evil. Very evil.

'The last time she appeared once again to kidnap Yvetta, she was here in New York as an illegal alien. You think the authorities are smart – but Fritzi is smarter. In her own, twisted way, she is very, very talented. I put nothing past her. Despite her illegal status, she managed to remain under the radar long enough to cause major damage. The whole thing was a nightmare, let me tell you. Fritzi shot Sasha and he was paralysed for a very long time. In fact, he never fully recovered. He was very lucky to be alive – and Fritzi was very lucky not to spend the rest of her life in prison, which is where she belongs. Safi nursed him to health, gave every ounce of her strength to his wellbeing, poured her heart and soul into his recovery.'

He lowered his face and his voice, too, fell. 'Poor Sasha, not long after he recovered, he had a massive heart attack and died in his pool one morning doing his daily swim. His poor son found him floating on top of the water. I can only tell you that Safi has been to hell and back. She suffered a breakdown after that. Now she is married again, to a wonderful man, and I must say very contented and happy. So, if Fritzi comes into all of our lives again it would be beyond Safi's endurance – and mine. I don't think any of us could stand it – or stand for it. For that reason, it is very, very important that Fritzi never show her face in this city again.'

It was a long speech and it was over now. The old man appeared exhausted. He remained quiet for some time, eating his crevettes and possibly recovering from his lengthy regurgitation of painful past events. Darius realised now that these people had been damaged beyond comprehension by Fritzi. He realised, too, that, under the circumstances, it was a tough call for one of them to understand why anyone would be trying to help her. Darius, who had not eaten at all during this tale, finished his food, and his wine. DuPont was no longer looking at him, seemed now utterly removed, in a different place, perhaps still lost in the events of the past. But Darius was no longer thinking solely about Fritzi. Instead, now thinking more broadly for the first time, he reflected that it was not Fritzi alone who had caused so much damage; she had, for a long time, been one half of an unbreakable partnership. Darius broke the silence by asking the question that had long been on his mind.

'After causing so much pain to everyone in her family, especially Safi,' he said, 'I wonder how Yvetta can now be reunited and, from what I have seen, so close to her sister-in-law.'

DuPont responded quickly, but still did not meet Darius's gaze. He still appeared firmly fixed in that other country, the past. 'Ah, yes, another crazy one,' DuPont said, almost wistfully, 'but Yvetta was loved, and the Rubicov family never gave up on her. That family is very loyal. For a long time, Yvetta thought the family was bad, but in many, ways they are, in fact, very noble, very good. When Sasha, Yvetta's, brother, was shot by Fritzi, it was a kind of catalyst, a breaking point. It was a significant emotional event in all of our lives, but for Yvetta, I believe, it was the lynchpin that brought about a dramatic change in her personality, and her life. Also, she fell in love with my assistant at the time, and that helped Yvetta a lot – helped both women, in fact. They are about to be married; you know. My assistant, Gina, persuaded Yvetta to seek help once more, and the doctor diagnosed bipolar disorder. Now she is on drugs for her condition, and they appear to be working. Yvetta is a different person, so much better in every way.'

'They never diagnosed this before?' Darius asked, amazed.

'Perhaps they did,' DuPont said, 'in one or all of the institutions she had been admitted to over the years, but it is my understanding that she never took her medication, unless she was forced to do so. Now she takes it wilfully, routinely, and it has been a miracle transformation. For so long she was against her treatment. She felt her family was forcing her into institutions, forcing her to take medication, for their benefit, not for hers. Now she acknowledges that she alone must repair her life, that it is her journey, her destiny, that no one but herself is responsible for running – not ruining, running – her life. For the first time in years, she wants to be stable and successful, to be good to others and to herself. She has learnt from her mistakes and now wants only to thrive.'

Darius shook his head. 'That explains a lot,' he said. 'I could not fathom how the two women – former enemies, as I understand it – could have reconciled after Yvetta tried to strangle Safi, and all the heartache she caused the family.'

'Yes, my friend,' DuPont said softly, and was staring at him with his soft expressive eyes once again, 'it's been a harrowing time for them – which is why I think no one really wants to revisit the events of the past. We all just want to move forward, you understand. And, I am happy to say, they are, as far as families go, contented at last.'

Darius and DuPont left the restaurant. It had been light when they entered, and it was almost dusk as they walked out onto the pavement. Still, the air was soft and warm, and the sidewalk was full of people walking to and from work, tourists, shoppers, stragglers, joggers, the city in the midst of another cycle. Darius watched the traffic and tried to get his head around all DuPont had told him.

'I cannot thank you enough, for your honesty and candour,' Darius told DuPont. 'The thing is, I have no idea how we are going to move forward once I return to Australia. Perhaps, under the circumstances, you'd prefer not to know?'

'Yes and no,' DuPont said kindly, but with a tight smile, 'so I will leave it to you how to proceed.'

They shook hands and Darius gave DuPont a hug. The man was, above all, a sincere friend to the Rubicovs and deserved respect.

As he attempted to cross the street, the late-afternoon traffic blaring around him, he decided that there was no reason to remain in New York a day longer. He had what he came for: a better understanding of Fritzi's character and life up until he had met her. What he had learnt here had disturbed him greatly, and surprised him, too. He wondered how much Fritzi had really changed, if at all. After all, she was still on the run from the law.

Chapter 11

Jared and Darius met in his offices. His desk was laden with papers, all serious-looking, legal documents. Fritzi or not Fritzi, he clearly had a lot on his mind. His cast had been removed and he was now only on one crutch until he built up enough strength to walk unaided. His face looked better, too: fuller, brighter, not as thin and wan as before.

'Well,' Darius began, smiling at his old friend, pleased at his improved health, 'I am sure you know why I upped and flew to New York. I have much to tell you about our mutual friend, before you decide to continue with her case.'

Jared leaned forward – he looked younger today – and Darius wondered as to what other changes there had been in his life with Fritzi, over the last few days. There were some things, however, he could not ask. 'I would like to hear everything in detail,' he said, 'but today I have a busy schedule. Can we meet over the weekend, at your place? It would be more private.'

'How has she been since I have been away?' Darius said, a little wary now, not entirely sure what to expect by way of an answer.

'Good,' Jared said, and his smile relaxed Darius, for it made clear that nothing terrible had happened in his absence, 'you will be surprised to hear that she has opted to stay with Maggie for a while. I believe they have bonded: maybe a mother-daughter thing, and Maggie speaks German. So that is quite a new development, and to be honest it suits me.'

Now Darius was smiling even more broadly – indeed, it was good to be home. Fritzi staying with Maggie, and away from Jared, was truly good news. Still, he wondered (newly suspicious after all he had learnt in Manhattan), what events – or emotions – had truly occasioned this change of events? He may never know, and wasn't prepared to ask.

Too shy to interrogate any further, Darius said simply, 'Have you spoken to the housekeeper about Fritzi's past at all?'

'Absolutely not,' Jared said with unusual firmness. He was smiling still, but the severity in his voice was disconcerting. Perhaps something had happened in his absence, after all.

'Well, do you think she might confide in Maggie?'

'Perhaps,' Jared said, sounding tired now, or – more likely – distracted by the large pile of papers on his desk. He was still behind his work, and still stressed. 'But I have no concerns about Maggie. In all the years that she has worked in the homes of high-profile politicians, she has, I am sure, seen and heard more than most.'

'Yes, you are probably right,' Darius said, feeling awkward again. Maybe things really were different between he and Jared now. They certainly felt that way. More distant, perhaps a little strained, cool, if not yet quite cold. Or perhaps he was just being irrational, suffering from some side effect of jet lag. Maybe the physical distance he had just suffered through had created the illusion of an emotional equivalent. Time to snap out of it. Time to return to a Sydney state of mind, whatever that was. 'I just wondered,' he added, rather inertly. No, he did not think that he was being irrational. He felt sure that something had changed between them over the last few days. The dynamics, he thought, the dynamics were certainly different. But how exactly?

'See you Saturday at 10am.'

Darius left wondering about the new development: Fritzi's change of address. He was sure Fritzi was safe with Maggie, but he thought the change a little strange nonetheless. Having spent several days learning just how cunning Fritzi was, he could not help feeling uneasy. Whom exactly he feared for (Jared? Fritzi? Maggie? himself? he wasn't exactly sure, and he reminded himself that there was no apparent reason for Fritzi to cause any trouble. But then, if New York City had taught him anything, it was that he knew nothing at all about Fritzi and her motivations. If Fritzi caused any trouble now, here, in her present predicament, she would be the one to suffer.

Refusing to give in to his jet lag, before he became a zombie in need of sleep, he decided to visit his mother.

His mother, as always, was thrilled to see him. She made him feel special, as if he was an only child, not just one of four sons. Well, he was the dreamer, the traveller, the free spirit, the innovative one, the unmarried son. She loved hearing about his life and he indulged her with antidotes about New York City, the new galleries he had seen, and Jacques, the good-looking Frenchman. Having no idea how many silk scarves she must have in a drawer somewhere from all his trips, she opened a brown paper bag containing yet another, showing surprise and delight. He, too, would indulge and let her spoil him with whatever she had baked or cooked that week, Italian favourites her boy's all loved when they came to visit were always on offer, lasagne, or meat balls in tomato sauce, and of course everyone's famous Italian deserts, tiramisu but his mom's was the best, and her cannoli was to die for.

And he had to admit he loved being back in his childhood home – in its own way it seemed as far-removed from his everyday life, and somehow as fantastical, as Manhattan. But unlike Manhattan it was calm – wonderfully calm. Not a care in the world here. It brought back wonderful memories of his dad and his other brothers. They were a rowdy bunch when together not without fights and, for that matter, arguments about almost everything, many windows ended up shattered and, being replaced, she seemed to take it all in her stride admonishing them but never punished them unfairly. His mom was the queen to all the men in her family and he dreaded to think of her not being there one day. They all fretted about her health and wanted her to take life easier, but of course she wouldn't hear of it. She didn't exactly live a quiet life.

Besides her endless grandma duties, she did charitable work at their local Catholic church orphanage, helping to bake with the kids, was her idea of a relaxing day. His mother was busier than he was right now. He often joked about having to make an appointment to see her when he wanted to visit, she was still an attractive woman dark eyes that sparkled with life, an open face with a ready smile for those she cared for, many would envy her thick wavy hair and, still a good figure, he had to admit for her age she took pride in her appearance, always a beautiful scarf to set off her outfit, hence his many gifts, so she'd never run out.

Sitting in her kitchen, where he had spent so many joyful hours as a child, watching her fuss over him, he wondered whether it was possible for today's woman to be like his mom in such a changed world. Was this the reason he was still single? He was looking for a woman like his mom, but in a world where this just wasn't possible? Lin was about as far from his mother as two women could conceivably be, which was one reason why his mother had disliked her so much. Well, the feeling had very much been mutual. No one had her ideals any longer; most woman today wanted a career, appeared to want everything, in fact. Feminist ideals were at the top of their list, kids were way down, and being a stay-at-home-mom almost right at the bottom. He didn't blame them for this prejudice: stay-at-home moms were not valued in society. It wasn't that he wanted a partner to have old-fashioned values. He liked strong, independent women – and Lin was certainly one of them – and he thought of himself as a feminist. He supported most of their values. Yet his mom was a feminist in her own way.

The ideals, definition, and even philosophy of feminism had changed over the last half-century, but this did not discredit the original feminists, the women who had paved the way for all of the women (and men) who came after them. Some of the later radicalism was difficult to stomach, but the philosophy of equality was inarguable. She believed in nurturing and she had taught her boys to value women, because she believed that both sexes needed something different from the other. These days, many feminists taught that men and women were no different from each other, that they were, in fact, exactly the same. This was not his mother's experience of the world – or his, for that matter, there had to be a good measure of chemistry. His parents complemented each other's strengths, and their differences made for a feisty exchange between them, always ending with his mother in fits of laughter, especially when his dad made fun of her habits, she had a great sense of humour and, was always ready to laugh at herself, his dad was a big bear of a man who doted on his mother and family, which made up for his absence's when they were growing up.

His mother had compromised her needs for her family and her husband, before he passed away, a few years ago now. Running restaurants – at first one, all-consuming, make-or-break restaurant, and then different restaurants in different cities; with success, the bank loans and reservations were easier to come by, but the pressure never seemed to really ease – used to keep his father away from home late into the night for many years. Darius reflected on the loneliness she must have suffered all those nights when he came to bed exhausted, way past midnight. (Indeed, Lin had had similar fights with Darius, when he was putting all of his time into his start-up and was, she said, 'putting your company above everything else – especially our relationship.' Which was quite an indictment, since Lin – who could stay in the office for days at a time, sleeping – when did sleep – on the couch – was far more obsessed with work than he would ever be.)

Saturday nights for his family were never like they were for his friends, when the babysitter came around because they went out. Due to the nature of running a chain of restaurants, his family had a different lifestyle. He never appreciated any of that when he was growing up, but now he felt in awe of his mother's selflessness. Not that she was a softy – far from it. She stood for no-nonsense at home and meted out the discipline. What she said was law. His dad was the softy, making up for his time spent away from home with cuddles and fun and ballgames in the back yard. They had a good balance and his mother never, as far as he could tell, resented her role.

'Mom, where am I going to find a woman like you to spoil me the way you do?' Darius asked. 'Darius,' his mother said, in her relaxed dulcet tones and, Ozzy accent. I think you are going to be the one doing the spoiling, when you find the right one – and you will. So make sure you find a girl who appreciates you.'

'So you think I'm a big softy?'

'I did not say that,' she said. 'You are my youngest. I indulged you, as did your brothers, and that gave you confidence to be yourself.' Darius had always found it easy to talk to his mother. If only it was as easy to confide in everyone else.

'Well, you know,' he said, 'I thought I would take a break after my relationship with Lin ended and my company went public. But I'm not ready to do nothing.'

'Well, none of you boys were ever good at sitting around, so I understand. Your father, bless him, was the same way. You have become successful very young. It must be hard to have so much time on your hands?' Darius had never thought about it this way: the freedom to do whatever you want being a kind of curse. Trust his mother to break it down like this, to make, in just a few words, a complicated topic seem so simple.

'Yup, it is,' he said, suddenly feeling (and sounding) like a child. But every adult reverted to being a child in the company of their parents.

He hadn't really stopped working, and he and Lin had arranged an extended break together. Now he wasn't sure it was the right way to go on his own. His company was always on the lookout for start-ups to invest in. When they found something, they would let him know; Fortunately, he did not have to be in the office 24/7, and was allowed the luxury of disappearing for weeks at a time. These days, anyway, everyone was always intimately connected over their iPhones and iPads.

Feeling bushed, but very much warmed by the reunion with his mother, he drove home to have a good night's kip. Tomorrow he would go through with Jared what he had learnt in New York about their girl.

Jared arrived bright-eyed and bushy-tailed, with bagels and fresh coffee, and they set to work at the kitchen island with its spectacular views of the bay. Back in his own apartment, well-rested for once, with his jet lag in the rear-view mirror, Darius felt in his element once again.

He gave Jared a rundown of his meetings with Safi, her gallery, and her life after Fritzi. He filled him in on Yvetta's life after Fritzi, and the remarkable change in her behaviour now that she had reunited with her estranged family. He made sure to inform Jared of Yvetta's upcoming same-sex marriage and her bipolar diagnosis, which she now accepted. Taking her medication had made a significant change to the lives of her family and to her own future, Darius stressed.

'Did you discuss Fritzi with them?' Jared asked.

'No.'

'Why?' Jared said, sounding amazed. 'After all, they would be able to give us information we could never glean from a document.'

'DuPont, an art dealer I had the good fortune to meet and spend a number of hours with, gave me in-depth details of everything we need to know about Fritzi. He made it very clear – in fact, he insisted – never to have her spoken of too Safi or Yvetta. Fritzi's actions through the years have caused untold trauma in their lives, to say nothing of the lives of DuPont and other art dealers.'

He opened his briefcase and gave Jared the file Bruce had collated for him about the Rubicov family. Jared held it for a moment, as though weighing it mentally, then placed it on Darius's desk. Unlike Jared's desk at work, with its small mountain of papers, Darius's desk was impeccably neat, almost empty; it shone.

'The reason I decided to go to New York to follow up this lead is in this file. I did not pass it on to you when I received it. I knew you were still building this case and, I must be honest, I wanted to find out for myself who and what these people were to Fritzi.'

Jared listened with interest as Darius explained his reasons for further investigation into Fritzi's life.

'When you read this file, you will have a clearer picture of what that family had to endure, and I am sure you will understand their reticence to have anything to do with her, now or in the future.'

Darius paused and stared at Jared. He wanted to convey how life-changing his decision was going to be for Fritzi. He had an image of the file being transferred to Jared's desk at work, where it would, no doubt, get lost amongst the other papers, never to be seen or read again. He had to stress its importance.

'The decision to go ahead with her case,' Darius slowly said, reaching over the desk and tapping the folder, and pushing it closer to

Jared again, 'might depend on what you believe to be the right thing to do after reading that file.' He glanced at the file, again. And again, Jared smiled at him, though somewhat indifferently.

'Well, thank you for making my work so much easier,' Jared said. 'If what you have told me is the case, we may well have to reconsider what to do.'

'I can relate my discussion with DuPont,' Darius said, speaking rapidly, sensing he was losing something in this conversation, 'and it might be prudent that I do.' He made a soft fist and hit the file with it, surprising them both. 'I think you need to read their side of the story first, in order to get a sound understanding of what these people suffered over the years due to Fritzi's constant attacks on the Rubicov family.'

Jared smiled again, but this time it was his sly, familiar smile. The robust, healthy, slightly cocky smile that Darius remembered from school. The smile he gave everyone when he had just scored a goal in rugby, or dunked a ball through a basket with energy and aplomb, whipping up the auditorium, exciting everyone. A winner's smile.

'To be honest, Darius,' Jared said slowly, 'I have withheld information from you, too.' Jared put his hand flat on the file. 'Since you have invested so much of your own time to help us solve Fritzi's problem, I will share a confidence with you. We are not nearly ready to put her case forward. This new information might enlighten you to her state of mind and as to why she was so obsessed with Yvetta – her previous pattern of behaviour, I mean.'

'I am all ears,' said Darius, who now had no idea what he was about to learn. At this point, after his conversation with DuPont, nothing would surprise him. 'But I must confess that not much is going to help change my opinion of her. Not after reading the file and meeting some of the people she has so ruthlessly tried to harm.'

Jared described to Darius the night Fritzi broke down at his place, and how she subsequently opened up about her childhood friend Erica, who her father had engineered to be admitted to an institution for degenerates and the politically undesirable. He told the story of her friendship from childhood with this girl, whose life was later ravaged and ruined, her intellect and abilities stolen from her – and so much else besides. Erica was bright, but, by all accounts bipolar and, more than likely, on the autistic spectrum.

He recounted how Fritzi had found out from her mother where Erica was being held. And how Fritzi had taken it upon herself to cycle miles out of town to see whether she could track down her friend in this institution – to save her, as it were. She eventually found Erica with the help of one of the inmates, a political prisoner himself. Jared went on to describe how Fritzi had found this girl, who had been a bright, sensitive, clever child from a musical family, tied to a bed in a vegetative state. It was here that Fritzi learnt from the inmate that her friend had been given a lobotomy on the orders of Fritzi's father, because this monster of a man did not want this wisp of girl to be influencing his daughter with degenerate political views.

Darius was visibly shocked.

'Fuck,' he said, struggling to find words, 'I can't believe what you are telling me. How old was Fritzi when this happened?'

'She was almost fifteen years old.'

Darius winced; he could tell that Jared was still shocked by the incident. 'What happened to her after that?' he asked.

'She went to live with her maternal grandparents for the duration of her school holidays,' Jared said. 'Then she lived with her sister and African boyfriend, in another part of East Berlin. She wanted to be nowhere near her father, understandably. Can you believe it happened just before the Wall came down? She never went back home, never saw her father again. On the day the Wall was being chopped down by the revellers, she went over to the West during the mayhem, and found her way to the house of friends, and the rest we know from the file on her life you brought to us.'

Darius had thought he knew almost everything about Fritzi – but now he realised, yet again, that in fact he knew almost nothing. He wondered what had happened between Fritzi and Jared, after or before she had confided in him. It was better not to think about it. Instead, he asked,

'Did you manage to reopen the subject about this awful thing that happened in her young life?'

'Well,' Jared said slowly, 'I suspect there is more than just one awful thing. I can only guess at certain things. There is what she has told me, and what, I am sure, she chooses not to speak about. But make no mistake, Darius, Fritzi has suffered and suffered greatly. And yes, we had quite a philosophical discussion that night, and I asked her whether she thought her obsession with Yvetta was because of what happened to her young friend and the similarities with Yvetta and her family. We spoke about other things, too. It was a long discussion. A long night.' He sighed, as though still exhausted from it.

'Yes,' Darius said, feeling oddly envious again all of a sudden, trying to shake the sting of jealousy and think instead of Jared's revelation, of how Fritzi herself had suffered, and not just Fritzi but the countless others destroyed by the abhorrent and inhumane actions of the communist state. When it came to recent European history, outside what they had learnt about in school and what he read about in brief in the international pages of the morning papers, Darius had to admit he was more ignorant than he would like to admit. The Berlin Wall, the two Berlins, the USSR, the Iron Curtain and the Cold War, all of it seemed like relics from the ancient past, but he understood now that to many it was still fresh, and the repercussions from those years were still being felt.

'I can see how Fritzi's relationship with Yvetta could be perceived as an extension of her relationship with this Erica, and for that reason, why Fritzi tried to hang on to Yvetta at all costs, and to hell with the law, with Yvetta's family, and with everything else. She loved Erica, she loved Yvetta, and who else did she love? For most of her life, she must have felt staggeringly alone. Her ease around other people – and then also her moments of suspicion, as though summing up a crowd – I always thought it was the result of something in her past. But I didn't know what. I knew she was broken, just not exactly how or why. I have to admit it makes a whole lot of sense. Especially Yvetta suffering from bipolar disorder, and, the fact that her family had Yvetta in sanatoriums – three, from what I have read. No wonder Fritzi went to such lengths to try and get Yvetta out of them.'

'Yes,' Jared agreed, 'it seems that, subconsciously, Fritzi was rescuing her friend repeatedly by helping Yvetta escape out of all these institutions. Like Oedipus doomed to forever roll his rock up a hill, Fritzi may have felt destined to rescue her lover, over and over, to save her life, but ultimately to lose her, too. She plotted against the Rubicov family, who had Yvetta committed, primarily to save her lover from a fate she believed to be worse than death. And, by all accounts, she was subconsciously engaging in the fool's errand of saving her childhood friend. But you can't save what's already been lost.'

You can't save what's already been lost. This was something that Darius had thought often after it was clear that Lin and him would never be together again. Their relationship was irreconcilably damaged – like Fritzi, perhaps.

Darius nodded, feeling suddenly humbled, and said, 'I will have to revise my thoughts on my findings now. And you should make yourself familiar with that document.' He pointed to it one last time. 'I will fill in any gaps you may find lacking.'

'Before you leave, Jared, just a few more details about Fritzi, if you do not mind?'

Jared nodded; he wasn't smiling now.

'Are you going to seek professional advice about her story?'

Jared gave it some thought. 'Yes, I will. And if I can persuade her to see someone, I will do that, too.'

'Good idea.' Darius sat for a while longer; it was a lot to absorb.

'How has she been since she opened up about this girl?'

'Remember how light-hearted and happy she was on that boat trip we took in the Bay.'

Darius smiled; he remembered that trip, that day, well. 'Well, I believe it was a whole load off her shoulders, sharing that story, that awful experience, with someone. Apparently, she carried the horror of that experience with her since that day, never telling a soul. Can you imagine the weight of that burden, and how carrying it would disfigure one? I am sure it manifested into something very unhealthy that catalysed when she met Yvetta. Anyway, that's my unprofessional opinion.'

'I agree,' Jared said, 'but the question is going to be: can one overlook her past behaviour? I am not sure you are going to be able to when you read that document, and see for yourself how she has impacted on the lives of others.'

Alone again and gratefully so, Darius sat for a long time staring out to sea. He had never before known anyone who had at such a young age experienced such evil – and to think that it was Fritzi's own father responsible for the state institution (masquerading as a mental-health facility) turning a child into a vegetable – it had to have huge repercussions for Fritzi for sure.

He grabbed a sweatshirt, tied it round his waist, and went for a run along the beachfront to try to clear his head of the hideous images he couldn't wipe from his mind. He was seriously disturbed by what Jared had told him.

He clearly wasn't cut out for this stuff; perhaps he was a big softy after all. Darius thought that it would be different for Jared, no matter how soft he often appeared. In his line of work, Jared must come up against this often; although, Darius reflected, even he seemed shocked by Fritzi's story.

As he ran across the beach, attempting to find some elusive calmness in the warm air and soft sand, his mind went over what he had learnt and he wondered whether Jared was regretting his involvement with Fritzi – and, by extension, with Darius himself. His other cases too the best of his knowledge were not, he was sure as personal, He was certain that Fritzi's case was very different to any other Jared had ever taken on. After all, Fritzi had saved his life and, there was no mistaking the risk to her own life in doing so.

For that matter, given the complexity of Fritzi's history, her background in prisons in multiple continents, and the crimes she had committed, there was no doubt that by representing her Jared was putting his own reputation on the line. Fritzi wasn't exactly a war hero – but she was certainly a kind of warrior. Still, after what Jared had told him about Fritzi's traumatic childhood, Darius was not comfortable thinking of her as a criminal. Technically, yes, she was a criminal, but there was so much more to it than that.

His heart pounded as he ran. He still had so many questions – after New York, more than ever – and no one to answer them. He was almost afraid to approach Fritzi now. It had been days since he last saw her, and so much had happened, to both of them. He wondered: was she redeemable or were her behaviours too ingrained for her to ever change for the better? Or had she proven as much already by putting her own life on the line for others, unselfishly and at great personal risk?

The questions weighed upon him. He wanted to be free of worry as he ran along his favourite stretch on the sand, with nothing but the beauty of the beach in front of and around him, the sense of endlessness and quiet freedom, his mind a wonderful blank space, but he was bothered now and couldn't get the thoughts and questions out of his mind. His worry reverberated and repeated itself as he ran. It was as if his jet lag had returned as a form of personal anguish, and he wondered what he could do to extinguish it. When you were stressed, it didn't matter where you were – you could be on a beach or in a bar – everywhere felt like nowhere, your problems front and centre, all else immaterial. As he circled back on his tracks, returning home after a jog that had felt altogether too long and not quite long enough, he began to feel a little better.

After all, he now thought, it wasn't his problem to decide Fritzi's destiny. But, was it Jared's? He had her freedom in his hands, so to speak. He wondered what Jared would decide once he had read all of the facts?

One thing was for sure: Fritzi, a free spirit, would ultimately decide her own destiny, one way or another. No one would dictate anything to her. Even some of the world's toughest prisons hadn't kept her still. Prisons, police, borders, Interpol, visa control – she appeared victorious against everything. But for how long, he wondered, realising yet again that he had feelings for her. That was the thing about luck (or even skill): eventually it ran out. As a businessman, and as an investor, he was acutely aware of this.

It had been a while since he had checked in at his office. He hadn't been back since his return from the States, almost ten days ago now. Sitting at his desk he had piles of mail; he put some of the personal letters aside to take home. The rest either went in the bin or were dealt with by his secretary; if, anything important needed his attention, she would contact him. After a conference call and a few meetings, he headed home, feeling better now. Work had at least taken his mind off of Fritzi. Sort of. Well, every time he told himself that his mind was off Fritzi, his mind returned to … Fritzi. Still, he wondered whether he would hear from Jared about the file he had given him.

Fritzi was still staying with Maggie, and he had dropped in a few times to chat and see how she was getting on. Maggie, to his surprise, had a beautiful home. Her husband, he learnt, had been a doctor of philosophy when he was alive, at Sydney's UNSW, and, was partnered with many foreign universities. Maggie had told him her husband had lectured and travelled widely, making her job a blessing through the years, and she loved all of it: the travel, the lectures, the faculty parties, the intellectual aspects, the experience of seeing and staying in new places.

She lived now in Mosman, a lovely, hilly suburb overlooking the bay. She encouraged Fritzi to take nature trails and they hiked together on weekends. Fritzi hung out at the pavement cafés, taking pleasure in being anonymous, in blending in, and wrote her journal. Other than that, she told Darius, her days were busy with healthy activity. Like him, she jogged every morning on the beachfront, and swam and surfed. She informed him excitedly that she had even been out on a deep-sea diving expedition.

He expressed amazement and she smiled and said she was just chilling and enjoying her life. But privately he worried if she wasn't getting out a little too much; he still worried about the media, to say nothing about Fritzi herself and her own inclinations and darker desires.

As though sensing his anxiety, she said softly that she hoped to go walkabout when the weather became cooler, if Jared agreed, of course – there was so much of the country she wanted to experience. She reassured Darius that she would, of course, be cautious and alert all the time, and, when possible, avoid other people.

This went some distance to assuaging him. He was still a sucker for Fritzi and her ways. In any case, he didn't see why Jared would mind if she went walkabout – or why she even needed his permission. She could not be watched closely, like a child, forever. That scenario was bound to backfire – on all of them. She needed her freedom – or at least a reasonable amount. And Darius needed to learn to trust her. She wasn't a prisoner. It was entirely up to her where she went. After all, she had a year's grace to do her own thing, before her visitor's visa was up. Of course, she needed to stay out of trouble – but if she hadn't learnt that by now, she never would. Perhaps this walkabout could double as a kind of test. It was nice to have her close by and safe, but they all knew things couldn't stay this way forever. They had to let go, and move on, and see what happened next.

Sitting in his office at home, going through his mail, he found two letters from the States. Opening the larger, expensive-looking envelope, he found a very formal, silver-embossed invitation. He laughed out loud as he realised on closer inspection that it was an invitation to Yvetta's wedding. He didn't mind if he did, and checked his diary to see whether he could make the month and date. He wasn't particularly busy in the upcoming months, but he did have a trip lined up with some mates to visit the Museum of Old and New Art (MONA) in Hobart, Tasmania, known as Tassie by the locals, something he had been looking forward to for some time.

He realised he had something in common with Fritzi: they both yearned to explore Australia, especially the wilder, less trodden, parts, the secret places, home to ancient peoples and ancient rites, where nature was its own terrifying god. Although a native Australian and a keen museumgoer, he had never been to MONA, the largest privately funded museum in the Southern Hemisphere, and was excited to experience it. In terms of its construction alone, the place was supposed to be beyond belief. The building was carved out of rock: a three-level subterranean cave.

He had met David Walsh, at a charity function, the owner and creator of the museum, a very eccentric guy by all accounts, and a very successful gambler. Checking his calendar, his heart suddenly sank. He was disappointed to see the dates clashed, too bad, but he already knew where he would prefer to be, and it wasn't in New York, even if it was the wedding of a kind of Russian royalty and, no doubt a memorable occasion – or (if enough vodka was consumed, he thought drily) impossible to remember. He made a note to send Yvetta an Aussie gift, and to inform her that he would not be able to attend. Among other things, his mother had instilled in him and his brothers at a young age the importance of good manners.

Now, he wondered, enjoying this distraction from work, what would make a good gift for a woman who possibly owned everything? Maybe a boomerang painted by a well-known Aboriginal artist? He tore open the second envelope, excited to know whether he had secured the Dax. The letter informed him that buyer had let the Dax go and, the painting was now his, it would be catalogued and crated, then shipped over by courier. He walked around the penthouse to see where the Dax would look its best. Originally, he thought it would work well in his bedroom, but on second thoughts he preferred it in the neglected entrance bathroom. The bare walls were calling out for something, and he thought the erotic canvas would lend a fantastic air of sophisticated decadence. The entrance guest toilet was not a small room. In fact, he had never given the space much thought, and neither had his interior designer. It was time for a facelift. This was his new life, his life without Lin, and his apartment deserved a new look.

He got the Rubicov gallery to send him some photos of the painting and sent it on to Lisa, his decorator. He did not have to wait long for a reply. 'Dasso, wow!' the familiar voice on the phone said. 'Where on earth did you find this amazing painting?'

'Hi Liz. I knew it wouldn't take you long to get back to me after seeing it,' Darius said, smiling.

'Guess where we are going to hang that beauty?' But he couldn't wait for her to guess. 'In the entrance bathroom!'

'Not a bad idea,' she said, 'very chic. We can have an accent wall in dark red. Fantastic, I can't wait to see it.'

Liz had been an old girlfriend, not long after college. Now they were mates, nothing more. She was superb at her job and had a thriving business in Sydney. He was pleased to count her as one of his first successful start-ups. 'I will let you know when it arrives,' he said.

'Probably in a month or so. Send someone to prepare the walls in the meantime.'

'Will do. I'll call you back later today.'

'Why don't you come round and see what else needs a facelift? I haven't seen you in ages; come for a coffee.'

'Sounds great, then you can tell me more about this Dax.'

Darius couldn't wait to see the painting up close again – this time on his own wall. And he couldn't wait for Liz to see it, too. She was always looking for exciting new stuff for her clients, and he wanted to remain in touch with DuPont, the art dealer, who had had such an unfortunate history with Fritzi. They might even do some business together in the future. Perhaps he would go to that wedding after all.

Chapter 12

Fritzi wanted to make the most of her year in Australia. After several weeks enjoying the hospitality and kindness of Jared and Maggie, she didn't feel confident that Jared would be able to help her without exposing her past, nor did she want to take that risk. At this point, there was no longer any need for her to hide from reporters. Time had passed, her story had been buried under other, newer stories, literally dozens of new headlines, and had, she hoped, been forgotten by now. She was old news, and happy to be so. And, best of all, she was free to travel again.

All the same, for some reason she didn't quite understand, she needed these people to be there for her when she returned. Right now, they felt like the safe centre of her world, a world which, she knew from experience, shifted and swirled like a whirlpool, never stable, always fragile, sometimes actively dangerous. It was a world that fragmented and rebuilt itself, over and over, but to what end? Perhaps with Jared and Darius and Maggie in her life, things would finally be different. It was not often in her life that she felt cared for; she did now. She did not want to lose that feeling, or these people.

Maggie had enjoyed Fritzi's company, Fritzi had overheard her tell Darius. 'Fritzi had been a pleasure as a guest,' Maggie had said, in her kindly, familiar, worn-in voice, 'and had mucked in with everything around the house, including sorting out Maggie's computer, which needed a good cleaning out.' Maggie's friends had taken to Fritzi immediately, Maggie had informed Darius; Fritzi was charismatic and delightful. Fritzi hadn't only overheard these things. Maggie had admitted to Fritzi that she would be missed, and had even managed, with Fritzi's help, to brush up on her German while Fritzi was under her roof. Overhearing Maggie's confession to Darius pleased Fritzi more than she realised. For the first time she felt someone trusted and loved her, not for how she presented herself, for the promise of a profit, or for a criminal job, or for sex, or for a ruse, or for a series of lies, but for who she really was.

'Fritzi felt like the daughter I never had,' Maggie had said.

Overhearing these words meant the world to Fritzi. She had been resolute about her independence from the age of fifteen; now, at almost thirty, she had become reliant and helpless. Was she going about life in the wrong direction? Well, it felt right. Perhaps, for the first time in many years, she was back on track. Her needs had changed without warning, she felt weirdly vulnerable, and, worst of all, had no fight left. She found that she wanted Maggie's approval; she needed it.

Feeling secure with the contacts she had forged in Sydney, Fritzi flew to New South Wales. She wanted to be somewhere she could indulge her passion for surfing and scuba diving. She knew she was trying to recreate her Bali experience, the beauty of having not much else to care about, free to explore what nature had to offer.

After laying low in Mexico for a few months after her failed attempt to capture Yvetta in New York, she had played with the idea of travelling through Central and South America, but her experiences with the tourists travelling that path didn't quite match with her own state of mind at the time, it was known to be a much loved party route for gap year students.

She wanted to go somewhere she might find a form of inner peace, but South America didn't seem to be that place. After losing Yvetta, the love of her life, to another woman, she needed headspace above all else. Travelling through South America, she realised, she would have to keep her wits about her, especially around the druggies who travelled that trail to Columbia; that kind of hassle she did not want nor need. She was thankful she had changed course, she was learning to listen to her inner voice.

India had been a good choice; it had given her what she was looking for at the time. She loved the people, colours and mix of spiritual philosophy of the Hindu and Buddhists who had a wonderful calmness about the hereafter and life in general.

On reflection, which she now did on occasion, she was doing okay. She had made it into Australia through sheer luck. Who would have believed that, after running from Bali to New Zealand, she would, through an act of God, end up staying with the prime minister's son no less, and get to meet with his father and other high officials in the Australian government, while staying with Jared. At this events she was introduced as a girl Jared had met in New Zealand after his accident.

Jared's father had visited from Canberra, where Australia's seat of government was. Fritzi did not want to intrude on Jared's parents visit while in Sydney, but Jared had insisted on her meeting them at a small cocktail party he held to celebrate surviving after the earthquake. It made no sense, Jared had told Fritzi, to celebrate surviving the earthquake without the presence at the party of the person who had been the very reason he had survived. He had gone on to assure her he would not reveal her true identity, and it was only after that, that she agreed to attend as his guest. She met Jared's friends and business associates and other members of the government. At this one-off event, which had been frenzied and fun she felt close to Jared, his confidante, and, in a way, his partner in crime.

At first Fritzi had to remind herself that the old Fritzi would not be making an appearance, at this time and at this event, she felt that being as inconspicuous, if that were possible, would serve her well, under the circumstances and, she conducted herself accordingly, playing another of her many personas, as the girl who saved Jared's life. Yet once Jared had returned to work, resuming both his social and professional life, she had become an appendage. Jared had made it quite clear that his relationship with her was purely professional. In a way she was relieved: she did not want to go down that road with Jared, it would only complicated matters further. She had at one stage thought they might get involved romantically – especially after the boat trip, when they had been unusually intimate, and joyful – but the atmosphere had quickly returned to one of lawyer and client.

Not that this was a bad thing. She was keenly aware that she couldn't afford to mess this opportunity up. She needed Jared and a failsafe route to a life in Australia. She was tired of being on the run. What she needed to be safe was connections, and it was difficult to think of better connected, people than Jared and his father. Darius had been her lucky charm in more ways than one and, she did not want to alienate him either, she had scarcely seen Darius he seemed to be keeping a low profile, but Fritzi was determined to keep him in her life, she needed friends like Darius, he had become a confidant and a trusted friend.

Maggie, who saw and felt most of what occurred in Jared's house and in Jared's life, could see that Fritzi felt left out once Jared's frantic work life resumed. Maggie knew, too, that Fritzi would, sooner rather than later, develop feelings for Jared, feelings Jared would probably (if his prior romantic history was anything to go by, and desire to dedicate himself to his work) rebuff. It was easier to see why Fritzi was attracted to Jared: sensitive, alert, humble, enormously intelligent, and very handsome, if Maggie was a little younger and not so much a mother figure for Jared, she would have had feelings for him herself. Much as she had taken a shine to the earnest, energetic, obviously pained Fritzi, she was devoted to Jared and would do anything not to see him hurt. She therefore understood Jared's need for privacy once he resumed his normal lifestyle.

Therefore, it was Maggie who suggested Fritzi move in with her until she set off on her travels. Good old, empathic Maggie – Jared had often joked that it was Maggie, not his father, who should have been a career diplomat. Well, in a way, she had been. The arrangement seemed to have turned out well for everyone – not least Maggie, who had had in Fritzi a firm friend and confidante. Maggie was sorry to see her leave, even though she thought that travel would do the young girl a world of good right now, to see the wonders of Australia and to clear her head at the same time. She had an awful lot to put behind her, Maggie reflected, and some of the pain would never go away. The child of German-Jewish immigrants, she thought she knew something of the nature of pain, loss, that which was difficult to forgive, much less forget.

Jared informed Fritzi one Sunday morning over coffee at Maggie's place that he would be in touch when he was ready to submit her case, and it would be her decision to go ahead with the case, or not. Fritzi wanted more than anything to trust her future in Australia to Jared, and respected his professional opinions, also the distance between them since moving in with Maggie, she was not about to spoil their relationship and, gladly followed his lead to place their relationship on professional basis only.

So here she was on the move once more, but this time it felt very different. For the first time in years, now, literally up in the air, on a plane to Byron Bay, she was a little more at peace with herself. Being there for Yvetta had always been her number one priority; it had kept her going through the hell she had endured during their time apart.

Physically and emotionally, she had travelled some distance away from the pressures of her previous life. And yet travelling through India had not helped dampen her need for Yvetta. Even though she now knew (though she tried not to think of it often, or for very long) Yvetta had moved on, the love of her life remained an obsession, and the only other person she cared for. She had revealed more to Jared and Darius than she ever thought she would to another human being. And confiding in them had felt good, a considerable relief, and release of the pain of the past. Emotions so long held stuck inside of her came rushing out, dissipated if not disappeared. She felt lighter now. And she trusted them – trust being something that came very sparingly to her. She had trusted Yvetta, perhaps to her detriment. She had trusted Erica, to Erica's detriment. And that was all. She had learnt over the course of her life to trust only herself.

Knowing her past as they now did, Jared and Darius were a constant reminder of who she actually was, someone stuck in the past. They knew (or at least she hoped they knew) the Fritzi of the past, and the Fritzi of the present, and that those were, to a large degree, two entirely different people … or maybe not. More than anything, they believed that everyone deserved the opportunity to be forgiven, and redeemed. And she wanted to believed that too.

Plane rides could cause nausea, but they also allowed one to breathe, too. And to look back, from high up in the air, on what you had left behind. Fritzi had lived so long running away from the authorities, it had almost become her default setting. Running towards them wasn't going to be easy. She would have to learn a new language, one of compromise, honesty, and self-improvement. She would have to abide by the law, which may be more difficult than many imagined. She couldn't afford to slip up anymore. One strike against her and she would be out, certainly out of Australia and her dreams of a new life. Or was it her own demons she had to stop running away from? Coming face to face with her childhood – long repressed memories of Erica and her father – had been a sobering experience.

Reliving the dreadful horror that happened to her childhood friend still haunted her when she least expected the memory to resurface and, many of her dreams as well, when she would wake nauseated and dripping in sweat. More than anything, she needed to come to terms with her own inability to cope with the past. To come to terms with her history, and with herself. And then to accept, to forgive, to let go. For the first time a window opened onto that painful horror that had so recently poured out in words. Through his probing questions and soft, knowing voice, Jared had touched a deeply hidden hell. Her overwhelming, insatiable need for Yvetta slowly began to make sense. Coming to terms with the damage she had caused through her own blindness to the truth would take time. And that was what she had: time, lots of it.

Maggie had been right: fresh air and a change in scenery did the world of good. It gave one a fresh perspective – and gratitude as well. You stepped out of society, and out of yourself as well. With this in mind, and in spite of years of anguish against the psychiatric profession (which had, Fritzi thought, treated Yvetta with such cruelty, treated her, in fact, as little more than a prisoner), Fritzi decided that when she returned to Sydney, she would ask Jared to find her a shrink. The psychiatric profession was a broad church, and, she figured, as with every profession, there were good shrinks as well as bad ones, and different ways of attending to patients.

If she had learnt one thing in life, it was that it was never fair to generalise. Take being in prison, for instance. You encountered all sorts of criminals: good ones, bad ones, bad good ones, good bad ones, ones you couldn't define one way or another, and rightfully so. The human condition was a complicated one – perhaps impossibly so – and defied easy classification. Fully understanding oneself was probably impossible, too, but one had to attempt the undertaking nonetheless. It was a crucial reckoning, for your own benefit, and others' as well.

It was time to come to terms, and to help herself, at last. She had waited long enough. It was time to stop blaming everyone for her inability to help Erica, or for the sins she had committed over the years, the lives she had damaged, the thousands of lies and dozens of selves, all in order to accomplish – what exactly? She did not yet know, but she was determined to find out. Perhaps blaming herself for what had happened wasn't the answer. Guilt wasn't exactly a proactive position. She had only recently become familiar with guilt (for so long blocking everything out, justifying or flat-out ignoring her deeds and desires), and she didn't like it very much. With thoughts of the past pouring through her mind like a torrent of water cascading down into her being, she fell asleep, until the aircraft touched down on the runway in Byron Bay.

Punching in the code she had been emailed, she walked into the spacious Airbnb townhouse she had found on a website. It did not disappoint. Pictures (especially on a website) were usually misleading – not this time, not at all. In fact, the place looked even better in person than it had on her tight computer screen. The house was beautifully furnished. She even found enough provisions in the kitchen to see her through to the next day. The shutters opened onto a sea view and a beach within walking distance.

Moving through the open-planned living area downstairs, she found through sliding doors onto a patio area with a BBQ, a lap pool in a small manicured garden. The large L-shaped soft furnishing had a large flat TV screen on the wall and a fireplace below. Making her way up the stairs, she found two comfortably furnished bedrooms on suite. Throwing her belongings onto the armchair, she fell back onto the king-sized bed, sinking into the sumptuous pillows.

She suddenly felt carefree once more – a glorious feeling. It was good to be on her own again, lighter than air, in a new place – and such a beautiful place, too. Sydney had been an amazing experience, but an intensely stressful one, too. Now she was free from that stress, and that freedom felt wonderful. Meeting new people was never a problem for her. Nor was being a stranger in a strange place. Indeed, there were few things she enjoyed more. She would join the scuba club, and no doubt, if she decided to stay, would find another yoga club to employ her. Fritzi splashed her face, shook her hair free, tucked a slinky silver vest into her jeans, threw on a paper-thin bottle-green leather jacket, donned her sunglasses, and ran down the stairs and out of the apartment, shutting the door behind her to begin a new day.

She had no desire to sit around on her own in the evenings. She had been alone long enough, and did not want to miss this opportunity to explore both Byron Bay and its community. The bars and clubs were places she could mingle easily, flitting from one group to another, dancing to the live music. no one thought twice about a woman on their own in this environment. This was a relaxed tourist town, and everyone had a relaxed attitude to mixing, chilling, and having fun.

Renting a car with her fake ID could be problematic. She didn't want to bring unnecessary attention to herself. Still, she needed a car.

Should she call Darius or Jared for advice? It was an odd feeling to worry about something she never gave much thought to.

The cell rang a few times before a groggy voice picked up.

'It's well past midnight here,' Darius said, 'this better be important.'

There was silence on the other end, and Darius suddenly knew it must be Fritzi calling.

'Fritzi, that you?'

'Yes,' she whispered, 'sorry to wake you. Where are you?'

'States again, on business. Not to worry, I got home in the early hours anyway.'

'Are you sure? I can call Jared, but I thought he'd be at work.'

'Everything ok?'

'I have a little problem and can't figure out how I should deal with it. I am in Byron Bay and need to hire a car, but as you know I have a…'

'False passport,' he said quickly.

'Yes.'

'Don't use it. The rental company will want all kinds of details from you, and if you have an accident – even a small one – you will be in trouble.'

'Oh, what should I do? I need a car to get about and to carry my scuba gear.'

'I will be back in a few days and will fly down,' Darius said. 'Can you wait until then? We can figure it out; even if I hire the car and take out insurance for you to drive it. If anything happens to the car, I will be responsible, not you.'

'Okay, thanks, Darius,' and her voice became soft again. 'Sorry for waking you.'

'Not a problem. Night, see you soon.'

And, just like that, there was silence on the phone again. Fritzi switched off the cell and sat staring at the empty TV screen for a while, her head resting on the back of the sofa. Suddenly she felt weak and insecure; needing help was still foreign to her. It wasn't a great feeling, but she had to take her insecurity seriously. She had to be careful here in Australia; things could get out of hand pretty fast.

Instead of signing up for scuba diving now, she would wait for Darius, at which point she would buy her gear and everything else she might need. Retail shopping was a great alternative, and she could pay cash; no trail to her could be made with cash. She suddenly wondered whether her accounts could have been infiltrated since Interpol had investigated her. With a shudder she realised that it was entirely possible.

She opened her laptop with her special code, and sent an encrypted email to her offshore bank, requesting that her bank codes be altered and for her accounts to be moved. She provided the bank with a new alias to use, this time a man's name, she didn't think twice Hans came to mind, Namibia was her last connection with Yvetta and, her past life. Once, satisfied with the bank's reply and confirmation of her requests, the anxiety she felt would be lightened and, she would head out for some serious retail shopping to further lift her spirits. She found a book on Byron Bay in the bookcase and curled up on the sofa, her cell pinged waking her, the book still lying open and unread in her lap. Her bank details, organised she headed out the door.

The boutiques were surprisingly chic and the clothes were worth spending money on. The shop assistants were more than friendly once they realised, she was a serious shopper who had some hard cash to burn. Intending to stop at a restaurant for some lunch, and not wanting to traipse around with shopping bags, she had the shop hold her purchases until she was ready to pick them up.

'No worries,' the perky shop assistant said. 'What name should we put on the bags?'

'Freya,' Fritzi responded, not missing a beat.

Fritzi had learnt to appreciate Aussie food; it was served with panache and a healthy twist. Mostly, it was fresh and tasty. She surveyed the people around her, noting most sounded Australian rather than foreign like her. This wasn't a touristy place, and therefore a great choice, she preferred to be amongst locals, gathering snippets of local gossip to gauge the mood. As the waiter took her plate, she ordered a flat black.

'American?' the tall, fresh-faced, athletic-looking young waiter asked.

'No. Why, do I sound American?' 'Yo sure do, ma'am,' he joked in his best – or, indeed, worst – American accent. Fritzi couldn't help smiling. He was obviously just trying to be friendly.

'German actually,' she said, before thinking better of it.

'Ah, right,' he said brightly, 'most Europeans speak English with American accents.'

'True.'

'But your accent is not very noticeable,' he continued. 'Very slight, now that you've pointed it out.'

Fritzi was pleased; she had never given it much thought, but obviously she didn't immediately sound German to those she met. All the better to disguise herself, and to elude those on her case.

The flat black was brought over by a perky girl in her early twenties, she was sure, bouncy and carefree. 'Sorry hope you don't mind me asking,' she said in her nasally Aussie twang, rather than the flat vowels of New Zealanders, 'but are you an actress or model or something like that?'

Taken aback she looked at the waitress in surprise. 'No, not at all,' Fritzi said. 'Just an ordinary joe, as they say.'

'We were so sure you were someone special,' the girl said apologetically, though not at all unkindly, but sounding a little disappointed nonetheless.

'That is very kind, really,' Fritzi said hurriedly. 'But no, I am not anyone special.'

Left alone to drink her black coffee and nibble her biscotti, she checked her cell for messages. She had given her number to Maggie and Jared, and of course to Darius.

Fritzi was pleased to find a message from Maggie, who was missing her. Jared had checked in to see that all was okay. It was a good feeling to be connected to others. She hadn't given it much thought before, the importance of having other people in your life, people who cared for and looked out for you.

She sent Maggie a selfie, raising her coffee cup in cheers, and pressed 'send.' Asking Maggie to delete it, she couldn't be too careful and Maggie would understand.

Her response to Jared was a little more sober, letting him know things were moving along nicely, that she was settling in and getting on with life. Before pressing 'send,' she wondered what emoji to use. She opted for the thumbs up it was friendly, but not as friendly as the hearts, Jared was an attractive man but out of bounds, Fritzi couldn't help wondering though, but immediately put the thought out of her mind, Jared was her lifeline to remaining in Australia, and, she was just a client to him, he had made that clear.

As she was about to leave the restaurant, one of the women from a table nearby stopped at her table on her way out.

'Hi,' the woman said, 'I just wondered if you were new in town.'

'Yes,' Fritzi said, surprised by the question but not displeased or unnerved. The woman was certainly attractive, and intriguing. She looked at the woman for some time before adding, 'Why?'

'Oh, just wondered,' the woman said airily, mysteriously. And then she surprised Fritzi with a smile. She moved forward, closer to Fritzi, and her body language seemed oddly intimate, as though they were old friends. 'We, collect people who take our fancy, and you seem interesting.' Fritzi wasn't quite sure how to respond. Never in short supply of charm – or flirtatiousness, for that matter, she felt obliged to be equally cute in reply.

'Ah, a favourite pastime, yes?' Fritzi said, returning the smile, and moving closer herself. 'What did you have in mind?'

'Well, we are having a sort of party at this address tomorrow evening,' the woman said warmly – and maybe a little slyly. Fritzi wondered what exactly 'sort of' implied – was this idiomatic Australian, or something else entirely? 'If you aren't busy, feel free to drop in for drinks at 6.30. We'd love to see you.'

She removed a card from her GG bag and dropped it on the table. Then, in a movement as fluid and elegant as the woman herself, she bent over and gave Fritzi a peck on the cheek. She walked off, looked back and waving, with a smile and a wink.

Not sure what to make of this woman, and how seriously to take her flirtatious behaviour, she stopped by the reception desk to ask if they were familiar with the lady who just spoke with her.

'Oh, yes,' the woman behind the desk said brightly, 'that's Missy. She is famous around these parts, owns a stack of places.' Smiling, leaning forward ever so slightly, she inquired, 'Why?'

'Well, she just invited me for drinks to this address,' Fritzi said, and waved the card at the woman behind the desk, perhaps a little boastfully, as if it was a kind of prize she had just been awarded.

'No worries,' the woman said, her voice still bright, 'that's fair dinkum. She's a really lovely lady. We'd all go in a flash if we were lucky enough to be invited, but then again that's not likely, but I hear her bashes are legendry you should go, If I'm not mistaken, that's the address of her house. I am sure she has a beautiful place.' She gestured out the window at a shiny new Porsche. 'That's her car out there.'

Fritzi walked past the Porsche and left a note on the windshield: 'We forgot to introduce ourselves. I'm Freya. Nice to meet you, Missy. See you soon'

The taxi drove up a long drive and stopped outside a villa with manicured gardens set back from the lawns. There were a dozen cars in the drive and people were making their way up the steps towards the entrance. Fortunately, she had hit the shops earlier that day, and had chosen to wear one of her new outfits. A gold lamé halterneck top loosely tucked into dark-green leather shorts, with the Roman sandals she had bought on her day out with Darius and Jared laced to her knees. She wore a small crossbody Gucci bag with a long chain. She felt comfortably chic, her long legs were tanned to perfection, and the leather sandals faded into her skin tone. Fritzi had put her hair into a high ponytail and wore long green feather earrings brushing her collar bone. Waiters were handing out flutes of champagne. Fritzi made her way down the stairs. Taking a flute in a seemingly effortless gesture, Fritzi stood to one side, peoplewatching. Most of the men were dressed fairly casually, and the women were in skinny jeans and evening tops.

Halfway down the stairs, she was aware that she had made an impression. A thrill passed through her; she could feel her heart starting to thump in her chest. She loved the feeling, and rose to the challenge; it was like being on the catwalk. Missy was there to greet her, and standing beside her was a startlingly handsome, smiling man who looked entirely familiar. It took a moment for Fritzi to register, and when she did, she surprised her shock with a smile of her own.

It was Jared, and now he was stepping up behind Missy to take Fritzi's hand.

'You keep popping up in the strangest of places,' Fritzi whispered in his ear as he led her into a crowd of people. 'First Christchurch, Sydney, and now here.'

'I could say the same of you,' Jared replied, still smiling. His touch on her arm, his breath in her ear, was warm. 'Who are we tonight?'

'Freya,' she whispered. 'Jared, are you following me?'

He did not respond, but simply smiled. Together they became one with the crowd, but never separated from each other's side.

A new pretty face, Fritzi knew, was going to attract attention amongst the locals, but she was not prepared for the welcome she received. Obviously, Jared had informed Missy, he knew her, after seeing her descending the stairs. She learnt that Missy's real name was Micheline. In fact, it was Micheline's birthday party Fritzi was attending, at the request of Jared, her cousin.

'I did not know I was going to be able to attend until very late last night,' Jared told Fritzi, 'so I flew in a few hours ago. And I certainly had no idea that you would be here,' he said to Fritzi's further surprise. There seemed no end to the surprises of the evening – or to the champagne on offer, or to the glamour. Still holding her hand, he said, 'And if you are wondering why my cousin approached you in the restaurant, she was informed by her shop staff that they'd sent you over to the restaurant for coffee, you'd spent a fair amount in her store. Missy, told me on her call to make sure I would be at her birthday, as she was inviting a stunning beauty she'd just met. She obviously wanted to surprise me, because I certainly was surprised when you descended those stairs like a movie star.'

Fritzi threw her head back and laughed, bared her near-perfect teeth. She loved attracting attention: it had been such a long time since she had enjoyed making an entrance into a room full of people. And how she had missed all of this: the glitz, the glamour, the heat and flash and flutter of flirtation, of bright light on bare skin, on quick touches in dark places, of seeing and being seen.

Missy had introduced her as Freya to, as Jared put it, 'the movers and shakers of Byron Bay.'

'You are not the only one who is surprised tonight,' Fritzi said, 'believe me.'

'How did you get here?' Jared asked.

'Oh,' she said, feeling suddenly humbled, even shy, 'I have not hired a car yet due to obvious complications. I arrived by taxi, and will have to call one to get back into town.'

'Don't worry about that,' he said with renewed self-assurance. It was as if he was his old self again, the Jared she remembered from her first week in Sydney, before he went back to work and she went to stay with Maggie, and they more or less lost contact with each other. 'I am staying here overnight, but I will organise for a friend to drop you off.'

Jared was about to say more when they were interrupted by a tall, good-looking, distinguished man in his early sixties. Unlike most of the other men at the party, he was extremely well-dressed, in a black dinner jacket, crisp white shirt, dark trousers, and expensive leather shoes.

'And this is my friend who will be your ride home,' Jared said suddenly, gesturing to the other man, who simply smiled. Fritzi was about to inquire the man's name, but suddenly she was in an altogether different place, encountering different people, and the older man was long gone. Even then, though, Jared remained at her side.

It was only some hours later that she saw the older man again, this time seated beside her in the back of a chauffeured black Mercedes, close to midnight now and nowhere near tired, the dark road and the glittering streetlights guiding her back to her rented apartment. The man still had not introduced himself. They sat in silence for some time, and she looked at him, tried not to look at him. He was very handsome.

'It's nice to see you again,' he said softly.

Again? He must he referring to earlier that night, when Jared had gestured to him on the stairs.

'You probably do not recognise me,' he continued, in the same slow but self-assured, educated tone, 'but I absolutely know who you are.'

Taken aback by this older man's bluntness, Fritzi suddenly felt an uneasiness in her stomach. Was this an ambush set up by Jared? Had she misjudged Jared all along? Had she walked into a trap? She had thought she could trust Jared, but perhaps he had been playing her all along. She had to think quickly before things got out of hand. Before she could answer he turned to face her, smiling.

'You are the Florence Nightingale who came to the aid of so many in Christchurch. And, not least, you saved Jared's life.'

'No, not really,' she said softly, turning away from him, looking out of the window, the sky above now as dark as the road ahead, 'I'm not that brave.' She felt hot again, as though she was blushing – or perhaps sweating. She had that not unfamiliar sensation of wanting to run. But she was trapped in a car speeding along the highway, with a man she did not know. But he seemed to know her.

'Please don't worry,' he said, and gently touched her hand, 'your secret is safe with me. I realise that you did not want to be a hero or a celebrity. And I respect that. Indeed, in this day and age, that is very respectable, even unusual.' Even without looking at him she could tell that he was smiling. 'So, I won't divulge that connection to Jared, if that's what you are worried about.'

Fritzi put her head back on the headrest, did not speak or turn to face him. Sometimes it was best to remain silent and allow the person with the upper hand to get to the point.

'The reason Jared agreed for me to drive you back into town was to thank you personally,' the man said. 'You see, I am the Australian ambassador to New Zealand. After you left Christchurch, so many people wanted to honour you for your selfless contribution on that day.'

Fritzi nodded but still did not face the man; there was no point in denying her involvement any longer.

'The Prime Minister wanted to thank you personally, as did the mayor of Christchurch. But since you want to keep a low profile – which, as I say, we entirely respect – maybe you will allow us to send you an official letter of thanks, signed and stamped by the Prime Minister of New Zealand.'

At last, Fritzi turned to face the man, and now she was overcome with joy. She could not deny her true feelings; she was overwhelmed by the recognition these people wanted to bestow on her for something she did without a second thought. It was the first time in her life that she felt she had actually made a difference in a good way.

'That would be wonderful, thank you,' she said softly. At that moment, this was all she could bring herself to say.

'Where should we send the letter?'

Her heart stopped again, and she wondered, again, if this was a trick. But no, she felt sure it was anything but.

'Well, it's complicated,' she said, the words uneven and uneasy to come by, tangled up in all of her fresh emotion, 'not quite straightforward. Would you mind if Jared guided you about the letter? I am telling you in confidence: he is helping me professionally, you see. For the moment, it would be best for him to deal with anything official.'

'Yes, I understand completely,' the man said, still looking at her with his unerring gaze. 'There is absolutely no need to be concerned. We will deal with everything through Jared – and may I say that you are in very good hands.'

They sat in silence for a few minutes, then fell into conversation about the party and Byron Bay. Fritzi finally relaxed, and found her words again. Gerald (as he wanted to be called) was a wonderful raconteur, and she was learning more than she could have hoped from him about Australia and New Zealand. He gave her his card and personal number for advice, offering her help in a professional capacity, should she ever need it.

She punched the entrance code into the keypad, fell onto her sofa shivering, not from cold but from sheer exhaustion. Since she had vomited out her innermost fears and demons to Jared and Maggie, several weeks ago now, her emotions had been all over the place. It was as though her confession had kicked open a door that she could no longer close. Images, over a decade old, came back to her and felt terrifyingly fresh. Images of Erica, her head lolling on her chest and the vacant look on her face when she held her on that day, so long ago now – but, evidently, in some ways, not so long ago at all. Images she hadn't so much as thought about since she was a teenager.

Certainly, she had had the odd dream and even woken up screaming once or twice, but all of that had stopped since she met Yvetta. For some reason she couldn't quite understand, Yvetta had made all of the pain and grief and guilt and fear go away. No wonder she had fought so hard to keep Yvetta in her life. Now Yvetta was gone – seemingly for good – and the old images and ideas, ghouls from the past, had come back. And she did not know how to deal with them. The fact that Darius and Jared knew the truth about her felt liberating – on the one hand. But on the other hand, she felt incredibly vulnerable.

Since the age of fifteen, she had made many bad choices, but they were her choices to make. Yet here she was not being able to use her credit cards, not being able to hire a car. She couldn't handle this level of restrictiveness. All of her life she had felt stifled and rebelled at any perceived lack of freedom, at authoritarianism, at attempts at control. And now, again, she could feel a familiar spark of rebellion. She needed to get her independence back, but at what price? Longing coursed through her – or was that just the booze? The champagne and vodka very much still in her system were impairing her thoughts. What she really needed was sleep. Tomorrow was another day.

Jared called from the airport on his way back to Sydney. He advised her to accept the official documents from the New Zealand Prime Minister. It was of the utmost importance to have positive character references, Jared stressed. And references from a Prime Minister and a Mayor of a major city in New Zealand were of a very high calibre indeed. Jared had taken the ambassador into his confidence about Fritzi's identity and her heroic role in assisting after the earthquake. He emphasised that Fritzi needed as much help as possible in putting her case forward to remain in Australia. Gerald was happy to oblige; Jared had known him for many years, he was a top bloke, someone you could trust with your skeletons.

As she put down her cell it rang again. She was surprised to hear Missy's voice on the other end.

'Freddie – that's what Jared calls you, so is it okay if I do, too?' she said in her characteristically lively, flirtatious manner. 'You were a huge hit last night. In fact, I'll let you into a little secret, but only over lunch. What do you say?' Fritzi barely considered the option before saying 'Yes.'

Missy walked into her restaurant, wearing dark sunglasses to no doubt cover her bleary eyes from the previous night's partying. The waiter put down two artistically decorated, mint leaved bloody Marys with a flourish, doctored he said with a secret recipe to combat any symptoms of a lingering hangover, Fritzi was happy to indulge her need for a pick-me-up. After ordering a naked hamburger and fries for lunch to soak up the previous night's booze, they sat chatting about how fabulous the party had been, and Fritzi was happy to listen to Missy chat away about her restaurants and, her passion for Byron Bay, over the years she had invested in properties and businesses never needing to return to the city, 'I have everything I want and need right here!

'I need a favour,' Missy began, after the food had arrived and the round of drinks had been completed. 'You have amazing style and I absolutely need you to help me.' She looked at Fritzi imploringly, with enormous and endearing eyes. In her own right, Missy was a very attractive woman. But then Jared was dashing, too, Fritzi reflected, so handsomeness must run in the family. 'Would you help with a charity event I am doing in a few weeks?'

'I'd love to,' Fritzi said quickly, feeling drawn to this woman's aura of enthusiasm and seductiveness. She sampled the food, which was fresh, unsophisticated and succulently delicious. 'In what capacity would you need me to help?'

'Modelling, for one. You'd be amazing,' Missy said sleekly. 'And I would love it if you could help me sort out what to show. It's all in aid of a charity dedicated to supporting disabled children. It's a passion of mine and it's so important, now more than ever. The event itself gets quite a turnout from the whole community, and I invite anyone and everyone who supports this charity.'

She couldn't help liking Missy, who appeared uncomplicated and a genuinely lovely person: sunny, optimistic, and, yes, quite enticing in her own way.

'What was the secret you wanted to tell me, by the way?' Fritzi asked.

Missy smiled coyly and twirled her fork. 'Ah, well, I couldn't help noticing my cousin Jared's body language around you. He is a known playboy, you know. Women flock at his feet, and he makes the most of it.' She put her fork down on the plate and her gaze now was even keener than usual. 'I think you may have what it takes to tame him.' She lowered her voice. 'He is very different with you – it's obvious he is quite taken with you.

Fritzi smiled. 'Thanks for the thumbs up,' she said, but her tone wasn't as buoyant as Missy's and she averted her eyes. 'Right now, I'm not really interested in any relationships. But I like Jared very much. Perhaps in the future … who knows?'

'Well, that's a sure way to keep someone interested,' Missy said sharply, still smiling. She gave Fritzi a conspiring look, as if the two women had known each other not for days, but for years. 'Quite clever, I'd say,' she said approvingly.

They both laughed. Jared was enormously important in her life. His having anything other than a professional interest in her pleased her.

'Oh, and he also told me you were once a supermodel,' Missy said. 'Not hard to believe, so I count myself lucky to have you onboard.'

The days passed in a haze of invitations from people she had met at the party. She felt, not for the first time, as though she was the flavour of the month. She was invited to lunches, BBQs, and had even been out on a yacht over the weekend to make up a party of six.

Feeling carefree and happy, almost her old self again, she arrived home late one evening to find a black SUV parked in her drive. Not sure who it may be and feeling a flash of anxiety, she asked the friend who had dropped her off to wait until she checked it out. Peeking through the window she found Darius fast asleep in the front seat, mouth open, his head lolling against the seat-rest. Wondering how long he had been waiting, she knocked on the window to wake him, waving that all was okay to her friend in the waiting car. Darius took a while to stir, opening one eye and then the other before he focused and remembered where he was. 'How long have you been here?' he asked.

'If you check your phone, you will find at least a dozen messages from me,' he said, almost angrily. She checked her cell and one message after another flashed up from him.

'Sorry, Darius, I was out on a boat in the middle of the ocean and my cell was in my bag.'

He clambered out of the car with some papers in his hands. Stretching his arms above his head, he said, 'Can we go inside? I think I deserve a proper bed for the night. Here, these are for you; all you have to do is co-sign them and the SUV is yours'

Fritzi made them both a coffee and they settled on the sofa to chat about the SUV and how things worked in Australia if one had an accident. 'The responsibility falls on the person who signs for the car, or who owns the car,' Darius said, now awake and alert again, 'even if someone else was driving. So, it's best that I am the main signature on the lease.'

'The last time we spoke you were still in Manhattan,' Fritzi said, finishing her coffee. 'Thanks, Darius, for doing this for me. I sent you my address a few days ago, hoping you would be able to figure something out from Sydney. I didn't realise you'd have to fly here to do the paperwork.'

He cocked his head to the side and looked at Fritzi. 'Well, I also wanted to check up on you. I did promise Maggie, you know.'

They both laughed. Fritzi could remember Maggie telling him to keep an eye on her before she left, when Darius dropped in on them unannounced one Sunday.

'I have a spare room,' Fritzi said, 'so you are welcome to stay. Unless you want me to drop you off at a hotel.'

'Fritzi,' he said, and the fatigue in his voice was evident, 'I am not going to foist myself on you. Even if we did have a fling, what seems like a million years ago now. I realise that since I had the audacity to have you checked out, we have been more than a little uncomfortable in one another's company. I don't blame you, but surely even if the status of our relationship has changed, we're still friends, right?'

Fritzi looked at Darius, the rings of tiredness around his eyes, his handsome, kindly face. She owed him a lot.

'I do realise that I had the upper hand when I seduced you in Bali,' she said. 'I wanted you to know that I did and, that I was in control of our relationship, I was at that time giving you the opportunity to run or to stay, by my aggressive roll playing seduction, I'm sorry. So, I owe you an apology, too. I think we are even on that score. Plus, you warned me to get out of Bali, and for that I will be forever grateful. If I were a superstitious person – which I am not, by the way – I would say that you brought me luck.'

'How so?'

'Meeting you has made me face certain truths about myself I may never have otherwise faced. I am still battling every day to face my ghosts from the past. Right now, I cannot afford to alienate you or Jared.'

'You mean by sleeping with either of us?'

'Yes,' she said bluntly. 'It would cause a schism between us, and we have, I believe, a good relationship right now. I would like to keep it like that.'

'So, you like Jared?' Darius said, almost afraid of the answer.

'Ag, not at all. I just want to remain unattached right now, until I work through this mess – my mess, you understand?'

'Perfectly. But, since we are being so honest, can I ask you one question since we are being up front? What did you do to me when you played around with me that afternoon in Bali?'

Fritzi knew she would have to answer, but she didn't like where this conversation was going. Getting up from the sofa she moved to the kitchen, where there was a good distance between her and Darius. She stared at him for a while, trying to figure out how she was going to explain something she herself did not understand fully.

'Darius, you must understand that I am a very complex woman – for reasons you have learnt about recently. Sometimes I need to be in control, especially when I feel out of control. Also, it's a way of giving pleasure to someone, yet at the same time you are showing who has the upper hand, and not only in bed but out of it, too. As it turns out, as a result of my behaviour, sexually and otherwise, I believe you felt the need to have me investigated, if you were to continue our relationship, am I right? So now you have the upper hand, and it's best we keep our distance from one another – for now, at least until I am able to sort out my life.'

'It did give me pleasure,' Darius said slowly, feeling confused all over again. He could feel, too, his renewed desire for Fritzi. He suspected now that he had never ceased desiring her. He wasn't sure anyone had ever got under his skin to such a degree. 'I was very naive in that department, and to be honest, I went to see a therapist to explain to me that I was not gay.' Darius smiled at the pained expression on her face, and laughed. 'You did me a favour,' he said, 'and for the record you can be in charge anytime you like.'

They both laughed; it broke the tension and they continued the conversation in a more relaxed manner.

'For the record,' he said, 'no, it's not one of the reasons I had you investigated.'

'Ya, okay, I understand. Let's leave things as they are for now. I am exhausted, see you in the morning, Darius. You'll find what you need in the spare bedroom – apart from me, of course. Only joking!'

'Ha ha, very funny, Fritzi. Be careful, don't try to be too smart. If you feel lonely in the middle of the night and want to play boss, I'm all yours, mine liebling.'

She walked towards him seductively, gave him a friendly goodnight peck on his cheek, and disappeared upstairs to her suite, shutting the door behind her, but not locking it.

Chapter 13

A week had passed since Darius's return from New York and, from Yvetta's wedding. He had decided to take up the offer to reconnect with the Rubicov's and DuPont, all had unknowingly contributed to his ambivalent feelings about involving Jared in Fritzi's case. Fritzi had as Fritzi does, crept under their skin, which irritated Darius, he felt responsible. Going to the wedding would perhaps galvanize his better judgement on how to move forward but he knew he was justifying his feelings, for Fritzi too. Fortunately, his mates had been gracious enough to postpone the trip to Hobart, Tasmania for a month giving him time to see Fritzi on his return from the States.

The night before Yvetta's wedding he had received a call from Fritzi to ask about hiring the SUV; he was relieved she had not used her false identity and he offered to hire the car for her, after his return from the States. Fritzi had made it clear that she wanted to make the most of her year the visa allowed her to stay in Australia, to travel, no one could persuade her otherwise. Seeing her again gave him an opportunity to put their relationship on a more even keel. Darius admitted since asking for the Interpol report on her, her attitude towards him had been one of restraint. and he had admitted to asking for the Interpol report on her.

And to be fair, though he often had to remind himself of this, he had not wanted to continue with the relationship at the time. But recent events had eclipsed this, and he felt as though he was in a different place with her now: not exactly better, but different. Everything (and perhaps everyone) had changed a great deal, and in a relatively short amount of time. He had been scared off by her past, perhaps rightly so, but he still desired her (enormously, increasingly), and he knew Jared found her intriguing and a provocative challenge, and perhaps felt other things for her as well.

Still, the trip to Yvetta's wedding had bothered him. Meeting and celebrating with the people Fritzi had gone out of her way to harm wouldn't be easy for him. Even though he thought he had some understanding of why Fritzi had done the things she had done (although this was in no way a justification for any of her actions), it was undeniable that she had wreaked havoc in their lives and not without consequences.

How could he reconcile what he heard and read with the images of Fritzi in his own life? And how, exactly, would he represent himself to the Rubicov family at the wedding? After all, they were entirely ignorant of his connection to Fritzi. And Fritzi certainly did not know he had met the Rubicovs, or that he was travelling to New York for the wedding of the woman she loved most.

Therefore, he felt he was deceiving everyone. It was somehow justifiable to deceive (or, at least, mislead) Fritzi, who had herself deceived him. But what of the Rubicovs, who had done nothing unkind to him, and even invited him, a stranger, to their big event? Still, he couldn't somehow help himself but go. It was all too enticing. Darius was not sure what he had to gain by becoming acquainted with the family on a more personal level, but becoming familiar with their backstory and knowing Fritzi seemed to make sense in terms of understanding what they were taking on helping Fritzi a master manipulator remain in Australia.

Now, he was putting himself in a position to get to know the family on a more personal level, albeit under false pretences. He was not comfortable with this. He wasn't altogether scrupulously honest (what successful businessman was?), but it also was not his nature to mislead or deceive. And, unlike Fritzi, he did not like playacting, pretending to be someone else. He felt comfortable in his identity, whatever or whoever that was. Apart from genuinely liking Yvetta Rubicov (and her beautiful sister-in-law, Safi), it was going to be difficult to explain away the reasons for his trip, or for his ruse. Perhaps by getting to know them he was hoping to prevent further heartache, in the event that he and Jared were able to help Fritzi come to terms with her past and her loss. Jared had reiterated his doubts to Darius about Fritzi giving up on

Yvetta; her obsession with her lover was extremely deep-rooted, intrinsically tied up with Fritzi's own identity and survival.

He hoped that he could come to more reasonable conclusions after meeting everyone at the wedding, and that the experience would somehow make him cautious about reigniting a relationship with Fritzi again – a desire that was becoming ever more compelling.

The wedding was held on a farm outside of New York, DuPont had arrived to give him a ride to the leafy Hudson River Estate about an hour's drive outside Manhattan. They chatted about the Dax artwork Darius had purchased and if it was a viable business proposition for the artist to show in one of the major galleries in Sydney. Darius was looking forward to meeting Dax and his partner Daniel at the wedding, he had admired Daniels architectural design skills, when eating at the Rubicov restaurant on his previous visit to Manhattan. They arrived at the farm where the car was whisked away by a valet hopefully to be returned with the hundreds of other cars at the end of the evening. The farm belonged to Safi's husband, which confused Darius, who had read that she had been married to Sasha Rubicov.

'Ah, well,' DuPont intoned in his now familiar, crisp, elegant, urbane European voice, his lips curling into a sly smile, 'that's another long story. So many of this family's stories are.' He gave Darius a long, keen look that seemed to mean something Darius wasn't quite sure of, before turning back to the road. 'Remind me if we have the time. I will fill you in, it's an interesting story.'

The reception was held in Janus's vast outdoor sculpture studio. DuPont was a most knowledgeable and wonderful host, explaining many of the gaps and inconsistencies in Safi's story after meeting Sasha Rubicov, he knew of so far, including the background behind Janus's work.

'Janus is a successful American sculptor. In fact, there is a show of his latest work in Germany right now; he is very popular over there. The work in this studio at the moment are chosen pieces from his last show, a number of years back. That was also a huge success. As you can tell,' he said, gesturing to the artworks above and around them, 'these monumental structures lend themselves perfectly to this occasion. They are so very tactile one has to run a hand along their smooth surfaces as the wood bends and twists.'

Darius, strolling among the sculptures with other guests, admiring the form and beauty of the wood carved from one piece, stopped to do just that. Waiters were offering on ornate trays champagne flutes, beautifully prepared Italian antipasto, as well as Russian treats on offer from their Rubicov Restaurant. It was a wonderful and seamless amalgamation of cultures, people, and food. And money – lots of money. There was an enormous vodka bar to one side, and Darius made his way over to the endless vodka pouring down the ice sculpture. The vodka would go down well with the Beluga caviar and French baguette slices being offered by the waiters. Darius had attended many expensive events, but nothing quite on this scale and, intrigue.

They were called to take their seats for the ceremony, after the reception, which had lasted an hour at least as everyone was given the opportunity to explore the art works. The ceremony was held outdoors in the grounds of the farmhouse. Darius was thrilled by the beauty of the grounds and the lush natural displays of grasses and meadow flowers amongst the trees lining the route to the Canopied Altar, itself decorated with the natural grasses and field flowers.

He took his seat with the other guests, only now realising how truly out of his depth he was. What was he doing here? He looked around him, as if for help, and found himself seated next to two interesting-looking guys. He introduced himself as a friend of Yvetta's from Australia, and they introduced themselves in turn. He was delighted to find he was seated next to Dax and his husband, Dan. He began excitedly engaging with the couple, but the wedding was about to commence so they had to stop talking.

Sitting back in his seat with a sense of great excitement, he was looking forward to learning more about the two men, Dax was too busy to talk, preoccupied with a little girl, with a mop of curly dark hair, dressed in a sparkly ankle length peach dress, he guessed around five, they were looking after. Darius was later to learn that the child, Raquel, was their daughter and they were the doting parents.

The female groom, he now knew to be DuPont's secretary waiting under the canopy was dressed in a tailored white satin skirt suit with a calf-length fish tail. As she turned around, he noticed a hint of breasts showing, presumably a waistcoat with no shirt underneath. The groom was a stunning redhead; she had a high ponytail pulled through a garland of natural field flowers. Darius was confused; he had never been to a same-sex wedding. As if intuiting this, Dan leaned forward to explain.

'Yvetta's partner is Jewish, so it's a joint religious ceremony. Yvetta is Russian Orthodox, which is why they have opted for a more traditional ceremony'

A small quartet struck up with John Lennon's 'Woman' and the guests watched as Yvetta made her way down the aisle on the arm of a tall, good-looking older man, a relative, Darius assumed.

Leaning forward and speaking in a whisper, Dan filled him in once more: 'That is Yvetta's older brother, Mika.'

Yvetta had a halterneck low-back heavy cream lace dress on, with a train beautifully attached to a small diamante belt around her tiny waist. Her veil was short and just covered her face, and in her hand, she held a posy of blood-red poppies.

As she proceeded slowly down the aisle, he noticed the people waiting on either side of the platformed canopy. This was obviously her retinue, and consisted of a number of young men and one woman on Yvetta's side. Apart from a man who formed part of an older couple (which he presumed were the redhead's parents), her partner's side had only females on it.

Leaning over again, Darius enquired who the people on Yvetta's side were. At this point, he had developed a friendly rapport with Dan.

'The young man standing closest to Yvetta is her nephew Alexander, Sasha's son,' Dan said, 'and the girl is Marina, her half-sister. The rest are cousins.'

The ceremony was beautiful and performed jointly by a female rabbi and a priest. Each partner recited their own vows to one another, and both stamped on glasses that had been rolled in napkins, laughing as the glass got caught up in Yvetta's high heels. The ritual of breaking the glass underfoot had become a symbol of the destruction of the Temple to be remembered even at times of great joy, we must remember moments of trauma and tragedy, what it means to be Jewish.

Once the ceremony was over and, the two women were officially and happily married, everyone threw sweets at the couple instead of confetti, and the guests made their way to the tables laid under a huge open tent.

Darius found he was seated at a table of ten. He was happy to note that DuPont shared his table, and, to his delight, Safi, her husband Janus, Dax, Dan, and other close friends and family. Surprised to be seated at a family and friends table, he later found that DuPont's wife had not been able to attend and, he had been given her seat, at DuPont's request.

'Yvetta wanted you to feel comfortable and, agreed happily for you to have my wife's seat so she put you at a table of people you have met, and already knew of, like Dax.'

Raquel was taken away by a nanny, now Dan and Dax had time to chat to Darius – and a wonderful chat it was, about art, design, life in Manhattan and Sydney. Darius had the most interesting evening, and left with an invitation to visit Dax's studio and Dan's business in Manhattan.

The wedding went on late into the night, and Darius, feeling entirely relaxed now, full of vodka and a celebratory spirit, danced the night away with everyone else. It was a relaxed fun wedding, the main courses being a mix of American and Russian food, all catered by the Rubicov restaurant.

Darius met many of Yvetta's family. He listened to the speeches, all tinged with sadness. Yvetta had lost both of her parents and her brother Sasha, and this was mentioned, fleetingly or in depth, in almost every speech.

Darius could not help wondering about Fritzi, it was almost impossible to imagine how this wedding he was attending would affect Fritzi, seeing the love of her life marrying another woman, sparks would surely fly one way or another, he was sure Fritzi would have a complete meltdown emotionally.

Safi, Darius learnt, had only recently married Janus, after knowing him for many years while representing his work in the Rubicov galleries. In the car, DuPont had informed him approvingly that Janus was more than he seemed: a very wealthy man with a business in computer intelligence. Something about DuPont's tone when talking about Safi suggested that maybe there was some sort of history between the Frenchman and the lovely British woman, too.

Although Darius did not get much of a chance to speak with Janus (who spent most of the wedding doting on his wife, who he clearly adored), he made a note to connect with him at a later stage. The two men had certain things in common. Darius's own company had a data collecting department, which assisted many companies in combating and preventing cyberwarfare and online espionage, new types of serious and sophisticated crimes that popped up with a frightening degree of frequency. Too often, the cybercriminals were one step ahead of the authorities, but Darius's company was attempting to correct that. His company had even done undercover work with the Australian government on occasion, watching what the Chinese and Russians were up to.

Darius arrived back at his Manhattan hotel in the early hours of the morning, still excited from the wedding and also more than a little drunk. But he needed a good sleep: he had two days left in New York before he flew back to Sydney and wanted to make the most of his time left.

Chapter 14

On the flight back to Sydney he reflected on how everyone he had met fitted into the puzzle. And how they were impacted by Yvetta and her affair with Fritzi. He hoped that the drama and trauma was all behind them now; Fritzi was, after all, securely out of their lives. Fritzi was, he reflected now, far away in Byron Bay. He would see her on his return to Australia, and make sure she was out of trouble.

Yvetta was happily married and had turned over a new leaf. She was, by all accounts, a vastly improved person, and, in her business success and in her personal life, on the right track – thriving, even. No one in her family believed this was possible. He wondered whether Fritzi would be able to turn the page in such a positive way too? The fact that she was still hung up on Yvetta, living too often in the past, was a bad sign. But what was her current trajectory? Was she moving in the wrong direction? He so wanted to make her right, but at what expense to himself?

He did not believe her to be an intrinsically bad person; damaged, perhaps. Sadly, Fritzi's relationship with Yvetta, it appeared, had fulfilled a psychological need, bringing out the worst in both parties. Together, the two women were like a perfect storm, both needy and on some level dissatisfied with their lives. But two wrongs did not make a right, nor did two broken people make a whole. Together they were like oil and water, and sadly the fire was extensive and many innocent people got burned, too.

Sleeping a fair amount on the first-class flight had its benefits, twenty-two hours of flying had its drawbacks but on this flight, it had given him time to reflect and would allow him to visit with his mom when back in Sydney, before leaving for Byron Bay. For the rest of the time, he reflected on the wedding.

The Rubicovs were warm and welcoming. Dan and Dax – the two D's, as everyone called them – were a creative power couple, both ambitious and successful in their own right. But they were enormously kind and helpful, too. They were also good company, and fun to be around. So was DuPont, Dax's agent, who had promised, to make contact with the gallery in Sydney Darius had recommended. Hopefully Australia could host a Dax exhibition sometime soon.

The night before he left for Australia, he had met the two D's, Safi, and Janus at a new Rubicov restaurant in the West Village area, which featured Dax's work on the wall. Darius was blown away by Dax's art once more.

Janus was no longer involved with the tech company in California, Darius learnt, but was happy to introduce him to the CEO, if he ever decided to visit the operation near Silicon Valley.

His decision to attend the wedding did not resolve anything in his mind, but it had made the actors in Fritzi's drama more real. Now he realised he was a player, too. He closed his eyes, drifting off again, his mind still consumed by Fritzi.

He picked up the SUV at the airport in Byron Bay and made his way to her apartment, hoping things would unfold between them one way or another.

Darius crawled into the spare room bed. The sparring match had been fun and revealed some important truths. He felt better for it. He wondered whether the thought of having Fritzi so close would interrupt his much-needed sleep, but as soon as his head hit the pillow he was away with the fairies.

Fritzi knocked softly on the door. It was past eleven and she had already been out to teach her yoga class at a local gym, leaving a note for Darius in the kitchen. Returning to find the note unopened, she decided it was time to wake him. Opening the door, she found the bed empty and perfectly made. Stepping into the room she walked over to the bedside table to check whether his belongings were still there.

Darius walked out of the bathroom, a towel wrapped round his waist, to find Fritzi opening the shutters. She spun round. 'Oh, hi there; for a moment I thought you had left.'

Aware of her eyes on his naked torso, not quite sure how to play the moment, he combed his fingers through his wet hair and off his face. He was about to move towards her, but she beat him to it, crossing the room in one fell swoop and ripping off his towel. They stood staring at one another, both waiting for the other to make the first move. Neither succeeded, instead reaching for one another simultaneously, stepping backwards towards the bed. He helped her pull off her exercise gear and they devoured each other with the heated passion of two people who had been denying their attraction for one another for some time. 'I promised myself I would not do that.' Darius, said.

They both laughed. 'Well, I tried my best to keep my distance, too, but obviously we both wanted what just happened.'

'Ya, and now I'm starving. I've just spent the best part of two hours teaching yoga. Get dressed and we'll go out and devour some delicious Aussie food. Are you going to stay for a while? I hope so.'

'Try and stop me,' he said. 'Now that I have you back in my bed, do you think I'm going to leave? I don't think so.' Pulling her back into his arms, he straddled her, but she picked up the pillow and hit him with it. 'Idiot, let's go and eat.'

Sitting opposite her in the restaurant, he had to catch himself from talking about the wedding and the Rubicovs – several times, it almost slipped off his tongue in conversation. He was now connected to her past life, and it was going to be damn hard to pretend he hadn't met her old lover, or any of the people she had so ruthlessly harmed.

Fritzi was more relaxed than he had ever seen her; she had none of the affectations he had previously noticed, the need for posing or pretence, was no longer part of her persona. He noticed she was no longer anxious or guarded; she did not scope out the people in the restaurant before entering Bayleaf, a popular breakfast place, or choose the most inconspicuous table in doors, from where she could keep her eye on who entered or left, if possible, in case of emergency, close to a quick exit.

She chose an outdoor table and people stopped at their table to chat. While eating his healthy homemade granola and yogurt with honey, he enjoyed watching the people and passing conversation with Fritzi who had obviously made friends quickly. As he was introduced, they nodded with approval, but the attention was all on Fritzi she was being treated with almost celebrity status and he judged as her appendage.

'You are quite the hit in Byron Bay,' Darius said, impressed with her all over again. 'Not bad considering you've been here for such a short period.'

'The flavour of the month,' she said, smiling, 'especially since Jared's been in town.'

Surprised, Darius's heart sunk a little and he said, suddenly talking fast, 'Really? I did not know he had been here. When?' He felt she had kept something from him, before remembering the wedding in New York and all he was keeping from her.

'A few weeks ago,' she said hesitantly, registering his surprise – almost his disappointment, she thought – wondering if she had made a mistake by saying too much. 'I had only been here two weeks when he surprised me at a party.'

'Go on, tell me more,' he said a little too sharply – and not at all happily, she thought.

Fritzi went on to explain the connection to (and her subsequent friendship with) Missy, a cousin of Jared's who had introduced her to a wide and interesting circle of friends, who had since wined and dined her.

'Jared made sure I would be well looked after while here,' Fritzi informed Darius, 'and tonight you will be meeting Micheline – Missy for short. She has invited me to a barbeque at her place. It's also to discuss the upcoming charity event she is hosting next month.'

'Wow,' he said slowly, trying to sound enthusiastic and put his momentary envy aside, 'you have certainly become involved with the community in a very short time. That is great.' But was it great, he wondered, feeling hesitant and anxious once more. What if her true identity was revealed? Or, worse, she fell in love with someone else, this Missy for instance?

'I am loving this feeling of belonging,' she said softly, 'of being accepted and not having to worry about my past catching up with me.'

Darius had an image of the wedding, of Yvetta and her partner hand in hand, the entire Rubicov family enjoying the occasion on Safi and Janus's farm. He thought of the two D's and their little girl, Raquel, and of course the inimitable, entertaining DuPont. He wondered how Fritzi would react if he were to tell her that only days ago, he had been with Yvetta's family.

Instead, he looked at her and said, 'Yes, that is progress, don't you think?'

Smiling, broadly she said, 'I think that for the first time in my life I understand what it means when someone says they are happy. This is a word and a feeling I never understood before, but now I do.'

'That's wonderful to hear,' Darius said, 'but what explains the change?'

'Because I feel at peace,' she said simply. 'Australia agrees with me: it has given me a family and friends I have longed for. I never found any real warmth or intimacy with Yvetta's family. I was always an outsider.'

Darius felt confused. 'When you say you have found family in Australia,' he said, 'who are you referring to?'

'Maggie. She feels like my family. I trust her and I speak with her all the time. She keeps me stable, you know?'

He didn't know and he felt sad for her. Yvetta had found true happiness with a romantic partner and a successful career, and here was Fritzi, for whom happiness was finding a mother figure.

Life, he realised, was all about choices. For example, he had just made a choice by getting romantically involved with Fritzi again. But the question was, did anyone truly know why they made certain choices? If the act of choosing was that easy, everyone would make the right choice every time. The truth was that so many important choices amounted to sheer luck; a choice that seemed a sure thing could just as easily end up being the wrong one.

Fritzi had chosen Maggie to rely on, and he had chosen, against all the odds, to resurrect his relationship with someone everyone had warned him against getting involved with. Every dossier on her he had read, all the information he consumed on her, all of the evidence, every shred of rational thought in his head – and he had ignored it all. Why? Because he liked to live on the edge? Because he was a sucker for punishment? Neither of these were especially true of him; so why? Because he was infatuated with her? Because he wanted to live dangerously? Because she was so unlike any other woman he had ever met? All of these options came to him, but none seemed to fit exactly right. Fritzi, he realised with a shudder, felt right in his arms; the fit felt right. And that, right now, was all that mattered. Or was it, or was he just following his heart not over thinking it?

When Darius and Fritzi arrived together for the barbeque, Missy welcomed Darius, to her luxurious home and outdoor area where the lawns slopped down to the bay beyond. But later he noticed Missy watching them on the sly, and wondered whether she would report back to her cousin Jared.

The evening went without mention of any relationship between the Darius and Fritzi, only that he was a friend from Sydney and, they left it that way, neither showing any hint or overtures of affection for each other during the evening. Darius had always enjoyed his visits to Byron

Bay, the laid back atmosphere so different to the fast pace in Sydney, here everyone including Missy he noticed wore relaxed clothing, less showy but quite sexy all the same denim shorts and cowboy boots with a white off the shoulder top not clingy, no overt figure hugging outfits he was used to seeing in Sydney, and he wondered watching the interaction between, Missy and Fritzi whether there was any sexual attraction, was he being especially alert to Fritzi's history, he hoped she had changed her sexual preferences for good.

'Well, you are a dark horse,' Missy said to her, in a low, almost seductive voice. 'I thought you weren't into any relationships right now?'

Fritzi was taken aback and did not quite know how to reply to her forthright personal question.

'Ag, no, Darius is an old friend. We like each other, but who knows … right now things just are … easy, you understand, nothing serious.'

Missy laughed, but it was a high, sharp sound. 'Yes, I do understand. It's been a while since I had that type of easy relationship.' She seemed to be hinting at something Fritzi couldn't quite understand.

No more was said and they got onto arranging the show with other members of the board of the charity.

That night Darius shared Fritzi's bed. All day with Fritzi he had felt a shared warmth, and he realised he had never felt happier or more content. He wanted her in his life, and he didn't care about her past any longer. He now believed her to be a different person, believed it every fibre in his body. He knew that some people would be more suspicious of his motives, of his desires, but he would leave that speculation to them. No one had investigated her past as thoroughly as he had, to his knowledge and, for personal reasons, not motivated for the sake of justice.

Whatever his justification was, he was listening to his heart not his head, that was for sure. If, after all he had learnt about Fritzi, he could come to terms with her past, he hoped DuPont, and perhaps even the Rubicov family, may one day forgive her, too.

Their plans came together naturally, suddenly, seemingly all at once and on the fly. Spontaneously, the way she liked it – and the way he liked it, too. They spent a week scuba diving, and decided to travel a little further along the coast, hiking and sightseeing wherever they stopped near Ballina to Lennox to watch the whales and camp out under the stars or slept in the camper van on the odd occasion.

He listened as she chatted on and on about where she wanted to go and what she wanted to see, as they sat on the beach watching the sun drop out of the sky as it sank below the horizon, both tired from a day out on the boat watching the whales and dolphins. The surfers' bodies outlined captured in negative space, catching the last waves as the last rays of sunlight hit the water. He understood her hunger for the limitless freedom and immensity the Aussie outback had to offer her. She was not sure when she would move on from Byron Bay, but felt it might be a good base to return to from various excursions.

He was waiting for Fritzi to invite him along, but no invitation came. He wasn't at all sure whether or not she took it for granted that he would accompany her when she decided to go on her travels around Australia. It had been a long while since he had been to many of the places she had on her list. Now that he had her to himself, he did not want her to get used to being without him. She was by nature a loner, and he wanted to encourage her to trust him, even become dependent on him, in their short time together in Byron Bay, over the last two weeks, felt so natural, to him anyway, Fritzi had come to enjoy him living with her, calling his name as soon as she got home, they had formed a close bond and, she was it seemed, depending on him more and more.

As they sat chatting in one of the outdoor restaurants on the beach, a cool breeze coming off the sea as the spray of the waves rolling in hit the sand, 'Well,' he said, prompting her, suddenly excited, 'it's been quite a while since I travelled to the places on your list. In fact, I am more than happy to be your personal guide. When do we leave?'

Fritzi stared at Darius; she had not expected him to want to accompany her. She was confused by his excitement, his hunger, even, to be with her. Perhaps she had misjudged him, and the wisdom of renewing their sexual relationship. Now he seemed to want to be with her all the time – and she was not sure that this was what she wanted. What she wanted was independence, adventure, and, above all else, personal freedom. Perhaps travelling Australia was something she should be doing on her own, that had been her plan all along. Feeling conflicted, she attempted to hide her hesitation, but Darius had already picked up on it.

'I tell you what,' Darius said, the old Fritzi he noted dejectedly was resurfacing a coldness pushing out the warmth he had felt was now creeping back. 'let's leave it for now. Sleep on it, If, you change your mind, I will travel with you. And if you go alone but find during the trip you want company, I'll fly out to wherever you are. How does that sound?'

Darius knew his feelings for her were overpowering his common sense to pull back, Fritzi he knew by now was her own person, yet he felt her need to belong, and, he wanted to be there for her when, and, if she admitted to herself that she needed and liked him in her life, even depended on him, was he imagining this new Fritzi, he wondered?

'I will sleep on it, she said, keeping her voice low, her eyes down adopting a thoughtful pose, and maybe, since you have put the idea into my mind, it would be a nice change to have company. I travelled through India and South East Asia on my own, so…'

But she did not finish the sentence, instead allowing it to hang in the air, along with her gaze and tousled hair. And noticing his questioning, vaguely bemused, slightly boyish face. Fritzi leaned over towards Darius and whispered in his ear sensuously, the sexual undertone unmistakable. He threw his head back and laughed, she was too much, but that's why he couldn't get enough of her.

'With a promise like that I am already packed,' he said, altogether too quickly.

She was laughing now, too. Her cell buzzed; checking who it was before answering, she smiled and showed Darius the caller ID. She walked off along to beach, to chat to Maggie, mainly to sound the housekeeper out on the idea of having company on her travels – Darius's company, in particular. And, again, Fritzi remembered Maggie's invocation to Darius to try and look after Fritzi. For that reason, Maggie's response hardly came as a surprise.

'Maggie thinks it's a great idea,' Fritzi said to an excited Darius, once she had hung up. 'She says she would feel happier knowing I have a knight in shining armour to watch out for me in the outback.'

'Good to know I have Maggie on my side.'

They made their way back to Byron Bay. Fritzi needed to be back for the charity show coming up over the weekend.

The fashion show and auction was to be held in a five--star hotel. The ballroom and seating was all arranged by Missy and her members a group of six women all from different backgrounds, but with expertise in various fields she could not have put any of the charity gala's together over the years and, Fritzi now added to her arsenal of experts; each had their role to play. The audience were sent embossed invitations for the big event of the season. The tickets were not cheap and the auction would be run by one of the many celebrities, this year it was a big star from the action movie industry who now lived in Byron Bay. Fritzi quickly found that the ever-resilient (pushy, but in a charming way; it was almost a pleasure to be pushed by her) Missy never took no for an answer. And most people (especially the wealthy Byron Bay set) were happy to give their time and money for a good cause.

Models were flown in from Sydney, and the boutique stores (many of which were just starting up and eager to get their name – and products – out) delighted at the opportunity for their clothes to be paraded down a catwalk, modelled by professionals from the fashion world. Both women and men's fashions would be exhibited.

Fritzi worked behind the scenes organising each ensemble. The wardrobe girl worked alongside Fritzi, and was, not only stars truck but grateful for her help. The two women sorted outfits for each model on the metal rails, developing a system so that there was no confusion when the models came off the catwalk for a quick change. Fritzi had her own rail of clothes chosen from Missy's stores. Each rail was attended by Design Arts students from a nearby college, who had the job of undressing and dressing the girls or guys as they came off the runway.

Everyone had given their services for free, and with an encouraging (and, for cynical Fritzi, surprising) amount of good will. Fritzi was beginning to realise that Australians were a nation of very kind people, who were as earnest and socially responsible as they were interested in others and interesting in their own right. The hair salon stylists from the salons and spas in Byron Bay (of which there were a surprising amount) had sent their makeup artists to help out. They were backstage hours before the show started, and each girl's hair was styled the same way: swept off their faces, combed and sprayed behind their ears into a low ponytail.

Besides clothing, the models were showing costume jewellery, fine jewellery and bags, all of which were for sale. A select few items would go into the auction, and punters would have their lots and their wands ready to bid as the they walked down the ramp. Missy would be standing off to one side, calling out the prices of each item. Members of the charity would be sitting at a table, taking the bids as the prices went up for the auction items. The whole evening was professionally managed and Fritzi was, she realised all of a sudden, more than a little honoured to be part of such a huge endeavour for a charitable cause.

The models were of mixed ages and sizes, some were just starting out, were given strict instructions to walk slowly and to remain standing at the end of the runway until each item for auction had been bid for, hopefully past the reserve price.

The twelve girls and eight guys were buffed, polished, and ready to roll by the time everyone had taken their seats at the tables.

The ballroom had been arranged with most of the tables positioned close to the catwalk, while others were placed at various angles to guarantee a good view. Obviously, those with deep pockets were seated closest to the runway.

Champagne was flowing and the noise and chatter could be heard in the changing rooms. The dinner would be served after the show was over; right now, Missy wanted their full attention. The buzz wasn't quite as thrilling as Fritzi had experienced way back in her catwalk days (after all, she was no longer centre of attention, but now quietly assisting those who were), but she felt the same butterflies and she noticed the eighteen-year-olds around her were like young race horses waiting to be let out of their starting gates.

She had confided in Missy that she had been on the catwalks in her youth, working for the top houses in the fashion capitals of the world. She did not want to be given celebrity status amongst the girls, or to be elevated in any way. She did not want to be treated differently, the show was about making money for the charity, and the focus should be on that. She was happy to be the lead model in the show, the first out on the catwalk and, the last at the end of the show.

The music would dominate the ballroom as they started, but would fade into the background for the bidding. Everyone from the lighting engineers to the sound engineers had their cue. Nothing was left to chance, everything was polished and had to be perfect Everyone who had worked alongside Missy in the past enjoyed the spectacle. The ballroom with its dozen low-hanging chandeliers, palm trees and troughs of potted flowers and, 6ft digital 3D screens capturing indigenous aboriginal paintings made for a spectacular atmosphere.

Even club disc jockeys and the guys who did strobe lighting for local bars and clubs had come on board; this was quite a production for Byron Bay, and you could feel it in the air.

Fritzi peeked through the curtains to see what to expect and was bowled over by the amount of people gathered. The ballroom easily held six hundred, and it was packed to capacity, with some even standing round the edges, chatting among themselves, with an air of anticipation and excitement about them. Fritzi felt that electricity of anxiety, too, and it was thrilling. She had, she understood now, missed the feeling a good deal. It was almost time.

Missy was making a short introductory speech, and once the music began again, they were on.

Behind the curtains stood Mr Larry. When Mr Larry said 'walk,' a retired musical director, paunchy and bald with piercing blue eyes, no one wanted to have blaze at them in anger, you were out there, no hesitating or procrastinating, no time for nerves or anything else; this was it, and no excuses would do. There was no room for error here; even the most minor slip-up or infraction was unforgivable, would slow everyone down and derail or even destroy the show. There was a science, as well as an art, to runway shows, and Mr Larry considered himself an artist, and had the temperament of one as well. Most shows lasted at most 60 minutes and this was a charity event so, Mr. Larry gave each model three minutes to shine on the catwalk; some would walk out alone for the auction pieces and others would step out in pairs. After that, they would double back for a quick change and the next walk-on, to showcase the 100 outfits.

After the auction was over and the charity aspect taken care of, everyone feeling good about themselves and their wallets hopefully a little (or even a lot) emptier, the dinner would be served and the entertainment would begin. Singers from around the bay would perform on the stage, as well as several rock bands from the area. Then the fun would start in earnest, with all those backstage joining in with the party. This was Missy's idea, an appropriately bubbly, all-in-good-fun flourish and something that certainly did not happen after high-end designer shows. The significance of her charity aside, Missy wanted the evening to be above all entertaining – for everyone, including the models.

Fritzi had been looking forward to the evening for days, and here it was, and her moment was imminent, and she could feel it now and it was dizzying, but wonderfully so. A great amount of work had gone into tonight, and Fritzi wanted to make it as special as she could in her small way.

She started her walk down the runway. At first her knees felt weak, but once that adrenalin-charge took hold, she was in her zone. In her catwalk days they walked like racehorses, one foot over the other, and that's exactly what she did. The gold one shouldered lame evening dress was long and slinky and hugged her curves tightly; the black shoulder brushing feathered earrings and art deco Judith Lieber evening bag were all on auction. She came to the end of the runway did a few turns and, then began her glide again.

As the auction progressed, she flirted, smiled and charmed, but kept moving, turning, walking a short distance and returning to the end of the runway. It all happened very quickly. The numbers were flying to dizzy heights. As the hammer came down on the last bid, she quickly made her way back up the runway. That was a unique experience, actually teasing an audience to bid for her clothing on the spot, but she could tell they were taken with her and therefore the bidding had gone sky-high, which was just what Missy wanted. She had known Fritzi would set the place alight. Fritzi, in turn, was pleased that she had pleased Missy, and that all had gone according to plan and the evening, already, was a resounding success and an occasion to remember – until next year's show, at least, at which, Missy joked later that evening, she would outdo this evening and herself.

Missy smiled and did a thumbs up as Fritzi proceeded up the runway. It was exhilarating, she felt lightheaded and happy – ecstatic, in fact – for the first time in how long she didn't know.

After that, the show went without a hitch, modelling the expensive items of clothing and jewellery down the runway each model doubling up as they passed each other down and up the runway to give punters a better look at each item, it kept the pace alive and made the runway buzz with glamour and energy. Lead by Fritzi, the models at the end of the show descended down the stairs on either side of the catwalk and into the audience. Private bids would then continue on unsold items, or those not reaching above the reserve price.

As Fritzi walked among the tables, feeling luminous and excited still, stopping to chat to those she knew and offering greetings to those she didn't, she noticed Jared and Darius for the first time. Sitting at one of the tables closest to the runway with them was Maggie, who looked as proud as a mother hen, dressed in a classic black trouser suit, her silver bobbed hair, cut an elegant version of Maggie Fritzi had not seen before, she was Fritzi thought a very attractive woman, when she made an effort to dress up.

Fritzi loved the recognition, especially from Maggie; it made her heart swell. This kind of affirmation, of validation, was something she should have experienced as she was growing up, but sadly she never had.

The absence of any kind of affirmation, and her experience with so much criticism and so much hardship and pain, had done a great deal of damage, damage she was still trying to heal and examine anew. Still, the past was the past, and this was a new moment, one in a ballroom of a grand building, and Fritzi had never been happier. It was never too late to have a mother in one's life, and Maggie was the closest she would ever come to having one, and her life already felt better for it.

While Fritzi made her way towards Maggie's table, the models, now back in their own clothes, apart from Fritzi, joined the dancing and feasting from the buffet. Her path towards them was interrupted by so many people (some strangers, some new friends) wanting to congratulate her on her performance; many just wanted to chat and some to flirt. She was relieved when Darius debonair in his tux came to her side to escort her through her adoring fans, she was grateful but also a little reluctant to have him take complete ownership of her, not with Jared looking on, and, she couldn't help but notice, looking dashing in his navy-blue velvet jacket.

Guessing that Fritzi would be hungry after the big show, Maggie had piled plates full of food and deserts.

'Ooh, thank you, Maggie,' Fritzi said, surprised again at how pleased she was to see the older woman. 'I need to eat. Apart from water and a few sucking sweets, I haven't had a thing since this morning.'

What with Jared and the rest of the male (and a good portion of the female) population drooling over Fritzi, Darius knew he would have to stake his claim. what with Jared and the rest of the male population drooling over her, he had gone to find her in the crowd. He knew she would struggle to find their table again, and desperately wanted her beside him now, and away from all of these other, almost uniformly attractive admirers. The music was pumping and everyone was whooping it up on the dance floor. The buffet table was groaning with food, and the catwalk had turned into a performance stage for the entertainers.

As Fritzi put the last delicious slice of chocolate mousse in her mouth, Jared, with a conspiratorial glance at Darius, arrived back at the table and whisked her off to the dance floor. They had already had a short conversation about Fritzi's case, while sitting at the table together.

'I leave early tomorrow morning,' Jared said loudly into her ear as he held her close, 'so I won't have much time to see you. I have been very busy at work.' His voice was apologetic now and he was looking at her oddly, as if he was taking in her beauty for the first time. 'But I have news about our case. But now is not the time for that,' he said with a laugh, gesturing around them, his hand coming back to rest on her hip, 'I will call you once I'm back in Sydney.'

If Fritzi had felt elated just moments before, now she felt only anxiety. Everything changed and even the room felt as though it had gone dark. Why had Jared come all the way to Byron Bay? To tell her what? To tell her nothing? To tell her that he would tell her everything later? What was everything? It was nothing. It was worse than nothing because not knowing was worst of all. Concern flooded her expression and changed the contours of her face. Holding her close, Jared took this all in.

'No need for that,' he said softly, but his hand was no longer on her hip and he was no longer whispering seductively in her ear. 'It's all going to be just fine,' and he surprised her with a smile. She had forgotten how good-looking he was, and tonight, in his tux, his hair neatly trimmed and his smooth face close to hers, he seemed more handsome than ever. It was a long way from the wounded Jared she had rescued in Christchurch, who had resembled a helpless, dying animal on the street. 'Better than you can imagine, in fact. So get your forty winks tonight, because we have much to discuss once I am back at my desk.'

She put her head on his shoulder, surprising herself, but there was nothing seductive about this gesture, it was one of trust and thanks, and also exhaustion. Jared pulled her in close. He knew she was with Darius, but he could not help feel her need for comfort, and he was happy to give it, Darius was a lucky bugger, he had to keep a professional distance but, he knew they had unfinished business, since their Bali relationship and he knew, he would have to keep his distance while her case was pending.

'I am so nervous going forward with this application you are working on, Jared.' And then, aware of the absurd seriousness of the moment which seemed so out of place here, now, looking around her again, she said, 'The show was exhilarating. I am relieved that it all went so incredibly well.'

'You did magnificently. Everyone is talking about it, about you. And Missy is over the moon.' He touched her face for a moment, then moved a step back, business-like once more. She didn't always know where she stood with him, and she enjoyed that ambivalence, their odd dynamic.

'I know you are apprehensive about the application, but I am positive we are heading towards a good outcome. Darius and I did a fair bit of bidding, by the way. Especially on items worn by one particular model. You probably don't know her. She is from Germany, far away from here, and she is a mystery even to me, and I suspect to herself as well.'

'Oh, you are right about that,' she said, feeling brighter already. 'And you came here all the way from Sydney to see me on the catwalk?'

'Oh, I never miss one of Missy's charity shows. Missy and I have always been close. And she always makes a huge effort. Actually, she always gives everything her all – and I mean everything. But then, from the look of it, so do you. Your contribution this year, I am sure, pushed profits up for her. Well done, you. She clearly knew what she was doing when she approached you.'

'Don't thank me,' Fritzi said, feeling elated once again, the anxiety fizzing away and disappearing like the champagne in the glasses of everyone around her, 'I loved every minute of it. And perhaps I will learn the ropes from Missy – as you say, she is incredible. Who knows, I may have found something I can do in the future.'

They made their way back to the table, where Fritzi sat with Maggie for the rest of the evening to catch up. She had little interest in her fanbase, the less she encouraged further attention the better. Maggie was leaving with Jared on an early flight. Fritzi learnt that Jared insisted Maggie accompany him, buying her a ticket as his date.

Before leaving for home with Darius, Missy told her that they made a killing tonight. In fact, this was the most successful auction the charity had had since its founding. Grateful, radiant Missy was insistent that it was Fritzi's contribution that had fired up the bidding war, and with brilliant consequences.

Back at home Darius asked Fritzi whether Jared had spoken with her about her case. 'Yes,' she replied. 'He told me I have nothing to worry about, that good things are happening. But he didn't say anything more than that.'

'Yes, he told me that, too, but I am also in the dark as to what he is referring to. We'll just have to go to bed, that's the best way to wipe all of that worry from our minds.'

'To bed but not to sleep?' Fritzi said.

'Oh, certainly not to sleep,' Darius said. 'I still can't get over how mesmerising you were on that catwalk. Everyone was enchanted.'

'Even you?'

'Especially me. You looked incredible. You look incredible still.' And her kissed her deeply and for a long time.

'It was exciting for me, too,' she said, realising that the event had very much aroused her.

Laughing, she allowed Darius to lead her up the stairs. It was time to give in to his wonderful caring all-consuming passion for her, and to give him what she knew he desired from her, what she needed from him, was to enjoy the heat of the moment.

Chapter 15

Dupont was panicked, he had tried to spell out in no uncertain terms what kind of person Fritzi was to Darius on both of his trips to New York, but as he well knew love and lust were about the only emotions that heeded no danger, but the sheer thought of Safi and Yvetta travelling to Australia, as the Americans liked to say, freaked him out! Darius had been back in Sydney two months since their last discussion.

What on earth could he say to dissuade any of them from making this trip? He could of course, come clean and tell them Fritzi was hiding out where they were going, but against his better judgement he did not want to, he wasn't sure why, but he felt protective towards Safi and, he did not want Gina to have a cloud hanging over her head, a Fritzi cloud was a very dark one, they were a newly married couple, it wouldn't be kind to give them all that anxiety to contend with, when they were so happy.

Safi wanted to visit her mother Fiona and brother Jake in Melbourne, and had every intention of doing business while in Australia. They intended to fly out to Sydney together, where they would meet with Darius to discuss the likelihood of putting on an Aboriginal art exhibition at Yvetta's gallery.

The very idea made him shiver: Yvetta and her wife, Gina, in Australia! And, for all he knew, in the same city as Fritzi, who had proven, over and over, that she would break international law and go to any lengths to get what she wanted? And what she wanted, still, always (if DuPont was correct in his suspicion) was Yvetta. God alone knew what Fritzi could do, out of jealousy, anger, and revenge, to Yvetta's wife. The three women were excited for the trip, looking forward to business opportunities, seeing the sites and experiencing a country that was unfamiliar to at least two of them, but DuPont saw only disaster ahead.

He had worried about it for days now, thinking through multiple angles and possibilities, many of them calamitous, at least a few even fatal. The smartest, most reasonable, least complicated solution he could come up with was to travel to Australia first. There, he would be able to gauge the level of danger for himself.

On his last visit to America, two months ago for Yvetta's wedding, Darius was hardly forthcoming about Fritzi's current state and, indeed, the status of his relationship with her. Darius hadn't exactly evaded any questions, but he hadn't answered them at length, either. In fact, DuPont (who knew much about the peculiarities of love, and even more about lust) got the sense that the Australian was hiding something, that he was perhaps in deeper with Fritzi than he would like to admit. Clearly, DuPont's warnings about Fritzi had not been heeded.

Fritzi was a master operator, unscrupulous and capable of breaking almost anyone. He had no doubt Darius had fallen under her spell (almost everyone did, at least at first). He couldn't blame Darius, either. Fritzi was a stunning woman, and a highly sexed one at that. DuPont had considerable experience in the subject of women – and sex, for that matter. A Frenchman, DuPont believed, could take one look at a woman and recognise her sensuality. Fritzi's was off the charts. So was her sociopathy, he thought, but that was another story. Her edginess and aura of recklessness and even danger made her more, not less, attractive. She had, he remembered with a sharpness that surprised him, a sensation of pleasurable pain, sensual charisma coming out of every pore. If she chose to seduce them, very few would be able to resist her charms – and very few did.

He pitied Darius, even as he understood his dilemma; he didn't even know how deep he was in it, and wouldn't until it was too late. Perhaps another personal warning could prevent a decent man from making the biggest mistake of his life. After all, after Yvetta's wedding and the shared car ride to and from it, the two men now knew each other far better, and DuPont may be in a better position to reason with Darius. It was worth a shot. The alternative was too terrible to think about, although think about it he did. With these thoughts in mind, he had his secretary find space in his diary to visit Australia after their summer season had ended and safely before Safi and Yvetta took their trip.

Once the bookings were confirmed, he would write to Darius to give him his date of arrival, and then implore him in person to step away from Fritzi. DuPont thought he owed such a warning to Darius – and to his own peace of mind. He had seen too many lives destroyed by Fritzi, and wasn't about to see her destroy one more. Especially not someone as upstanding and quick-thinking as Darius.

But quick-thinking, intelligent men, DuPont reflected, were stupid in love, like everyone else. Love did that, it levelled people and was democratic in its way: from kitchen staff to kings, love made fools of us all. It was, therefore, superficially, better never to fall in love. But never to fall in love was a fate worse than death. So, either way, you lost – or won, depending on how you looked at it. Being French, DuPont always, always sided with love, no matter how reckless or insensible. Insensibility, he thought, was overrated, even delicious – but now if it was going to cost you your life. At some point, even the most adventurous person had to draw the line. The line was here, DuPont now thought, it was now, it was in Australia, and it needed to be drawn between Darius and Fritzi, drawn in the sharpest, most indelible way, drawn forever.

How he wished that evil woman was still in jail. He imagined she had seduced her captors somehow. Prison guards were fools for love, too – or, at least hungry for money. DuPont, in his many years in New York and Europe, with his many notches on his many expensive belts, thought he had seen it all – but Fritzi, with her ingenuity and her cunning, always, always surprised him. In a weird way, he respected her. Still, he feared and detested her like no one else. There was no way in hell he would allow her to enter his life again. He would do anything to prevent that.

DuPont had travelled the world, visited so many countries he had lost count (more notches on more belts), but oddly he had never had an interest in visiting Australia. It was just too far – or (culturally) not quite far enough. He had heard amazing things about Australia, of course, but life was short and there were many amazing places, many amazing things. So he, too, had drawn the line – until now, at least. Down Under had never held much allure, all those jumping kangaroos, odd-looking creatures (he much preferred women to animals, the city to the bush, a long meal at a good restaurant with expensive wine to a night in a tent under the stars somewhere) and dangerous spiders gave him the shivers (despite his bravura, he was jittery and neurotic in some ways; a Frenchman through and through), not to mention crocodiles.

He had read more than a few accounts of horrific tourist incidents. He thought it much safer and more pleasant to be in Europe or the States, where one only had guns or terrorists, or rats to worry about. But he would travel urban Australia, the two big cities, which, from what he had heard, weren't very much different from western Europe. He would opt for only city tours, where the closest thing to danger would be coming face to face with Fritzi … a dreaded thought, worse than any amount, of spiders or crocodiles.

It was now time to alert Darius to his trip, and ensure he would be in Australia at that time. Looking up the time zones, DuPont realised he had 11hrs of day time to figure out when to call during the 15hr difference between Sydney and New York. He was regretting his decision to fly over already; how on earth was he going to get over his jetlag. No, it was surely not worth travelling all that way to meet with someone who probably wouldn't listen to your heartfelt advice. He resolved to email Darius instead. It was a pity: he would have preferred to speak to the young man, and Australia's by all accounts attractive cities had even begun to appeal to him. Another time, perhaps.

DuPont met the two D's and the newly married Yvetta and Gina for brunch. The newlyweds were waxing lyrical about Safi's idea for a Australian trip. It would make a perfect working holiday. Thank goodness Gina wasn't working for him any longer, his offices would have come to a standstill with everyone away. DuPont was relieved to learn that Dax, at least, refused to consider making the trip. Neither of the two D's would leave their little Raquel for that long. As for bringing the child along … a trip of that duration would be a nightmare for one so young, and, indeed, a nightmare for her parents as well.

DuPont thought that Dax had a point: it was madness to sit on an aircraft for hours. Flying to France twice a year was bad enough at his age. DuPont couldn't believe Safi and the others would have to fly to LAX and then catch a connecting flight directly to Sydney. One flight lasted six hours, and the other fifteen hours. The mere thought made him feel ill. Again, he had the urge to cancel the trip. What was the purpose of the trip to Australia, really? Had he been crazy to pursue the idea this far?

His secretary, Helene, Gina's replacement, tried her best to humour and placate him with thoughts of catching up on movies he intended to see but never quite found the time. 'Well,' DuPont told Helene, 'I can certainly think of better ways to spend my time, but the trip is booked now. I will visit my doctor for a check-up before I go; he might be able to give me some sleeping potion.'

'Great,' Helene said, now used to DuPont after eight months as his personal secretary, and his surprising array of anxieties and second thoughts, 'get him to check you out.'

As she said it, she checked him out, with her eyes, herself: DuPont was in his senior years, certainly, but he was still handsome, still charming, incredibly so. If circumstances were different and he wasn't her boss… No, she put it out of her mind and smiled a little too broadly.

'I hear thrombosis on long flights are a danger. Some of those medical support hose might not be a bad idea.' Helene giggled to herself at the thought of the debonair DuPont in elasticated support stockings under his personal tailored French trousers.

He put his head in his hands, feeling a sharp and sudden pang, perish the thought, support hose was a step to far. This was getting worse by the moment. He knew it was a bad idea the minute he had booked those flights. Why had he gone through with it? For Yvetta? For Darius? For himself? Right, now he could think of nothing, his mind – not unpleasantly – blank.

Darius had mailed back that he would be in Sydney on DuPont's designated dates and was excited about the visit. He had already arranged for DuPont to meet with all the top movers and shakers in the art world. He also wondered whether DuPont would consider a trip to Tasmania; he had sent him the link to the website of Mona.

DuPont distracted himself from his anxieties by viewing the photos of Mona and reading David Walsh's biography. It made fascinating reading, and he was beginning to feel more positive – even excited – about the trip again. Mona was a place he would love to exhibit the work of Dax and his other artists. The building appeared an awesome endeavour, and certainly worth a visit.

He mailed Darius right back about meeting Walsh. Putting Fritzi aside, this excursion would make his trip almost bearable.

Since his conversations with Darius at Yvetta's wedding, DuPont had felt uneasy. He regretted his openness about Fritzi. Perhaps he had said too much – or perhaps he hadn't said enough. The anger, he realised, was still very raw, not only for him but for his dear, dear friend Safi.

She had lost her husband and father Leonard in the same year. Fiona had sold the business and moved to Melbourne to be closer to her son. Safi understood her mother's reluctance to live in America. Fiona had friends in Melbourne, and a younger sister, so the move made sense, but it added to her feelings of loss.

Fritzi was not the cause of Sasha's death. No one could pin her down directly, but indirectly DuPont blamed her all the same. She had caused six months of hell for the whole family when the gun she fired hit Sasha, almost paralyzing him for life. During that long, lonely, traumatic time, Yvetta was a silver lining while her brother was bedridden. She had made peace with Safi, finally developed a relationship with Safi's two children, her nephew and niece, and had sat at Sasha's bedside his daily during his convalescence. Their mother Anna had moved from Cannes to New York to help. At last, through great tragedy, the Rubicov family pulled together, giving Safi support at a very dark period in her young life.

After the Rubicov patriarch, Alexi, and son Sasha's death, the Rubicov empire – still enormous in its global reach and profits – was run by the extended family. All decisions were passed onto Mika, the older brother and now de facto head of the Rubicov organisation. DuPont believed Mika would, without a doubt, have Fritzi taken out if he knew where she was. She had been the cause of his father's heart attack, and, Sasha's kidnapping and the family's resultant panic and pain, sped up his death. Yvetta was a problem the entire Rubicov family came together to deal with, the best way they knew how, but they were thwarted at every turn by Fritzi.

With the help of Janus's intelligence agency, Mika had been responsible for her capture. Knowing Fritzi was out there free, to cause more harm and even attack the Rubicov family again, perhaps still obsessed over Yvetta, would not wash with Mika. Mika was nothing if not a man of action. DuPont had a difficult decision to make: would he let Mika know Fritzi's whereabouts once he was sure of his facts? It was something he would have to consider.

DuPont owed the Rubicov family a great deal; they had been loyal friends and had made him a very wealthy man. And Safi remained one of his closest friends in New York, someone dear to his heart, almost a surrogate daughter. When he heard about Fritzi in Australia, without a care in the world, travelling about freely and enjoying her life, meeting (and, no doubt, manipulating) everyone she came into contact with, never properly punished for the hell she had wrought, DuPont became intensely angry.

Fritzi, he believed, did not deserve to have a life of freedom. She had ruined others' lives, and yet she was somehow free, thriving (if what Darius said was true), without a care in the world for the harm she had caused, very much living in the now and with a healthy distance from the lives she had destroyed. Even in an obviously unfair world, where money could buy freedom and crime paid, this upset DuPont more than he cared to say. He had lost sleep over Fritzi and what she had done to the Rubicov family and his friends – and, indeed, to him, too. She had tried (unsuccessfully, thank God) to destroy his reputation, too. Did she feel guilty at all? Did she feel anything? Or was guilt immune to her, was she a sick sociopath to her core? Perhaps she was more sensitive now, perhaps she had changed.

DuPont believed in the capacity of self-improvement, and believed in second chances, too. But somehow with Fritzi it was different. He had never loathed or feared anyone as he did her. And he felt personally responsible now, after receiving Darius' information, which made everything more complicated. Unlike Fritzi, he did have a heart, he did have a conscience, he did care. He had to stop her from harming anyone else with her lies and duplicity. Just because she was in a new continent did not mean she would instantly become a new person, no matter how generous and forgiving Australians may be. More than likely, at some point, sooner rather than later, she would be up to her old tricks – and everyone would suffer as a result. As long as he lived, he thought, he would make sure that her evil behaviour would someday catch up with her. How he would do this he did not yet know.

It pained him that he could not warn the Rubicovs about Fritzi. It would take just one telephone call, one conversation, just a few words ('Fritzi is back'), but somehow, he could not bring himself to do it. After a long period of angst and pain, the Rubicov family were finally settled, moving forward with their lives at last, happy even. He did not want to bring that dark cloud back into their lives, to turn everything upside down. Telling Mika (who was always the most pragmatic, and also the family member DuPont was least friendly with; their relationship had always been primarily business) was his only real option. Or he could tell the stoic Janus, but no, Janus was too close to his wife, the wonderful but still fragile Safi. DuPont decided he would not take them into his confidence just yet, not before he was sure of his facts and got a chance to investigate for himself. And there was reason to be hopeful. After all, Australia was a huge country, hopefully Fritzi would be elsewhere when they made their trip over Christmas and New Year.

Walking home from the office, the streets slanted with the beginning of evening, fall still strong in the crisp, warm air, DuPont reminisced about his past. His wife had never taken to New York or his career here, and they had lived their separate lives, which suited him well. They only had one daughter, and she was now settled with her own family in Lyon. He had mistresses from time to time, certainly, and enjoyed the good life always, but old age had made him selfish and he was set in his ways. Art had always been his life, his first and true love, and he felt sure that it would continue until the day he died.

His wife and daughter wanted him to move back to France to grow old with his grandchildren around him, but that was DuPont's idea of hell. He did not see himself as an old man ready to be taken for granted, almost ready for the grave. No, thank you, he wouldn't move back while he still had his wits about him, that was for sure. He loved his independence, his life, in New York. This sprawling, massive, cosmopolitan city kept him young – but still old enough to know better. Manhattan was part of him, a part of him that was large and vital (like the city itself), a part of himself he was proud of.

After all, he had been in Manhattan far longer than he had lived in Paris, and the city had been kinder to him, and perhaps him to it. Here, he knew everyone who was anyone in the art world. He had a full life and was widely respected; even at his dotage he was still a force to be reckoned with. Seventy-eight these days was young, not that he looked his age. Indeed, he was still able to turn a head or two, and charmed the odd young thing (each generation seemingly prettier than the one before), much to his delight – but that was about all.

In spite of himself, he thought often and with much enjoyment about the dalliance with Safi all those years ago – ooh la la, what a beauty she was. (Well, that was not a surprise; she was extremely beautiful still, and had aged with her characteristic grace.) The affair had been totally out of character on her part, but he never said no to good sex, and when it ended, they had remained good friends. She was one in a million and he would do anything to keep her out of harm's way. A more, loyal and kind person of Safi's calibre was hard to find today, he would rather die than see her hurt again, that was the truth, he loved that girl.

Still ruminating on his decision, going back and forth and in crazy semi-circles in his still overactive brain, he now knew without a doubt he was doing the right thing by travelling to Australia. He had to make sure Fritzi remained as far away from the Rubicovs as possible.

It was dark by the time he returned home. When young his days seemed endless, now he wondered where the time had gone.

Reading and clearing the correspondence in his inbox and glancing at the Sydney papers online (something he had started doing a few weeks ago, and which had quickly become a habit to familiarise himself with current news stories and the country at large), his eyes fell on an article. He read it through, not even skimming like he usually did. Then he looked at it again, this time more closely, every word. He had to reread the article several times to be sure he wasn't hallucinating.

It was not a major story, certainly (to the best of his knowledge, it had not appeared in the international press), but it was certainly a headliner.

The son of Australia's prime minister, a human rights lawyer and an estimable citizen in his own right, had been saved in the recent New Zealand earthquake by a tourist from Europe. That was interesting on its own, but there was something else here – something that had made him take a closer look. The tourist, a woman, had put her own life on the line for not only the son of the prime minister, but other victims of the quake as well.

The article said that this unidentified woman had (according to the many survivors she had rescued, resuscitated, and cared for on the site) worked tirelessly without any thought for her own safety. The article went on to state that the tourist's name could not be revealed due to an application pending for citizenship in Australia.

'It has been revealed that letters of thanks from the Prime Minister of New Zealand and the Mayor of Christchurch have been sent through diplomatic channels to the Australian department of immigration,' the article noted. 'We wish the young lady in question the best of luck with her application. Given her heroic actions on the day of the quake, she would certainly be a great asset to this country now and in the future.'

DuPont sat back in his favourite chair, flabbergasted, most of his reflections from his evening walk wiped clean from his mind. The unidentified woman in the article could not possibly be Fritzi. If it was, the Australian media and the diplomatic services (to say nothing of, potentially, the immigration department) were giving high praise and commendation to a criminal, a sociopath, an outright and irredeemable scoundrel.

Darius had informed DuPont of her bravery during the Christchurch earthquake and he had given it short shift. It had seemed so unlike the Fritzi he knew and detested, and he did not want to alter his negative opinion of her, not one bit. Now, he viewed even her actions after the quake with suspicion. She was no hero at all; the opposite, in fact. She had excelled even his expectations of duplicity and fraud by reinventing herself. It would be almost impossible to debunk the media's widespread high praise, but by God he would give it his best try when he saw Darius and met the Prime Minister's son, he would request a meeting, with Darius's help, to enlighten the man Fritzi saved, who he was in return trying to help, through misplaced feelings of gratitude!

DuPont printed out the article and put it in his safe. It would be evidence to hand over to Mika when the time came to involve them. There were, he saw in a quick Google search, many other articles, much more acclaim for the unidentified hero of the quake. It made him sick to his stomach.

DuPont was not sure how he would broach the subject of Fritzi when out in Australia. It was not going to be easy to persuade people who thought she was a paragon of virtue that she was, in fact, a fraud – and worse. Someone who would not save your life, but quite possibly destroy it.

If the Australian authorities were in possession of the file Darius had shown him about Fritzi's life and had excused her behaviour by virtue of her bravery on the day of the quake, when she put the lives of others before her own, it would be almost impossible to have them see her any other way, DuPont realised.

If the accounts were true, she had done something selfless, he had to admit (and it pained him to do so), yet she was also capable of treacherous behaviour still. He doubted Fritzi would ever truly change.

He would have to think this through carefully. When he arrived in Australia and met with Darius, he did not want to alienate his new friend, or anyone else for that matter. Now he knew one thing for sure. He needed to get his facts straight about Fritzi before he set Mika and the Russians on a collision path with her.

DuPont needed confirmation, and the only person he knew who it was safe to speak with was his old friend Jacques.

They met at an old favourite uptown: a French brasserie they had both long frequented. DuPont was fond of bringing French acquaintances, new to New York, here for one drink that inevitably turned into many. Jacques was a dear friend from college days, and one of his oldest clients. Jacques had a particular fondness for lithographs and prints on the art-deco period. Besides the Picasso prints and Miro lithographs, he was also an avid collector of African art. His beautiful apartment on the Upper East Side was filled, in almost equal measure, with his love of books and art.

Jacques arrived to find DuPont at their usual table, accompanied (also, as usual) with a bottle of rosé on ice, light and sparkly, perfect for a fall heatwave. A heavy French red gave DuPont a headache, and there were too many sparkling Californian Chardonnays on offer to consider any of them, without also getting a headache in the process.

Jacques breezed in and (as usual) didn't waste time looking over the menu, which was comfortably familiar to both of them. They both ordered favourites and, after exchanging pleasantries, settled down to discuss DuPont's upcoming trip to Australia. This conversation quickly evolved into a discussion about what DuPont had read and heard about Fritzi, and how it may impact the Rubicov family's visit to Oz, as well as his own planned trip to try and pre-empt or avoid any unpleasant surprises.

Jacques understood his predicament. He made understanding sounds from time to time, but mostly he listened. DuPont's dilemma was a tricky one, for sure. He knew DuPont needed another ear, and he had always been happy to lend his friend that courtesy. DuPont, he knew too, was emotionally far more complex than many suspected. Like Fritzi, he, too, was fond of putting on a front of sorts, in his case that of the urbane, articulate, charming Frenchman. The two men had known each other a long time and had, from time to time, shared many years of family ups and downs, confided in each other about infidelities, business problems, and emotional episodes that were unknown to anyone else. For this reason, Jacques was only too familiar with DuPont's feelings for Safi, a very beautiful young English woman and one who had been threatened by Fritzi on multiple occasions.

Jacques did not think that DuPont could do much to change the situation in Australia, apart from insisting that Fritzi be thousands of miles away when the Rubicovs visited. More than that, Jacques told his friend, was unlikely at this juncture. Jacques said that if DuPont had an opportunity to meet with the Prime Minister's son, he should listen carefully to his point of view on Fritzi, and to his experience being saved by her. The Australians were clearly convinced that Fritzi was a very different person than DuPont knew her to be.

DuPont was rightly sceptical, of course. Still, he was pleased to have another opinion, and promised he would report back to Jacques on his return, He also confided in Jacques his idea about informing Mika about Fritzi's whereabouts, and the news about her possible immigration status.

'I am not sure you – or, for that matter, Mika – could legally manage to do anything once Fritzi becomes a bona fide citizen of Australia,' Jacques said. 'And the article you showed me, certainly seems to indicate that she will shortly become one.'

'Legally, probably not,' DuPont replied. 'But Mika doesn't always do things legally.'

'I see,' Jacques said simply, unsurprised, raising his glass.

'But,' DuPont continued, raising his glass too, 'I too think there is not much that can be done at this point. For that reason, I believe my best course of action is to try and prevent any further distress or harm befalling any of my dear friends.'

Together they finished the last of the rosé. It was DuPont's turn to pay. DuPont left the restaurant more confident than when he entered, but still could not shake the foreboding he felt about being on the same continent as that crazy woman. Was this upcoming trip a huge mistake? Almost certainly, but it was too late now to change his mind. For Safi, for Yvetta, for Sasha, he had to make the trip – he knew that much.

Chapter 16

Although his heart would always be in Russia, Mika had grown used to his life in America. After all, it was hard to complain too much when you lived in a palatial mansion in Florida. The family had successfully extricated most of their assets out of Russia and had reinvested in the West, refashioning themselves in the process. The Rubicov restaurants in St Petersburg and Moscow were their only link left to Mother Russia. This helped to smooth over any bad feelings with the authorities, who continued to receive, of course, a healthy kickback.

Mika still had dealings with his close associates in Russia, and his finger was kept very much on the pulse. The extended family on both Anna and Alexi's side ran the restaurants; they loved their mother country enough to put up with small inconveniences that arose from time to time, mostly from unsavoury henchmen working for the government. Loyalty never came into negotiations, but money spoke volumes, and that was a small price to pay for a continued presence in Russia.

To honour his father's memory, the family gave generously to religious charities in Moscow, to feed and help the older generation who were floundering under the new freedoms and a resurgence of some of the same old problems that had haunted Russia for centuries. The old social infrastructures were no longer in place, and the elderly needed whatever help they could get, especially food. The synagogues and churches provided these people with private donations.

When back in Russia, Alexi visited both the synagogue and the Orthodox church; he was a tartar and believed he was half Jewish. The Jewish community had a vibrant and active social life in Russia where ever a synagogue was being kept active, as long as the right palms were greased, they were left alone, but still kept security tight. many attended Friday night prayers and, the Sabbath dinners hosted by the synagogues after, for the community. Alexi encouraged his family to attend on occasion. After the family left Russia, they continued to give generously to support the community in Moscow, which fed and looked after many of the elderly.

Mika had spread the family assets far and wide, never missing a chance to invest in new ventures in the Far East, South East Asia, or in

India. They had built hotels and high rises and were happy to be part of new infrastructure that needed financing.

Mika's mother, Anna, had handed over the mantel, and Mika had taken full advantage of his powers. His father, Alexi, had never made a move without consulting Mika, the most business-minded and hard-headed of his two sons, and Mika now found that without Sasha or his mother to consult, his only alternative was to trust outsiders. That outsider had become Janus, Safi's second husband. Sasha, Mika's younger brother and Safi's first husband, had trusted Janus implicitly, and Safi had remained a loyal wife while Sasha had been alive. When Safi married Janus sometime after Sasha died, Mika had had no bad feelings towards his sister-in-law. Safi had suffered a great deal; she now deserved a good and untroubled life. Indeed, Safi was one of the most loyal outsiders Mika and the rest of the Rubicov's had taken to their hearts. His brother Sasha had been right about Safi, who had been barely eighteen when they first met, all along, Safi had shown time and again where her loyalties were and – even in the face of his Sasha's indiscretions from time to time, and long periods of considerable anguish and adversity.

Even after Sasha's kidnapping and Yvetta's (Mika and Sasha's sister) violent attack on Safi, the no-longer-young British lass had steadfastly and unwaveringly supported the family, remaining faithful to Sasha after his release from a Russian jail and eventual return. To Mika's amazement, Janus had not fought for Safi once she had made up her mind to return to Sasha, but instead had remained a loyal and loving, faithful friend. Indeed, next to Safi, Janus was the most loyal person Mika knew. On Sasha's death, Janus had supported the family in their time of grief. In her own time and after months of grieving Sasha, Safi had returned Janus's love, and the Rubicov family blessed the union. Now Mika considered Safi and Janus to be honouree family, tied to the Rubicov family through Sasha's two children.

Although a successful artist in his free time, Janus had made his fortune in the intelligence community. He had owned a successful surveillance technology company, and he had done intelligence work in Russia, where Mika had first come into contact with him. Mika and Janus had much in common and had become firm friends over many years, working on various cases together. It was Janus who had helped Mika free Sasha, and track down Fritzi.

Despite Mika's old-fashioned, hard-earned Russian values, living in America had mellowed him considerably. In fact, there was much to celebrate of late. Yvetta had remarkably turned a corner; Mika was the first to recognise the change in her unpredictable nature, from manic states to one of calmness and stability. Like all the Rubicovs, Yvetta had a strong work ethic, and with her lifelong passion for art she had excelled with her new Rubicov gallery in Brooklyn. Mika's support financially and fraternally was pure; she now had his complete trust.

Due to Yvetta's anger and jealousy over the years, Safi, had suffered the most, and her subsequent forgiveness was to be admired. Now married and settled and the Rubicov empire thriving, Mika had little to worry about any longer where the family were concerned. Still, he wished his father was alive to witness Yvetta's success and change, and to see how she had embraced the family once more. Admittedly, old-fashioned, conservative Alexi would have found his daughter marrying another woman hard to understand, but like Mika, Alexi was at heart a pragmatist, and knew that social change was constant, that nothing ever remained the same. Yesterday's opinions were today's taboos (and vice versa). Look at the formerly glorified Communist party and its propaganda machine that never seemed to end – until it ended, absolutely, in 1991

Mika had a long-term partner now, Daniella, an American who was twenty years his junior, but he liked it that way. He had no intentions of marrying or having a family. His life was devoted to work, and to having a good time when he wasn't working. Daniella suited his lifestyle; they dined lavishly and entertained on a grand scale. She was tall and long-limbed, enhanced with a little help (all of this cost money, too, of course), but, more to the point, as far as he was concerned, she had a softness about her that, he thought, counteracted his harder, more pragmatic business side.

She was sweet in nature, and he preferred that. He didn't have time for any of that feminist bullshit; he liked his women to enjoy life, go shopping, and come home to him, he had to be the centre of their lives, and Daniella did all those things. She loved cars and fashion, and he saw to it that she had whatever she desired. There was no limit to her budget; when she looked good, he reasoned, so did he.

What Daniella did in her own time was okay with him and she certainly kept busy. Over the five years he had encouraged her to become involved in charities, and to build a social circle that suited their standing. Now she attended meetings to plan fundraisers, played tennis three times a week, and participated heartily in all of the activities available to women of means. This suited Mika perfectly. As a Russian émigré in Florida high society, many doors were not immediately open to him; now, with Daniella by his side and in his life, they were. He was generous with his donations.

Daniella came from a wealthy professional family herself, and he got on with her parents, who had not accepted him at the beginning, although things had got easier when they realised, he adored and was capable of endlessly spoiling their only daughter. The only bone of contention with Daniella and her parents was Mika's determination never to marry. To get over this hurdle, and being nothing if not a severely and famously practical man, Mika knew that sooner or later he would have to come through for Daniella and her family in some way, though what that way was he did not yet know. They needed to know that Daniella was not going to be left on the shelf for a younger model.

He had his lawyers draw up a legal document which left Daniella with a substantial sum if he ended the relationship. If she left him, it would be a lesser sum, but she would not leave emptyhanded.

After that, they both felt more secure, and the relationship flourished. He believed that Daniella loved him, and that was enough for Mika.

Being the oldest son to Anna and Alexi, in what was soon to become an empire, meant that Mika grew up to be the family trouble-shooter, taking over the running of Rubicov Industries even before Alexi's death. Sasha was born after perestroika, at which point the Rubicovs were well on their way financially in the new Russia. From there, the family industry and its attendant fortune went global and sky-high.

Mika, on the other hand, was born in Soviet Russia to barely adult parents who worked day and night to support their first child in impoverished circumstances. By the time Sasha and Yvetta were born, Russia had changed absolutely, the business was thriving, and Mika had left home, already an adult. Unlike his siblings he was educated at college in Russia, after which he automatically went straight into his family's business, becoming his father's right-hand man.

Life had thrown the Rubicov family many curveballs, yet through all of the upheavals and disappointments, despite anguish and significant pain, they were still a family, forging ahead with a new generation that would carry the Rubicov mantel forward, to even greater success. And, after the dark times, Mika envisioned only happiness ahead – for everyone in both the immediate and extended family.

Alexi's heart attack and Sasha's kidnapping, was a dark period in an otherwise enlightened time for the family; they were out of Russia, living a comfortable life in Europe and America, yet the most unlikely of dark shadows hovered over them in the form of a slip of a girl from East Germany, who went by the name of Fritzi (among many other names and aliases). She had attempted to destroy his family (not once, but over and over), and done a damn good job of it. Worst of all, she had shot Sasha, precipitating his death sometime later. In business and in his life, Mika had met many people that he disliked, but none he detested like he did Fritzi. She was pure evil, he thought. It had taken his sister, Yvetta, years to heal from her poisonous spell, to become her own person once again.

Mika had sworn to himself and to others in his family that if he ever found Fritzi, he would mete out the harshest punishment he could devise. Death would not be too cruel for her – indeed, it may not be cruel enough.

Mika had many contacts around the world. It had recently come to his attention that Fritzi was roaming the globe, a free spirit, living large once again, without a care in the world. In a way, her ingenuity was impressive; nothing seemed to stop her for long. For example, escaping a Russian jail was almost unheard of, an impossibility, yet she had managed it. No one knew how or why, but she had freed herself, or, more than likely, manipulated someone to free her.

He didn't like to think about Fritzi, but think about her he did, all the time. He reflected on how she had turned up in the States to cause havoc in their lives, and untold suffering for Sasha, who almost died of his wounds after being shot by her. All Mika's efforts to run her down after her attack on his family in New York had come to nothing. Mika had an infinite amount of resources, the best intelligence agents in the world at his disposal, and still he couldn't find her. Her, a slip of a girl, a near-nothing who had come close to destroying his family empire, the life of his parents and two of his siblings.

Mika's close associate Kolya had gone over the Mexican border with some of his men, in order to follow a lead into Central and South America, where Fritzi had reportedly been seen. But Kolya had come back emptyhanded; Fritzi, if she had been in the area at all, had once more disappeared into thin air. He had a watch out on Fritzi, to keep him informed if anyone meeting her description was sighted.

Kolya had been given another lead by one of his people in the field.

Looking again at the printout on his desk, Mika felt vindicated. Fritzi had been tracked her down to a small island called Bali, but since then she had once more vanished. Time would be on his side, he thought. He had no doubt that she would turn up like a bad penny eventually. And that day would be sweet for Mika and for the entire Rubicov clan; she would not be given another chance to harm his family.

Kolya would be dispatched to do his job and would be in and out of the country before anyone was any the wiser; that was how Kolya had always done things, quick, clean, and above all professionally.

Mika resolved to discuss details with Janus, and together they would with precision take her out.

Chapter 17

That Monday morning Fritzi returned to Sydney with Darius, for a meeting with Jared alone, who had, in the intervening weeks, discussed her case with human rights lawyers who could give impartial opinions on the matter. The Interpol dossiers on Fritzi Darius had submitted to Jared, and experts Jared had reviewing the case, and human rights lawyers had doubts about her chances to become an Australian citizen.

Jared was not one to give up on a client, especially not on Fritzi, who had saved his life – and who, he now had no doubt, was a different person than she had been in the past, utterly rehabilitated and unidentifiable from the Fritzi described in the dossier at such length and in such alarming terms ('dangerous,' 'cunning,' 'criminal,' 'almost endlessly deceptive,' 'possibly sociopathic'). Several days before Missy's fashion show, he had flown to Canberra to speak to a member of parliament in the strictest confidence. Jared's great hope was that this person, after interviewing Fritzi in person, would be able to make the final decision on her application to remain in the country.

Fritzi sat opposite Jared in his pristine and characteristically impressive (but not showy or pretentious) office. The office, with its neat rows of impressive- and identical-looking legal volumes, soft décor, and stylish, black-and-white photographs of urban and rural Australian cultural sites, would make anyone – from a penniless illegal immigrant to a high-powered politician – feel instantly at home. And as Jared leaned forward, smiling at her, Fritzi felt at home, too. Yes, she thought, Australia can be home. But would it?

Indeed, it was not his usual, casual, boyish, thoroughly authentic smile, but something she had not seen on his face before. A forced and perhaps fake smile, a smile of courtesy and convenience that he probably gave to all of his clients before commencing a legal meeting. A smile that signified nothing – or perhaps something, but something wrong. A worrying and worried smile. A smile that perhaps indicated news ahead that was not exactly favourable or especially easy to deliver.

As his smile waned and she saw fatigue and perhaps even anxiety under his warm blue eyes, Fritzi felt a cold shiver run up her spine. Even hours ago she had still felt elated from the fashion show, the rush of being on the catwalk again, the adulation of the crowd. But now that had gone, replaced by trepidation and angst. The comedown from the catwalk to Jared's office was so sudden and drastic, she felt as if she had fallen down a flight of stairs. She could read the atmosphere in a room – even in a room as bright and artful as this one – and now had the distinct impression things were not progressing in her favour. Despite the forced and uneasy smile, Jared's stern manner and facial expression as she entered was easy to read, but there was something else she could not put her finger on, That something, whatever it was, was hovering somewhere in the ether, warning her to be careful.

Fritzi expected that Jared, to whom time was valuable, would commence speaking immediately, as he usually did, but this morning was evidently different. He was silent, as though assessing her now, back in Sydney after weeks in Byron Bay and the success of his cousin's fashion show. She felt extremely uneasy and wondered if he could see her hands, which were shaking slightly in her lap.

Jared sat for a while, staring at Fritzi, his fingers peaked in a pyramid in front of his face.

'Now don't look so crestfallen,' he said after what felt like an inordinately lengthy amount of time had passed, 'we are still in with a chance.' But his voice sounded flat. She lifted a shaking finger and said,

'What do you mean a chance?' She had to check her voice, in case her anger was apparent – after all, Jared had done everything in his power to help her and could not be blamed – but it was possibly too late. His smile was now positively gone, and he looked a little hurt, or nervous, perhaps. 'When we last spoke you were positively upbeat about my chances.'

'I didn't say I was positively upbeat,' Jared said. 'I just said …' But he stopped there.

Hesitantly, he opened the file on the desk and turned it about for Fritzi to read. She glanced at it, but did not attempt to pull it closer.

'Fritzi, I have arranged an interview with a member of my father's government. I had to call in a few favours to do so.' His voice was as severe as she had ever heard it. 'You must understand that if he feels for any reason we cannot proceed, there is nothing more I can do to help.

The document I have asked you to read is a series of questions; it would be prudent to answer all of them honestly.' He tried, not entirely successfully, to soften his voice. 'I will help you through the process. There will be time to expand on the answers at the interview, you understand?'

She nodded, her anxiety nowhere near abated. He was looking at her keenly again, and not in an admiring manner. She thought back to how he had looked at her just a few days ago, at the fashion show, with ravishing eyes and his full attention. That seemed a lifetime ago. Everything was different now.

'It is still your call to go ahead with any of this,' he continued. 'As we discussed, you can remain here, without a problem, until your visitor's visa is up, and then leave.'

She looked away from him all of a sudden, downhearted, wishing (for the first time since she had arrived in Australia) that she was somewhere, anywhere, else. She felt his uneasiness and it made her want to cry. She didn't have a fallback plan, or any other options. Certainly, she was good at thinking on her feet and coming up with a plan, but she was also tired of living that way. She had hoped that Australia would finally be her path to a stable life. Perhaps she had been wrong all along. Rather than her final destination, Australia had been another step in an endless game of evading the authorities, running from the law, and running – she realised now – from herself as well.

'Do I have to fill that in here,' she said, touching the document between them, 'or can I take it away with me and then return it to you? That would give me some time to think about what to do, and the best way to progress. I would also have to think about where I would go next, you understand. I will have to rethink my future.'

Secretly, she hoped that the prospect of losing Fritzi would frighten Jared, and she hoped to see signs of this on his face. But he only looked tired and he shook his head and said, 'Sadly, I do understand, and yes you may take the this with you, absolutely.'

He was sad, she realised suddenly, without a doubt, and frightened, too. He didn't want to lose her, and was fighting his fears about that. His cocky self-certainty, which had for so long been his trademark both as a lawyer and at school, was gone, absolutely wiped clean. He was silent again for a long moment, before saying,

'Our interview will be in Canberra on Friday. That means you have exactly four days to complete the form if we are going to go ahead with the application.'

'Is it worth even going ahead with this application?' she said.

'Yes,' he said, 'yes, I think it is.' But his voice had slipped once again into its slightly indifferent, professional tone, and she felt sadness as she stood, thanking Jared for all his help and work. She grabbed the form, tucked it under her arm, then turned abruptly and left, closing the door behind her before he could probe any further.

Jared realised Fritzi was shaken and disappointed. He called Darius on his cell phone. The two men needed to bolster her morale, and together they could work out where she could go if the interview did not go well.

Fritzi rode down in the lift alone. She didn't feel anxious anymore. Instead, her mind was numb. Outside she made for the Ferry terminal, she needed to walk and the best place for that was along the beachfront. Now that she was back in Sydney she was staying with Darius. Was that, in retrospect, a bad idea? All she wanted now was to escape to Maggie again, to stay somewhere calm and unpressured, to think things through, to scheme and plan and worry in peace. She didn't want Darius's empty reassurances, or his barely stifled stress, or him second guessing the good work Jared was doing, or the forthcoming interview, or anything else.

Darius would be as anxious as she was, and she had felt Jared's disappointment in the office, too. He had been so lively and confident just days ago. He had clearly believed that, with the letters from the New Zealand authorities and her well-publicised and much-applauded heroism in Christchurch, she had citizenship in the bag. But Jared, Fritzi reflected, hadn't reckoned with just how complex and criminal much of her life had been. Her past was catching up with her, and no matter who or what she was, or how many identities she tried on and pretended to wear, like so many outfits at a fashion show, nothing and no one could erase that blot on her character now.

It was dusk when she finally walked into the flat, only to be surprised once again. She opened the door to be met by … Maggie, sitting on an overstuffed armchair, smiling broadly. And Jared was standing behind her, giving her his old, warm, intimate smile again. And, of course, Darius was there, too, kissing her on the cheek, as though he was the husband she had just come home to after a long day at work. She wasn't used to people being concerned for her welfare, and now she felt overcome with emotion, and gratitude, which was largely unfamiliar to her but felt wonderful nonetheless. She felt – it took her a moment to find the right word – loved. Maggie forever the mother hen, shot up out of her seat and moved towards Fritzi. Taking Fritzi's hand, Maggie noted how dejected and dishevelled she appeared. So far removed from the supermodel on the catwalk in Byron Bay just days ago.

'Where have you been all this time?' Maggie asked in a voice of deep concern. 'You are frozen! But don't worry, I have a cure for that. My homemade minestrone will warm you up, I brought it with.'

Thank God for Maggie, Fritzi thought, a hero in her own right.

Fritzi knew how to fight for someone else, but felt at a complete loss when it came to fighting for herself. She had always preferred to run or to plan or to scheme or to work hard, put her head down and just get on with stuff, worry as little as possible (what good did worry ever do? if anything, she thought, worry was a sign of weakness, and weakness was the beginning of one's downfall), move forward and move fast.

This philosophy, tested and perfected over years, made the significant pain in her life recede, and she barely thought about loss and the many dark events that had marked out her life and set her on this path. Her father's unconscionable evil, the loss of her family, of her childhood friend, and the loss of Yvetta loomed large as she walked along the pier, the wind whipping at her hair. She couldn't run from the past anymore, it was everywhere today. It had found her even here, in Sydney.

And, in a way, she was done running. She had found peace here in Australia, and found people who believed in her – who believed she was good at heart and had what it took to be even better. She wanted to stay here, but her past was working against her. Worst of all, there was no one to blame but herself. What else could she do to turn her life around?

The answer did not come. She was tired of running, her head hurt from pure frustration; even her feet, that had run so often and so far (literally and figuratively) hurt sympathetically. She slowed down on the pier, breathed in the air. Even the air here was fresh and new, full of possibility. Not like the air in East Germany, in her childhood; even that had felt and smelled soiled, still heavy with the crimes of the past, as well as those of the present. The whole sorry history of humanity – and of herself. Yes, she thought, leaning over the pier and gazing across the ocean, she was done running. This was it. The end of the pier. The end of the line.

It all felt terribly unfair. She had been foolish enough to think she was free, and that too was an illusion, like so much else in her life. The illusions that she had created, the illusions created about and around her; the illusions she had invented in order to free herself, and the illusions others had oppressed her with, in order to imprison her, to keep her trapped, to keep her down. Things had felt so different these last few weeks – but now she could see it for what it was, a respite, a mirage, like a shadow on the water, perhaps even a cruel trick of the kind she herself had played on others in her life. It was so easy to say someone was easy, but less easy to live with that designation, that stigma and that shadow – and to overcome it, she now understood, was near impossible.

She had come so close – so close to belonging, really belonging, fitting in, making a difference even in a small way to those she had met and who appeared to love her unconditionally (something new for her) and who, yes, she too loved.

She breathed in that Australian air – raw but clean; optimistic, immigrant air – and tried to summon her optimism. This was a country, unlike any other, that was practically founded by criminals, that promised people from around the world a second chance, a better life. Wanted in both North America and Europe, familiar to both Interpol and Scotland Yard, Australia, far away from everything, truly the new world, was the perfect place for her. No, she decided, to hell with it, she had to stay, she had to somehow convince this man who was to interview her that she had changed, served her time, metaphorically speaking. Didn't they all agree that she deserved a break? Was she being a fool for beginning to believe it, too? Confused with the thoughts racing through her mind – impossible to control, ceaseless and frightening and wild – cold and hungry, she made her way back to the flat, where she was greeted by warmth and affection by Maggie, Jared and Darius.

Jared, Darius and Maggie waited nervously in the flat for Fritzi to return, after her meeting with Jared earlier that day. It had been two hours since she had left his office, and everyone was worried. They hoped she had not decided to run, and quietly discussed her problem.

Maggie said that she was prepared to be a character witness for Fritzi if Jared thought it would help.

Jared confided that, in the event that her application was rejected, the only other course of action to ensure that she remained in the country was for Fritzi to marry an Australian. But, Jared stressed, it wasn't quite as simple as that. Even if she married an Australian, she would still have to satisfy the authorities before she would be allowed to remain - still, it would be a less complex and vexing process than the one they were currently struggling with.

Of the three in the room, Darius spoke the least. He was at a loss for words. He, too, had thought that Fritzi's citizenship was in the bag. His feelings for her were intense, and increasing by the day. The mere thought of losing her gave him no small amount of pain. Could he live without Fritzi? Yes, of course. Did he want to? Absolutely not. He did not want her to leave Australia, but was he prepared to marry her?

He thought about it for a moment. The answer came to him with surprising ease, and felt right and good. Yes, absolutely, he would marry her – and there was another option he hadn't thought of up till now. If Fritzi had to leave, he would leave, too. If she wanted him, of course. He had his fortune and could live comfortably and anywhere – and he could always visit his family and friends in Australia. Still, he was careful not to share his thoughts with the others. For his part, Maggie noticed how Darius was unusually quiet, but decided not to embarrass him by address it. Jared seemed too preoccupied discussing Fritzi's situation to notice much of anything around him.

After an hour of waiting, the three of them stopped speaking. They had run out of options, of words, of energy. Instead, they waited for Fritzi, eager to comfort her and persuade her, with their help, to fill in the questions on the form, to comply with whatever was asked of her, and to boldly face the future, whatever that future held. Darius wanted to make Fritzi strong again – like the Fritzi he had met in Bali; it seemed like a lifetime ago now – to give her confidence to believe in her ability, her potential to do good and be better and to thrive, and to convince those with the powers to say yes to her new life in Australia – a life with him.

Maggie was practical and warm food and cold drinks were a help in moments of need.

Quietly letting out their breath in relief, after Fritzi's return, they sat around the kitchen counter watching Fritzi eat.

The scraping of chairs, soft breathing, and Jared drumming his hand on the side of the document as he read through the questions had them all on edge.

Eventually, he read them out loudly, one question at a time, and looked directly at Fritzi, indicating for the others to remain quiet.

'I do not know how they want me to answer those questions,' Fritzi said. 'Is there a special way I should do that?' asked Fritzi

'Yes,' Jared said.

'But they are so open-ended,' Fritzi protested. 'They could be answered in so many different ways, don't you agree?'

'Yes,' Jared said again.

Darius was looking angry and frustrated, but he kept his mouth shut. This was Jared's expertise, not his. Suddenly he began to doubt the very man he had placed so much trust in, in whose hands he had entrusted Fritzi's future – and, in a way, he now understood, Darius's own. He had thought Jared would do the best at ensuring Fritzi citizenship. Now, suddenly, he wasn't sure.

Maggie did not speak now, she simply looked encouraging, as if to say 'trust him, Fritzi, you need to learn to trust, it's your only option now.'

Fritzi read all of their expressions and decided to take action.

'Okay, I am ready. I will answer with the first thing that comes into my mind, and if it's wrong, please do not write, just question me until I get it right – or whatever you feel may be the right answer, or at least the answer that will best represent me and my case.'

She looked at the form properly for the first time. The first line asked her to state her full name and address.

'What address am I supposed to give?' she asked.

'Maggie's address would be good,' Jared said. Then, turning to Maggie, 'At least if that's alright with you, Maggie.'

'Of course.'

Fritzi wrote down, 'Frieda Maria Dietrich.' The next line said 'Country of Birth.'

'East Germany,' Fritzi wrote, followed by her date of birth, her age, her sex.

It was the next question that stumped her. 'Is there any reason you should not apply for citizenship?'

Fritzi looked lost.

'Yes,' she said, 'past criminal records.'

They all stared at Jared, but he wrote her answer.

'Excuse me,' Darius said slowly, indignation and confusion rising within him 'but surely that is not going to help her case to remain?'

'Darius, she has to answer these questions,' Jared said, 'and I believe honesty to be the best policy. If it's discovered that she's lied on this form, she won't have a chance.'

'Elaborate if the answer is yes.'

'Selling stolen artefacts,' Fritzi said.

'Okay,' Darius said slowly.

'Wait, I'm not finished,' Fritzi said. 'Accidently injuring someone. And kidnapping.'

No one spoke for a long while, and then Jared read,

'Why do you want to become an Australian citizen?'

'It has changed my life for the better and I love the country,' Fritzi said simply, feeling good for the first time in a while.

'Will you be able to support yourself? If your answer is yes, elaborate.'

'Yes, I am financially independent.'

'Would you contribute to Australia? If the answer is yes, elaborate.'

'I intend to devote myself to charitable work and fundraising.'

In all, they spent an hour on the questions. Some questions were impossible to answer, but Fritzi managed to dig deep to find answers that were both honest and inspiring.

It was well after midnight when Maggie and Jared closed the door to the apartment behind them, leaving a confused and frazzled Darius and an exhausted Fritzi.

Darius was angry, but did not want to show his true feelings about Fritzi's dwindling chances to remain in Australia. He did not want to upset Fritzi further, and would do anything to keep her safe. The answers were incriminating, he thought; barring a miracle, he could not in all honesty believe it possible that she would be awarded full citizenship.

He hoped the member of parliament she was seeing with Jared had the power and the foresight to give her a betting chance, at least.

Darius and Fritzi spent the following few days around Sydney, meeting Darius's friends and family.

His mother, to his amazement, took to Fritzi at once; they spent a good half-hour chatting when he left the room, and both were in fits of giggles when he returned.

It was no doubt at his expense, but he did not mind in the least; it was a welcome sight to see Fritzi laughing again. These were the two most important women in his life, he realised with a radiant feeling.

They flew to Canberra on Thursday evening. Jared had booked them into a hotel, while he would be staying at the prime minister's residence. They did not meet with Jared until the following morning, on the steps of a modern, low-slung building with a glass front overlooking a lake.

Darius sloped off to the bar, leaving Fritzi in Jared's safe hands, praying the meeting she was about to have would not ruin her chances of remaining in Australia.

The evening Jared had Fritzi answer the questionnaire showed what a long way she had come. There was not an ounce of subterfuge or duplicity in any of her answers; she took every question head-on. Some of the questions he would have balked at, but Fritzi had forged right on: it was, he believed, a testament to her character in the face of not only adversity, but almost certain failure to get what she now desired so much. He was sure that in the past she had never been able to accept this level of likely rejection, of probable failure. But now she had no choice. She was, indeed, a different person. It bothered Darius, too, that the man who would interview Fritzi, in whom they were all placing so much hope, did not know her the way he or Jared or Maggie did, and he would not understand the nuances of her situation. Still, Fritzi was adept at first impressions, and perhaps the interviewer's lack of intimate knowledge of her would work to her advantage. Darius hoped so.

She had laid her clothes out the night before (he had an image of the good little girl she had possibly been, in East Berlin, before Erica disappeared and everything went wrong in her world), and he watched as she went through her morning routine. At breakfast she had only had a coffee and, at his insistence, nibbled a croissant. Jared gave a nod of approval, and Darius had to agree that Fritzi had dressed perfectly for the occasion. Her hair was scraped off her forehead into a high ponytail. She wore a navy pinstripe suit, high waisted Oxford baggy pants, and a double breasted jacket, only Fritzi could carry off with her long legs and narrow elongated frame, all bought in Missy's boutique and, she paired it with a white T-shirt, LV bum bag slung low on her hips, with flat, pointed quilted navy and cream Chanel pumps. He knew exactly what (or who) she was wearing, because she had pointed it out to him, given him a short history of her outfit, including the LV bum bag, which contained her cell phone, credit card and lipstick. Jared, she hoped, had with him the documents containing her ticket to freedom, and would dissuade the authorities from kicking her out of the country.

And now it was finally time to present herself at the Canberra (ACT) Legislative Assembly a one hour and fifteen minute flight from Sydney, to state her case. She had been in front of a lot of authorities in her life – school principals, prison guards, police, criminal investigators – and mostly managed to keep cool. Today she was unusually uneasy, as if this interview was more important than all those other interrogations that had preceded it over the years. She tried to wipe fear from her mind, and relax her body; the mental equivalent of a yoga pose. She had lived her life with self-confidence (some would say altogether too much) and she wasn't going to change that now. She considered herself a better person than she had been in the past, but she maintained (and, she thought, would never lose) her self-respect.

With that thought in mind, she took a deep breath and entered a room not unlike the interview rooms she had been in on a number of occasions while in prison in various countries. Oddly, no matter which country you served time in, the bland rooms and hard stares were the same everywhere. Authoritarianism, institutional cruelty, and those deemed different (such as Erica) were shockingly similar – uniform, anonymous, intolerable – all over the world. Even in New York City, supposed bastion of freedom, the last place she was interrogated in a room just like this one. Breathing out, she stepped into the room to see a long wooden table with four chairs, two on either side, a bland, anonymous, officious, largely unwelcoming room. It wasn't entirely unwelcoming, though; unlike the other rooms where she had pled her case, this one contained, in the far left corner, a console with fresh coffee, still and sparkling water, fruit juices, biscuits, and numerous jars of candy on offer.

She had to remind herself that, unlike her previous meetings in rooms like these, she had not come as a criminal – not entirely, anyway. She was the hero who had saved the life of the prime minister's son, among other people (several of whom had been Australian citizens), she was, in a way, a guest of honour – but perhaps not for very long. Even the residency of a guest of honour had an expiration date. Another nice flourish that she noticed, a pot plant in the other corner of the room, in a clean white tub. Fritzi registered with an increasing sense of anxiety that Jared himself was unusually nervous. Instead of immediately taking a seat, he poured Fritzi some ice water and made them both, an espresso.

Not since the earthquake had she seen him so unrelaxed. She could tell he did not want her to detect his nervousness, and was doing anything he could to conceal it – unsuccessfully, of course. They sat at the table and neither spoke. Jared wasn't looking at her now, instead he glanced at the document he had placed on the desk, while occasionally taking joyless little sips of his espresso. She wondered whether he was especially nervous for her, or this was simply his natural state of being when he was minutes away from presenting a case as dismal as hers.

Did he smell failure? Judging from his posture and his avoidance of her gaze (his eyes usually welcomed her), she thought the answer was yes. Was his anxiety purely professional, then, or was it tinged by his personal relationship with her, his deeper feelings for her, even? She knew that Jared was an esteemed lawyer, and that he prided himself on being, at all times, professional and discreet. But surely this case, this woman (Fritzi), was different? He had flown to Byron Bay (twice), not for Missy, Fritzi thought, but for Fritzi herself. She had spent hours with him, and certainly there were some professional discussions about her case, but mostly it was personal time, conversations that were even intimate and, she thought, mutually enjoyable. But perhaps she was wrong about that, too. Perhaps he merely felt enormously grateful to her for saving his life, and had been paying off a kind of debt. In which case, if her citizenship and continued residency in Australia was denied, that debt would be null and void soon enough. And she would never see Jared – or Maggie, or even loyal, caring Darius – again.

And where would she go from here? Nowhere good, she knew that much. Prison again? Backwards, retreating into her past life and past crimes? Into the deep recesses of her sinful past; a kind of decadent and thoughtless hell. Throwing her fixed and solid identity away in exchange for multiple personalities, multiple lives, multiple lives, all of them bad. Nothing positive came from lying to others, or to yourself, she knew this now. Erasing all of the good work of the last few months. The warmth and reward of at least attempting to be a good person, loved by others, beginning even to love her own self.

She was thinking fast now, her mind all over the place, in different countries and states of being – but suddenly she stopped thinking entirely. The door opened and Jared jumped up to greet the neatly and professionally dressed man and woman who entered slowly, methodically but also rather automatically, as though they had entered this room, in this manner, countless times before.

Fritzi stood to be introduced, and Jared dutifully performed the introductions, seeming, in this moment, every bit as practised and professional (and even fatigued) as the two who had just entered. The woman complemented Fritzi on her suit, which made her seem more human, but only for a moment: Fritzi had been up against officials many times, and she knew a tough negotiator when she saw one. She knew many of their tricks, had tried out a few herself when she was negotiating with criminals and members of various underworlds. The woman sat slowly, affectless but nonetheless bristling with a quiet electricity, her face now shorn of its smile.

Her male counterpart had a silver grey brush-cut closely shaved to an inch of his skull and, wore red-spectacles a very fashion consciously-dressed man, but his expression cut a don't mess with me attitude. He, and Jared chatted for a brief moment about the rugby game against New Zealand while they unloaded their briefcases, neatly fanning their documents out on the table. Fritzi noted the woman did not wear a wedding ring, and there was a palpable frisson between the two authorities now sitting opposite her, who she learnt were Civil servants from the Foreign Office and, colleagues of Jared's.

Neither had yet spoken to her directly about her application; they were trying, she realised, to put her at ease, while also weighing her demeanour, her temperament. Jared had not coached her in any way; he wanted her to present herself as the Fritzi he knew – complicated, yes, but also human, sympathetic, full of potential and deserving of a second chance. He did not want her to portray an over-confident or arrogant persona – to put on another act. She understood that, yet she felt defensive and uneasy nonetheless, being put under a microscope by two people who knew nothing about her life. She doubted they had time in their busy schedule to study her file in depth. One thing was for sure, it was going to be an interesting morning.

'Fritzi – may we call you that?' asked the woman, as Fritzi leaned forward to take a sip of her iced water. Was this an overconfident move, she wondered? Perhaps, but she was beginning to wonder who she was supposed to be. This moment, this situation, was hard to read; feeling relaxed was one thing that could not be faked, it was beyond natural behaviour.

Her thoughts reverted to a performance she gave: she was playing the role of the head of a hospital from Zurich about several years ago now, in order to con them into releasing Yvetta into her custody. That had been one of her great successes, and she had given it everything she had, of course. But her aim then, the raison d'être for the performance, was to free Yvetta, the woman she loved. Now she was not acting at all, and the person she was trying to free was herself. Reality could be its own kind of prison, its own kind of joyless void. Ultimately, you could not run away from your true self forever.

She had to win these people over and, under such intense pressure, she wasn't sure what side of her personality would come to the fore. During high-pressure moments like these, when she felt sometimes like she was tilting dangerously close to madness, the planets orbiting away from the sun of herself and into altogether unpredictable and uncontrollable places, she felt afraid for herself – and for others as well. She fell out of time, felt herself tumbling through a forest of memories and images, real and unreal, floating free at last, almost dizzy now. The way she had run free in the woods, with Erica. That was all.

It came to her then, a single word, a name, an image from the past. Erica. Her childhood friend. A lost soul, destroyed by the communist government and Fritzi's own cruel father, and authoritarian who was also, almost certainly, a murderer. Did she hear the name Erica, or was she having an out-of-body experience? Playing with Erica in the woods behind her house when they were in grade school, still so young and fast and fresh. And then later, Erica in that horrible place that pretended to be a hospital but was really a torture chamber.

Erica. Was she imagining it, conjuring her up out of the magic dust of the past? Had Erica come to help her now, to get her out of this mess? To save her as Fritzi had saved Jared? No, it wasn't an illusion at all. The man with the red spectacles was talking about. Suddenly she was alive in the present moment once more, sitting erect, all of her attention riveted on what the man opposite her was saying. Realising that she had not been concentrating, that he had lost her for a long moment, Jared had softly touched her arm, bringing her back.

'So sorry,' she said, struggling to find words again, fighting against the reflex to speak in German, the language of her childhood, the language she had shared, along with so much else, with Erica, 'could you repeat that, please.'

'In the light of your character references from very important dignitaries,' the man said slowly, and in a flat, almost bored, voice, 'not to mention the people who you have impressed here in Australia, we have taken a different approach to your application. Jared here has written a very comprehensive document about your childhood. In addition to that, from our end, we have taken the unusual step to investigate some of the references in the documentation. I would like to speak, in particular, about your childhood friend Erica.

Still finding her footing in the present and more than a little confused, Fritzi listened with shocked awe as they continued to enlighten her about her past.

'We had an Australian government employee in Germany investigate the institution your friend Erica was imprisoned in. We were curious whether we could unearth what had happened to Erica and her family in the years since perestroika.' He stopped suddenly, looked at her more intently. His voice was no longer flat; it was somehow now alive, even interested.

'Fritzi, we have come up with very interesting findings that we would like to share with you. Your father was indeed the officer who institutionalised Erica. That has been confirmed in documentation from the former East German state. I know, too, from your document, that you suspected as much. Well, I take no pleasure in informing you that you were correct in your suspicion. Our staff did quite the thorough investigation into what actually occurred during Erica's stay in the institution – what happened, I mean, after your visit, when you so nobly went to find her.'

He surprised her now with something akin to a smile. 'We have some excellent news for you. Erica was not one of the many in the institution who underwent a lobotomy. In fact, she was spared by a doctor who knew her family. When you saw her she was being kept in a state of heavy sedation.'

Fritzi nodded, remembering, trying not to remember.

'As you know, at the time of your visit, the political situation was changing at a very fast rate. Not long after you saw Erica in the institution, many of the political inmates, who were being held against their will, were allowed to leave. Erica was released in the care of the doctor who saved her life. Her parents, unfortunately, were not as lucky. They were sent to an extremely harsh prison, and most likely tortured. Once the wall was demolished, chaos reigned and many people were misplaced. Erika was reunited with her family only years later, when she had already become a doctor of psychiatry. In fact, we were able to make contact with her, and she has provided us with an in-depth report on her friendship with you and your family. We will pass on all of the relevant details to you. She would like it very much if she could contact you.'

Fritzi sat back, visibly stunned. Her whole demeanour changed from one of indignation to one of complete frailty, confusion, even gratitude. She felt more vulnerable than she had felt in her life, and more emotionally alive than she had felt in many years.

'No, this cannot be true,' she said softly. I saw her with my own eyes, all of those years ago. She was a vegetable, I tell you; she was completely limp like a zombie.' The recollection made her shudder. Was this some kind of sick joke on the Australian officials' part? Where they using this obvious lie about Erica to try and extract some information or confession out of Fritzi? Would they stoop so low? Surely not, she thought, steadying herself. She breathed in deeply, tried to slow down her heart-rate.

'I realise this must be a shock,' the man said. 'Up until this moment, you have believed that, because of the actions of your father, and as a result of your close friendship as children, Erica had been punished in the most horrific manner imaginable.'

This was not a lie, she knew it now, knew it instinctively. It was the truth. She felt a lightness in her heart, a wonderful heady sensation overcome her.

She whispered, 'Oh my God, Erica is alive and well.'

All three people around the table shook their head in agreement. Jared poured her a drink, this time he gave her something stronger than water or even an espresso: a yellow liquid that made her splutter but also calmed her. Not realising it was whiskey, she asked for another.

'What happened to her parents,' she asked, 'do you know?'

'According to Erica, her parents were eventually united. Her mother recovered from her imprisonment. However, her father was never able to play the violin again; after hard labour in a harsh winter climate his hands were ruined. After the wall fell, the government paid formerly imprisoned political dissidents, reparations, and in this way Erica's parents were able to survive.

Finding Erica, their only child, who they too had thought was dead, was the most joyous moment in her parents' lives. Erica never married and looked after her parents until they both passed.'

Warmed by the alcohol and stunned by what she was hearing, as if deep in a dry, Fritzi began to cry, at first quietly, and then with huge shuddering sobs. A cry from her soul that had been waiting to escape at least since that day when she visited Erica, that day that had framed so much of the rest of her life. Like a person sinking in the ocean, waving helplessly from above the water, she put out her hand to apologise, but could not stop crying. Her whole body was wracked with shock and relief. It was a miracle, she felt sure of it; her mind was consumed with this information, this revelation; she had completely forgotten her own plight and why she was appearing in front of these people.

They sat quietly until she stopped. 'I am so sorry,' she managed to get out through her tears. 'Forgive me, this is the most wonderful news; really wonderful.'

The woman spoke now. 'Fritzi,' she said, in a surprisingly bright, friendly voice, 'there is so much more, but we will pass the document on to you to read at your leisure. Now,' and her voice became slower and more thoughtful, 'as to the reason we are all here today. Your application for Australian citizenship.

In light of our finding – and, indeed, your sympathetic, selfless, and thoroughly humane response to this news – we are going to recommend that you be given full citizenship when Jared sends in your application. We believe that people deserve second chances, and you as a person, despite your mistakes in the past, have a great deal of good in you, and potential to do even more, and be a productive member of our society.

There should be no further problems – but if there are, Jared will seek us out, and we will go to task with anyone blocking your application. But we very much doubt it will come to that.'

Although Fritzi realised that this was good news, she found the information confusing. She understood that these two officials would support her application, but that meant she still wasn't home free.

'Excuse me,' she said abruptly, 'sorry for asking this, but you mean I am still not home free, so to speak?'

Jared took her hand in his and squeezed it gently.

'Fritzi,' he said, the relief evident in his voice, 'believe me, you truly have nothing to worry about. Your application will just be a formality now.'

Smiling weakly, she shook hands with the senior officials from the foreign office, whose names she could not remember, thanking them for supporting her and for giving her such incredible news – the news about Erica, and the news about Fritzi's own likely future as an Australian citizen. They had sought out and interviewed Erica to investigate Fritzi's full story, find out if it was truth or fiction, but had discovered so much more in the process, news that shone light on everything and made her heart light, too.

On seeing Fritzi's expression when Jared and Fritzi arrived back at the Canberra hotel they were staying in, where Darius and Maggie were nervously waiting for their return. Darius feared the worst, but Jared was smiling broadly and clapped Darius on the back. A more confused message wasn't possible, and Darius was full of anxiety himself – he hadn't slept the night before, could think of nothing but Fritzi and her application and her future in Australia. 'What the hell's going on, mate?' he asked.

'It's a long story,' Jared said, his voice still bright, one arm around Darius now, and the other around Fritzi. 'Fritzi has got the best recommendation possible. There should be no holdup when we apply for her citizenship. But she has also received news – news which, I am sure from looking at Fritzi, she would like to break to you in her own time.'

Darius was unnerved by this last part, but Jared's enthusiasm was enormous – and infectious. 'That's a relief,' Darius said. 'Considering the time, you two took in there, I was under the impression things were going badly. I have never been so glad to be wrong.'

'Fritzi,' Jared said, and his arm was only around her now, 'I know you have suffered a tremendous shock, so it's your call: would you like to fly back this evening, or have dinner at my father's residence here in Canberra?'

She sat perched on the edge of the armchair, in the quiet hotel lounge for a while, trying to focus on the present still getting back her breath, trying to re organise her thoughts and priorities, which were very much in a state of chaos. Still, she had enough wits about her to realise it would be rude and downright stupid to pass up an invitation from the PM himself.

'No, no,' she said quickly, 'I will be fine – after a nap this afternoon and a talk with Darius and Maggie, (who she noticed, had a concerned expression and, were watching her closely) that is. Dinner with your family sounds perfect, and thank your parents for the invitation: I would love to accept.'

Delighted with the way the morning had turned out, now not wanting to acknowledge how fearful and sure of failure he had been, still tingling with the warm energy of recent success, Jared left them to continue his, meetings. Although he would admit it to no one, Jared had had no idea what to expect from the meeting – and certainly was in the dark about the earth-shattering information they had passed on to Fritzi. With the benefit of retrospect, it was evident from that moment forward that Fritzi would receive their blessing, plus all the other beneficial factors involved in her recent case history. It was, as far as he was concerned, a good morning's work.

Maggie, he knew, would be over the moon for Fritzi. He remained surprised at how his faithful and long-serving caretaker had taken to this German girl, albeit one who saved his life. Well, now he felt he had gone some distance to returning the favour. He felt vindicated; the least he could do was fight her corner, not only for his own peace of mind but for Maggie's, who he knew had fallen in love with Fritzi as much as he and Darius had. She was definitely one of a kind, the proof of the pudding was still very much in the eating. Time would be the judge of whether they were correct in their belief in her; they would find out from practical experience and not from appearance alone.

He was excited about the evening ahead. His parents had only met her once, and at that time they did not know she was the person who had saved his life. Tonight, he would tell all.

Darius went on a shopping spree with Fritzi, who wanted to look her best for the dinner. She hadn't brought any suitable clothing with for the occasion, and certainly wasn't going to wear her pinstriped suit again, still redolent of so much anguish and unease. While they were back in their suite at the hotel, he read the dossier they had handed to Fritzi, which documented facts that the Australian investigators had uncovered about her childhood.

He read about Erica, the childhood friend he had heard about from Jared. Erica, whose life had been cruelly cut short by the East Berlin authorities. Except, thankfully, according to the document, things had turned out altogether differently. It was an astonishing finding, and for Fritzi had the potential to be revelatory. Now, after all this time, Fritzi might be able to lift the dark shadow hanging over her every waking moment and move on from her nightmare past.

Erika's telephone number loomed large on the page; Darius knew that this would be on Fritzi's mind, so he encouraged her to call Erica as soon as it was a decent hour in the States. After the death of her parents, Erica had moved to Washington State; according to the documentation, she had still had not married. She lectured at a university college and had her own private practice. Darius knew that Fritzi could not enter the States; he hoped that Erica would be able to visit Fritzi in Australia at some point. A reunion between the two old friends would be healing for Fritzi, and might make the torment of her friend's experience at her father's hand less guilt-ridden and unbearable.

Darius encouraged Fritzi to text Erica; even if at first they could not speak, texting was a good way to break the ice, and when Fritzi did eventually call, both women would be more relaxed, the shock of hearing one another's voices a little less daunting.

He watched Fritzi deliberating over the text she was going to send to Erica – if, that is, she could ever decide on the right words. She was sitting on the edge of the bath, her hair wrapped up in a towel after her shower, preparing for the evening ahead. The noise the text made when it was successfully sent was obviously a relief to Fritzi, judging by how she came bouncing into the room, full of the joys of spring. He hoped the call would bring more joyous moments she deserved them.

Her hair almost dry, she loosened the knot on top of her head and allowed it to fall free over her shoulders. She fastened the taupe wrap dress around her slim frame, the low front showing her breast bone. She sat on the armchair to slide her feet into the dull gold slingbacks. Darius took in this vision of beauty; she certainly knew how to make the most of her attributes, which were plentiful. Fritzi grabbed her clutch and wrap. The hotel reception had called to say a car had arrived from the PM's residence to pick them up.

On the drive, Darius gave Fritzi a short history lesson. 'The Lodge, here in Canberra, has been the official home to all Australian prime ministers. They also had a residence in Sydney – Kirribilli House.' They were welcomed to the official residence, The Lodge used as the residence in Canberra by most Australian Prime Ministers. Jared, in a navy velvet jacket, which suited his blonde hair and physique well, welcomed them as the car pulled into the drive. The Georgian revival styled house was set in lush landscaped gardens, hidden well from the road it cut an unassuming natural style. He lead them into the Colonial styled wood beamed entrance, with a strong Mediterranean, feel inside.

'At my request, my parents have kept it an intimate dinner. I felt it would be appropriate for this evening, but nothing is ever quite intimate when you are the PM, so we do have a few other guests, but thankfully not many.'

Fritzi was greeted warmly by Jared's parents, who were both tall and elegant, his mother was blonde and had a natural friendly air. They were introduced to the other couples, who consisted of Jared's older sister, a brunette who was rather plain, compared to her handsome brother, her husband was a jovial red faced rotund man and, to Fritzi's surprise, the man who had interviewed her that morning with his girlfriend, who was not the woman interviewer.

A waiter served drinks and finger foods while everyone stood around chatting, in the off white elegantly furnished reception room with dark wood panelling. The PM gave Fritzi a personal tour of The Lodge, and she took the opportunity to study the Aboriginal paintings and artefacts. Once all of the guests were seated at one end of a long highly polished wood dining table for dinner,

Jared, raised his, glass to make a toast. He gave a short speech and introduced Fritzi as the 'the young brave European who saved the PM son's life, straight from the headlines.'

All heads suddenly turned towards Fritzi, and she wasn't sure how to play the moment. Smiling nonchalantly, pleasantly nonplussed, she raised her glass, too.

'It was my pleasure,' she said simply. Everyone laughed, raised their glasses, then suddenly spoke at once, wanting to know all of the details straight from the hero's mouth.

'Ah, really,' Fritzi said, still surprised by the sudden acclaim, finding her way (a little uncomfortably) into this very busy moment, 'it all happened so fast,' and her voice quickened at the thought of it – that moment in Christchurch as crowded and chaotic as this one, but unlike this one a full-scale emergency in which there was barely time to breathe, let alone think her actions through. 'A haze, you understand. I did not have time to think. I just did what was needed at the time.'

In the months since the earthquake, she had read and heard a great deal about the events of that day, and her actions in particular. But oddly enough, the truth was she had spent very little revisiting those moments. It was as if her actions, the events of the day, the unfolding situation, was too enormous to contemplate with any degree of meaningful insight. To this day – more and more, day by day, in fact – it all felt like a dream.

But she thought about it now, and became agitated and excited at her recollections, her voice quickening and body straightening even more. She felt oddly breathless, as she had on that day – a day which felt like it had been half a century ago, but was really still fresh in the past, central to her own story, to the rupture between her wayward past and her hopefully promising future in Australia.

'Jared was hanging on for dear life,' she said, watching the faces around the table as she described these details, almost savouring the anxiety and excitement, lengthening the moment and taunting the tension between each word, 'and he was so close to me I had to try and help.'

Sitting on one side of her, Jared was smiling, happy to have this tale, with its blessedly happy ending, relived.

'That is really all I can remember,' she said, suddenly feeling tired for the exploit of narrating this tale. 'The rest is history, as they say.'

'Well,' the prime minister began in his earnest, polished, practised, deep and thoughtful voice, sounding as though he was about to begin a political address, 'my wife and I will be forever grateful to you, my dear.'

It was a TV-trained voice, a familiar voice. But as he looked across the table at her a funny thing happened. Both his voice and his gaze softened as he said, 'We are truly in your debt.'

In a moment, the façade of the experienced politician was gone, replaced by the words of just another father who was grateful for the life of his son.

'The secret was safe with us,' he said, his voice lighter now, almost joyful, anything but the slightly severe, fatherly figure he played in the clips they showed on the nightly news. 'We realised when Jared first introduced us to you, some weeks ago, that you had to be the girl who saved him, and we were correct. Of course, if we had voiced our suspicions of your true identity, Jared would have denied it on your behalf, and rightly so. He would do anything to keep your anonymity from the press hounds. He's a good boy, my son.'

'That he is,' Fritzi said.

'But then you are good, too,' the prime minister concluded.

Everyone – apart from the man who interviewed Fritzi – joined in the conversation. Of the four dinner guests, he alone knew the true reason for Fritzi's reluctance to be named in the press. She had been introduced to him at the meeting, and now was at a loss for words, having taken nothing in at the time. She quietly leaned over to Jared, to ask the man's name once more. Fritzi did not want to seem forward or to put the man in a professionally complicated position, but privately she wanted to thank him personally for setting the wheels in motion to find Erika; this action had, she hoped, unshackled her from her ugly past and set her free from a life of guilt, doubt, and self-punishment.

She would, she hoped, be speaking to her childhood friend in a couple of hours, bridging a gulf that until very recently had seemed insuperable, reconnecting with her past and, perhaps in the process, healing herself as well. This was something she could never have imagined that very morning. But then she was changing as a person, and quicker than she had ever thought possible.

Indeed, the whole day had been dreamlike, too, both daunting and incredible. On the ride home, going over it in her mind as best she could, the last few hours felt like an out-of-body experience. Perhaps it was a dream, and she was asleep still. She had to ask Darius, sitting beside her in the back of the car, his arm around her shoulder, to pinch her. Ah yes, a soft, intimate, not unpleasant pain. Thank goodness, she was alive and awake. The events of the day had been real after all, even if she could not comprehend them still.

She spent a restless night waiting for dawn to show through the curtains. The cell phone with Erica's number on it was sitting on the low table next to her bed.

She knew her friend could not see her for the moment, but she ran into the bathroom all the same, to prepare for their meeting, to brush her teeth and hair, and splash water on her face. A face so different from the last time Erica had viewed it – older, hard, with more contours, even slight lines around the eyes – but also, perhaps, at heart, not so different at all.

Darius woke to find her staring at the cell and then the clock. She was a complete bag of nerves. He rose to make them both a cup of coffee, and at that exact moment her cell pinged. In shock, as though she had never seen or heard a cell before, Fritzi dropped the phone on the floor. She was half in and half out of the bed, scrambling around looking for the phone, when Darius picked it up and opened it to the message for her. Handing the phone over, he whispered, 'It's from Erica.'

The message was in German so he could not read it, but instead stood waiting for Fritzi to translate. Fritzi was overwhelmed. In the months that he had known her, he had never seen her behave like a child, but that was exactly what she was doing now. For some reason, hearing from Erika seemed to have thrown her mind – and even her body – all the way back in time to when they were children. Her eyes were wide and her mouth moving, but no words came out. Her hands were flailing about without a purpose, and she was dancing next to the bed on the spot, jumping up and down like a young girl in merriment.

'Hey,' Darius said, almost angrily, in a state of agitation himself, 'what did she say?'

'She still loves me and I am still her best friend. She asks that I please call immediately.'

'Well, what are you waiting for? Call.'

With a shaking hand she passed the cell to him. 'Please dial for me.'

Erika must have been waiting, for the phone hardly rang. Once Fritzi heard Erika's voice, she whispered in German, 'Erika, is that really you?' Darius could understand this much, and realised, too, that Erika had answered back. Then there was a pause and both women were crying, sobbing into the phone. Feeling strongly that this was a private moment, he walked out of the room, leaving them to bond with one another again.

Eventually, from where he was seated in the other room, he heard them begin to talk slowly, at first one syllable answers, then sentences, and then it was no stopping them. He smiled, understanding now that the two women's friendship had never suffered or died, it had somehow sustained itself over time, during periods of emptiness and even loss, and he felt sure that Erika had been aware of Fritzi's visit when she was in the institution. Even if Erika was not alert enough to recall it herself, someone would have told her, he hoped.

Fritzi poured her heart out to her friend. They had so much to catch up on, which was impossible to do on a single call. They resolved to resume their conversation on WhatsApp, once Fritzi was back in Sydney, when they could relax and, actually see one another, after their first moment of anxiety about reconnecting once more, had passed and, they were less shy of physically seeing each other once again in the flesh.

Fritzi came into the small lounge and fell onto the sofa next to Darius. 'I feel reborn,' she said, and rarely had he heard her sound so happy, not even after the conclusion of yesterday morning's meeting, when she was essentially granted her freedom in Australia. 'There is no other way to explain how I feel. Really, this is a gift from heaven … to find Erika, a gift.'

'Maggie would be so happy for you, too,' Darius said. 'Are you going to share this with her?'

Nodding, still smiling, Fritzi said, 'Yes, as soon as we return I will call her; there is so much to tell her.'

'Happy stuff for a change.'

'I'm starving,' she said, checking the time on her phone. 'Let's go down for breakfast; our flight is in about four hours.'

Wearing jeans, boots, and a scarf tied in her hair, she looked younger than he had ever seen her. She was obviously light-hearted and happy, and her energy was infectious. She had finally relaxed, allowing her guard to drop, and it suited her to be carefree for a change. No more scanning rooms nervously whenever she sat down in a public place. He liked the new Fritzi.

Back in Sydney, Fritzi spent her days with Darius and, much to Darius's faux-chagrin, every evening with Maggie. Still, she knew he did not really mind, he loved her and was happy that she was happy.

Erika and Fritzi renewed their friendship on social media and were astounded by the change the years had brought about. Erika, dark and petite, had remained as cheeky and intelligent as ever. Her dark curly hair was long and unruly, and her features had matured into an adult's, but her eyes remained the bluest Fritzi had ever seen. She had grown into a beautiful strong woman. Her childhood had been cruel, but she had found her place in the free world as an adult and, her adopted carer, the doctor who had saved her life, had given her the confidence she needed to succeed.

She had had a boyfriend, but they had parted after Erika decided to give her aging parents her full attention until the day they died. She owed them that much, and her father was able to teach, which gave him pleasure in his last years. Her mother's health had suffered especially; she had never quite recovered from the harsh conditions in the work camp. As it happened, both of her parents had passed away within a few months of one another – a blessing as far as Erika was concerned. Her parents needed each other until the end; she could never have filled that void for either of them.

She had been seeking and, was offered a teaching job in the States and it was the best decision she had ever made several years ago. Being away from Germany had recharged her battery. She loved the American lifestyle and had many close colleagues and friends in the States.

Erika thought Fritzi as beautiful as ever (indeed, she was surprised – and even a little envious – at how youthful Fritzi still looked). She had always admired Fritzi's loyalty and wanted to thank her for being there for her when she was a child. Most people from her childhood had wanted nothing to do with her; only Fritzi had stood by her through many years of torment – torment from both the other children and the adults who viewed her as a danger to their offspring.

Eventually, bit by bit, very much in her own time, Fritzi disclosed her life, and Erika gave her valued opinion. Even though Fritzi felt sad for her friend, she was as always forthright about her answers, not sparing Fritzi's feelings. Fritzi found it difficult, but soon learnt to accept Erika's harsh criticism of her various past episodes with the law.

Erika appeared shocked at learning that Fritzi had spent time in an American jail, and was not allowed back into the States, to say nothing of Fritzi's need to protect Yvetta at any cost. When it came to Fritzi's relationship with Yvetta, Erika agreed with the opinions of the other professionals who she had therapy sessions with while in jail, about her past and, her attachment to her childhood past, but never agreeing with Fritzi's methods to protect her lover at any cost.

Erika had been on lecturing tours to Australia in the past, and promised she would find one that suited her again in the future. They promised to remain connected now that they had found one another once more. Erika had not approved of Fritzi's past lifestyle or her choices; this did not, however, affect their lifelong friendship. She was relieved her friend had found strength to rely on the help of others, and approved wholeheartedly of Fritzi's present choices. Erika believed, above all, in redemption, in second chances at life. She believed in this from personal experience. She felt strongly that Fritzi was finally turning a page in her life, and beginning a fruitful and positive next chapter.

When Fritzi moaned about Erika's harsh words, Maggie gave her the motherly attention she needed, never taking sides but allowing Fritzi to relate her feelings of frustration or anger at being judged.

Darius suggested they return to Byron Bay and Fritzi was happy to oblige. He had persuaded her to begin her trek around Australia, and he promised that he would catch up with her from time to time. The visit by DuPont, Safi and Yvetta was a few weeks away now, and he decided it would be best if Fritzi was many miles from Sydney out of harm's way. Darius himself had to return to Sydney, too.

He did not want Fritzi to be confronted with her past; any encounter with Yvetta would not bode well for either woman. He knew, too, that DuPont would never understand his relationship with Fritzi, who the Frenchman blamed for so much of the trauma the Rubicovs had suffered.

Darius felt underhanded keeping secrets from Fritzi, even more so than when he had investigated her behind her back. He knew that it would not be to his advantage if she was confronted by these people, who he had only recently befriended and under what Fritzi would surely see as suspicious circumstances. He could not think of any way to defend his choice to seek them out – after all, he had known from the start about her history with them. All he could do was to try keep Fritzi from their anger or any possibility of a reprisal. He had understood from DuPont that the Russians had never given up looking for her.

This knowledge was not comforting. He decided to share his fears with Jared.

Many Russians had settled in Australia over the years; if it became common knowledge that Fritzi had settled there, it would not be beyond the Rubicovs' reach to target her.

Awful events happened in every country, of course; daily people were found dead in mysterious circumstances. According to Jared, the Australian police had dozens of unsolved murder cases on their books, some were the result of contract killings, while others had political motives.

In the course of conversation Darius voiced his concerns, over coffee at a cafe, close to Jared's offices. he had fears for Fritzi's wellbeing, together a plan could be formulated to dissuade anyone from seeking revenge.

'Darius, your connection to Fritzi's enemies might be to her advantage.' Commented, Jared.

'How so?' Darius asked.

'Well,' Jared said, 'you would have to convince the Rubicov family that Fritzi has given up her revenge on them – and that she has given up her relentless struggle to save Yvetta.'

'Perhaps I could persuade DuPont of these things, although I'm not even sure of that. You should hear how DuPont speaks about Fritzi. Even the thought of her upsets him. And how on earth would I explain my connection with Fritzi to Safi – or Yvetta, for that matter?'

Together they came up with different scenarios, but none made any sense.

Darius in deep thought threw out various suggestions 'What if you debrief them in a professional capacity in your office, while they are here in Sydney?'

Jared was inclined to play along with Darius's throw away ideas hoping that some sensible solutions could be found.

Jared, smiling half-heartedly, said, 'I will think about it. I have to say, it's not strictly, a lawyer client privilege rule, but nothing about Fritzi's case is ordinary, 'Maybe if I ask Safi and Yvetta, for permission to discuss a matter I know is of interest to them, that has come up, we might be able to persuade them that Fritzi has been rehabilitated.'

'Well,' Darius said, 'we are leaving for Byron Bay in a few days, and then I have suggested Fritzi begin her travels to the various sights she so badly wants to see. I will try and join her from time to time. Due to work issues I won't be able to be there for the whole trip.'

Jared enquired, 'I take it that 'work issues' refer to the Americans visit?'

'Yes.'

'Keep me informed while DuPont is in Australia, and if he challenges you at all about Fritzi'

Chapter 18

DuPont was picked up by a car at the airport. His PA had organised everything for him; she did not want him to fret once he arrived. She knew that a smooth entry into Sydney would be a good start for her boss. She had booked him into the Four Seasons Hotel that overlooked the Harbour Bridge and the Sydney Opera House – all could be reached by foot. Better still, the Museum of Contemporary Art was literally next door to the hotel; that should make him feel right at home.

He unpacked, showered and called room service for a light dinner. After one of the longest direct flights of his life, he had decided to sleep his jet lag off, in order to start his antipodean experience, fresh the following morning. Eating an Asian chicken salad for supper, DuPont pulled back the curtains which had been drawn for the evening. His first impression was the stunning view of the Bridge at night, and the Opera House was beautifully lit. When his PA had told him how close he would be situated in relation to the city's cultural highlights, she had not been exaggerating. He felt perfectly positioned, and the elegant hotel was to his taste, too.

Setting his watch to Aussie time, he decided a tour of the sights within walking distance would occupy him the next morning. After that, once he felt a bit more Aussified in his new surroundings, a call to Darius.

DuPont woke at dawn the following day. A sharp sunlight was filtering through the gap in the curtains he had partly closed. Doing his morning stretches, he pulled the curtains open, only to be momentarily blinded by the sunlight. Immediately placing his hands in front of his eyes, groping for a pair of shades, he stood in awe, staring (when he was able to) at the stunning view that was unfolding in front of him.

He felt great, no jet lag, well rested, invigorated by the view and excited for the sights and experiences ahead of him. Even his sense of trepidation at the gravity of the Fritzi situation excited him a little now. It would be a challenge, certainly, but then challenges were nothing but exciting, they got the heart-racing and the brain working overtime. He dressed and headed out of the hotel for breakfast along the pier.

After that, he quickly decided, his first stop would be the Museum of Contemporary Art, then onto the Sydney Opera House, an architectural marvel he had seen so often in photographs. It felt electric to be in touching distance of it, at last. The morning was fresh and the heat of the day was still at bay. People were up at dawn; Sydney obviously woke earlier than Manhattan.

DuPont had barely sat down at the restaurant when his cell pinged. It was Darius, who clearly wasn't wasting any time in contacting him. Darius obviously took his duty of care seriously; having a foreigner in his hometown from New York City wasn't an everyday occurrence, and he insisted on joining DuPont for breakfast. So much for his morning alone, gathering his thoughts, breathing in the foreign air, and experiencing the city for himself. Oh well, Darius was a great guy and good company. Manhattan was still asleep, so he did not have anyone else to talk to yet.

He gave Darius the name of the restaurant and indulged in a flat black served by a waitress who took her job far more seriously than he had experienced at diners or cafés in Manhattan. Ordering coffee here appeared to be a big deal; she tried to entice him to try many of their roasts and various different coffees on offer. She was both convincing and charming, suggesting that one of their many espresso roasts was the perfect solution for jet lag. Even though he had never felt less fatigued, he relented and was savouring the aroma when Darius walked in, embraced him briefly but without any of the usual macho awkwardness, and ordered his exotic daily brew with artistic, decorated froth on top.

He persuaded DuPont to indulge his taste buds in the restaurant's macadamia nuts and, bircher muesli – or how about some banana bread, followed by smashed avocado on toast with feta. 'If I indulged in all of that,' DuPont said in his amused, urbane voice, 'I would have to go straight back to bed.' He smiled, happy to see his new friend once again. 'But the smashed avocado with the trimmings sounds perfect, thanks.'

Darius opted for the acai bowl of muesli and banana bread. He had flown back to Sydney to meet with DuPont, while Fritzi had left to visit

Uluru, one of the must-see sights in Australia and thankfully some distance from Sydney and the possibility of catching sight of DuPont. Darius had organised a full day for his friend, and hoped DuPont would be able to keep up with the schedule he had arranged. DuPont was no spring chicken, but he was still extremely athletic and fitter than most people half of his age.

And, best of all, Darius was pleased to learn, he had lost none of his urbane enthusiasm, and his interesting chatter. DuPont appeared knowledgeable about almost everything – except Australia, about which Darius was more than happy to inform him. (Not for the first time, Darius marvelled at how many otherwise educated and well-travelled Europeans knew so little about Australia, the country's history and many cultural landmarks.)

Their first stop was the Museum of Contemporary Art, housed in a waterside art deco building, where Darius had the curator waiting to show them around. Then he whisked him off to the Sydney Opera House for a tour. After that, a long and very pleasant lunch at one of the many restaurants on the pier. If DuPont had enough energy, Darius planned to take him on a cruise around the harbour, a stunning architectural experience for a first-time visitor Down Under.

It was well past noon when they disembarked from the tourist boat, and DuPont could feel his body going into sleep mode; jet lag, or some shadow of it, was obviously catching up with him. Even the expresso at lunch had not stopped his body and mind from fogging over. It was time to return to his hotel for a much-needed nap and a chance to reflect on all he had seen and heard in what had already been a very busy day.

Darius put DuPont into an Uber, and arranged to meet him early the next morning for their noon flight to Tasmania, where they were due to meet David Walsh, who owned the Mona in Hobart.

DuPont decided not to check out of his room, but instead to pack a small roll-on suitcase for the two-day, visit away from Sydney.

He knew his PA would scold him for the indulgence and for wasting money, but he liked his comfort and hated the idea of having to settle in again. He was a creature of habit in that way, and besides it was his money he was wasting, and what was wrong with that? After all, even if he did not look his age, he was much older than most of the people he was dealing with these days.

The Subterranean Museum was a delight to the senses. They approached the museum by boat and docked at a jetty with a 90-step assent to the entrance. To DuPont's relief, Darius had him remain on board to alight at the second jetty, where they were met by David Walsh, who was driving a golf buggy. He whisked them off up a steep hill to his folly of wonder – and what a wonder it was. The three men descended in a lift to the first floor and entered between two massive stone walls hung with large paintings. Further along the entrance bridge was a long bar, where his host had iced gin and tonics waiting.

They travelled a long stone passage with antique armchairs and sofas along the walls, so that people could sit and listen to a small chamber orchestra playing classical music. But there wasn't time to stop – or even to take in all of the wondrous sights. And sounds – for the classical music receded as they travelled further and deeper. Following the stone passage between mountainous walls of rock, water could be heard splashing from a waterfall of words descending in cascades from high up in the rocks above.

David explained that this was a sculpture of everyday words and a permanent exhibit. Other permanent exhibits included a broken-glass installation by the German artist Ansel Keefer, a favourite of DuPont's. In fact, the exhibitions were eclectic and diverse throughout the gallery, and all were reached by a glass lift, which descended further into the vast cavernous spaces.

They alighted into daylight to be led through a garden of sculptures, a tennis court, and outdoor restaurants. They followed their host into a restaurant, where outdoor tables were covered in growing grasses instead of tablecloths, each sprouting tiny white and red daisies. It was a delight to the senses. They ordered lunch while on the grass far below a rock band played for an audience of whoever happened to be lazing around on the lawns below. DuPont was blown away by this self-contained and completely wonderful world. He was in complete awe of his host, who had created this artistic heaven against all the odds. Walsh had funded the museum with his own money – money he apparently made by gambling, using an algorithm he had devised.

Their evening was spent at the Art Hotel, where the walls were hung with indigenous Aboriginal art. The hotel's restaurant was a delight, and DuPont was enjoying himself immensely, indulging in the best wines Australia had to offer, not to mention the delicious alternative menus. All thoughts of the endless journey to get here were long forgotten. It was well worth the trip, that was for sure.

Darius had booked over a weekend when the local markets were in town, and the two men spent a leisurely day going from stall to stall. They met with the bombastic art dealer near the hotel, who was an expert in Aboriginal art. The two dealers exchanged business cards. Advised by the dealer, DuPont bought and organised the shipping of a number of works. DuPont also let the man know that Yvetta and Safi, who both owned galleries in Manhattan, were visiting Australia shortly. He was happy to be the intermediary if they set up any shows.

Food was another Tassie must; they dined with the art dealer and his wife at one of the many highly recommended places in the town. Another alcohol-fuelled evening out, not good for DuPont's liver or general health, but great fun nonetheless.

Back in his suite at the Four Seasons hotel, DuPont sent off various emails, including to Safi and Yvetta, extolling the wonders and incredible time he was having in Australia. He prepared them for the most humbling and awesome experience when they visited Mona in Hobart; they were in for a marvellous treat. He loved everything about his visit so far, and he found Sydney especially beautiful.

Back in Sydney, Darius had persuaded Jared to dine with DuPont the following evening, and together they would broach the Fritzi question.

If they were to get through to any of Fritzi's enemies, DuPont was surely their best chance of a Fritzi conversion.

DuPont had another week left in Australia; he needed to make contact, with some of the galleries, and do some schmoozing of his own when visiting the major dealers. It was important to make new contacts in the art world whenever he visited abroad, to grow his network, and his place in the world. Dax's work, he thought, would go down well in some of the larger galleries here, and Janus's sculptures would strike a chord with the naturalists of the day.

Jared met them at a fish restaurant, a large open space facing the water. DuPont was comfortably dressed in a casual French navy pinstriped shirt, a yellow cashmere jersey slung over his shoulders, chinos and suede loafers, no socks, of course. Darius and Jared were both in jeans; Darius wore a pale pink polo shirt, while Jared had on a crisp white open-necked shirt. DuPont had been briefed by Darius that they were dining with the PM's son, a human rights lawyer. DuPont was under no illusions about this dinner. It had to be about Fritzi; he could see no other reason for the meeting.

The bar was a long affair; all the way along the centre of the open space there were glasses hanging upside down. One could view the bay from either side of the bar; it was a spectacular sight. The three men were shown to a table overlooking the water. The tables were of rough distressed wood, and the chairs were upholstered in bright velvet colours to add glamour. The menu was vast and the smells of fish and crustaceans, shrimps and other sea creatures he had not previously encountered, grilled on an open fire, was heavenly. DuPont allowed the waiter to advise him in his choices and wasn't disappointed when his first course arrived: giant grilled Portuguese shrimp, crevettes in France, served with an Aussie twist and accompanied by a basket of varying colours of grilled cherry tomatoes and thinly fried zucchini frittes.

Jared did not waste time with small talk, he launched right in with his sales pitch – at least that was how DuPont perceived the speech. But DuPont was not going to be brainwashed by these two; no matter what they had to say, he knew the truth about Fritzi, this paragon of virtue they were trying to present to him, painted up to resemble the new Virgin Mary; it was a joke – and a sick one at that.

The second course arrived and he could tell Jared was only getting started with his sales pitch. DuPont decided his best option was to listen, be polite and, focus instead on this feast of the senses and the spectacular view of the bay as the lights began to twinkle in the distance. Night was settling in as the sun dropped behind the horizon. The wines on offer were the best anywhere; he was enjoying a light fruity white wine with his grilled fish and fresh salad – all the while Jared's voice was droning on opposite him.

'I understand how she has behaved in the past,' Jared said, 'but I assure you we have had her thoroughly investigated. There is not a thing we do not know, that the authorities have uncovered about her past. But what almost no one knew was what happened to her as a child growing up behind the Iron Curtain. If you will indulge me for a little longer, I would like to fill you in on that.'

DuPont shook his head, enjoying the last mouthful of his delicious, freshly grilled sea bass. 'This food is truly outstanding,' he said diplomatically. 'The view and the ambience alone is five-star. I must commend you on your incredible food here in Australia: it is an art and a great challenge to beat the French for delicate flavours, but in freshness

and taste, I think I must sadly admit you have achieved the impossible.'
He smiled before taking on a more sober, tone.

'On the other hand, I cannot see how a story of Fritzi's childhood could possibly make up for her past treachery – but, by all means, enlighten me.'

Darius and Jared made eye contact, both agreeing they were fighting a losing battle. Still, the famously tenacious Jared was not to be put off by his guest's charming, polite, nonchalant French manners.

They ordered fresh fruit and a selection of sorbet made from the craziest flavours he had ever experienced, but he was prepared to have his palette savour all the new tastes in this down-to-earth, surprisingly unsophisticated, yet beautiful city with its culinary marvels.

Over desert and coffee, Jared made steadfast eye contact with DuPont. He was determined to move this man (even if in a small way) to show some empathy.

He told Fritzi's story about Erika in the only way he knew how: with honesty and horror, emphasising Fritzi's guilt for the sins of her father throughout the years. He ended by giving a summary of Fritzi's interview with the immigration officials, and the honesty she had exhibited about her past; and, finally, Fritzi's discovery that her childhood friend was alive and well, and informing DuPont how Fritzi and Erika had made contact in the last few weeks, had rekindled their friendship. Jared made sure to describe the wonder and delight – and most of all peace – from the years of horror Fritzi had suffered, not knowing what had happened to her very best friend.

DuPont felt a shiver run up his spine. The story Jared had just told was inhumane; more than pitiful, it was criminal beyond belief, a crime against humanity. The one thing he found difficult to comprehend was that it was Fritzi they were talking about. DuPont sat in silence, drinking his wine and mulling over what he had just been told. It was beyond his capability, at this point in time, to take all of this in. He empathised with the child-Fritzi so vividly described in Jared's tale, but not with the woman Fritzi he knew altogether too well. To see these two Fritzi's as one would take time, DuPont was sure. But Jared and Darius seemed to require an immediate response.

'It is the most shocking story I think I have ever heard,' DuPont said finally, uneasily. He shook his head slowly, using the gesture to buy time to find the right words, not that, there were, under the circumstances, any right words. 'The depravity of it all. No one –

especially not a young person – can come out of this story unscathed. I see that, of course I do. The thing is, I cannot see the child and the adult as the same person – not yet, anyhow. I need time and distance to absorb what you have just told me. I must play everything through in my mind, before I am able to truthfully know how I feel about Fritzi, and respond accordingly.'

'That's fair enough, mate,' Jared said. 'To be honest, I had sleepless nights going over this conversation in my mind. You understand, all of this was told to me in the strictest confidence, but as her lawyer I had to find the linchpin that would save her.'

Darius interrupted; he hadn't spoken much all evening, and now felt he needed to add his opinion.

'Well, since Fritzi and Erika's story has had a fairy tale ending, I hardly think that matters any longer.'

They continued on a lighter note, enjoying the atmosphere and what was left of the dessert. Still, DuPont felt light-headed, well-fed, and disorientated about their meeting. Before he met with Jared he had thought that he knew exactly how he felt about Fritzi; now he would have to reevaluate. It would be churlish and unkind to ignore the younger Fritzi: her past, her scars, her growing pains, how her sad and destructive life had shaped itself. The story about how Fritzi and Erika's reunion had come about was in itself worth thinking about; one could only imagine the relief it must have brought Fritzi.

DuPont returned to his suite, mellowed from the delicious food and wine, but disrupted by thoughts of Fritzi still. The person he hated to think about was occupying his mind tonight. Tomorrow he would walk and think; it was the best way to sort out one's muddled thoughts.

He turned off the lights, pulled the heavy curtains shut, and settled down into the downy pillows, waiting for sleep to find him; it did not. Instead, he lay for hours staring up at a ceiling he was only aware of until he woke with a start to a dull knocking at his door. Pulling on his gown and slippers, he found the service maid waiting to clean his room. 'What time is it?' he asked groggily.

Shocked to find he had slept through both breakfast and lunch, DuPont returned to his suite to shower, his mind full, once more, with thoughts and images of Erika and Fritzi and, the father who nearly destroyed a young mind. He spent the rest of the day and night walking, eating, and chatting to people he randomly met along the way at cafés.

He felt peculiarly outside of himself, isolated and removed, standing around watching others enjoying themselves.

Walking back to his hotel he decided he would not call Jared or Darius for a few days. He was not finished working through how he felt about Fritzi, and wasn't sure he would ever resolve this conundrum. Still, he resolved to speak to Darius about last night's discussion before he returned home.

The days flew by, packed with appointments set up for him by his PA and friends of friends who wanted him to meet various people in the Australian art world. He was wined and dined by many, got to see fantastic, priceless private art collections in beautiful homes, and felt he had made many valuable contacts for the future. This certainly was not a wasted trip.

On his last day in Sydney, he had a date to meet Darius and view the Dax artwork in his home. Looking out of the penthouse apartment windows at the views along Bondi Beach, the Frenchman was blown away by the sheer joy and freedom people here lived their lives with; a part of him yearned to be young again.

They settled down at the long slate kitchen island with two beers, lox pickles and bagels. 'I can tell you are preparing me for my return to Manhattan,' DuPont said softly. 'I will miss the delicious fresh food, I can tell you that as a true convert to all Aussie grub.'

They both laughed at DuPont's attempt at Aussie slang.

'Darius, I have spent sleepless nights, and days walking, thinking about this whole Fritzi issue. But as much as I want to, I cannot bring the two people together as one person. I keep viewing one with the utmost empathy, and, the other with the utmost disdain.'

Darius thought about what DuPont was struggling with, and thought that, in a small way, at least, he understood. He, too, had tried to wrack his brain to solve the puzzle, how to help him merge the two Fritzis into one homogenous personality.

'Maybe distance will bring about some kind of solution?' Darius said.

'Listen, let's go and see the Dax. Then we can settle down to our bagels and go over this. What I can tell you is that for Jared, myself, and for Maggie – who you have not met – Fritzi has become an important part of our lives. I know you find that hard to comprehend at this stage, but it's a fact.'

'Who is this, Maggie?'

'She works for Jared and has become a mother figure for Fritzi. Maggie gave Fritzi a much needed, non-judgemental kindness and understanding at a very low point during her time here.'

They walked towards the guest cloakroom. Darius swung the tall oak door open for DuPont to enter into the space. DuPont was about to remind Darius that the light had not been turned on, when – to his delight, once the door was closed behind him – the painting came to life. It hung against a deep red wall that was facing him. A sharp light washed over the image, giving it the appearance of an old master. The hues in the figure were illuminated to perfection while the background faded away gently.

'Magnificent,' DuPont said, stunned. 'Who did the lighting and hanging for you?'

'An old girlfriend. It was the last room in the apartment we had not paid much attention to, and once I received the Dax I realised it was the perfect place to hang it: hidden, yet very much alive once revealed.'

'I couldn't agree more. A fantastic sense of drama. Dax himself would approve.'

They tucked into the bagels, cream cheese, and lox. The beer was ice-cold and the view mesmerizing. It was a shame to spoil the evening by discussing someone he had no time for and couldn't imagine changing his mind about. But this was clearly exactly what his host had in mind.

'May I ask where is she now?' DuPont said, hesitating even while he said it.

'I prefer to remain stum, on that point,' Darius said. 'I'm only too aware that she has her detractors, some of whom are obviously a clear and present danger. If these people knew how or where to find her… Thankfully, Australia is a vast country, easy to get lost in.'

DuPont remained silent, knowing Mika would be that danger if DuPont were ever to divulge where she was. Australia might be vast, but so were Janus and Mika's resources. After all, it was their profession to track down rogue elements, either in governments or other, equally distasteful characters he'd rather not know about. DuPont knew that both Mika and Janus did intelligence work for conglomerates and other agencies. They were no longer personally involved in this line of work, yet they could no doubt utilize their databases and significant resources if need be.

'I won't pretend the thought hasn't crossed my mind whether to take Mika into my confidence about Fritzi and the new developments here in Australia.' He brought out the news article he had printed out from the Aussie paper. 'I imagine this is about Fritzi?'

Darius read the article. 'I wouldn't be at liberty to disclose the name of the person referred to in that article,' Darius said slowly, 'even if I do have the answer to your question.'

'You know, Darius,' DuPont said, and his voice was firmer now than it had been since his arrival in Australia, I have grown fond of you, but this obsession of yours with Fritzi I cannot understand. The only thing I can recommend is be very careful: you are dealing with a duplicitous personality. She may appear to be wonderful now, but mark my words, she can change on a dime, When she does, watch out: she knows how to strike where it hurts.'

'Yes,' Darius said, suddenly feeling tired and irritated, 'you have given me this advice before: I have taken it on board and, I have examined her past. I am fairly sure that no one has gone into her past as thoroughly as I have. The government has gone into her childhood, all those stories have been corroborated as authentic, and what's more Erika has now substantiated all of them.

So, you will have to do better if you're going to insist that she's this demon you believe her still to be.'

DuPont shook his head, took another swig of his ice-cold beer. They had reached an impasse. There was nothing more to be said; he was incapable of changing his mind or feelings about that woman, no matter what these people had told him. Perhaps age had made him less forgiving, unable to believe it was possible for her to be anything other than what she was: a devil dressed up in sheep's clothing.

He hoped they would not suffer when she reverted to her former self.

'Oh, well, I leave early in the morning for the airport. My visit has passed all expectations – apart from our impasse on Fritzi, that is. But, who knows, I might have a eureka moment or even a religious experience on that front. When it happens, you will be the first to know.'

Darius gave a weak smile at DuPont's attempt at humour, which, he felt, was in bad taste on Fritzi's behalf. He had tried hard to convince the Frenchman – and clearly been unsuccessful. And Darius's failure stung him for a moment. If Fritzi's childhood experience of horror had not changed his mind about her past, nothing would, he thought.

They travelled down in the glass lift together, Darius waved as the car left the curb. The night was beautiful and Darius headed for the pier and the bars; he needed some company tonight. Tomorrow he would fly out to meet Fritzi, the woman he was in love with. Travelling in the outback was good for the soul.

Chapter 19

Before he left to meet Fritzi on her travels, Darius met Jared for an early morning breakfast, meeting. Over eggs and coffee, Darius recounted what he jokingly referred to as his 'last supper' with DuPont.

'The problem, as I see it,' Darius began, unconsciously tapping the fingers of his right hand on the rim of his coffee cup, 'is that DuPont cannot reconcile the old Fritzi, whom he detests, with the young version, for whom he feels obvious empathy. But,' he paused, took a sip of his coffee, tapped the rim again, 'merging the two women into one human being appears to be a step too far for him.'

They both agreed, the situation was way too complicated for the two of them to handle, and certainly not this early in the morning. DuPont would ultimately have to figure out the conundrum for himself – or not, as the case may be. 'That's my hope, anyway,' Darius concluded, 'that, with, the benefit of more distance and time, our chat with him will bear some fruit.'

'I like the French art dealer,' Jared said, after placing his knife and fork together on the plate (he did this, as he did everything, with swift efficiency). 'Why do you call him by his surname only?'

'I'm not sure,' Darius said, finishing the last of his coffee, pushing the cup away. 'That's what everybody I met calls him. Perhaps he doesn't like his Christian name. One day I will have to ask him what it is.'

'You mean, after all of this, you don't know his first name?' Jared asked, amused.

Darius was embarrassed to admit that he did not, but his embarrassment was good-natured, and the two left the restaurant in good spirits.

After breakfast they both went their separate ways: Jared had a busy day in court, while Darius had a flight to Alice Springs.

Heading into the city Jared sat thoughtfully, staring out at the busy sidewalks. The traffic was horrendous; what should be a short trip was going to take time. After his stay in Canberra, he'd corresponded with the immigration team who were studying Fritzi's case.

The team informed him that the letters of recommendation would be taken in the highest regard and given the respect they deserved. All the same, Jared was informed, the team would be conducting further investigations and, would let him know if they required another interview in due course. If not, he would hear from them after they had completed their work on the case.

After his meeting with the minister of foreign affairs, Jared had hoped the remainder of the process would be cut-and-dried. He now suspected there was some hiccup they were not sharing with him. He would have to call Bruce and enquire if anything further had come to light that he wasn't aware of. The letter had only just arrived on his desk and he was not ready to discuss its contents with Darius until he had a clear picture of where they stood on the issue of Fritzi's citizenship.

During a harrowing interview with the minister and psychologist, Jared had been in awe of Fritzi's ability to be both vulnerable and quietly poised at the same time. In fact, the psychologist had confided in Jared afterward the interview how impressed she had been with Fritzi, in whom she said she had not seen any sign of guile or false bravado. Indeed, the psychologist said, she had seen only a girl who had grasped at straws to overcome what was, by all accounts, a dreadful and disastrous experience as a young teenager.

Now the immigration team were sitting on all of this information, as well as many favourable character witnesses and professional reports. Yet, for all of that, they appeared to still be at an impasse; one way or another nothing had been resolved. And Jared knew that this was not good news.

He could not help but feel a little uncomfortable about the outcome now. If an appeal were to be processed through the courts it could take years, and there was always the possibility – perhaps even a likelihood, at this point – that her application would simply be rejected. He prayed it would work out in her favour, but he no longer felt so optimistic about her chances. What he knew for sure was that Fritzi's case was exceptional.

He knew no other applicants who had been given such a high-profile hearing. As a close friend of the family of the PM, the minister had done Jared a favour a hearing of the kind Fritzi had enjoyed would have otherwise been unheard of.

After Fritzi and Darius had left the dinner party, Jared's parents and their friends had remained to discuss the evening. They had all looked upon Fritzi favourably. Indeed, it was hard not to – Fritzi was a beautiful and accomplished European, with impeccable manners.

Jared's mother, always straight to the point, had taken him aside, wanting to know whether Darius had definitely won Fritzi's heart. His mother thought that Fritzi would make Jared an excellent partner. Jared had swiftly disabused her of that notion … but still, he wondered. Was she correct about there being a spark between them? A mother always knew what and, who was best for her son.

He had initially laughed off his mother's suggestion, but he had to confide a soft spot for her. After all, she had saved his bacon during the earthquake; the least he could do was give her his best shot at becoming an Australian citizen.

At the front door of his parents' residence, his mother had kissed him gently on the cheek and given him her usual parting words of advice, which now rang in his ears.

'Well,' she had said, 'if there is a spark between you two, I suggest you fight for her.' And Jared had surprised himself by responding, 'I am, Mother, the best way I know how.'

'Jared, darling,' she had said, with an unusual but not unfamiliar sternness, 'you know exactly what I mean.' and he had, too.

The car pulled up outside Jared's office block, abruptly breaking off his thoughts of that conversation and bringing him back to work mode. His personal life would always take a back seat to work, to fighting for the oppressed and for those less fortunate than himself. Perhaps she was better off with Darius, who appeared to have great reserves of both time and money after spinning off his company. Jared would never have the luxury of affording her the attention his friend could.

Back at his desk, his day became the usual whirlwind of meetings, with most of the afternoon spent in front of a judge, pleading for the freedom of another soul at risk of being thrown out of the country, deported to one of the many unsavoury countries around the globe, countries that did not safeguard democracy and individual liberty the way Australia did. And yet Australia could do better, too – some of its immigration laws seemed cruel, and much of its cruelty felt, to Jared, anyway, unforgivable. And yet he was nothing if not forgiving. Many would-be refugees never even made it in front of a judge. It was tragic, even inhumane, but Australia had some of the strictest immigration laws, even when someone was seeking asylum, as was the person whose case he was about to plead.

He hoped to God Fritzi would have none of the complications he dealt with on a daily basis, and always struggled to overcome. He had certainly given Fritzi's case his best shot; now they had to play a waiting game. They had no other options at this point, and no backup plan should her application be rejected. The afternoon felt long, dull, heavy, with Fritzi's case very much in his mind.

As the hours passed, he felt more pessimistic, resigned to losing Fritzi's case – and, with it, Fritzi herself. He decided that it was best he told Fritzi nothing until he had the utmost clarity on her situation, and had heard from the powers-that-be about her status, one way or the other. If it was good news they would celebrate Fritzi's freedom, with Maggie and Darius, the only people he knew who cared as much as he did about her future and her fate. The bad news, at this juncture, was not worth thinking about yet.

Until the day arrived that they found out Fritzi's fate, he knew that Maggie would be as anxious as he was . He had never seen two people bond the way the two women had over the last few weeks and months, since Fritzi had entered their lives. Maggie spoke with Fritzi on a regular basis, and entertained Jared with antidotes of Fritzi's travels, which he was eager to hear about.

Every morning, when she brought in his paper and they sat together to go over the daily needs of running his household, had now become a slightly more intimate affair than in all of the years previously. Maggie would enquire how he was, and then, her voice become softer, ask if there was any news about the status of Fritzi's application.

If she had heard from Fritzi, she would regale him with tales of their friend's wonder and delight travelling through the outback.

He had become attached to Fritzi, just like Maggie and Darius. It had happened slowly, steadily, and then seemingly very quickly, had overcome him absolutely. And, as his mother had intuited and he now had to admit (if only to himself) he was completely infatuated with her.

His mother always saw right through him, right through his bluster, machismo, and nonsense; he had to give her credit. He understood that she wanted to see her youngest son settled; it had been five years since his breakup with Natalie, with whom his mother had a close bond. He thought about Natalie now, and with a pang that surprised him. She had long ago moved on, and, as far as he knew, was happily married with twin boys, living in Perth. At least she looked happily married in her Facebook pictures – but then almost everybody did.

Jared, on the other hand, spent his time studying and working his arse off; his job paid handsomely and was enormously fulfilling in many ways, but it had not brought a life filled with the companionship and, children his mother clearly hoped he would be receptive to.

He felt that he was letting his mother down, and a part of himself down as well, but this was the life he had carved out for himself, through considerable study and sweat and toil, and, up until now, it had suited him well. He had achieved great esteem in his field, and in a relatively short amount of time. Success wasn't only about the marital home and the photographs of one's children on the mantel. His sister was married and her and her husband had given his parents four grandchildren; it made up for Jared's tardiness in that area, and perhaps he owed his sister a thank you.

Time would tell. He never believed in anything working out the way one imagined. If he and Fritzi were meant to be together, it would happen. He wasn't aggressive in that way; love was meant to find you when you least expected it – perhaps it had. All the same, he was happy to play the waiting game. Or perhaps he was just cautious, even a little afraid. In any case, the verdict was still out on Fritzi's future in Australia; until then he had time on his side.

If it did work out between them – and, he had to admit, he was giving their potential relationship more and more thought – he would have to keep them on a tight reign. If left to their own devices, the two women, both busybodies in their own rights, would make sure cupid's arrows were pointed straight from Fritzi towards him, rather than towards Darius.

If things went the other way, and Darius won out, well, Jared would be the first to congratulate them. Darius was a good bloke, and a long-time friend.

Maggie interrupted his thoughts with her usual chatter. Today she was less talkative than usual, and he guessed why. He had noticed that whenever Darius was on the scene Maggie became a little less forthcoming. He guessed she, like his mom, had a vested interest to see her charge married to the girl of his – well, actually, her – choice. He found the whole thing quite amusing and often teased Maggie about being his surrogate mother instead of his housekeeper.

When he did spend a weekend with a woman at the house, Maggie had always been discreet; but so many women had passed through since her employment that he suspected she had given up hope of a permanent female presence … until Fritzi came onto the scene.

Now he was reluctant to bring anyone back for fear of Maggie's disapproval. He was being quite ridiculous, he knew. All the same, he valued Maggie's judgement and craved her approval; she had his best interests at heart.

Perhaps it was time to throw a spanner in the works. He decided to ask Gabi, his latest love interest, to spend a weekend with him. If nothing else, he needed to get Fritzi out of his head – and fast. He needed to normalise his life; he felt that he was in danger of becoming oversensitive, too eager to please and comply with the wishes of others, less independent and free-spirited somehow, too. It had to stop. It was time to be the old Jared again.

Gabi was a pukka Aussie Sheila (whatever that was thought to be now, since pop stars had become all the rage). He preferred the outdoor life rather than the showgirl type. The two of them had a great time jogging, trekking, and both had a passion for windsurfing. She was a natural beauty, with short, cropped blonde hair, zero makeup, and low maintenance. She was happy to spend nights in front of the TV watching box sets, rather than being seen in the latest hot spots. Her life as a GP was hectic; weekends were when she relaxed. They both had the same needs in that respect: a hassle-free relationship, with as much sport and sex as possible on the agenda.

Once divorced, with no children and no responsibilities apart from her work, she was a perfect partner to hang with. Gabi had tried the married life for only three years, her response to why it had only lasted through the honeymoon phase, was a straight forward answer, ' We were not soul mates, our needs ended up on the chopping block, I wanted only a career he wanted kids right off, end of story, why waste more time together.'

She now opted for independence, freedom, fun. In his eyes, she was perfect, he couldn't ask for more. And yet… she wasn't Fritzi. But maybe that was a good thing. There was much to look forward to this weekend.

Maggie's expression when she realised, he had brought another of his lady friends to spend the weekend, would be worth the wait. To Maggie's credit, she managed to ignore all the tell-tale signs: wet towels in the bathroom, both sides of the bed a mess, and the dishwasher full of plates, coffee cups and cutlery; not Jared's usual low-maintenance, hardly-there existence.

What's more, Gabi remained with him until Monday. Far from being in a hurry to shoo her out (as he had been with other girls in the past), grateful for the company and warmed by her body and her fun personality, he had encouraged her to stay, and even to leave for work from his place at the very last minute. Was he trying to prove something to her? Or to himself? It seemed the best way to show he had resumed his old lifestyle once more. His injuries were completely healed, Fritzi had moved on with her own life, it was time he did the same. He needed to bring normality back into his social life, not only to ward off the motherly concerns from his mother and Maggie, but for his own sanity. His mother and Maggie's stranglehold on his love-life had to be broken.

Chapter 20

Fritzi's relationship with Darius had become uncomplicated and carefree. He was dependable and kind, caring, a welcome constant in her always unpredictable life. They both enjoyed one another's company. Still, she had to admit that Jared was never far from her mind.

They had never so much as kissed, but whenever he was around, she felt her heart beating that little bit faster. While Darius was comfortable to be around, this was not the case with Jared, who was, despite outward appearances and his charismatic manner, surprisingly reserved. His thoughts were private and hard to read. Did he know how much he meant to her? He was her ticket to freedom, which was a good reason to be on her guard around him. It wasn't difficult to work out why she might also be infatuated with him. No one (not even Darius) had ever tried to help her as much as Jared had. Right from the start in Bali, Darius had been upfront about his feelings for her. Yet Darius had had her investigated by a private eye he hired while they were in Bali, and opened her up to dangers best avoided now, while she was on the run from her previous life.

The warning Darius had sent her once her cover was blown had probably saved her life. Well, her life was now a mess anyway, a complete disaster, her future uncertain once again, which stung all the more because in recent weeks she had found a kind of peace. If Australia turned its back on her, which was looking increasingly likely, it would be a devastating blow.

Indeed, she could not bear to think about it. Better to live in the present moment, enjoy her life right now, keep her fears and doubts at a considerable distance. Easier said than done. At the moment her only saving grace was Erika: the two women text daily and, called often during the first few weeks of finding one another. It was still so hard for Fritzi to believe Erika was well-adjusted, happy and alive. She had suffered more than Fritzi, but her adult years had been so much smoother, less complex and criminal. It had taken a while to believe that reuniting with Erika wasn't a dream she might suddenly wake from.

Hiking in the outback gave her mind time to reflect on her life with more insight and intensity than she had previously. Some days were harder than others. Images of her past were often overpowering, growing up behind the iron curtain her childhood had been stilted by oppression and, her escape to the free world came with mixed blessings, she was ill-equipped to deal with, she now believed.

Her moods these days were a rollercoaster, as they had been so often in the past. But this time, for once, much of her anger and resentment was turned inward, on herself. On some days she felt great shame; on other days optimism would buoy her and happy thoughts would rush in, sweeping away the darkness and feelings of despair. She had to be realistic about her fate, as unpleasant as it was to consider. There was little doubt that in the past she had done a good job of being bad, and in the process made powerful enemies with a long reach; it was only a matter of time before they tracked her down.

After her years with Yvetta and living in Moscow, a city that to many foreigners was as alien and alienating as it could be icy and unforgiving, Fritzi understood the Russian character only too well. When you crossed a Russian, they did not, perhaps could not, forgive you. And Fritzi had crossed that line more than once, with Yvetta's family, who were no strangers to taking violent revenge when they thought the situation warranted it. She knew, too, that she was on the list of Mika Rubicov, who was now the sole heir to the Rubicov empire.

Fritzi spent hours trekking along well-travelled paths, sometimes with a guide, other days alone. She tried without success to formulate an apology to her enemies. In her mind, she apologised especially to Yvetta and to Safi; they did not deserve what she had put them through, she saw that clearly now and at great emotional cost.

Her feelings about DuPont were more complex; he had invaded Yvetta's territory, and Fritzi had wanted to punish him for aiding and abetting Safi when she took over the Rubicov gallery in Moscow. It was both a shameful punishment and a massive slap in the face for Yvetta to discover that her brother's no-nothing, barely adult fiancé had, in Yvetta's absence, been brought in to run and eventually take over the Rubicov galleries. DuPont had mentored Safi, guiding and instructing her until she was able to run the Rubicov galleries on her own, expanding and establishing them in the States. Fritzi had wanted to punish him on Yvetta's behalf, and she had almost succeeded.

Because of Fritzi's tactics at Sotheby's in London, DuPont had suffered client loss and his reputation had taken a dive. Unfortunately, DuPont had got his revenge, double-crossing her in the States. For this she paid a high price, doing time behind bars. Now they were even (to her mind, at least), but she knew that DuPont would hold a grudge against her for hurting Safi, whom he loved and was, she thought, very possibly in love with, too. She spent hours in the outback considering one question: how was it possible to persuade these people to let sleeping dogs lie? They would never change their opinion of her, and she had little right to expect anything less.

In the intervening years Alexi and Sasha had died, but Mika was alive and he would not hesitate to take her out. She had caused his family much heartache. She had, among other things, masterminded the sabotage of the Rubicov restaurants in Moscow and London. Alexi's wife, the ballerina, had been brutally attacked by people Fritzi paid to rough her up. It seemed too awful to contemplate, but it was true, all of it. The memories shocked her even now, under the wide Australian sky, in this very different, but still frighteningly connected, world. These terrible thoughts of her past actions filled her every waking hour.

She had orchestrated Sasha's kidnapping, but had saved his life, for her own self-interests. Feeling self-pity or indulging in self-examination was ridiculous, she thought, and in the past, she had been largely immune to it; even in the yoga retreat there had been little or no introspection on her part. But here in the vastness, strangeness, and barren beauty of the outback, with only herself as company for long days on end, her past came rushing in, filling her soul with despair. For the first time in her life, she hated herself, or the person she had become in her adult years.

The anger directed at the Rubicov family, she guessed, was to dull her own pain and guilt. Now that she knew Erika was alive and well, she no longer felt any need to harbour resentment towards anyone; she had been set free. Free to a point, because she still felt like a prisoner of her past. Now she was dealing with another kind of guilt, that of her own making.

Over the telephone and in her messages, Erika had tried to help set Fritzi on a path of introspection of the spirit. She had tried to teach Fritzi to accept her shortcomings and her sins, to forgive other people (her father, for instance) and, most importantly, herself. Standing alone on a hill overlooking a valley in the outback, a place both barren and fertile, dense with possibility, Fritzi realised that she had reached a place of no return. Now she needed guidance and she – who had always been independent and elusive, and kept herself to herself – needed other people. All of this had been alien, to her in the past; but everything was different now. She had to learn how to accept her truth, the old Fritzi was her story, too, and would always be part of who she was, no matter how far she travelled or the distance she put between then and now.

When Darius arrived, he found Fritzi in a state of mental anguish, out of sorts in her manner, she was he observed in a state of deep introspection. He realised that the solitary bush existence had played with her mind, and thrown her emotions into a state of upheaval. The bush could do that to anyone. This was tough terrain: emotionally tough, and physically brutal as well. Rewarding, certainly, but all-consuming and exhausting, an exertion that could feel more of a punishment than a pleasure. Going into the outback made you face down yourself, and some people never fully returned. That's why the term 'walkabout' was used when someone had some deep thinking to do.

Still, despite his protestations, Fritzi did not want to give up on her walkabouts, and he joined her trekking into the wilderness. At first, they walked in silence; only the water bottle was passed between them as they hiked up steep hills and down inclines. Still, he could tell that she was immensely grateful for his company, for the presence of another human being.

She had saved Jared's life, and perhaps, in a way, Darius could save Fritzi's life now, and not for the first time. He had gone to great lengths to tip her off in Bali, once he got wind of her criminal past. Now he could attempt to save her from herself. Tired of cactus-bashing, he encouraged her to break for some tucker the outback lodge he was staying in had prepared and, which he had packed in his rucksack. Both ate ravenously. The food was pretty basic, but it revived them. Best of all was the mango juice, the sweetness bringing colour back into her face.

Even during times of intense anxiety, Darius realised, Fritzi looked stunningly pretty. He marvelled at her attire: laced hiking boots, cargo pants, a bush jacket with a backpack, and an old leather outback hat with a wide brim. Her hair was in a thick braid down her back. Only one word could describe Fritzi, he thought, and that word was 'magnificent.' Simply put, she had style; everything she threw on her body became an instant fashion statement.

They had been hiking for some time in silence when she spoke. At first, he didn't realise she was speaking, thought he had heard an echo or a rustle in the brush, but then she spoke again. 'Darius, can I talk to you?'

Shaken out of his own reverie, he smiled, grateful to hear her voice again and encouraging her to continue. He knew it was best to say little in moments like these; he had been on many bush hikes and meditations, and he understood how the human mind worked: it needed to offload all of those thoughts, images, and ideas that were bursting to get out like steam from a kettle.

He listened without comment as she emptied her mind, going back and forth over the actions and events of her past, never shying away from her worst moments or deeds. He was relieved to have read her background files; without them, he did not think he would have been able to keep up.

What seemed like an hour later, but was really only several intense minutes, she suddenly stopped. She was obviously exhausted, both mentally and physically. He turned to stare at her and was surprised to see that there were no tears, only a dejected sadness, as if her spirit had been broken. Her expression was flat, empty, affectless. And now he felt an emptiness and a yearning within him, too. The emptiness of the horizon, the emptiness in Fritzi's own soul. The almost endless divisions around them, within them. Were these divisions insuperable, impossible to repair? He hoped not. It was impossible to build bridges, to heal and to help others, to restore the soul. Not sure whether to break the silence, exhausted himself, he waited. It was time to head back, they did not want to be caught out here in the dark.

'We need to make our way back,' he finally said. 'The sun will be gone in two hours, and tour guides will be waiting for us at the centre.'

She followed as he hiked back, hurrying at first, then settling into a swift step. Silence fell between them once more. He wanted to make the hike hard, so that there was time only for putting one foot ahead of the other. Above all, he wanted to make it back before dark. He knew from experience that out in the bush the sun had a habit of falling out of the sky much faster, surprising even seasoned hikers and, plunging amateurs into panicked darkness. This time of year, the warmth would be sucked out and, the desert cold was to be avoided at all costs; neither had proper gear for a sudden temperature drop.

Mulling over her outpouring of guilt and anguish was one thing, but he knew the danger was real. DuPont could not get his head around the new Fritzi, and Darius had to admit that neither could Fritzi herself: she was stuck with old guilt, unable to move forward until she forgave herself for all of the dark deeds she had done. And, yet she could not find herself worthy of forgiveness. He neither wanted to nor had the skills to help her help herself, beyond listening without judgement.

At the centre the last bus was waiting to give them a ride back to the lodge. Both were bushed from the hard hike, with little energy for anything but a hot shower, and a cold beer.

Darius lay on the bed while Fritzi was in the shower. It felt good to be horizontal after a day of walking and climbing; the full length of his body supported by a soft mattress. He shut the world out, giving in to sleep.

Aware of movement around him, he forced his eyes open to find her fully dressed and ready. The sadness was still lingering around her eyes, but she had regained her energy and dignity. He made his way into the shower.

'Give me half an hour,' he said, 'and I'll meet you downstairs in the bar. You look great, by the way. Hopefully that hot shower will work its wonders on me.'

A little more than two hours later, back in bed, both tired but refreshed and more than a little drunk, he took Fritzi in his arms. If ever there was a time to give her comfort, it was now; she needed to feel loved. Again, he marvelled at her beauty, and the depth of his love for her. Had he ever loved anyone this much? Not Lin, certainly not Lin…

He felt shaken up by Fritzi still, but shaken up in a good way. Being with her made him feel buoyant and positive, and he therefore hated to see her sad and would do anything to set her right. But this would not be an easy process, as so much of the crimes she had committed in the past had been so severe, and the people she had hurt along the way felt that pain still. And now Fritzi felt it, too.

They flew out to Byron Bay the following morning. Fritzi wanted to reconnect with the friends she had made during her stay there. It was time to put her troubles on hold and to call her friends. To take a breath and to learn how to smile again The Australian outback had given her much to think about, and lying in Darius's arms after gentle lovemaking had helped to lull her into a dreamless sleep. Now she was ready to fight for what she wanted – and to seek professional advice. She had no idea what the future held, at least she knew that much. Still, she had much to feel grateful for. Darius was a godsend, and Maggie a comfort. Her friend Erika was holding her together. Fritzi and Erika talked for hours; she guided Fritzi with her professional knowledge, and persuaded her to keep moving forward. The past could not be changed, but the present could. Being positive about her future wasn't easy, she had so much hanging in the balance.

Chapter 21

Erika danced around her apartment, holding herself tightly. She got out one of her childhood albums, hidden amongst her memorabilia from the past, locked away in an American eagle topped cupboard in her study, a treasure she would never give up. It was battered and faded, but she loved it that way; it held remnants of her old life, both happy and sad ones, but both kept her in touch with her past and grounded in her new reality.

Truth be known, she did not recall much of what took place in that institution. Arriving there was the worst, knowing she was being locked away, possibly forever, and not knowing what had happened to her parents, and if they were even alive.

Her parents had received a stark warning from an unknown source to get out of East Berlin – or suffer the consequences. Her father had panicked (he admitted to Erika, years later, when she was reunited with her parents); as a result, he had not taken long enough to arrange the family's escape to the West. His main priority was Erika, his daughter: she had to escape Herr Dietrich, who had an insane hatred of Erika's outspokenness, especially in front of his own daughter, Fritzi.

They had paid a courier to help them cross over Checkpoint Charlie, but when it came to the day of the escape the plans suddenly changed. They were led down a long tunnel under the ground to a point near a barbed wire fence. Unaware of the searchlights flooding the area, they were caught like deer's in the headlights. Due to some sort of divine intervention (though none of them believed in God, He clearly believed in them), they were not shot. But what happened to them afterwards was almost worse than death. Maybe God – if He did exist – did not care for the family so much after all.

Her father had been taken off to be tortured and thrown into prison. All of their possessions and worldly goods were taken away. Her mother had not been tortured, but stripped of her dignity and thrown into a workers' camp. Erika had been dispatched to a holding cell, from where she was driven to the institution for the mentally insane (many of whom were, in fact, political dissidents and degenerates shunned by the communist regime and locked away from respectable society) to meet her fate. If it were not for the kindly doctor who saved her from becoming a lobotomised zombie at the age of fourteen, the remainder of her life wouldn't have been worth living.

The doctor had diagnosed her to be on the autistic spectrum, high functioning but incapable of reading societal nuances, especially in the repressive climate they were living in at that time. Erika voiced her disagreement of any laws she deemed unfair. She had been especially rebellious as a teenager, and her rebellion was compounded by the fact that she came from a liberal home, where it was considered healthy and acceptable to challenge existing notions and mores, and to discuss solutions to social problems. In the environment of her adolescence, in the DDR, nothing seemed to make sense to her.

She had been kept under continuous sedation for weeks in the institution, until the patients (or, more accurately, inmates) were all set free. Then, seemingly overnight, every single person who chose to was suddenly liberated. When it did happen, finally, it happened very quickly. Every Communist satellite country from Czechoslovakia to Poland were suddenly tasting freedoms they had previously only dreamed about. East Berliners were once more reunited with the rest of Germany; it was, at last, true unification.

When her parents crossed over to West Berlin, they were met with a live concert: Leonard Bernstein and his orchestra playing at the Brandenburg Gate. Many years later her father spoke about how elated they had felt; he had shed tears on hearing such wonderful music once more, music that somehow represented freedom, the sound of lightness and brightness and joy.

The doctor who had rescued her in the institution had given Erika a new lease of life. While her parents were being nursed back to health, the doctor had taken full responsibility for her wellbeing and education. Her parents had by then relocated to West Berlin, and Erika visited with them most days.

During those visits, her sensitive, progress, academic-minded parents encouraged her to study, and to get her degree. Once Erika was on her feet financially and able to support them, they moved in with her. Now they could be a family once more, but in a free and tolerant environment, able to ask questions and engage in political discussions, as was the family's earnest, intellectual nature. Life was good for a long while – until her parents passed, within a few months of one another.

The job, offer in the States came about at the very moment she most needed a change, and she grabbed at it with both hands. She had never wanted a family nor had any interest in marriage. She had seen enough awfulness in the world to question the wisdom of raising a child, a child who could possibly suffer the way she and her family had. The life they had led was not a life at all, more like a death sentence, and she wanted now only to move forward, to live in the now. She cohabited with a scientist and they had made a life of academia together. Both travelled on the lecture circuit. She had her private practice, life was now good and getting better.

Finding Fritzi, her childhood friend, had made Erika take stock of her own blessings. Certainly, Erika had suffered a great deal of tragedy in her life, but others had suffered even more, and at least she was alive, and intact. Yes, she was lucky, more fortunate perhaps than she could ever realise.

These thoughts flashed through her mind as she paged through the album, studying the pictures of herself and Fritzi. As children they had been the closest of friends, and perhaps not all that much had changed, now that they had found one another again. In fact, if it had not been, for, Fritzi, who came to her rescue time after time, when she was bullied or punished by teachers or unfairly picked on simply for being different, for not fitting in, her life would have been even more of a misery.

As it was, Erika had lived in constant dread of punishment by the state, had squandered her youth in a state of anxiety, self-doubt, and stifling depression. So much of her youth had been hell in itself. That was over now, and she had Fritzi to thank for her relative sanity. Now, it was Fritzi who appeared to be in a bad condition, Fritzi who needed her help. And Erika was eager to return the favour. She owed it to her childhood friend.

Fritzi and Erika had been drawn to each other early on. They had a lot in common; they were both very different from everyone else at school. Fritzi had a tough home life; she lived at Erika's parent's home most weekends. Her father was a Stasi officer and, strict authoritarian, and her mother was a typical German hausfrau: brisk and efficient, but all too willing to be submissive to her cruel and controlling husband, to toe the party line and to preserve, at all costs, the East German status quo.

Fritzi's sister, who had always appeared to Erika to be an older version of Fritzi (fiercely independent, and sometimes just fierce; a rebel in a place where overt rebellion was punishable by death, a deliciously subversive non-conformist with artistic temperaments of her own) left home the moment she met her boyfriend (a black man, no less) from Cameroon.

Erika was, therefore, thrilled to hear from Fritzi, having tried to track her down over the years without success, using Fritzi's birth name had not helped, Fritzi had long ago changed her identity becoming less Germanic and more western. By all accounts, Fritzi had done well for herself in her early years, attaining considerable success as a runway model. It was what had happened after that that confused and disturbed Erika. It appeared that Fritzi's later life, after meeting the Rubicov girl, had affected her psychological state and had possibly left deep scars.

Erika was shocked to the core to learn how dysfunctional Fritzi's life had become.

Both Erika and her partner were avid art collectors. Although Erika had read much about the Rubicov galleries, she had never visited any of them and it was something she was eager to do. She was not yet sure how she could assist Fritzi in her quest to repair her life and unburden her soul, but she thought it may help to meet with Yvetta and the other key members of the Rubicov family. She had read the files on Fritzi's life; the major players in her drama appeared to be from the Russian family.

Fritzi had asked Darius to send Erika the files, and Darius had, in turn, consulted Jared. Jared had left the decision to Fritzi's discretion, but had mentioned that, under the circumstances Fritzi had described to him, it was a sound decision. Fritzi needed positive feedback from those who had her best interests at heart. As someone (possibly the only one) who knew Fritzi's background intimately, Erika thought that she was in a unique position to help.

She read the files with alarm, realising their childhood had so much to do with her friend's state of mind and, ultimate decision--making processes, it was hard to ignore, that, some of her acting out, was shaped by her past. Since Erika was in New York City with her partner, Rob, a visit to the Manhattan Rubicov gallery seemed a good idea. She discussed the possibility with Rob, who was happy to indulge her. Not even half an hour later, they ventured into the gallery.

The artwork on exhibit were mostly sculptures, but they were displayed with a simultaneous exhibit that, was screened on monitors throughout the gallery. These images were of another exhibition, that was concurrently on at the Brooklyn Rubicov gallery. Rob had struck up a conversation with a French gentleman who was viewing the sculpture exhibit. He introduced himself as an art dealer. He was obviously intensely familiar with the work they collected at the gallery, which was in itself impressive, since the work here was so diverse, stretching more countries and forms than Erika could count.

The Frenchman, who was every bit as charming as he was knowledgeable, informed Rob that he was happy to assist the couple if ever they needed advice. He was charismatic and good-looking, with a somewhat youthful temperament and charisma, despite the fact that he appeared to be in his sixties. There were lines on his brow and around his eyes, but his manner was otherwise smooth – perhaps to a fault.

Fritzi's file still fresh in her mind, Erika thought she knew who the French gentleman was. She walked over stridently to introduce herself. It wasn't the right time to broach the subject of Fritzi with him, but she had every intention of doing so in the future. She just had to maintain a connection to him. As it happened, he had helpfully and coincidentally made the first move. It was almost too good to be true.

Rob had taken the Frenchman's card – it was, indeed, DuPont, she realised with a satisfying shiver – and she resolved to contact him when the time was right, even if she had to do so under false pretences. Investing in art wasn't a hardship, and DuPont was well respected in his field. Erika suddenly felt tremendously excited. But informing Fritzi – or, for that matter, the Australian human rights lawyer, or her boyfriend – could wait until she had something positive (or at least constructive) to tell them.

She did not know what she could achieve by introducing Fritzi's childhood friend, but she felt strongly that it would be easier to empathise with a narrative when faced with one of the actual people involved, and a person who – unlike Fritzi herself – had not negatively impacted on any of their lives, Fritzi's antagonists may be less inclined to dismiss Erika's version of Fritzi's story out of hand.

She realised that Fritzi's, enemies were all victims one way or another, their lives connected by and to Fritzi, through Yvetta Rubicov. Erika was no stranger to how this must feel. Erika's own family had suffered because of Fritzi's father – indeed, they had been almost destroyed by the ramifications of his actions and his inherent and irrational dislike of Erika.

Erika had come to terms with this now – to the degree that anyone could ever come to terms with such trauma. The Rubicov family, in turn, Erika had learned, had suffered great pain, due to their daughter's connection to Fritzi. All of Yvetta's immediate family (even her British sister-in-law) had been tormented, not just Yvetta herself. As Erika perceived it, there was an incestuous connection linking her with the Rubicov family, with these people she had never met and about whom she had only recently heard about.

Erika's career and reputation were flourishing, and she found herself much in demand. She only had a few lectures coming up in Australia, one in Perth and the other in Melbourne, which would allow her to see her friend in the new year – which was in itself contingent on whether Fritzi would be permitted to stay in Australia. Before this year was out, though, she had a lecture tour in Berlin. followed by a lecture in Tel Aviv.

She was most excited to return to Israel, a country she had only recently begun to become passionate about, as her distant connection to her roots became known to her. Her hectic schedule left very little time for her to concentrate on the immediate problem of Fritzi, a problem that had begun to occupy her as much (if not more so than) her lecture tour and her work. She desperately wanted to help her friend resolve her predicament with the Rubicov family.

She understood from Fritzi that, after Alexi Rubicov's untimely death, the leadership of the family empire had passed onto Mika Rubicov, the oldest brother. Yvetta Rubicov, Fritzi's beloved, was the only sister and by far the family's most troubled member, although she too seemed to have been reformed. Fritzi, Erika felt, could be reformed, too, and was well on her way, taking the first necessary steps to making peace with both herself and her conflicted past. Surely, she could make peace with the people she had hurt, too?

Perhaps the larger question was, could they make peace with her? Fritzi had told Erika that Mika was not to be messed with: he called the shots, and those shots could, in fact, be literal. He was not above breaking the law to achieve the family's ends, and he was familiar with the Russian mafia, and with other mafias as well. Without a doubt, Fritzi had sabotaged that family, and caused them much pain in the past.

This was a highly complicated situation, and Erika wanted to give her involvement in it, even and especially at this early stage, more thought. She was nothing if not thoughtful, rigorous, academic, cynical even (in no small part because of the events of the past) second-guessing herself often, and the actions and judgements of others as well. She would think the situation through from every angle, decide her part in it and prepare as if for a lecture, in order to best get her point across.

The aim was this: she would try to get the Rubicov family to empathise with someone they detested, namely Fritzi. This would, by all accounts, be a very hard task, a huge ask on their behalf. Would Erika be successful? She had her doubts. Still, what did she have to lose? She owed Fritzi at least an attempt at mediation, even if it would prove to be impossible. She was prepared for this outcome, too. As cynical as she often was, Erika could often be unreasonably optimistic – she had lived in America long enough to have a healthy faith in both herself and even those around her. She therefore believed that she had a better than average chance of achieving the impossible with the Rubicovs. When she put her mind to something, she was like a terrier with a bone, she wouldn't let it go until she had the required results.

Not long after her stint in Manhattan, and her decision to take on the Rubicovs and DuPont, Erika flew off to Berlin for the lecture tour. On the long flight over she gave the Fritzi situation her full attention, even drawing up notes on a yellow legal pad and strategizing her initial, imagined meetings with the family. As if compiling a case history on each subject, she compiled a thick sheath of rigorous notes, delving as deeply as possible into the background of all of the people with whom she planned to meet, in order to familiarise herself with their strengths and weaknesses, and to come up with a winning plan. When dealing with unpredictable personalities, it was always good to know as much as possible about your subjects. But first, Berlin.

Each time she visited Berlin she was pulled back to her childhood. Life had moved on, and so had Germany, a truly modern and thriving democracy and economy now. The old days were well and truly in the past. Germany had moved on from its acts of savagery to become an economic powerhouse. Berlin's past was commemorated with holocaust memorials, a stark reminder to build a better future. Germany could not, allow its past to be forgotten. Nothing less than the fate of humanity was at stake.

Not so long ago, the world had come dangerously close to destruction, had been pulled back from annihilation only at the very last moment. Germany had tried to face up to that time with determination, and its citizens were now forced to learn about their atrocities, so that they would never repeat them. Archives were a testament to what had happened, and the awful past was enshrined in the German education system.

Erika's parents had survived the war, largely because her great grandparents had assimilated. the family were thought to be Catholics like everyone else in their neighbourhood. The family's link to the Jewish faith was present but weak and never, never spoken of. Not until her father and mother were once more, safe and living in the new Germany with her did they reconnect to the religion of their forebears, the religion and ethnicity that the German nation had tried (and almost succeeded in) wiping off the face of the earth. Sadly, her parents never got the chance to make the journey to Israel. Erika had made sure to take their ashes with on her first visit; it was what her parents would have wanted, and what Erika wanted as well. She was pleased her parents were now resting in a place they believed was their natural home.

She had never given religion much thought, and there was a reason for that. She had been brought up during the communist era – her childhood shaped, and misshapen, by that failed and futile ideology – in which the state replaced religion, which was outlawed and frowned upon. But she still had no religious affiliations. A visit to Israel changed her ideas and, made her, if not a practising Jew, then, at least one who was proud of her lineage and connection to Israel. Friday nights were now observed, and she attended a liberal synagogue once in a while, on a religious holy day. This level of observance was enough for her; it made her feel closer to her father and mother, who had become observant in their old age.

When in Berlin she would visit familiar places, it was like returning home. She loved Berlin, which had become a vibrant city. Tel Aviv offered another feeling of coming home; her parents were buried there. Gaining permission to bury their ashes had not been easy. She had to jump through many hoops before she was able to lay her parents to rest in the country of their wishes. Returning each year to visit was something she would do until the day she died, she decided, or moved to Israel herself, to be close to their spirits and their spiritual home.

She would return each time feeling renewed in the knowledge that she had fulfilled a promise to her mother and father. Should she feel responsible for Fritzi, too? The question kept popping up in her mind, and the answer was always the same: yes, she should feel responsible – it was the least she could do for her only childhood friend. Long ago, Fritzi had saved her life, and now it was time for Erika to do the same. This time she wanted her promise to enable her friend to live a long and fulfilled life. That was what she prayed for when at the Western Wall in Jerusalem, with all of her heart. Perhaps Erika and Fritzi could visit Israel together one day soon. A new life for Fritzi, a second chance for both of them. Spiritual renewal.

The political situation in Israel had cropped up in conversation many times with Erika's colleagues in the States, and she, too had discussed it with Israelis. A wise person once advised that the three major religions should be viewed as one, and in much the same way as a person viewed a house. The foundations were the Jewish religion, the walls were the Christian religion, and the roof the Muslim religion. Erika had given that deceptively simple-sounding statement much thought, and decided it contained a great deal of depth and truth. After all, if one removed the foundation of a house, nothing would remain standing. It was a sobering thought to hang onto; the foundations of monotheistic religions, the so-called Abrahamic religion (because they shared a fabled ancestor – and much else besides), began in the Middle East.

Back in the States, renewed in her mission to help Fritzi, she made a decision to visit Safi and Yvetta, and also Mika and the Frenchman DuPont. She was not going to balk at her responsibility, or feel intimidated by these people's fathomless wealth or considerable power. Social and material trappings like wealth and power did not impress Erika, who had grown up with nothing and been to hell and back before the age of seventeen. She had, she thought, a stronger grip on life. What she had on her side was reason, generosity, and forgiveness. The foundations of something special.

If she was going to appeal to the Rubicov family to hear her out – if she was going to launch an intimate, impassioned defence of Fritzi – she had no choice but to do so in person. Erika realised that she herself was the living example of her friend's good character. And Erika was also living proof (possibly the only, objective proof still in existence) that the story told by Fritzi was the truth.

Erika made up her mind about a lot of things fairly quickly. She would not reveal her sources, and certainly not where Fritzi now resided – at not until (or if) she received permission to do so from Fritzi herself. All Erika wanted, at this stage, was to plant in their minds the seed of doubt that had festered over the years about Fritzi.

Rob was away on a lecture tour in Ireland, one of his favourite countries: he loved the green hills, the pubs (he loved these maybe a little too much, Erika sometimes suspected), and the Irish sense of humour. Erika was very different from Rob, which was perhaps why they got along so well. Most of the time, anyway, they got along extraordinarily well. She was lucky to have found him, and she had heard him say much the same about her.

Their differences kept them at peace (albeit sometimes apart), and the similarities of their interest (human nature, psychology, the arts) brought them always close together. She was more passionate about Israel than Ireland, which she found an interesting, enjoyable trip, but hardly life-altering. She preferred to visit places with a less old--fashioned approach to feminist issues like abortion. The Catholic Church had a hold over so many rights, if not laws, making it difficult for true progressivism to flourish in the country, or for many taboos and restrictions to be relaxed.

The reality was hard to ignore; many women still suffered – in Ireland, and certainly elsewhere as well. Everywhere, she sometimes thought, had its own peculiar problems. Nowhere was safe from suffering of some kind. All over the world women suffered, and life was harder than it needed to be. The pain of other people gave Erika pain, too. She was empathic, perhaps overly so; she couldn't help but be. She knew what it meant to be in pain, an outcast, a subject of shame, and she knew how it felt to be liberated, and she wanted desperately to help others to liberate themselves. But it wasn't always easy, and she often felt that she failed.

She had seen patients, unmarried mothers, who had given up babies needlessly. It was hard to believe so many still had the same stubborn and destructive attitude, even though the times had long ago changed, and so had society's conception of the rights and resolve of single mothers.

Her mind kept drifting from the issue of Fritzi, which was tantalising complex and, for that reason, both frustrating and enticing. She could not fathom how to approach the Rubicovs. It was like a jigsaw puzzle, the pieces of which were always jumbled, though each time in different ways. It was still a struggle for Erika to rein in her immediate tendency to blurt out, what was uppermost in her mind. It had taken determination and, self-discipline to keep a civil tongue in company, or, when challenged, to answer questions with which she did not agree.

Most people (interested only in themselves, as so many – perhaps too many – were) did not notice that she had a stilted manner about her movements, or that she could sometimes be a little too honest when dealing with emotive issues in a more pragmatic manner.

It was an occupational hazard she had to be continuously aware of, to show the empathy she felt. Living in New York made it slightly easier; she found her anxieties and often anti-social behaviour to be more acceptable here. There were others like her here, a whole community of others. That was the nice thing about New York – there was plenty of everyone (and, seemingly, everything – well, everything except available real estate and moderate rent) here. It was an easy place to blend in, if not exactly fit in.

And she enjoyed the anonymity and enormousness of the city, too. It sometimes seemed that every New Yorker was outspoken, never shying away from confrontation, indeed relishing all but the most extreme exchanges. And then there were others who kept themselves to themselves, who shied away from everything, and stayed in their tiny apartments alone for days, afraid of the sunlight or the darkness or whatever their peculiar phobias were.

On a day-to-day basis, Erika's was, she supposed, at the low end of the autistic spectrum her self-diagnosis for her awkwardness. But, these days, more and more people were coming out as autistic, and the condition was – thankfully – more socially acceptable and, at least superficially, better understood. One reason why she adored Rob so much was that he not only accepted her occasionally anti-social, even abrasive behaviour, but was sensitive to her moods and moodiness, her rituals and routines, and seemed to love her in spite of her affliction. Certainly, he had his own foibles – everyone did – at least that's what he always joked. 'Nobody's perfect,' he would often say, quoting the last line of one of his favourite films, Some Like It Hot. Well, to Erika, Rob was pretty close to perfect, most of the time, anyway.

She preferred not to speak directly to the Rubicov family and DuPont before notifying them, but how to contact them was a dilemma. Her attempts at writing a letter was scrunched up and thrown into the very quickly overflowing bin under her desk, handwritten would have to be rejected, although her calculation was to send an embossed sealed envelope, that would not be discarded out of hand.

She never mixed alcohol with her anti-anxiety medication, but tonight she felt a small schnapps would not go amiss; she badly needed to relax. The schnapps was kept in a drawer in her study desk, reserved for moments when life became a little too tense; it was her way of reconnecting with her German roots.

Some people relaxed with an illicit cigarette or some hash, but she had schnapps (but never more than two shots), always followed by an espresso freshly brewed from the machine. This too was a ritual, one of many. In this way, she had rigorously organised aspects of her life. Unfortunately, to help organise other people's lives was not nearly as easy.

Sipping the espresso she surveyed the overflowing bin, and decided her best course of action would be by invitation. Her conundrum was, should the letter be handwritten, or should she communicate via a personal call, or by today's preferred method of email? She quickly decided that handwritten letters were classier but could easily go astray (more unnecessary anxiety, wondering if, or when the letter would ever arrive), while a personal call was out of the question (what would she say and how would she even begin to say it?) No, she thought, it had to be by email, which was, in any case, her preferred method.

A joint email to Yvetta, Safi, and Mika would be best, but she did not have, and could not locate, Mika's email address, another stumbling block. Her, communication would have to be with Safi and Yvetta to begin with, and hopefully she would progress from there, depending on the outcome of the initial email.

DuPont was someone she could tackle at a later date; as far as Erika could tell, the Frenchman did not pose a threat to Fritzi's life.

Tired and tipsy from the schnapps after deleting numerous emails, she decided that bed was a priority. She had the whole of tomorrow, Sunday, to figure things, and then she could do so with a clear mind, not at all inebriated.

Returning from her Sunday morning run, Erika opened her emails and was shocked to find one from DuPont. But how … she had decided against making contact, with him, for now.

Reading the email over several times, she realised he was keen on selling her and Rob some art; it was a surprising, but very welcome, coincidence.

Erika shot off an email to DuPont, inquiring whether he was free for brunch. Rob was away, she informed, but she had questions, would he be available to meet?

As it happened, DuPont had saved her from another wasted day figuring out how to correspond with the Rubicovs.

Erika arrived early, settling into a corner banquette in the midtown restaurant he had suggested. She hadn't been there five minutes when she noticed a handsome older man make his way across to her table; he didn't look quite as suave in his casual attire as he had during their initial encounter at the Rubicov gallery.

DuPont studied Erika as she ordered her brunch. He found her alarmingly petite, almost birdlike, with piercing blue eyes, attractive in a serious, studious manner. He leaned forward, his voice appeared to change, and there was a hard glint in his eyes now.

'Erika, I am going to come clean,' DuPont said. 'I know who you are. Forgive me, but after you introduced yourself at the Rubicov gallery, it took some time for the penny to drop You are Erika from Fritzi's childhood, am I correct?'

'How would you know that?' Erika asked, bewildered.

'Ah, well,' the Frenchman began slowly, his voice unusually gravelly now, 'I am now going to fill you in.' He smiled thinly. 'It's only fair that I meet you before I can settle an irritating psychological question. It has been uppermost in my mind since my return from Australia, some weeks ago now – far too long, in fact, for me not to do something about it.'

Now it was Erika's chance to feel in the dark, confused, conflicted, as though she no longer had the upper hand of being in control of the conversation. To be surprised was to be in a position of subservience, to be dominated, she now understood. She had no chance but to listen in stunned silence. It did not take long before she realised that Darius, Fritzi's love-of-the-moment, and, more alarmingly, Jared, her lawyer, had shared highly personal information with the Frenchman. But why? She felt outraged on Fritzi's behalf. And she felt angry with herself for being so ignorant about a situation she had dived into with such speed and, she now understood, vulnerability.

'I understand Darius's reasons for investigating Fritzi,' Erika said, 'although my verdict is still out about his invading her private life in this way.'

DuPont did not speak, but now nodded for her to continue.

'Why would they take you into their confidence about her childhood,' Erika asked, taking care not to raise her voice, 'and share something with you that is none of your business?'

'Ah, you may well ask,' DuPont said. 'This is precisely why I so wanted to speak with you face to face. And it's why, after determining who you were, I sent you that email, trying to establish communication.'

'Explain, please,' she said flatly.

DuPont was initially taken aback by her abrupt, even abrasive tone, but then he recalled both the reason and the degree she had suffered throughout her childhood, and decided against becoming offended. He wanted information from this woman, and it would not pay to antagonise her, or to be antagonised himself in the process.

'Darius and Jared, who I met while in Australia,' DuPont began, 'wanted me to empathise with Fritzi's experience as a child, with what they believed shaped her personality and her life. They believe the reason for her fanatical behaviour towards the Rubicovs, not to mention towards me, stem directly from that time.'

Erika kept staring at DuPont, waiting for him to come to the point. She was not prepared to fill in the blanks for him; surely, he knew her story. She had not forgiven him for inviting her under false pretences, even if she had met with him with similar intentions, it still irked her. He no longer seemed quite so smooth, and not nearly as charming as he had appeared at the gallery.

'I am so sorry and horrified about what happened to you, Erika,' he said, his voice and face downcast. 'It's a monstrous thing that Fritzi's father intended to do to you.'

'Yes, but he did not succeed,' Erika said, warming to the Frenchman once again.

'Dear God,' he said softly, 'that would have been tragic, a crime too awful to imagine.' He smiled again, but it was a small, strange smile, as though it pained him to do so. His eyes, though, were soft, warm, sensitive, she observed, not for the first time. No wonder she had been drawn to him at their first meeting. 'Sitting here with you today, I realise now how miraculous it must be for Fritzi to find you are alive and well. The guilt must have been overpowering.'

'Yes,' she said simply.

DuPont was struggling to warm to Erika; she was difficult to read, unpredictable, very possibly inflexible. An intelligent woman, certainly, perhaps far too intelligent for her own good, he reflected. He did not know how to continue this discussion; she appeared to be hostile towards him, looking at him with cold, wavering eyes – or not looking at him at all. What was she thinking? He did not know and it scared him. He tried out a change in tone.

'Perhaps now,' DuPont volunteered, 'Fritzi feels free from some of that guilt, some of that pain. I hope so. You are clearly one of the most important people in her life, one of the few people with whom she can be herself.'

But Erika did not reply.

'May I ask, Erika, do you know about Fritzi's life since she left Berlin?'

'I do,' she said, 'and, with Fritzi's permission, I have read all of the files that were passed on to me; they are, to say the least, comprehensive.'

'What is your opinion,' DuPont said, almost afraid now to make eye contact with this inscrutable, almost intimidating, woman, 'if I may ask?'

This was Erika's opportunity to lay out a defence for her friend, to say all of the things she wanted to, an argument she had been rehearsing for days … yet she hesitated.

'I know you hold Fritzi responsible for everything that happened here,' she said, 'and, worse, what happened to the Rubicovs.' She made a point to gaze directly into the Frenchman's soft eyes, to implore him, from one human being to another, to forgive her friend. 'And yes, she did without question do all of those things. But I have a different story to tell, if you would allow me. I have known Fritzi from the age of five. In fact, and as I think you know, she was my only friend in a very hostile environment, in what was a country and culture – now extinct, thank God – that was, if you'll forgive me, quite ugly.'

The Frenchman nodded, and she noted again the kind eyes.

'Fritzi's loyalty to me, right up until we were fourteen and I disappeared, never wavered. She protected me, over and over, in the face of grave danger. It is not a stretch to say that she saved my life. The finger of the law – a crooked, ugly finger; a law that was utterly criminal in so many ways, and that was bereft of forgiveness or humanity – stretched a very long way. It was frankly suffocating, that finger, those laws, that country, that time. Many people couldn't survive it – I know I barely did. Only the ideology of the communist era was valued. People certainly were not, especially not those who were deemed to be an enemy of the state, like my father and myself. If one person in a family was seen as a political renegade, or suspected of a crime against the state, a family would lose everything. There were spies everywhere – everywhere. In your neighbourhood, in your community, in your school even, under the cover of darkness and in broad daylight. No one was safe. Everyone was watched, even young teenagers. The state knew everything about everyone, and everyone watched everyone else. Paranoia is ugly and infectious, like a virus. It destroys entire communities. We were all spies.'

She took a gulp of her water. Her voice was trembling slightly now. DuPont did not want to interrupt her, he could tell she was emotional. He had read, of course, how life had been in East Germany, but he had never before spoken to anyone who had suffered first-hand, and Erika had most definitely suffered.

'I believe that Fritzi was without a doubt affected – as am I, from our experience. As a child, I actually got off lightly, compared to Fritzi.'

She stopped, surprising even herself, saw the look of doubt on DuPont's lined and handsome face.

'Even in bad times, there were good people. Never as many good people as one would like there to be, but good people nonetheless. The doctor who worked in that place of horror saved me. Apart from my fear on arrival, and my anxiety that I would never again see my parents, were, they dead? or that I would never see them again, I do not remember very much. The doctor did me a favour by keeping me sedated, to save me from a fate worse than death. Once we were free, that doctor became my surrogate mother and provider, until I was able to support myself, and support my parents, with whom I thankfully reconnected. Like Fritzi, that doctor saved my life. I owe her everything.

'Fritzi, on the other hand, had nothing: no parents to prop her up or wish her well, no safety net, no provider, nothing but self-doubt and darkness and despair. And intense, unsparing guilt, guilt most people would find difficult to live with. She was a child only fifteen, alone, who had to make her own way in a very tough world.

'I believe when she met Yvetta, who, from what I have read and heard, was suffering from bipolar disorder, and who, to Fritzi's mind, needed protecting at all costs, her childhood trauma and fight-or-flight experience and guilt kicked in. She wanted to be a kind of mother and saviour to Yvetta, and maybe she went about it all wrong, but her intention was good, believe it or not, it was pure. Yvetta took my place in Fritzi's mind. Yes, I believe Fritzi was reliving her past in a different time, with a different person, but reliving it nonetheless.' She stared closely at DuPont. 'It was Yvetta, but it wasn't Yvetta. It was more than Yvetta, it was more than anyone. Fritzi was protecting me.'

DuPont did not speak for a long time. He found Erika's unsparing gaze disconcerting. The restaurant had emptied out in the time that they had sat there – seemingly forever, but really just thirty minutes or so – and now felt altogether too quiet.

'I see where you're coming from,' DuPont finally said, when it became evident that Erika had finished speaking, 'but why on earth did she need to attack me? Or Alexi's wife? Or poor Safi, who was entirely innocent? Or others, for that matter, who were not directly involved with Yvetta? Her behaviour was criminal, it was pathological, it was sick. It was, one could say, inexcusable, unforgivable.' He returned her hard gaze with a stare of his own.

Now, Erika was the one to turn away. She looked back at the restaurant, as though just noticing that it was now empty. She looked at the front door, as though plotting her escape. Then she said softly,

'The way Fritzi saw it, you helped Safi to take Yvetta's galleries away from her. In her mind you were to be punished for indirectly hurting Yvetta, robbing her of her passion, and taking her career, her reason for living, away from her. The galleries were everything to Yvetta, and then she had nothing, and Fritzi wanted to avenge that.'

'But why?' DuPont asked, genuinely not understanding.

'Safi had to be punished for taking Yvetta's gallery. Everyone Yvetta saw as her enemy had to be punished – by Fritzi, on Yvetta's behalf. And, yes it was inexcusable, unforgivable, but maybe you can see her true intentions, the demented logic behind the attacks. Fritzi saved Yvetta from every institution the family locked her away in; it was a pattern for a long time. Until it eventually stopped, that is, because Yvetta no longer needed Fritzi's protection.

'And, that realisation broke Fritzi, it destroyed her anew, because, like Yvetta without her galleries, she suddenly had no purpose in her life, she was full of rage and guilt and lashing out everywhere, not knowing where to turn. She had to flee from this realisation, much as she had to flee from the law. She had behaved badly for a long, time her life of crime was catching up to her. She was desperate. Time was running out. Running away from the authorities and from her crimes, travelling overseas, with a new identity, her life began again. Without realising it she yearned for salvation, for forgiveness from her enemies. But first and most importantly she needs to forgive herself.

'When Fritzi and I reconnected, for the first time in decades, I spoke to her daily, sometimes twice a day. Even now, when a day goes by that we do not speak, she still texts me every day, without fail. She needs me in her life, and it's become apparent that I need her as well. Like old times, when we were children, in a different world, a world that in many ways no longer exists, but in some ways, psychologically, continues to loom large. I always answer her, because she needs to know every day that I am alive and well. She has almost no one in her life, you must understand, and she desperately wants and needs people to care for, to give her life meaning, to help keep her afloat.'

DuPont nodded, waiting, not sure she had finished speaking.

'I did not approve of her methods,' Erika continued, her voice now steadier, more relaxed, 'or her involvement with the stolen artefacts, for which I believe she has been punished. I have told her honestly what I think' – DuPont well believed this, he had had a taste of Erika's unwavering (perhaps even unbearable) honesty – 'but I do wholeheartedly believe that Fritzi has changed. She deserves to be left alone to start again, and, most importantly, she deserves a second chance. She is still young, she deserves to live her life without looking over her shoulder all the time, constantly in fear of reprisals from the Rubicov family. I am now fighting for her, after all she never stopped fighting for me, through Yvetta, that is. I do believe this to be the case.'

'Is that your professional opinion,' DuPont asked.

'No, it's what I understand to be the truth.'

He did not know how to respond. After all, this had happened to Erika and Fritzi, it was their story, everyone had a story, much like he and Safi and Yvetta and Mika had their own story, too – and who was he to judge? All the same, Fritzi had caused many people a great deal of pain. Much of that pain remained, and he knew that people lived with its ramifications, the echoes of the past, every day, much as they tried to move on with their lives. Perhaps he needed to soften his stance on Fritzi after all; in time he believed that he would. But not quite now. He wasn't ready.

'Honestly,' DuPont began, 'I empathise with your story, but I find it extremely hard to empathise with the Fritzi I know, to reconcile your Fritzi with my Fritzi, as it were.' He looked to see if Erika understood, and from her eyes, her posture, he believed that she did indeed understand. 'The Rubicovs have been through enough hell. I do not believe they should, or need to, know anything else about Fritzi, including her whereabouts. She is out of their lives now, and it is best if it remains that way.'

He waited for Erika to nod, or respond in some way, but instead she said, surprising him, 'Perhaps you are not the one to make that decision for them.'

He shifted uncomfortably, now ready to leave: the conversation, the encounter, Erika herself, had left him feeling exhausted and uneasy. It was never, even after all of this time, easy to relive his experiences with Fritzi. And many people had been wounded by her far worse than he had, carried greater wounds, deeper scars. It was important, therefore, to keep those people safe.

'I feel protective towards, Safi, my dear,' the Frenchman said, somewhat uneasily, his usual charisma and self-confidence seemingly dissipated, 'she is a very dear friend.'

Yes, Erika thought, from what I read, at some point, she was more than just a friend. But instead, she said, 'I have no doubt, but I still think the Rubicovs should know Fritzi's whole story. After all, we are all adults – even Fritzi, now more so than before. The Rubicov family forgave their own kith and kin, who wreaked havoc, too, I believe.'

DuPont leaned forward again, but now he had very little energy left in him, and certainly was in no mood to argue, or even entertain.

'How do you propose to tell them?' he asked.

'I have not worked that out yet,' Erika said, but she seemed distracted still. 'Don't you think there is a direct link between all of us, through Fritzi. Though we don't know one another, she has affected all of our lives one way or another.'

'If you look at it that way,' the Frenchman said, 'I suppose that she has, yes.' He surprised her with a smile, but it was a thin, almost bitter, smile. And the soft eyes looked tired now, too.

'I am the living proof that she is not the monster you believe her to be,' Erika said finally.

'Erika, please talk to me before you contact the Rubicovs. They may not be open or prepared to view Fritzi as you wish them to.'

'Well, I have tried,' Erika said. 'Perhaps when you have given it more thought we can come up with a solution together, a kind of proposal to bring to the Rubicovs, something that will cause the minimum amount of damage.'

'Oh, there will always be damage,' DuPont said wearily.

'I am afraid the head of that family may try to harm Fritzi. I cannot allow that to happen, you understand? I have lost Fritzi once, I don't intend to lose her again. Not under any circumstances.'

DuPont could not deny this; he knew it was only a matter of time before Mika tracked her down. And possibly, since so many now seemed to know Fritzi's whereabouts, Mika was closer than ever.

'I will give it thought, Erika, but please do not attempt to appeal to them. I cannot see it working in Fritzi's favour.'

She could tell DuPont was overwhelmed by the conversation.

'Now I must go,' he said softly, fatigue evident in his gentle voice, 'I am quite exhausted after this discussion, my dear, quite exhausted. I need fresh air and a very long walk.'

Chapter 22

Mika sat at his desk, methodically going through mail, as he did every morning. This morning, in particular, was a pleasure. It was winter, the best time of the year to be in Florida. The patio doors to the terraces were open, and a light breeze was tugging at the voile covering the open doors, in order to prevent any mosquitoes from entering. Still, they still hung around annoyingly when the temperature rose.

The maid had just been in to bring him his usual midmorning coffee accompanied by a bran muffin. Up early and out of the house before six-thirty, he was ready to indulge after a competitive game of tennis with his coach, followed by a swim in his pool. Mika loved his home on Star Island: it was secure, and offered the best views of the coastal waters on both sides.

He had bought this palatial mansion sight unseen: one of many properties his agent had scouted for him to invest in. The moment he laid eyes on the property, in fact, he had the workmen move in to adapt it to his taste. He was one of those wealthy people who received as much pleasure from property as from other people. This one had given him untold pleasure during the winter months; the summer, on the other hand, was far too humid.

Mika and his girlfriend preferred Europe, where they had a portfolio of properties to choose from. A villa near Geneva was his favourite choice, but Daniella preferred to holiday on the continent, or to stay at his mother's small chateau on the French Riviera. The properties were all part of Rubicov Industries impressive (and ever-growing) portfolio. Once Anna passed away, now almost four years ago, the chateau remained as a holiday home.

Tuscany was another favourite destination; the food, all farmed by the locals on his property, was delicious. Here, they produced their own olive oil and wine, not to mention bright, abundant and very tasty cherry tomatoes, and other fresh produce besides. The hardworking staff maintained the grounds. The gardens were kept throughout the year by the locals, who were thankful for the work. Mika liked to think of it as a team effort: he had bought the old castle in disrepair, and the artisans from the area spent many months bringing it back to life. It was a jewel on a hill looking down on the valleys below. The scenery and colours changing from hour to hour, one could sit on the terraces with their overhanging bougainvillea, watching the beauty of those rustic hills as the sun set, hearing the sounds of the birds and crickets. A treat for the senses and for the self, those were long, lazy, mesmerising days spent languishing outdoors, enjoying fresh simple dishes prepared in the kitchen.

The family all spent their holidays on the continent. Safi preferred the rustic Italian castle, while Yvetta loved the French Riviera. It was the only time they managed to spend a full month together as a family, with – most importantly (Mika thought) – the Russian, English and American cousins getting a chance to grow up together. Inevitably, Mika and Daniella spent most of their time in Tuscany with Safi.

After that, the family chose to spend the rest of the summer at the portfolio's other properties, but separately, and never together. It was a perfect arrangement for everyone: just enough time to catch up and enjoy the reunion, and not enough time to get on one another's nerves, to squabble, or fall back on old feuds and petty politics (of which there were more than a few).

More recently, Mika had been enquiring about properties in Greece, another unspoilt part of the world the larger family could enjoy as a group holiday. But Mika was more specific in his demands, and had the capital and resources to realise them, too – and to settle for nothing less. What he wanted was a property with its own private beach. More specifically still, he wanted to moor a small yacht, with which he would cruise around the islands with the family, often and at their leisure. This was the dream he was currently busy trying to turn into a reality, an ideal distraction from more pressing, work-related politics.

Mika ruled his empire, growing the family's assets. But it wasn't about the family's assets, it was about the family itself: they were his passion and his reason for living. He would do whatever it took to keep them happy and safe, as his father Alexi had done before him. He had learnt it from an early age and he would never forget it: family was everything.

Now he was home, surrounded by a staff who catered to his whims. He liked to joke that Daniella, his partner, kept him on his toes, but the truth was that he secretly enjoyed the charity events she organised – so many charities! so many events! – it gave him an opportunity to be generous. He understood only too well the kudos and respect this level of philanthropy had afforded her. Indeed, she had become the queen of her social circle.

Between tennis and his travels – and what Daniella termed his 'workaholic ways' – he kept trim, privately admitting he wasn't a bad-looking for a man in his mid-sixties. Since leaving Russia several years ago he had learnt to relax more, to be more American in many of his pursuits (which included the pursuit of leisure) and less Russian in certain other pursuits (the pursuit of plentiful vodka, for one). He had seen his father die before his time from stress, and had no intention of following suit. He had begun to take life easier.

It was shortly before twelve when he set his mail aside and opened his laptop to view his personal emails. Among a clutter of names, he knew and work-related queries from friends (and one or two foes), he was surprised to find a message from a contact in Australia. The contact had attached to the message a newspaper article, which Mika scanned, then read in full, and then read again. It was only then that he read the explanatory message below.

After rereading the article for a fourth time, he returned to the message once more. At, first he scratched his head – certainly his attention had been caught, but he was still confused. The article (from an Australian paper) and the corresponding message did not seem to make any sense– but the contact was a reliable source. The article was about a very brave person who had saved the Australian prime minister's son etcetera, and about a woman waiting for her Australian citizenship, and they were, apparently, one and the same.

And that person, according to his contact, was Fritzi. Before allowing his immediate feelings of anger at the mention of her name, to rise to the surface. He needed details, places, people – everything he could find on her. If this person was indeed Fritzi, he wanted to know when she woke up, and when she went to bed; every piece of information that could be dug up.

The truth of Fritzi's whereabouts, and whichever identity she was now assuming, had to come through sooner or later, Mika was certain of that. He knew enough about intelligence work (through his long history working with people like Janus to know that no one fell off the face of the earth or went into hiding for ever; certainly not someone like Fritzi, who was (both at the best of times and at the worst of times) a larger than life personality.

Yvetta and Safi were about to make their journey to Australia and Mika wasn't happy about it. They did not know about any of Mika's suspicions – nor should they. Indeed, if he insisted, they be accompanied by Kolya, or other protection, they would become suspicious, something he wanted to avoid at all costs. He did not want them to know Fritzi was in Australia, nor did he want to spoil this long-awaited visit for them.

And if they found out about Fritzi (with all the attendant trauma and horror – the complicated and still resonant pain of the past – that her very name brought up) their holiday would be ruined. He knew Safi wanted to visit with her family out there and to see Australia's considerable wealth of art museums and cultural history. Mika himself, already overstretched and thinking of Greece rather than Oz, had no desire to accompany them on this trip himself – nor did he have the time to do so. Still, something needed to be done, some sort of security system or defence mechanism put in place before they arrived in Sydney.

The Russian underworld contact he had in Australia were reliable, but Mika was not sure whether they were capable of keeping a low profile, of being unseen by Safi and Yvetta's suspicious eyes – eyes that,

Mika feared, were already prone to paranoia, and with good reason. No, he needed someone who could shadow them covertly rather than obvious bodyguards. Mika called his Israeli contact Yuri, with whom he often did business; Yuri's company were used for the high, profile protection of dignitaries from all over the world.

Mika would send Yuri his sister's and Safi's itinerary, and once Yuri's company had the information, the resulting protection would not be a problem to organise. Mika called Yvetta and then Safi, asking them to send a copy of their itinerary. He said that, for business and familial reasons, he needed to know when and where they would be at all times.

Yvetta did not argue; she knew how cautious her brother could be. Safi and Janus likewise agreed that it would be prudent if Safi and Yvetta's whereabouts were known at all times. Janus called Mika to sound him out and, to figure out the subtext behind his sudden and surprising request. Knowing his friend, Janus had a strong suspicion there was an underlying reason for this request, and that it wasn't the one that Mika had provided to Safi on the telephone. No, something else was going on.

For his part, Mika had decided to play this on his own terms – for the moment, at least. He did not want to alarm Janus without further proof; if it came to that, in the future, armed with sufficient information, he would inform Janus, for sure. But he didn't have enough to go on quite yet – nothing solid, anyway – and he didn't want to unnecessarily ruin Safi and Yvetta's trip. He knew only too well how much they were looking forward to it. If more came to light before the two women departed, or while they were abroad, he promised himself that he would alert Janus.

But something else was different now, and he felt it in his gut. He could not decide if this trip to Australia was an omen, and for the remainder of the day it sat uncomfortably in his thoughts. Perhaps it was up to him, Mika, to stop them from going, and he would blame himself for ever if he let them step onto that plane. Was he making a grave mistake? Flashbacks to that fatal day when Fritzi had attacked Sasha reverberated in his mind.

Of all the places they chose to visit in the world, they had opted for the very place that Fritzi likely was. It seemed too close for comfort. Perhaps he was being overly anxious – it certainly wouldn't be the first time when it came to his family and, his desire to protect them at all times. After all, Australia was a vast country, Yvetta and Safi might never glance, to say nothing of meet, Fritzi. Nor did Fritzi have the information that Mika had – at least Mika hoped to God she did not. For example, there was no reason for Fritzi to know that Yvetta would soon be on the same continent as her. Perhaps he was overreacting – he hoped so.

The women's itineraries were sent on to the Israeli company, which assured him all protection had now been arranged both in Sydney and Melbourne. The company informed Mika that if he wanted the detail to follow them to other places in addition to this itinerary (or even after their due departure date) they would make the necessary arrangements. As for remaining undetected throughout their assignment, the security detail would appear to be tourists, which would not be notable in the tourist-heavy areas the women would be visiting; no one would take note of them. Mika organised for the detail to shadow through their complete itinerary; at the very least, it gave him peace of mind, and money was not exactly a problem.

According to Yvetta, DuPont had just visited Australia. Mika had a premonition that their friend the art dealer might know something – and not just about Australian art. Opening his cell phone, Mika scrolled through until he found DuPont's number. The coincidence of DuPont visiting Australia (for the first time ever, no less) in such close proximity to Safi and Fritzi's visit was in itself suspect. Once Mika's logical, rigorous, problem-solving mind was set on a trajectory – and his was now firmly focused on Fritzi – everything, he hoped, would fall into place, and he would soon find out what was going on (and something was, for sure – he knew this now, deep down).

DuPont picked up the call with a bright greeting, his urbane voice, a little rough around the edges, warm and kind – but … Mika could tell there was an inflection in his voice that said, that something was a little unusual, a little off. His usually calm, level, even voice now had a nervous edge.

Also, the wait to be connected by the front desk had taken much too long, Mika now reflected. DuPont was hiding something for sure, and Mika was going to find out exactly what that was.

The usual pleasantries out of the way, Mika came straight to the point. He began by mentioning Darius, the young Australian man he had met at Yvetta's wedding in upstate New York. What about Darius? DuPont inquired. Well, Mika asked, why had this previously anonymous person suddenly become everyone's best friend?

DuPont began a lengthy and rather awkward explanation, which Mika, not only still suspicious but now impatient as well, soon cut. Mika explained his concern about the newspaper article he had been sent this morning. If the article was accurate, Mika said, it meant that Fritzi was currently in Australia and may be an Australian citizen soon. Did Fritzi know this Darius, and also the prime minister's son?

DuPont changed his tack. He very quickly decided that there was no point in being evasive: Mika was far too versed in that game. And besides, he and Mika were old and close friends – they had gone through a great deal (not least of all the chaos caused by Fritzi) and he owed him the truth. He owed Mika a great deal, in fact. Besides, if his disclosing information meant that Mika would use it to protect Safi, this was imperative, too. If anything happened to Safi in Australia, DuPont would never forgive himself.

'Can I fly down?' DuPont asked, surprising Mika with his change of tone. 'It is best we discuss what has recently come to light.'

'Is tomorrow too soon?' Mika said.

'Perhaps over the weekend, if that will work. There is something I need to arrange… I would like to bring someone with, who you should meet.'

'Who?'

'Dr Erika Shultz,' DuPont said simply.

'Is she connected to this Australian article?'

'Not directly, no.' DuPont hesitated, then said, 'She knows Fritzi rather well.'

'In that case,' Mika said, 'I will meet this Dr Erika Shultz.'

Erika and DuPont flew down from New York City to Fort Lauderdale early on Friday morning. They put their bags into their separate rooms at the Lowes, freshened up all too briefly, and then hurried down to the car, that had been sent by Mika to drive them to his luxurious estate.

Erika had only been to Florida once before, and was impressed again by the beauty of the State. The weather was seasonally perfect, making a welcome change from the cold spell the East Coast was suffering this fall.

Both spoke little on the drive, each staring out at the scenery as they made their way to Star Island. DuPont had been to Mika's home with Safi many years ago, and was looking forward to the opulence and art, to say nothing of its palatial Floridian architecture, which was something he had grown to enjoy over his years away from France.

Memories of his last visit so many years ago now, flashed across his mind: Yvetta had been the main antagonist then, she had choked, and almost killed, Safi in a rage of jealousy. At the time, Sasha was still missing, presumed dead but never by Safi. Alexi Rubicov's will had bequeathed her the deeds to the Rubicov Gallery in Madison Avenue. It was this revelation that pushed the already unstable Yvetta (who had founded the Rubicov Gallery in Moscow) over the edge. It had been a terribly fraught period for the Rubicovs, Alexi's will, leaving many, like Yvetta, left out in the cold.

On DuPont and Erika's arrival at the elegant palm-tree-lined estate, with its circular drive and water fountain, in front of an impressive entrance, where they were greeted by Mika. The tall Russian dressed casually in white linen lead the way to his office. The determined expression on his handsome rugged face and his formality made it clear that this was not a social call, they were here to enlighten him to the most recent findings on Fritzi.

Mika had them facing him in high-backed green leather armchairs on either side of his maple art-deco desk with black inlays. It was a stunning Biedermeier that DuPont was admiring anew, it was a rare find from a French Chateau that was up for auction, as so many were these days.

DuPont introduced Erika once more with a brief history after which they were offered coffee with biscotti while Mika explained his fears for his family while they were visiting Australia. It had come to his notice, he said, that Fritzi was involved with the same person who had recently befriended his sister and Safi, and even attended Yvetta's wedding in upstate New York.

Mika stressed that he needed to know every detail: if Safi and Yvetta were to run into Fritzi down under, Mika could not, in all honesty, guarantee Fritzi's safety. The welfare of his family, he said, was far more important than a renegade from the law, one who should, if there was any justice in the world, still be languishing in a Russian jail.

Erika swallowed, not expecting the severity and intensity of Mika's feelings towards Fritzi. She could see by his expression, his dark eyes and low faltering tone, how important this matter was for him, and how much he felt was at stake for both his sister and his larger family unit.

Leaning forward in the armchair, trying not to reveal her sudden anxiety (Mika, and his mansion, was nothing if not intimidating), Erika knew this was her chance, probably the only one she had, to put Fritzi's story to this tycoon, who had been only too blunt in his assessment of Fritzi just moments before. Mika was clearly a no-nonsense, straight-to-the-point, tell-it-like-it-is kind of man (not unlike many Russians) and she would have to honour that now. Taking a deep breath, and with a thin smile, Erika began her story by talking about her own life in East Germany never mentioning Fritzi by name, only – in as brisk and dispassionate a manner as she could - recounting her horrendous experiences from beginning to end.

Mika watched and listened, not a patient man, but careful not to interrupt her, either, making sure to hear her out, to absorb every word. He appeared blunt, yes, but fair, she reflected as she spoke, feeling more confident as the story of her time in East Berlin drew to its conclusion, and she spoke about the collapse of the Wall and the beginning of her new life, a new person in a new, liberated country, but still haunted by old images from the past, the trauma she had undergone and the few heroic people who had helped her survive it. She had to give Mika credit, he did not interrupt her until after she finally ended her story, describing her reunion with her childhood friend, who she now revealed to be the very same Fritzi Mika spoke so unfavourably about.

Silence fell over the room. Mika shifted in his chair, looked over at DuPont, who himself said nothing. Eventually, after what seemed an inordinate length of time, Mika stood up, came around to Erika, and took her tiny hand in his.

'Thank you, Erika, for sharing with me so honestly the horror you suffered during the communist regime. I am very happy that you were spared – many were not, and for far less. They were sent to gulags, never to be seen or heard from again. It was a dark time in Soviet history. As a Russian I am only too aware of what happened in the past – of what should never have happened; of the upheaval, oppression, and insanity of life under communist rule – as, of course, are you. You are an enormously intelligent, enormously resilient, passionate and inspiring person. That much is clear.'

Sitting down again but not breaking his eye contact with Erika, clearing and then lowering his Russian accented, voice, he said, 'What I find difficult to comprehend, or reconcile, is the person you are describing with the one we know only too well.'

Erika knew that this was the moment when she would have to defend Fritzi – explain her psyche and speak up about her rehabilitation and atonement for the many sins of her past – and do so in a full-throated, compelling, and compassionate manner. She hoped that when she came to the end something in her sincere heartfelt delivery would miraculously hit a chord with Mika, and give Fritzi the second chance that Erika believed Fritzi so clearly deserved. She had no time to waste, and started speaking immediately, and perhaps a little too quickly, adhering to the comprehensive, in-depth knowledge and understanding she had of the details relating to the Rubicov Fritzi case study. She was more nervous than she had imagined she would be, and felt like a young child again, called to speak at school, unprepared and wishing she was anywhere else.

This time she began at the end rather than at the beginning, briefing Mika on another side of Fritzi her selfless deeds in New Zealand, heroic acts that had resulted in her being represented in immigration court by the prime minister's son, himself an esteemed human rights lawyer.

She briefed Mika on Darius relationship with Fritzi in Bali, when Fritzi was traveling under an alias, of his suspicions that she was not the person she said she was, how he discovered her true identity, the reason he flew to the States to find out more about her past and the people she had harmed. Continuing to brief Mika, whose gaze, somewhat offputtingly, never wavered from Erika's, Erika recounted Darius' in-depth enquiries here in the States, which culminated in him meeting the Rubicov family, and those she had so callously and grievously harmed. On Darius return to Australia, he had shared his findings with the human rights lawyer Fritzi had saved from the earthquake.

She now mentioned a more personal grievance against Fritzi. Anna Rubicov, their mother who was terrorised during the ransacking of their home in Moscow by Fritzi and Yvetta. She believed Anna Rubicov reminded Fritzi of her own mother – a mother she both loved and despised, deeply and unfathomably resented, and ultimately had wanted to destroy, she believed Fritzi empathised with Yvetta. Understanding Fritzi's childhood trauma (and her own), Erika detailed a pattern of behaviour that recurred when Fritzi fell in love with Yvetta. Erika believed that Fritzi had substituted saving Yvetta for Erika, (herself) and that anyone who harmed Yvetta in her eyes had to be punished. Fritzi's guilt had twisted her misplaced need to save Yvetta from what she conceived as the same fate that had befallen Erika years before. Yvetta being institutionalised, suffering from her own severe demons and significant depressive episodes, imprisoned in one cold and unforgiving mental institution after another, had triggered Fritzi's protective instincts, she had gone to unimaginable lengths to free her lover and soulmate from being institutionalised and, to her mind, slowly starved of life and love, doomed, destroyed.

It was only when Fritzi realised Yvetta had moved on with her life, and had another lover, stability, even independence and success, did Fritzi, acting out of irrationality, obsession, and perhaps even insanity no longer conscious of her actions, shot wildly into the crowd on a busy Manhattan street to cause maximum chaos, enabling her own escape. That's when Sasha, panicked and acting out of instinct, true to his ever-fraternal, loyal, loving self, leaped to protect his sister Yvetta. Tragically, accidentally, the bullet hit him. In fact, Erika stressed, Fritzi had told her often that she had meant to fire the bullet into the pavement, perhaps it bounced she did not know.

Erika folded her arms and closed her mouth. She was finished talking. She was also exhausted, and felt emotionally drained. It was not easy to relive (as she had been doing these last few weeks, after years of neglecting her past altogether as a form of sanity and self-preservation) her own trauma, and now she felt she was reliving (and, bizarrely, having to defend that which did not always seem defensible) Fritzi's tormented past as well.

Still, she was committed to defending Fritzi – who had defended Erika when she was most vulnerable and most alone – to clearing her name and setting her on a new and better path. But there was nothing more to be said about Fritzi's misdeeds and damaged youth, she had tried her hardest, told the story in the clearest and boldest way she could, and she had nothing left by way of a defence: this was it. Her mouth was dry and her hands were shaking slowly.

She looked at Mika, who sat in stony silence. Erika could not tell what he was thinking, gave up trying. Instead, she took a sip of water, summoned her last iota of energy, and felt compelled to continue speaking. Her voice now flat, she spoke of her renewed relationship with Fritzi after all of these years apart, the goodness, grace, and surprising generosity of her childhood friend, their daily contact, and Fritzi's slow but steady, and ultimately all-consuming realisation about the crimes and chaos she had caused in the past, and her deep desire for salvation from the Rubicov family.

Erika explained how, once Fritzi (as a result of a file compiled by the Australian immigration team, in Fritzi's defence) had learnt that her childhood friend, Erika was, alive and well, Fritzi slowly stopped suffering from the crippling guilt of her father's unspeakable cruelty.

'Slowly but steadily, over time, Fritzi began to heal, thanks in no small part to the love, sympathy, and stable presence of Darius, Jared, Maggie and myself. We gave her unwavering support, we believed in her, we have grown to love and respect her,' Erika continued, her voice breaking slightly. 'We have witnessed her suffering, not for herself, but for what she had inflicted upon others.'

Erika mentioned that Fritzi had confided in Erika her need to write to each and every one of the Rubicovs to apologise – and write to DuPont as well. She did not want their forgiveness, she had said, but she wanted them to know that she understood their anger and, that she acknowledged the consequences of her actions and the pain she had caused.

Now she was waiting to hear whether her application for Australian citizenship had been successful. She had letters of high praise for her selfless work during the earthquake from the New Zealand prime minister and the mayor of Christchurch. She had the prime minister of Australia express eternal gratitude for saving his son, and at great danger to her own safety.

Nothing about Fritzi's past, Erika said, would have come to light if it had not been for Darius's investigation into Fritzi's past. He had found her in Australia, where she had found herself after running from Bali to New Zealand. She had ended up in Sydney, having been evacuated from a disaster zone.

'Now she has found, even with all of her contacts and the significant goodwill from her actions during and after the earthquake,' Erika continued, 'she still has to wait for the immigration authorities to process her papers, in order for her to begin a new life in Australia.' She took a deep breath, looked at her hands, which were shaking softly, and then away from them, in order to steel herself and find some confidence that may have escaped, and said,

'I beg you, not for Fritzi's sake, but for my own, please do not harm her. I would never survive if she were to be killed, because it's me she was saving when she freed Yvetta. In fact, it seems to me we are all linked one way or another through Fritzi. She has affected all of our lives.'

Mika stared at Erika. She had piercing blue eyes in a small sharp angular face. Her frame was like a child's, but her mannerisms were stilted, her speech clear and direct, void of charm or guile. She was exactly as she appeared, he thought, honest to the point of rudeness. It was obvious she suffered from some mental disorder, but she was compensated by being blessed with a sharp, brilliant brain. It would have been a tragedy beyond humanity had she been given a lobotomy by the East German regime; he shuddered at the thought.

Erika took Mika's stare and his corresponding silence as an adverse reaction to her direct pleading for her friend's salvation, and for her own need for Fritzi's freedom from harm. She had miscalculated, she now thought, or been overwhelmed by emotion when emotion was least desired. Russians were cold, she reminded herself, even more so than East Germans.

Her speech was all much too emotive, she decided, she should have been more professional, she wished Rob had been here with her. Lecturing was one thing, but she did not know how to deal with such personal, emotional affairs, it wasn't in her nature. The only thing she did know was that, above all else, she needed Fritzi in her life, loved Fritzi like a sister, one she'd never had and, in fact, the only family she now had. She did not want to – could not afford to – lose her again. She would do anything to prevent that from happening.

She lifted her head off her chest, trying to control the tears she did not know she still had in her. Feeling utter desolation and failure, in a voice so soft it was almost inaudible, Erika spoke once more.

'I have no family anymore,' Erika began, not just her voice trembling but her whole body. 'Fritzi is my only link with the past. My only family, you understand. I love her like a sister.'

DuPont had been moved to tears. He had never seen anyone try so hard to fight for someone else – or witnessed anything that was as selfless as it was passionate, utterly authentic, heartfelt and hard-won. He felt her pain: it was pitiful, yet so brave, to watch this girl who, by all accounts, did not have the tools with which to be persuasive, or enable her to give the most riveting account of her own and Fritzi's life.

They sat in silence for a long time. Mika did not move but his stare, directed at Erika, was unbroken. She nervously looked away, but when their eyes met again, the weight of emotion was so great that DuPont held his breath: what was said in that fleeting moment was beyond words. It was the understanding of another's pain, a realisation of one's own frailty when it came to loving one's family more than life itself.

He reached for his phone on the low glass desk between them. As the phone connected, they heard on the speaker a man's voice with a thick Russian accent.

'Dasha,' Mika began, 'I want you to cancel the operation in Australia; it is no longer needed.' DuPont and Erika both experienced the long, almost painful, pause that followed, a loaded silence, heavy with anticipation, hesitation. No one in the room moved.

'Do I understand you no longer need the target removed?' said the voice with the thick accent.

Mika's response was blunt, almost abrasive. 'Correct,' Mika simply said.

Again, a heavy, uncomfortable silence descended on the telephone line, and reverberated across the room. DuPont looked at Erika, who was looking at the ground.

'You will be paid in full for your services, of course,' Mika continued – but he did not move, or so much as glance across the room. DuPont thought that Mika was finished speaking, but then he said, 'The target must be left unharmed at all costs'

The man with the heavy accent clearly had nothing more to say, not even 'Dos vidanya.' Instead, a click could be heard over the speaker, and Mika replaced his phone on the desk, flexing his muscular arms, his sleeves rolled up. He was not smiling and his face wore no expression.

Looking around at last he found four pair of eyes staring at him. Not only that, but the normally restrained DuPont's mouth was hanging open. Then everything happened at once, and with great speed.

Erika jumped up, knocking her glass of water over the expensive silk Persian rug. It took her a moment to realise the previously unimaginable: she had succeeded, she had managed to repay some of Fritzi's favour (Fritzi, who had saved her life all those years ago), Fritzi was safe, she was free.

Looking often over the course of their meeting at Mika's hard face, thinking that he had, too, a cold heart, she had not thought such a reversal would be possible, and now that it was, she felt dizzy and in disbelief. It was as if the ornate, elegant room, the low desk, the expensive tasselled silk rug, was spinning, and she expected at any moment the floor to open up and swallow her entirely, or to wake up to find it had all been a dream. Perhaps appropriately, therefore, the moments that immediately followed felt dreamlike, at once painstakingly slow and very fast.

Elated tears running down her face, Erika reached over the desk with an outstretched hand. At first Mika felt shock, as though this gentle and obviously broken woman was about to assault him, before realising she simply wanted to shake his hand. Extending both his thick hands, pulling her towards him, as he walked towards her, she found that her feet were off the ground as he gave her a bear hug, like only a Russian could. She felt like she was dancing again, only this time in mid-air.

As he released his hold, her feet slowly sank down until she was on solid ground once more.

'Well, that calls for a toast,' Mika said, and DuPont did not think he had ever heard Mika sound so happy, with the possible exception of when Sasha reappeared in his life after an absence and imprisonment so long that everyone in the family had thought he was dead. And, of course, Fritzi had been involved in that ordeal, too. But now was not the time to reflect on this.

It was time to live in the present, and to celebrate – which is exactly what they did. Mika poured them each a vodka from the art deco drinks cabinet behind his desk. Neither of the two guests (from very different places in the world, and their relationship to Mika wholly different, too; only one person, at this point, drew them all together, and that person was Fritzi, a name that, until a few moments ago, DuPont could barely bring himself to speak) could not refuse, knocking the fiery but oh-so-satisfying liquid back, Erika feeling even more heady than she had just moments before.

Mika surprised Erika by throwing his shot glass into the fireplace, indicating they should follow. It was an old Russian custom to celebrate after a deal was struck, Erika was entertained to learn, throwing her glass and, in the process, feeling a rush as though she had just consumed another two shots.

'Now you will join me on the terrace for lunch,' Mika said brightly, his voice no longer quite so serious or severe, rising from his chair and placing both hands, momentarily, on the desk. He glanced at the cabinet and the vodka bottle once again, but then determinedly looked away, at his still-seated guests.

Surprising them again – this time with a smile – he said, 'I won't take no for an answer.' Gazing fixedly at Erika again, her no-longer-so-cold but still very beautiful blue eyes and neat, curious, angular face, he said, 'I want to get to know this young lady. She has the determination of ten men, and with guts to fight against the odds, I have learnt something very valuable and that's never to give up on hope.'

On the flight back to New York that evening, still feeling deflated but also exhausted and very much absorbing the experience of the last few hours, little was said. DuPont was deep in thought about their incredible day. Erika, utterly drained, with not an iota of energy left in her lithe, little body, fell asleep as soon as the plane took off.

This left DuPont, the only conscious one in the aisle, to reflect, and to play back the day's events. Indeed, shocked still at Mika's ability to take a contract hit on someone's life – but on this point, battle-hardened, East German Erika had not seemed to turn a hair. He made a note to question her about this when they were on solid ground again, when she was awake and they were alone again. She was a fascinating person and he wanted to get to know her better.

He had to agree with Mika: she certainly put her whole body and soul into fighting for Fritzi. He only hoped she would not live to regret it. Perhaps it was his French pessimism, coupled with a large dose of cynicism – but then one would think that East German Erika would be every bit as cynical. And yet she came across as buoyant, optimistic, full of hope and excitement for the future. Like an American, he thought. As soon as he arrived in New York, he would call Darius with the news. Darius, who, along with Erika, had been instructive in saving Fritzi's life, deserved to hear a blow-by-blow account of the day's events.

In the hours that followed, it was decided that Yvetta and Safi would leave for Oz none the wiser about Fritzi's current place of residence, and least of all about Erika's visit. They simply did not need to know any of this – nor should they, Mika had quickly decided (a decision with which DuPont agreed). Still, he would keep the Israeli shadow on the trip for his own peace of mind. Fritzi would continue travelling in the outback, or staying in Byron Bay, where Mika learnt she had made many friends, honing her skills (learnt from the prime minister's niece) organising charity events.

At Kennedy Airport, Erika and DuPont exchanged cell numbers; if any news was heard about Fritzi's immigration status, DuPont wanted to know. Considering the time and energy he was affording Fritzi again (Fritzi, who he had once sworn he would never spend another second thinking about; who he had once hoped would rot in hell), he was curious to follow her progress, or perhaps demise; time would tell.

'By the way,' DuPont said, as Erika turned away from him at the exit, about to go outside and wait in line for a cab, 'you did not seem to be shocked at Mika's openness about taking a contract hit out on Fritzi's life.' Erika turned and smiled at him again, giving him the full gaze of her blue eyes, eyes that had once seemed so cold but now were full of warmth, even gratitude.

'No,' she said, 'he's Russian, that's how they do business. Memories about that time are still deeply entrenched in my psyche, I guess.'

He waited with her in the queue but now they did not speak. There appeared to be nothing left to say. Although both going into Manhattan, neither offered to share a cab: they were going to very different places, to continue very different lives, and besides any further contact, after this extraordinary day, it suddenly seemed, would just be awkward. Both appeared to concede this by their silence.

Then her cab pulled up and he was curiously relieved to be alone again after such an intense and dramatic day. People had an image of DuPont as an uber-sociable, extroverted, people-person, but privately he had always suspected it was a front, and that he was a little bit of a loner. Certainly, he enjoyed his own company – long stretches of silence, to gaze at works of art or consider life's larger subjects, and the comfort of his own thoughts – and relished the prospect of it now.

He waved Erika goodbye as she stepped into her cab, thinking how tough she was under that frail exterior. He, on the other hand, had French sensibilities about such things, he liked to imagine all subjects were philosophically discussed, or ended up in bed a much more persuasive endeavour to get one's way, whether or not those sensibilities were naive, he preferred to hold onto his old-fashioned idealistic beliefs. Part of him knew Mika as the pragmatic, relentless, even fairly ruthless, stop-at-nothing trouble-shooter, yet experiencing it first-hand had unsettled his western morality. If he had to choose between Baudelaire's Poetry or Walter Benjamin's modernity, he would be in the Baudelaire school of thought for sure.

Chapter 23

The option of returning to Sydney did not grab her. After experiencing the magic, mystery, and near-infinite expanse of the outback, big cities (one so much like another, with the same franchises, brands, looming buildings, and big-block shops) had little appeal to her. The wildness, spareness, and empty fullness of the outback still held its tranquil charm over her; the mere thought of it enchanted her anew.

In any case, Darius would be too busy with clients (clients she suspected he had long neglected in order to travel with, assist, and advise Fritzi) to spend the kind of time with her that she so badly needed and wanted. Still, Fritzi needed to spend some quality time with Maggie, and, with that thought (and Maggie's sympathetic, understanding face) in mind she decided to call her right then.

'Maggie, hi!' Fritzi said, delighted to hear that familiar, but intimate, affectionate, ever-understanding voice on the line again, and smiling as she said it, 'I was wondering whether a long weekend in Byron Bay with me – just the two of us; while Darius is in Sydney – appeals to you? I'd love to see you, it's been a while.'

Maggi, who was almost as happy to hear Fritzi's voice as Fritzi had been to hear hers, thought it a great idea, and pencilled in a tentative date for the coming weekend.

'I will have a word with Jared,' she told Fritzi, though she did not think Jared would be at all opposed to the idea. 'If he can spare me the time I would love to come.' Indeed, her voice made clear how excited she was at the possibility, not least at the opportunity to catch up with Fritzi, whose life had undergone so many changes in a short amount of time.

Though she had not seen Fritzi, she had kept up with the young German's life through telephone conversations, text messages, and the odd email exchange. Jared had a hectic schedule of late: his interest in Fritzi had not waned, but there was not much more he could do until the department had reviewed her case; as a result, his daily conversation with Maggie about Fritzi's future had petered out.

On the other hand, Maggie noted (not unhappily) that his social life had become hectic once more. The young female doctor was still on the scene, staying over most weekends at Jared's place. Though the doctor was neat enough, as always it was Maggie who was left cleaning up everyone's mess – and sometimes doing a little extra work, lending an ear or a shoulder, when the mess was heavier on the emotional side.

The doctor was nice enough, if a little too brisk, even blunt, with the staff. Maggie had put this occasional abrasiveness down to nerves, the doctor, who was otherwise unassuming and not at all entitled or ungracious, not knowing how to deal with Jared's domestic entourage, the machinery that kept his life running smoothly. Still, all that soothing, scrubbing, sweeping, listening, vacuuming, and arranging of odds and ends grew exhausting.

For this reason, Fritzi's idea of a weekend away was enormously appealing. Besides, flying down to Byron Bay would be a welcome change from the heat settling over Sydney. You knew that the city was unseasonably humid when even the January morning felt almost as hot as mid-afternoon. Indeed, Maggie's early morning walks were becoming a little too warm for comfort. The very idea of being with Fritzi, undertaking longer walks in a cooler climate, in an environment new to her, beside the sea, was refreshing. A much-needed break from the steamy oppressive city heat. Living close to the water did not help much in urban areas, and certainly not in Australia's biggest city; it seemed to trap the heat.

Despite her desire for fresh adventure, to explore new places with new people, Fritzi was happy in Byron Bay. Her new townhouse, closer to the centre of town, suited Fritzi's needs to a tee. This area felt hip and lively, younger, more compact and social. Here it was easier to walk everywhere, and driving to the beach took no time at all. Through one of her many contacts, Missy, Jared's cousin, had found the perfect apartment for her, which went a long way in a small community.

Arriving late on a Wednesday morning, Maggie put her things down in the hallway and walked through to survey Fritzi's new abode. 'It's cosier than the last place, especially this time of year.' The days were warm, but when night set in the cold from the sea made everything feel damp, not least because she lived a stone's throw from the beach.

'I love it here,' Fritzi exclaimed, embracing Maggie for a second time. 'It's so much more convenient, I can now walk to most places. At first I was lonely without Darius for company, but here, so close to everyone and everything, it's almost impossible to be truly lonely.' Indeed, looking at Maggie, surprised at how much she had missed the older woman, a mother in so many ways, Fritzi felt less lonely than ever before.

Fritzi walked Maggie through the apartment, which spread out from the main living areas. Having been converted and modernised, the flat had character, and was surprisingly spacious for this very much in-demand area of town. The floor space was all on one level, which suited Maggie, who no longer had either the energy or flexibility she had had in years past. The beech floors covered in Persian rugs made a nice change from the marble flooring in Fritzi's last townhouse. There was a small veranda with an overhanging pergola covered in sweet-smelling blossoms. Terracotta pots filled with flowers lined the few wooden steps leading to a yellow front door with rocking chairs on either side. The place was romantically charming, too. The three rooms were all on suite, chic and comfy, and decorated with warm fabrics and four-poster beds. The fourth room had been converted into a small office and library, and Maggie noted that Fritzi had made this her hub. Maggie could certainly see why. The room had large shuttered windows that overlooked the street. The desk faced the window, which had a comfortable sofa below it.

The kitchen, which was small yet ample for Fritzi's needs, was countryfied with a black refectory table and wooden benches, and led onto a spacious sitting room furnished with leather armchairs, sofas, and a fireplace.

Carrying their coffee into the small office they settled into the sofa under the window. Fritzi usually took a while to warm up to company, but this was never the case with Maggie, who she felt she had known her whole life (the only other person she felt this way about was Erika; indeed, the two women had become her de facto family unit). She always looked forward to her conversations with Maggie, conversations that could sometimes stretch on for an hour or more, and which allowed her to chatter away knowing she wouldn't be judged. Fritzi knew that whatever she chose to share would remain between them.

She wanted to share her latest news with the woman who was like the mother she never had. In fact, one of her unstated reasons for bringing Maggie out here was so that she could meet Erika on a FaceTime call (Erika and Fritzi now spoke at least four times a week; and, in spite of the time difference, sometimes as often as once a day).

It was the waning hours of the afternoon in Byron Bay, but the sky out, and the airy flat within, was still as bright as day. It was late at night in New York, but Fritzi knew that Erika would be still, finishing up her last cup of coffee or a leisurely final glass of wine, waiting for the right time to call Fritzi (still an East German in some respects, she was nothing if not punctual) as she slowly got ready for bed. Fritzi put the iPad on the coffee table while she filled Maggie in on her latest news, ready to answer the call from Erika as soon as it rang.

'I had a call from Erika in the middle of the night with the most unbelievable story,' Fritzi told Maggie excitedly. 'You just cannot imagine what has happened.' Gazing at Fritzi more intently, waiting to hear more, Maggie suspected anew that there was indeed something different about her friend, something brighter, a new light around and within her. Smiling, Fritzi continued, 'Erika has taken it upon herself to tackle the head of the Rubicov family, a man called Mika, who apparently had a contract out on me.'

'A contract?' Maggie asked, thinking this sounded different from the contracts Jared was always signing for his work.

'A hit,' Fritzi said, 'on my life.' Shocked, registering this news, Maggie reminded herself to never be shocked by anything Fritzi told her. Still, it was difficult sometimes. Seeing her friend's fright, her voice softening, and still smiling, Fritzi continued, 'It was the reason I feared most for my safety when I was travelling. It was the reason I was so paranoid, so petrified, so uncertain all of the time. I could never be relaxed, even when I was alone. I always, always had my guard up. And I always had to cover my tracks.'

Maggie listened with interest, reminded why it was so entertaining, and satisfying, to have Fritzi in her life. One gained an education of a sort. But this new news, despite her initial fright, seemed good, even wonderful. Fritzi was so animated about this new, life-changing development. And Maggie, for her part, was horrified and amazed as the story unfolded.

'I have not spoken with Erika since she called yesterday,' Fritzi said, touching Maggie's hand as if to calm her nerves which had so suddenly been rattled, 'so when she calls, she will give us more details, and you will hear when I do – but it appears that the contract on me has been cancelled. How Erika managed to convince him, we will have to wait to find out. She was too exhausted to fill me in on every detail, but she wanted to let me know that now I can finally relax. I no longer have to live in fear. I can be at peace, at last.'

Smiling herself now and still taking in this news, Maggie said, 'That is a momentous shift, Fritzi, especially now. It will set you free to live your life without fears of reprisals. And the timing, with your hopefully approved immigration status and your new life of stability, happiness, love.' Saying this last word, her thoughts turned away from Fritzi's life alone. 'Have you told Darius and Jared?'

'No, not yet,' Fritzi said, her smile fading but her hand still holding Maggie's, indeed tightening her grip on it slightly. 'I wanted you to be the first to know, Maggie. Erika will fill them in too, no doubt.

Perhaps when she calls with the details, I will find out whether they already know.' She finally let go of Maggie's hand, but her voice was flatter as she said, 'Hopefully, there are no unpleasant surprises or strings attached.'

Maggie turned to reach for the hand again and at that moment the ring tone sounded, invading their moment. They both jumped in surprise.

It was a good line and Erika's face filled the screen. Erika paused in a manner that Fritzi had not anticipated, taking a moment when she saw Maggie, not having met her before. Fritzi had told her the day before that Maggie would be on the next day's call, but Erika had clearly forgotten.

'Erika, this is Maggie; Maggie, this is Erika,' Fritzi said with a huge smile, delighted all over again, and long-anticipating this special moment. They both nodded greetings, both feeling a little more awkward than their gregarious shared friend.

'So wonderful to meet you Erika,' Maggie said warmly, smiling herself and seizing the moment to go first. 'I feel I know you well through Fritzi, of course. I would like to say how incredible it is that two you have once more found one another after many years of separation and pain.'

Erika understood why her friend had adopted this older woman as her family: she was warm, honest, and motherly, just what Fritzi needed at this moment.

'Thank you for being there for Fritzi now and in the past few months,' Erika said, sensing that it was her turn to speak. 'Without you in her life Erika may have suffered more than she already has. She has told me what a comfort you have been during her time in Australia, and, indeed, how important you are to her life. We will meet when I visit, that would be good.'

Maggie, a little taken aback at this woman's direct way of speaking, her precise and unemotional manner, and her blunt, almost affectless stare into the camera, remembered Fritzi mentioning that Erika had been diagnosed on the autism spectrum – or was it bipolar disorder; she could not immediately recall, but it certainly accounted for her brisk mannerisms.

Erika did not wait for a reply but focused instead on Fritzi.

'Now that I am less tired, I will fill you in on the details,' she continued in the same brisk, rather dry, manner.

They both listened to her dramatic story told in the most undramatic way, as if she were giving a lecture. To Maggie it sounded more or less like this: 'This is what happened… that is what happened … this is what I said … and this is what he said.' With a spattering of DuPont thrown in for good measure, since this DuPont fellow (Maggie recalled that Darius had mentioned him too once or twice) was apparently the catalyst of Erika's meeting with Mika the Russian. When Maggie tuned in again, Erika was saying,

'I have no doubts about his sincerity, Fritzi.' She paused for a moment, in which Maggie could clearly hear Erika breathe a sigh of relief. But Erika was not yet done. 'Whether he has changed his mind for my benefit, or for yours, it does not matter. What matters is that he no longer has someone searching for you to take you out.'

Maggie held her breath, wanting to put her hand in front of her mouth. Erika's unemotional recitation of the story, her brusque delivery with little if no empathy in her tone, was shocking to hear and difficult to connect with on an emotional level. It was good news but it might as well have been bad, or at least indifferent, news. It was all very confusing. Erika was direct to the point of resembling a rude, unattached stranger, not Erika's longest and closest friend, sharing life-changing news.

Fritzi, no doubt used to Erika and gaining comfort from her (and perhaps even from her blunt manner) seemed to take it all in her stride. Indeed, she was still smiling, more broadly than ever. 'Erika,' she said, 'I cannot find the words to convey my gratitude. How did you manage to track down DuPont, to say nothing of get him to listen to you – that alone is a miracle.'

'I met him at the Rubicov gallery,' Erika replied with her by now characteristic flatness. 'I visited the gallery after speaking with you. I guess I just had a hunch – or at least a hope. To my surprise he was there, on the very same day, viewing an artist's work.'

It is, indeed, a small world, Maggie thought, gazing at Erika facing the camera all the way from Manhattan. How had Fritzi brought her and Maggie, two people who had very little else in common, together – it seemed nothing short of a miracle now.

'I cannot imagine he cared one way or another what happened to me,' Fritzi said wryly.

'No, he doesn't – but I do,' Erika said. 'So I told him I would hold him responsible if Mika succeeded in having you killed.'

They both looked at one another's image on the screen. Erika wasn't someone to mess with. When she had her mind focused on a problem, she tackled it head-on.

'Mika was more difficult to convince,' Erika continued, 'but obviously I must have do exactly that. And you can now move on with your life.'

Fritzi spoke to Erika for a few more minutes before she ended the call, with Maggie and Erika biding each other a somewhat strained farewell. Afterwards they sat in silence for some time, Maggie uncertain what to say or do next.

'Well, I truly don't know what to say after that call,' she finally said, deciding, Erika-like, to speak her mind. 'Erika certainly is not someone who suffers fools gladly.'

'Oh, that's just how she is,' Fritzi said happily, and Maggie could see first-hand how large Erika loomed in her life and how the very thought of her brightened up Fritzi's day, 'she has always been that way, even as a child. But she is a wonderful person – once one gets used to her direct manner, that is.'

Feeling the need to say something more, Maggie said, 'Erika has gone above and beyond to spare your life – which is precisely what you tried to do for her all of those years ago.'

Uncharacteristically looking away, no longer smiling, Fritzi dismissed this suggestion out of hand. 'I failed her,' she said simply, bluntly, and now the happy surprise of the last half-hour appeared to have been wiped away and she was miserable and remorseful once again.

'You need to forgive yourself,' Maggie said. 'After all, you were merely children in an adult world. What happened was beyond your control – that you survived it, that you have thrived of late, is all that matters.'

Surprising Maggie by standing up, shaking her head, her tone now almost as flat as Erika's, Fritzi said, 'Come, let's get out of here.' She tried out a smile, but this time it sat flatly on her face and did not last long. 'We have the whole town to explore, shopping to do, and I have a wonderful place to take you for a late lunch.'

Not even two hours later, enjoying the best naked burgers anywhere in the world, with zucchini frittes, Fritzi confided, 'I wanted you all to myself this weekend, but Missy, Jared's niece who you met at the charity auction, has insisted that we dine with them at their home tomorrow evening, if that's alright with you.'

'Sounds perfect,' Maggie said, feeling suddenly exhausted from the day's events thus far. And the day wasn't even close to being over. Who knew what else Fritzi had planned. 'We will have the whole day together tomorrow,' Fritzi said, registering her friend's fatigue and taking in her hesitation with a sharp eye. 'You might need a break by evening.'

Laughing, they ordered desert. It was well past nine before they returned home; by the time they had finished browsing through the stores, lunch had turned into an early dinner. Maggie enjoyed it all immensely: she never indulged in browsing from store to store in Sydney (she didn't have the finances, to say nothing of the time, energy, or inclination); it was much more of a chore finding what she needed when shopping, either for herself or as gifts for others.

Byron Bay was full of life – and shops. It had alternative novelty stores, gift stores, and beautiful houseware stores from which Maggie could not resist buying odds and ends. The bookstores alone could have taken her all day to browse through – thankfully, Fritzi was there to steer her away. Books had been Maggie's passion for as long as she could remember.

By now it was evening, after a long and profitable day, and the mist had rolled in off the sea. Fritzi lit the fire and tucked Maggie up in a mohair throw in one of the high--backed leather armchairs. Finding an old movie starring Marlene Dietrich, they settled down to watch as Dietrich charmed Gary Cooper in Morocco.

The weekend raced by as the two spent time enjoying one another's company. Fritzi tried not to dwell on her citizenship issues, but they could not be avoided. Jared had called to brief Fritzi about her hearing during the week.

Maggie tried to be encouraging after the call. Although Fritzi did not know it, Jared had encouraged Maggie to visit Fritzi; knowing the authorities had requested an interview with Fritzi, he wanted to break the news while she was in Byron Bay with Fritzi. He was keenly aware that it was not healthy for Fritzi to deal with all of this tension and self-doubt alone. She needed company, and she needed Maggie, who seemed to want to reconnect with Fritzi just as much.

The interview was for the first week after the new year. She had four months left of her one-year visa, and the months were now going fast. Fritzi's mind was racing, too, and not always in a positive direction. Things were becoming urgent and Jared wanted them resolved. He understood that Fritzi was at a crossroads, that events were entirely out of her control and that this caused her considerable anguish, and that if bad news ensued the results could be disastrous – at the very least, it would undo all of the good work Fritzi had done on her self-control, on her psyche, on her present and her future.

'One moment I receive brilliant news from Erika,' Fritzi informed Maggie after Jared's call, 'then the day after I receive this news. One moment I am flying high, the next I'm struggling to come up for air.' She held up her hands in disbelief, and the confusion and upset on her face was clear.

'Fritzi,' Maggie said softly, 'I believe your life is more important than your status to remain here in Australia. I have complete confidence in Jared – so must you. I have known Jared for years and he has the utmost integrity, as you know. He is the most loyal boss – and friend. He won't allow any other outcome; and while his father is still the PM, I think your application will more than likely be successful. Not many people get character references from the PM himself, not to mention one from the PM of New Zealand PM.'

Fritzi looked at Maggie and then at the floor, clearly still uneasy. 'If there is a hitch, do you think I would be allowed back into New Zealand?' she inquired. 'I could try again after a few years. I believe some find that an easier route.'

'Perhaps,' Maggie said, 'but I do not think you will have to resort to that. I have every confidence you will be allowed to remain. If there are complications, I am sure you will receive an extension to remain until they are duly dealt with.'

She tried a smile but Fritzi wasn't having any of it. Instead, Maggie changed the subject. They spoke about Christmas and the New Year, but Fritzi was not sure she was in the mood to discuss either. Maggie was eager to steer clear of the immigration problem, not wanting to invite anxiety or to dwell on any potential for failure and to increase
Fritzi's fears.

'I would love for you to spend Christmas with me in Sydney,' Maggie said softly, touching Fritzi's hand. 'It would give me so much pleasure. What do you think?'

Softening suddenly, regretting her outpouring of anxiety and her sour mood, she hugged Maggie, feeling thankful once again to have such a caring person in her life. 'Sounds wonderful,' Fritzi said, 'thank you.'

Not wanting to be alone after Maggie left, she invited herself to Missy's for dinner. Maggie's visit rekindled feelings of her past self and, she much preferred her present self, a self that was prepared to be vulnerable with those she trusted and, even loved. After the fashion show (and, indeed, in the days leading up to it), Fritzi and Missy had become firm friends. Missy was great company, something Fritzi needed right now. Darius would not be back in Byron Bay for some time; he had clients arriving in Sydney from the States, who, he had told her, were expecting his undivided attention.

Resigned to some alone time, her life lurching from one dramatic episode to the next, and no longer able to put off what appeared to be inevitable, she needed to prepare for the following instalment: if they issued an unfavourable result to her application to remain in Australia. It was time to put a positive spin on a troubled situation: being alone to work out an alternative plan would give her breathing space. She needed to consider all of her options (and, right now, there did not appear to be any at all), and quickly. When backed into a corner, with seemingly no hope in sight, she had come up with some of her most ingenious ideas – and some of her most awful ones as well.

For the first time in weeks, she remembered her time in Bali with Darius. Beautiful, self-contained, idyllic Bali. She wondered if Darius would return to the island with her, if it came to that? Mika, no longer posed a threat to her and, Interpol seemed to have put her Red Notice on the back burner, according to Jared.

Having a plan formulated, thinking things through carefully and independently, gave her strength to face the interview. And the more she gave the subject considered thought, the less bleak it appeared to be. Yes, she would find an option, there were always options, and she was nothing if not resilient. Indeed, there was a great deal to be thankful for. She was free to go almost, wherever she chose, no longer having to look over her shoulder any longer.

Of course, visiting Erika in the States was off the agenda, but they would have to meet somewhere else. Erika returned to Berlin from time to time, whereas Fritzi had not returned home (since her fallout with Alexi and Mika, when she was unceremoniously put on a plane back to Germany accompanied by Kolya, a dark episode from her past she preferred to forget, it had set her on a path to save Yvetta from one Institution after another, meeting in Germany was an option they could consider.

The more she thought about this option, the more attractive it became. They could reunite in unified Berlin, in the city that pushed them together and tore them apart, they would be able to retrace their childhood together, both the special moments and the considerable trauma, it might give them both, closure. As if on cue, and to Fritzi's great relief, Erika called, and they settled down for a long chat about Fritzi's future with the idea of meeting in Berlin now firmly on the agenda, a very real and exciting, upcoming possibility.

Suddenly visiting other countries became an option once more. She could breathe easily, and travel under her own name once again, rediscover her true self, whoever or whatever that was. For the first time in her life, there were no consequences to worry over, the pressure on her, that insufferable and enormous weight, had finally eased, and she felt instead lighter than air, liberated, footloose and fancy free. It was a good feeling, albeit one that took some getting used to. Whatever happened at the interview, and she had come to terms with possible failure, she was feeling more optimistic about having a future. If she had to upend her life once again, so be it. At least she had a life, and she was nothing if not adaptable.

Her preference was a new beginning in Australia, a country she had fallen in love with and felt at home in. It wasn't just the country, it was the people as well.

Neither Jared nor Darius had been in touch about her momentous news regarding Mika's decision to essentially pardon Fritzi. Erika had mailed the two Aussies a full--blown report of her meeting with both DuPont and Mika.

After returning home from Missy's, a wise decision on her part, there were as always new people to meet and, lively conversation, just what she needed after Maggie's departure to keep her from over thinking about what lay ahead. She thought of calling Jared, needing some positive input on her situation from him, but she was hesitant to do so, always feeling a little unsure of their relationship.

She picked up the cell to call, but in the end her nerves got the better of her, and she called Darius instead, he wasn't directly involved with her immigration status, but he was always she felt, someone she could count on, Darius she knew still liked her, and was still infatuated and fascinated by her, he was always there for her.

Within seconds of his picking up, she could tell he wasn't alone, and for the first time she noticed a nervous strained edge, as if he didn't or, couldn't speak to her, he sounded preoccupied and distant. Voices could be heard in the background, she was sure she heard an American accent. His visitors must have arrived.

Trying to eavesdrop on their conversation as Darius moved away to speak with her, she thought it impossible, but was convinced she had heard the name 'Safi'! Surely not … but she was almost certain she had heard it. That word struck her, chimed at a bell deep within. And that sound kept reverberating.

An accident, another, similar-sounding word, something else entirely… She tried to comfort and distract herself from suspicion, but the irritation and the echo of the word would not go away. She decided that she had heard the right word, but that it fit the wrong identity. One of Darius's guests was referencing another person with the name of Safi. But how many people had that name? None she had ever met before encountering the British Saffron, the one and only … well, that thought stopped her heart cold. Putting it at the back of her mind, she had a quick, unsatisfactory conversation with Darius.

Sitting back after hanging up, her head a confusing buzz of mental noise and echoes from the now-dead call, she pondered on who his guests were. Her mind went flying off in all directions, as restless as it had been in the past, which, she knew from experience, was a dangerous thing. What if it was that Safi? What if she (or someone who knew her) was dining with Darius? What if Safi was in Australia? Who else would have accompanied her? And how could they possibly have come into contact with Darius?

The world was small, she knew from experience, but it wasn't that minute, surely? There was still space for people to never bump into each other, she hoped, now deeply unsure of herself – and unsure of Darius as well. What would he learn about her from this visit? And how would it change his opinion of, and relationship with, Fritzi? And what if Safi was there and wasn't travelling alone? Could Yvetta be there too? she wondered. Her heart began to throb and her head felt light, again dangerously so.

She felt dizzy and stayed seated, hunched up and cowering, almost afraid to move. Was it possible that Darius's guests were the Rubicovs? But how? Why? All this time she suspected that it was her who kept information from others, and that with Darius she had finally, wonderfully opened up… But what if he was keeping information from her again? Much as he had when he tracked down and read her Interpol file? Or had her warned about staying in Bali? Was trustworthy Darius playing her? Was he not who he seemed – and after all this time? More than anything, she hated the feeling that she was being kept in the dark, that others knew things she did not, that she was not even remotely in control.

She would tackle Darius when he called her back to have a longer conversation, she decided, the sense of resolve strengthening her. Some of the dizziness eased, as did the fear; she shifted in her chair. Even if he thought her mad, she had heard what she had heard – Safi – and, now that she thought about it, the voice she had heard sounded like Yvetta's, she would surely know that unapologetic strident manner and, her Russian intonation anywhere.

Bewildered, she remained frozen where she was in her small study, staring out of the window as shadows of life passed by under the street lights outside. What would she do if her suspicions were true? What could she do?

She decided to call Erika right away. She didn't care what the time difference was, she had to satisfy her strong feelings and suspicions. Speaking with someone else might help her figure out why this new, crazy development was crashing down on her.

There was no reply only an impersonal voicemail message. Frustrated, needing to talk to someone, she dialled Jared's number. She didn't care about how she might sound on the phone, or her nerves, which were, at this point, beyond shot. She was so fixated on frustration, so driven by anxiety, that she was almost surprised by some small measure of success when she heard Jared's voice on the phone, answering on the first ring.

'Hi, Jared, thank God you answered,' she said so hurriedly that she wondered if her words even made sense. Safi, she thought. Yvetta. My past. And, God forbid, my future, too. 'Why what's happened?' he said, sensing her anxiety.

'You are going to think this is mad,' she began. 'In fact, I think it's mad.'

'Well, I'm listening,' he said kindly.

'I called Darius – well, he didn't want to speak, because he had people over. But that's the thing, in the background, I heard voices, American voices and English voices, and I heard someone say 'Safi.''

'Are you sure?' Jared asked.

'As sure as I am talking with you.' As she spoke, she recalled again what she had heard, and the sounds, the experience, seemed to clarify, to become whole and real and undeniable. 'I heard Yvetta's voice in that Russian--American accent I know so well, and that voice said 'Safi,' and then I heard Safi answer in her English accent.'

'And then?' Jared said.

'And then I put the phone down. I felt bewildered, even frightened, completely shaken up. I tried to call Erika, but she didn't answer. Then I called you because after going over what I heard in my head, I had the strongest premonition it had to be Yvetta and Safi. I mean, it makes no sense that it could be them, but it must be, it must be, I just feel it.'

'If it were them,' Jared said slowly, gently, 'what would you do?'

There was a long pause, her mind raced in all directions suddenly she felt unsure could she trust anyone, even herself, her emotions were all over the place, before Fritzi said, 'I don't know, but I need to know if it's true and, if so, why are they with Darius.'

She took a deep breath, looked out the window at the dark street, looked around the room, which was dark now, too. She still felt a little dizzy. The previous feeling of warmth, comfort, homeliness that had been so present when Maggie was around was gone, all gone, replaced by anxiety and unease. Everything was upside-down and uncertain now. She had known for a long time that it was uncertainty, more than anything, that could weigh you down and crush you if you allowed it to, what was she missing, and why did she feel so angry, it seemed as if her present and past were colliding without her knowledge, and, it was pressing all her fight or flight buttons her antennae were in sharp focus once more.

'It's starting to freak me out, Jared,' she said, trying not to gnaw down a fingernail. 'Why on earth, or how on earth, could Darius be with them? It's not possible, right?' Seeking reassurance, or trying to sound him out, she said again, 'Right?'

Then he heard a deep intake of breath; she was nobody's fool.

'No,' she said slowly but with surprising firmness, 'he couldn't have, on those trips to the States, could he have, made, contact with, any of the Rubicov family? Did he take it upon himself to be Mr Sleuth after knowing of my background; he did, Jared, didn't he?'

Her mind was in sharp focus, dredging up all Darius's previous interventions through various sources, into her life, so this fell neatly with his meddling into her past, Darius was thorough if nothing else, but she wasn't at all sure why, or whether it was for his benefit or hers, what game was he playing?

She heard him sigh, resigned to what may follow. But the silence only seemed to strengthen her case.

'He did, didn't he,' she said, as though Jared had confirmed it merely by saying nothing at all. She felt humiliated, confused, and, worst of all, betrayed. 'What a bastard – how can he do this to me, entertain my enemies without even telling me. How far does this intrigue and betrayal go? I mean, are they as much in the dark as I am? Do they know that he knows me? No, I don't suppose they do.'

She spoke rapidly, not even allowing him to speak, which was just as well because he did not know, at that moment, what to say. 'I can't believe this, Jared, it's my worst nightmare come true. The man I trust absolutely goes behind my back yet again! I mean, he knows everything about me – everything! God knows what he's doing with that information, even as we speak. This time he befriends my foes without telling me while he is having a relationship with me. What kind of man does that, Jared?'

'Fritzi,' Jared said quickly, 'listen to yourself: you are surmising all these scenarios without even giving Darius a chance to defend himself to you – but perhaps you should. If, what you are saying is, indeed, true, give him the benefit of the doubt and allow him to explain it to you personally before incriminating him. Perhaps, if it is true – and I have no idea if it is - Darius is doing this for your benefit, knowing the situation between you and the Rubicovs?'

'Ja, perhaps,' Fritzi said, wondering how much, if anything, Jared really knew, 'but still, it's frustrating, Jared, to be here while he is there with Yvetta. Can you imagine how I feel?'

'No,' Jared said gently, 'tell me how do you feel.'

'Horrible, frightened, angry, I don't know,' Fritzi said. 'Jared, tell me honestly, how much do you know about this?'

'Nothing,' he said, 'honestly.'

He knew he had to keep her from doing anything stupid to jeopardise her immigration status.

'Really?'

'Really. And maybe you are mistaken, Fritzi, and that it wasn't really them you heard on the phone. Allow me to give you some very sound advice as your lawyer.'

This time Fritzi said nothing, there was no response, just silence, so he went ahead.

'I know you are upset and confused, but please listen to me carefully. This is the most delicate stage of your status here. If you were to do anything to jeopardise that interview, all would be lost. Now is the time we have to keep a sound head and heart; now is the time to test your resolve, to be the Fritzi you claim you want to be, that choice will always be yours but never has it been so crucial.'

There was another long silence, he waited patiently, breathing and steadying himself, using the dead air to think of how he would respond to whatever she suggested next. What worried him was how unpredictable she could be.

'You tell me what I should do,' she said, her voice breaking, 'what would you do in my situation – no, don't answer that.' Fritzi had crawled to a corner of the room wedged herself into the corner on the floor, like a frightened wounded animal, she felt herself being enveloped by feelings of helplessness for the first time, her future seemed to be in the hands of others, yet she knew inevitably her future lay in her hands, Jared had just reminded her, and she understood her actions now spoke volumes, she was the master of her own fate.

Now it was Jared's turn to be confused. 'Do you mean I should only answer what I think you should do?'

'Yes,' she replied, almost curtly.

'You are smart, intelligent and loyal,' Jared began, 'but Yvetta is not the one you should be loyal to any longer, Fritzi. The person you should be loyal to is yourself. Yvetta has a partner, she has moved on with her life, and so have you. As I said earlier, it's your call.'

'Yes, I suppose you are right,' Fritzi still slowly, still wondering how much exactly Jared knew, 'I know this, but still to imagine they are here in Australia … it's hard not to feel conflicted.'

'If they are here,' he said.

'Yes, Jared,' she said, 'I am sure they are.'

'Should I let Darius know about this call to me?' Jared asked.

'Please, yes,' Fritzi said, 'I am not sure I can call him again. I'm not sure I can trust him – or who, exactly, I'll be talking to if I do call. I'm not sure of anything right now. I wish Maggie were here. She left at exactly the wrong moment. Everyone seems to be in Sydney but me. Or maybe I shouldn't be here.'

'In Byron Bay?'

'In Australia. Anywhere, I don't know…'

She was beginning to crack at the edges, Jared thought, and at the worst time, with the immigration interview coming up and so much at stake. And now Darius had brought her enemies into her safe space, throwing everything into question. Fritzi's standing had felt so solid to her just hours ago, and now everything was up in the air, charged with a terrible, almost electric, uncertainty. Jared understood only too well how insecure she must be feeling, and, indeed, felt some of that insecurity now himself, her call to Darius at an unfortunate inopportune moment could be fatal for Fritzi, he felt a certain amount of chagrin, he and Darius would have to talk.

'Well, it's probably best if you stay in Byron Bay for the moment, but if you feel you need us, come to Sydney – you can stay with me, or with Maggie. I am sure they won't be here for long, anyway; they will be traveling like most tourists do – if they are even here, that is.'

This time Fritzi answered almost immediately. 'I will sleep on it,' she said, 'but please let me know as soon as you hear anything – and, Jared, on second thoughts, don't tell Darius about this call. If I'm wrong, he will think I've gone mad. It's better for him to tell me himself when the time is right about what's going on.' She breathed easily again for the first time in over an hour.

'That wasn't the only thing, Jared. I wanted to tell you about Erika's call to me about Mika Rubicov. Did you receive any information about this from Erika?'

'Yes, it's certainly excellent news,' Jared said, grateful for the change of subject, for something brighter to end the call, 'how do you feel about this news? Perhaps it's changed your mind about remaining here?'

'Never, I love Australia. But why didn't you contact me about Erika's report on the situation with Mika?'

In fact, knowing that Erika would have filled her in, Jared had wanted Fritzi to digest the news before speaking with her.

'I wanted to give you the space to internalise the consequences this has for you,' he said, choosing his words carefully, as both his profession and disciplined, diplomatic temperament had taught him to do, 'not having to fear for your life any longer.'

She smiled now, surprising herself. Perhaps the voices on the phone had been in her head, or at least misconstrued by her. Perhaps everything would be all right after all. Certainly, she was anxious about the hearing, and that anxiety and uncertainty was getting the better of her. She needed to relax and calm down.

'I will meet Erika in Berlin as soon as I hear about my immigration application. It's uppermost in my mind to be together with my closest friend in our place of birth. It may give us both closure to visit again.'

'That's a wonderful idea, Fritzi. I am sure it will have a beneficial outcome for you both. And, perhaps it's prudent to dwell on your future now rather than on your past, if you can.'

He was right, of course, she knew he was. And maybe she was wrong about the voices on the phone – although she didn't think that she was wrong at all. An awful feeling continued to enclose her and it was hard to breathe now in the dark. Hearing that familiar voice had thrown her right back to her past, and all her old feelings had resurfaced.

'Yes, my past came back in a torrent of emotions. It frightened me momentarily, but I'm over it now, thank you, Jared, for listening to me. I might have done something I'd have regretted if I hadn't spoken with you. Not for the first time, you saved my life.'

'That's what we do,' he said, 'you and I, Fritzi, we save each other's lives. I wouldn't be here if it wasn't for you.'

'And vice versa,' she said, ending the call.

After putting her cell down, Fritzi poured herself a much--needed vodka and walked back to her hub, where she sat behind her desk, stared at the keys on her computer for a while, and then began to type.

Chapter 23

Mika felt sure that calling his hounds off Fritzi had been the correct decision; and yet he did not feel comfortable with his family on the same continent as that viper. For this reason, he had put provisions in place to prevent any unpleasant surprises.

He now knew where in Australia Fritzi resided. He had made contact with Bruce a private investigator in Sydney who had worked for Darius, the Australian he had met at Yvetta's wedding.

DuPont had been drawn in against his will by Darius while in Manhattan and, once more when in Sydney. Darius and Jared had pleaded Fritzi's case but DuPont had not changed his mind about that despicable woman. Now Erika pleaded Fritzi's case trying to involve DuPont personally, it was hard not to be moved by her childhood horror in East Berlin. DuPont felt he had to inform Mika about Darius, including his recent visit to Australia, and his involvement with Fritzi's case.

In spite of Erika's interruption in his life, and dredging up old, bad memories, Mika had taken a shine to Erika. She was a straight talker and had made a brave effort to help her childhood friend, Fritzi. He admired her loyalty, her dedication, her obvious and considerable intelligence. The Russian satellites at that time were as brutal, if not more so, than Russia itself. Erika did not have to convince Mika of that. Her father might have been a young teenager during the Second World War, but her grandparents were more than likely foot soldiers for the Germans, if not worse. The Nazis were scum of the earth; as far as he was concerned, the apple did not fall far from the tree. Being a member of the official state security apparatus, one of the most repressive in the history of the world, Fritzi's father was not unlike an SS officer during the war. The Stasis were feared by all who had the misfortune to live under that regime during the Iron Curtain in Eastern Europe.

It was therefore Erika who deserved his empathy, not Fritzi – but he understood that their childhood had been influenced, shaped and also scarred, by events beyond their control. Now he understood so much of the background and context to the person who had almost succeeded in destroying his family. It was as though Erika's tale had illuminated the darkness, made much of it clear, but it remained terribly dark nonetheless.

Living under her father's roof, Fritzi, he feared, had learnt more than she realised, and had used clever manipulative antics at every opportunity to sabotage his own family.

The story told by Erika had been a convincing one, he had to admit. Fritzi had been relentless in her pursuit to save his sister Yvetta from every institution they hid her away in – albeit for misguided and sick reasons of her own. Still, Erika's explanation had not been entirely convincing. For one thing, Mika hadn't bought into Erika's psychobabble about Fritzi's mental state, he doubted her emotive reasoning, that Fritzi replaced Yvetta for Erika.

No, Erika was obviously too emotionally involved and unobjective, even if she was a psychiatrist by profession. Fritzi had been a bad influence on his sister, almost killed his brother, attempted to ruin the family and come damn close. He could not, under any circumstances, allow her influence to continue – if it meant having to have Fritzi 'taken care of,' he would have done it, and she had been spared simply because he had not been able to track her down. All of this was water under the bridge now. His sister had miraculously changed for the better. He was not one to dwell on how or why; she was a different person today, that was all that mattered. Perhaps he should afford Fritzi the same opportunity.

Still, Mika requested his own investigation, in order to know as much as Bruce was able to find on her new life since arriving in Australia, and all of her contacts. He wanted to make sure she wasn't still a threat, wasn't running a new scam or scheme – and, if she was, to be safely on top of it. Too often, Fritzi had been two steps ahead of him with her plans. Things would be different now. And he had leverage, too. If, Fritzi made contact with Yvetta and Safi, Mika would ruin her chances of getting what she so badly wanted: her Australian citizenship. He had been duped by her cunning methods before.

While his family were traveling round Australia, they were vulnerable. He instructed Bruce to keep as close to Fritzi as was possible. He wanted to know every move she made until Yvetta and Safi were safely back in the States.

While they were in Melbourne things had gone smoothly, but now that they were in Sydney, he felt less sure about the visit being uneventful. They were staying at the same hotel DuPont had stayed in, close to a major art gallery. He was in possession of their business itinerary, and had the names of the art dealers in their line of work they would be making contact with while in Sydney. Mika would be relieved when his sister and sister-in-law flew home; his life was busy enough without having to keep a constant vigil over their visit.

His friend (and Safi's husband) Janus, who he held in high regard, was in Germany, where he had work on show that had travelled from the Venice Biennale; the exhibition happened to coincide with Safi's trip to Australia.

Most of all, he valued Janus's opinions and friendship. Russians were often suspect presences in foreign countries, and knowing Janus had proved a sound investment. Through Janus's many and important connections Mika had been able to avoid throwing any suspicions his way or becoming involved with any dubious investments.

After Sasha had died, Janus had been a first-rate stand-in father to Mika's nephew and niece. Janus had always loved Safi, without envy or resentment, even after Sasha returned to Manhattan after being held captive in Russia for years. Up until that point, Safi had turned to Janus for comfort, but once Sasha returned, she had gone back to her husband. Through it all Janus had remained a genuine friend to both the woman he loved and to his brother Sasha.

Now that Sasha was gone the responsibility of family was squarely on Mika's shoulders, and he needed to repay that respect to Janus, ensuring that nothing happened to Safi, or, for that matter, to his sister, Yvetta.

The time was almost over for his family in Australia; nothing had occurred thus far. They had forty-eight hours to go before flying home, which meant that Mika himself was almost home dry and beginning to relax.

Sitting at his computer after his morning exercise routine, which included playing a punishing game of tennis with his coach (who he had not yet managed to beat – but he would), followed by a refreshing swim in his pool. Now, after towelling himself down and changing into comfortable clothes, he browsed through his personal emails.

Opening up his junk-mail folder in case he had missed correspondence with a realtor on his Greek venture, he opened an unknown letter to check the subject.

'Dear Mika,' the letter began.

Only personal friends addressed him as 'Mika,' so he clicked to open the email, only to find a letter written by Fritzi. He sat up straight, his finger poised to delete the email, wipe every trace of it from both his computer and his mind, sheer anger rising in him at her gall. He breathed, removed his trigger finger and ran it through his now-dry hair. Then he scanned the letter, his finger still trembling in anger above the mouse. He did not want to read it, but he read it, all of it. Fritzi was trying to apologise for her past behaviour to his family. His brow knitted and again he had the urge to delete. But he continued reading, but not without great distaste.

The letter was impersonal, mostly honest, even judicious, not apportioning blame or finding excuses for her treachery towards all of the Rubicov family. She took full responsibility for her actions. Sasha being shot had been an accident, she had never meant to harm him, although she admitted putting his life in danger more than once. Her sole motivation had always been to save Yvetta. She now understood how vengeful her actions against all of the Rubicovs were, and had no reservations with regards to her guilt in this respect. Even her involvement with the art smugglers, she admitted, was to damage the Rubicov reputation.

She did not ask for forgiveness, but hoped that, in time, she could, if it were at all possible, atone for her past sins and mistakes.

He reread the letter a few times, looking for signs of treacherous duplicity. After all, the old Fritzi, he knew, was without a doubt cunning enough to hide her true malice towards the Rubicov family, to try and exploit an apology to operate a new scam, but he found none of that here.

She signed the letter 'Best Fritzi.'

He wondered whether a similar letter had gone out to Safi and Yvetta. If it had, he hoped they had not received it while in Australia, lest she mention where she was residing, or was it hiding? Yvetta, even though travelling with her wife, Gina, might (in spite of all reason and their tragic and maddening history together) try to make contact with her old love, he did not want that to happen under any circumstances. Such a reunion would be disastrous – for everyone.

Mika had given Bruce strict instructions to intervene if any personal contact were to take place. If that were to occur, Mika could not vouch for Fritzi's safety.

Finding her email an affront, Mika had no intention of replying. Indeed, he was still angry. He hated thinking about Fritzi, and now she had consumed most of his morning, ruined a post-workout endorphin high, and soured his mood. And her gall, it appeared, had not lessened at all over the years. She had taken it upon herself to invade his privacy. If her mission was to be the centre of attention, she had succeeded yet again In, all likelihood, he decided, now shifting the target of his anger slightly, she had acquired his email address from Erika.

Mika wondered whether Fritzi had taken advantage once again, relying on his weakness and empathy towards Erika, her childhood friend. This thought caused a further bout of anger. He should have obeyed his instincts and deleted that email before reading it. And perhaps he was, indeed, partly to blame, too. Perhaps without realising it, he had excused Fritzi's actions towards his family. Interestingly, Fritzi had not mentioned Erika or their meeting in her email. But he knew without a doubt that the letter was a direct result of his meeting with DuPont and Erika. The email, the message, and most of all the author, none of it pleased him.

So be it, for all he cared, Fritzi could go to hell – but he knew he would be hearing from Yvetta in due course, and from Safi, too, if they both received messages from Fritzi. What course of action (if any) would be taken in response would depend on their reaction. More than anything, he did not want either of them to be hurt by Fritzi ever again. Until then he would print out the email, adding it to the growing folder he had been sent by Bruce.

This done, he went to find Daniella. He hoped she did not have a million things to do today; he needed some distraction – and right away. Fritzi had ruined enough of his day. Time for something different. It had been a while since he and Daniella had been out together on an impromptu lunch.

Mika found Daniella doing laps in the pool, her early morning swim. Checking his watch, he realised it was only nine-thirty, long before she started her day. Fritzi's email and his reaction to it had made it seem so much later than it actually was.

They settled down to breakfast together on the shaded, pillared portico leading out onto the terraces below.

'I want us to spend the day together,' Mika said, looking at his partner, touching her hand. Daniella in a white kaftan looked as ravishing as always with her long blond hair drawn back off her face and her almond blue eyes fixed on him, always made his heart flutter. 'Do you have a busy day?'

Daniella was always busy, she never allowed a day to evaporate without appointments. She consulted her iPhone diary. 'I have a lunch date with Cindy,' she said. 'We, were going to discuss the upcoming fall charity ball, but I will postpone it. After all, we still have a few outstanding invitations to agree on.'

Mika enjoyed spending time on his boat – it was relaxing, and today especially he needed to relax. He instructed the boating crew to prepare his yacht for a day out on the coastal waters. They would stop at his favourite place for lunch.

After his conversation with the crewmember, Mika and Daniella both retired to their suite. Mika was in the mood for romance and love. He adored Daniella; she, above all else, made his life here in Florida one of pleasure rather than work. He never demanded she gave up her time for him at a whim, but whenever he suggested they spend time together without prior notice, she had never found an excuse not to please him.

Twenty years younger than Mika, Daniella, not yet forty, was in excellent shape. Admiring her tanned, long-limbed body as she stepped into the shower after making love, he wondered whether his roving eye would get the better of him once she started showing her age.

She had become indispensable to his lifestyle, and he was more than a little in awe of her ability to keep their social life and personal family life running so smoothly and without the smallest sign of conflict. The festive season was around the corner, and that meant a hectic schedule for Daniella to organise. Still, Daniella never complained, and all Mika had to do was sign the gift cards and show up.

Stepping onto his sleek sunseeker yacht, the skipper at the helm, they set off for a day out at sea, visiting the bays along the way. A clear blue sky with low humidity this time of year would be perfect for a day on his yacht.

Mika never took his fortune for granted; everything belonged to the family businesses, nothing belonged to any individual when it came to high-expenditure luxuries. The yacht, the houses, all of it belonged to the family not to him alone. The homes on the Riviera were shared by the Rubicov family, including Safi: that was the way Alexi ran his life, and Mika continued his legacy.

Being the patriarch of the family, now that his father Alexi was no longer at the head of their empire and Sasha had died tragically young,

Mika did not take his responsibilities lightly. Above all else, it was up to him to keep his family safe.

Chapter 24

Daniella had every reason to believe she was the centre of Mika's life. She was treated like a queen, and she enjoyed every moment she spent with Mika.

At first her family had balked at her involvement with a Russian oligarch (the Russians had a notorious reputation). The media coverage of Russian Oligarchs who owned prime landmarks in major American cities and, no one forgot the Cuban crises, apart from the cold war era, their prejudices were ingrained, but Daniella had fallen head over heels in love with Mika and, there was nothing quite like meeting the charming Mika in person to give them a change of heart. He was a charming soft spoken, tall, attractive cultured European educated gentleman who won them over in no time at all.

Her single regret was not having her own family or being married to Mika. Instead, he had worked out with his lawyers an agreement to suit her the best way he knew how, and she had readily accepted the deal. Secretly, she would have remained without a deal, yet she knew it was in her best interest to accept one; after all, she did not come without brains or talent and, it did not hurt to let Mika know. Mika believed in keeping his life simple, his family business was in itself complicated and, he preferred to stay out of American legal ramifications where marriage was concerned, having children was never on his radar, it would complicate his otherwise perfect lifestyle.

She had figured out early on in their relationship what was of the utmost importance in his life. His family were always number one to him and, she was under no illusions about this. After all, the Rubicov business empire was run by the family. Mika was the caretaker, keeping everything running smoothly; he ironed out any knots.

Living in America meant he needed to be seen in the right circles and the right places. She was able to provide all of that through her family connections and contacts. She was, after all, from old money, even though her family did not have the means Mika's had had. Still, they had breeding, which opened doors for Mika.

Thus, from a social perspective the relationship was mutually beneficial – but happily they loved one another as well. At least Daniella hoped Mika loved her the way she loved him – he was certainly wildly attractive and caring. Her family being a fixture in Miami social circles for over a hundred years, Daniella knew everybody who was anybody in Florida. Mika's finances behind her and her charisma and philanthropic endeavours, she had become a force to be reckoned with in the community.

Through her charity work, the couple entertained politicians and movie stars, sports personalities and those who were in the arts. They gave generously to all. Mika and Daniella were feted by the highest echelons of society, and Daniella loved every moment of her work. She considered it a fulltime job keeping up with their social diary.

Mika only asked to be told well in advance when and where to be at any given time. She made sure his clothes were tailored to perfection; Mika did not like loose fitting clothes or to dress casually, like most Americans, and was only interested in European designers. Mika often said that he liked the best of the best, which is why he had chosen Daniella, who was just that. She made sure they were at his beck and call whenever he needed a new wardrobe. His shoes were designed in Rome and London, where they kept his Cedarwood shoe lasts, if he needed a new pair they had what was needed.

His shirts and polo shirts were never worn for more than a month before a new lot were delivered for him or Daniella to choose from.

Their fleet of cars were exchanged regularly. Mika preferred not to have his cars recognised by the paparazzi or any unsavoury people; one could never be too careful, he often said.

She had a free reign in indulging wherever and whenever she chose. She often took her mother with on shopping expeditions to New York. They would both shop for the season, but of course it would all be charged to Daniella's credit card, with Mika's compliments. Mika encouraged Daniella to spoil her mother; it reflected well on him. It was, as he saw it, a win-win.

Her parents would spend every Thanksgiving with them, as would Daniella's extended family. No one ever turned down an invitation to spend time at the Star Island mansion. Mika's family spent Christmas with them each year. The Rubicov clan would fly in from all over the world, it was an awesome extravaganza. The tree tall enough to touch the sky would be in the double-height hallway. Bergdorf Goodman would send a team down from Manhattan to decorate it. The gifts were boxed and packaged by Neiman Marcus and Bergdorf's. The gardens were lit with fairy lights and Mika would have a fireworks display every new year, one of the most impressive in the city.

Mika and Daniella never travelled abroad until after the seasonal festivities were over; the holidays were a standing invitation to all their friends and Mika's associates to join them for one of the most sought-after parties in the Bay. Daniella's life was glamorous and filled with love: instead of children she had her two miniature Schnauzers, Maisie and Oliver, who fulfilled her cuddling needs. Even though fifteen years her senior, Mika was more than enough man for her; he had boundless energy. He was lean in build and handsome, no paunch on him; he kept trim and healthy.

Today they were alone out on the open water. When Mika asked to be alone with her, she would drop whatever arrangements or appointments she had, understanding exactly what it was he needed from her, her undivided attention. it was the least she could do to repay his loyalty, love and, the generosity he bestowed on her and her family.

She never inquired or asked questions about his business arrangements or meetings, which were often held at their twenty-four-seat dining table, with the doors of the dining room firmly shut. Tripods with maps were used and lectures in Russian were given. Once or twice she recognised high-powered politicians amongst those who attended the meetings.

She knew only too well that this was Mika's world, and one that she had joined out of her own free will. In fact, she did not regret one minute of her life with Mika. She could not remember ever being as happy as she was with him. As far as she was concerned, his business connections were not her business. Besides, she trusted Mika with her life.

Over the years Daniella had heard many stories about the notorious Fritzi from East Berlin. She had heard, for example, all about her and Yvetta's attack on Mika's beloved mother Anna's home in Moscow. She had heard about Sasha's kidnapping and how the family had suffered afterwards, resulting in the tragic death of Alexi, Mika's father and the family's patriarch. Daniella noticed where Fritzi was concerned Mika had a blind spot, just the mention of her name instantly darkened his mood.

Mika never discussed much along business lines with Daniella, but once in a while they would discuss the subject of his family.

The yacht pulled into a bay, where Mika had reserved a table for lunch. After a leisurely lunch, over coffee and dessert, Mika began to share the most recent story about Fritzi and her childhood friend Erika, a name Daniella had not heard before. This new story was astonishingly macabre, shining a light on Fritzi's paranoia and behaviour towards Yvetta over the years the two women were together, wreaking havoc wherever they were.

'Are you still searching for her?' Daniella asked.

'I have found her,' Mika replied softly but firmly.

'Oh,' she said, trying not to sound surprised. She put down her dessert fork. 'And?'

He went on to tell her the rest of the story, including the tale (an intricate, fascinating story within itself) of her saving the PM's son from an earthquake in New Zealand. The more she heard about Fritzi, the more conflicted her thoughts about her were.

He ended by describing Erika's visit to their Star Island house, begging Mika not to harm her childhood friend.

'What did you say?' Daniella asked, intrigued. Leaning in towards Mika as if, what he was about to reveal was highly sensitive. Daniella's blue eyes didn't stray from Mika's, as she blew the stray hair away from her forehead, with her breath, the light breeze from the sea had tangled her otherwise perfect hair.

'I had to agree,' Mika said slowly, his voice still low and gravelly, his gaze hard. But Daniella knew that beneath that tough exterior beat an often surprisingly soft heart. Mika was many things, but he was always reasonable. His thin lips almost smiled, a moment of silence ensued, which was broken when he said, 'Fritzi's attempt on Sasha's life and the extraordinary lengths she went to extricate Yvetta from every institution we hid her away in was, if not maddening, certainly quite a feat and to be admired.'

He paused again, realising he had never described Fritzi's activities as admirable before. He had always seen her as the exact opposite: evil, reprehensible, inhuman even. Now he was beginning to accept her as, if nothing else, a human being with authentic feelings and emotional complexity. Of course, he was a human being with feelings, too, and he had his own prejudices against, and long, sordid history, with Fritzi, but he was beginning to reconsider her from every angle, Daniella could detect as much.

As if in response to this, Daniella gave him a soft but interrogative look, assessing her partner anew. She loved him deeply – there was no doubt about that – but he was an enormously complex, often unpredictable, challenge but nonetheless rewarding personality. Full of masterful charisma, energy, intelligence, raw sexuality even.

'Once I realised, she was saving Yvetta from the same fate she thought Erika had suffered, I could no longer continue with my original plan.'

'Oh,' she said, grasping his hand. 'I can't say I am not relieved.'

'Oh,' he said, surprised, 'why is that?' He gazed at Daniella, impressed anew by her always surprising, always graceful beauty, her soft, emotional eyes and delicate features. He always found her sincerity and warmth a turn on, she was absolutely adorable.

'I know she has done some awful things,' Daniella began slowly, squeezing his hand, 'but so has Yvetta, if you don't mind me saying so,' she knew to be especially sensitive now, since in Mika's world only a Rubicov family member was allowed to say anything critical about one of their own, 'from what you have shared with me. So perhaps Fritzi can change, too, under the right circumstances – especially given that she no longer has to carry that mountain of guilt, which must have been a punishing burden, for her father's sins, sins she should never have felt responsible for in the first place.'

'You are right, as always,' Mika said, finally allowing himself to smile, albeit fleetingly, and squeezing her hand back, 'I agree.' Then the smile faded, he pulled his hand away (he did that gently too), and he said, 'All the same I have a tail on her while Safi and Yvetta are in Australia. It is strictly a precautionary measure. Who knows what Fritzi might do if she hears that Yvetta is on the same continent? We think and hope that Fritzi has changed, but what if she hasn't? Or what if hearing that Yvetta is in Australia triggers something within her – no, I won't allow that to happen.'

'As you've said,' Daniella whispered, sensing the change in Mika's voice, his mood, but having the sense not to reach again for his hand (he had pulled away from her, albeit unconsciously, in a posture of anxiety again), 'she wants to become an Australian citizen and has high--powered people rooting for her. That must mean something. I cannot imagine she would jeopardise her chances.'

'That may be,' he said, softening, realising that he was now being unnecessarily physically aloof and that his loved one deserved none of this (after all, Daniella had done nothing to him except have the utmost love and confidence in him and his business dealings, and kept him afloat during the many difficult periods that came with his position), 'but it's my job to look after my family, even – and especially – if there is the slightest chance they may be in danger.'

Daniella shook her head; she understood Mika only too well: family always came first, the consequences could be dealt with later.

'Well,' Mika continued, 'today I had quite a surprise. I received an email from Fritzi.'

'Really.' Daniella scolded herself for being surprised; she should, she told herself, by now used to the endless twists the Fritzi saga had to offer – and yet she could not help but be fascinated by the outcome, and the character of Fritzi, at once so vulnerable and so conniving, so insidious and so seductive, but most of all so indelible and, by all accounts, unforgettable. 'What did she say?'

'She apologised,' he said, sounding surprised himself, and his voice was now resigned, jaded even. 'I don't want to go into it in detail, really, but she admitted to her attacks on my family – for the very first time. Maybe that's progress, self-awareness, a kind of atonement. Or maybe it is yet another ruse. I am not sure … yet.'

'Are you going to reply?' she asked.

'Absolutely not,' he said firmly once again. I will wait and see what happens, confer with others. Perhaps Yvetta and Safi received the same email from Fritzi. If Fritzi does write to them, I hope they receive the message after they have left Australia. I most certainly do not want Yvetta getting it into her head to track Fritzi down – or vice versa, for that matter.'

'That would not be good, I agree.'

'Well,' he said, trying for a smile, 'it's only a day before they fly back, so I think we are out of the woods. After that, I will be able to call off the dogs, and Fritzi will be home free, so to speak.'

The rest of the day was spent in idle chatter, this story leading to other stories about other people from Mika's past. Daniella always felt important and pleased on the rare occasions when Mika shared confidences with her. It made her feel wanted, an important part of his life rather than how she often cynically saw herself, which was as his highly paid personal secretary with fringe benefits. Of course she never let Mika know she often felt this way. She kept her feelings to herself most of the time, just like he did. In fact, they had a lot more in common than either of them would ever admit.

Daniella had got used to Yvetta (who she only spent real time with during the Thanksgiving gathering, Christmas, and a few other holidays, and who, in any case, kept herself to herself, preferring her own company and that of her wife and sister-in-law Safi to Daniella and the rest of the larger Rubicov clan), but was still wary of her.

Yvetta could be prickly, mercurial, unpredictable, aloof, intimidating, intellectually haughty, and oh-so-sensitive (often for mysterious, even arbitrary-seeming reasons, so Daniella (who considered herself a less complicated) minded, her p's and q's around her, and often avoided her company altogether, if she could help it. Safi, on the other hand, was a proper English lady and very beautiful. Safi was often earthy (with a dry sense of humour), always friendly, engaging, sensitive, intelligent, outgoing, refined. She was the magnet of warmth that Daniella had always been drawn to; not fully an insider to the family, but certainly not an outsider either, Daniella felt she could learn a lot from the much-loved Safi.

The Rubicovs were a handsome family; all the cousins were well-educated at the best schools and colleges, but Daniella liked to keep her family separate (they were, after all, so very different) and avoided joint celebrations. This separation, suited Mika and, Daniella to have her family at Thanksgiving and Mika's at Christmas and New Year's, which was fast approaching, time just flew.

So far she had managed to keep everyone from both families happy, and given the variety and prestige of the various members, that was no small thing. Most families had tense moments at these large festive occasions, but she prided herself on her party-planning and problem-solving abilities, to say nothing of her steadfast, almost stubborn, diplomacy, avoiding conflicts and even minor disruptions by organising each occasion to suit each family.

Really her real concern was only ever Mika, the man she loved. He was always uppermost in the pecking order, and she had every intention of keeping it that way.

What Mika wanted Mika got; as she was treated like a queen, so he was served like a king. She would organise with the staff the smallest details to suit him. When out at restaurants she would call ahead and have his preferences taken care of. Only Pellegrino would be served, while the most expensive caviar would be brought in and kept on ice. His favourite vodkas would be delivered if none were available.

It wasn't often Daniella thought of herself as lacking in the looks department, but she did when Mika's family came over. They were without exception the most groomed and surgically chiselled females she had ever met.

Daniella was thankful she still had the glow of youth on her side and a body to match. She worked hard to keep it that way. Daniella never wanted to give Mika a reason to discard her for a younger model. She loved her life, knowing her position in the community without Mika would make her just another pretty, well-connected American. But with Mika she had become someone everyone needed to know. She was the queen of their society and relished each and every moment of it.

It was dusk when they returned home from the ocean. The lights were on in the house. Mika thanked the crew and they made their way back up the terraces to the air--conditioned comfort of their magnificent home. She never tired of seeing it from a distance: it was truly a beautiful property she was proud to live in, much as she was proud to call Mika her other half, to have him in her life and in her heart. Daniella often wished Mika would include the mansion in their agreement: she would hate to lose it to another woman, perish the thought.

She could not understand her negative feelings of late; something was niggling at the back of her mind. Usually she never dwelt on maybe's or if's, but that had begun to change, and only very recently. It had happened over time, but it had happened nonetheless, it was undeniable, and she was afraid it would be impossible to reverse. She did not understand why a feeling of foreboding had crept into her otherwise loving, safe, and certainly successful life. Mika had never given her any cause to worry. She had not put a finger on any cause for her doubts, so she put it down to fears should her happiness evaporate overnight. Perhaps the real reason unsettling her equilibrium was her next birthday, when she would be turning forty, not that youthful any longer.

Chapter 25

It was their last full day in Sydney. The trip had been a great success for Safi, her mother Fiona, and the rest of her family living in Melbourne. Yvetta had met Safi's immediate family at functions in the past. Her brother Jake had done well in the tech world out in Melbourne, but Yvetta noted Safi did not seem to want to impose on her family's lives, so opted to stay in the hotels that were booked by their travel agent back in New York.

Fiona accompanied Safi and Yvetta to Hobart, Tasmania for three days. Grateful to see her daughter after what had been too long of an absence, Fiona confided that moving to Melbourne had given her a new lease of life. Indeed, she was looking brighter – even younger – than she had in years. She wore her hair loose and fashionably styled, her face was nicely tanned from the Australian sun, and, best of all, she was smiling widely and happily once again. It wasn't the fake, flat smile she had delivered (and, even then, all too sparingly) in the long years after Safi's father died.

She found life in Melbourne exciting, and spent much of her day as a mature student doing water colour painting and pottery courses she had always thought were out of her reach. Being independent had opened whole new horizons she never thought possible. She had met a retired Surgeon through friends, and, with surprising speed, they had become an item. This was another shock finding for Fiona, one of many in her life: after forty years of marriage, she was still desirable.

Safi confided in Yvetta that it was a relief to find her mother so animated, with a renewed zest for life, but, as happy as Safi was for Fiona, she found it hard to imagine her mother in a romantic partnership with someone besides her father, Leonard. Yvetta assured her that such mixed feelings were entirely natural, thinking of her own mother, Anna, and the German-Jewish psychiatrist she had been in a serious relationship with after Alexi died. And still, both Safi and Yvetta agreed, it made it easier for Safi to return to America knowing that her mother was happy.

Not for the first time, Safi felt blessed to have the open, peaceful, confiding relationship with her sister-in-law (and partner in the Rubicov galleries) that she had always craved. These days, it was as if the two women could tell each other anything, at any time of the day or night. Nothing was out of bounds or inappropriate or taboo.

As for the misdeeds and mistakes of the past, the trauma of the Fritzi years, well, those were well and truly in the past, and never spoken about. For so long such a fearful presence (even in her absence), Fritzi had become an afterthought, little more than a bad memory, a brief and fleeting sense of pain. She was, it appeared to Yvetta, at least, for ever in the past. Little did Yvetta know how close to Yvetta she in fact was – closer, geographically, at least, than she had been in years. And her proximity was made that much sharper by her obliviousness to this fact.

Although this trip to Australia was a working holiday, Yvetta saw it also as a honeymoon and a well-deserved break from their hectic lives in Manhattan. On his trip to Australia just six weeks ago, DuPont had made many new contacts; through his resourcefulness, attractiveness, and considerable charm, he had laid an easy path for them in Sydney. Both women were enormously grateful: for DuPont, for each other, and for the opportunity of this incredible adventure down under. Each day was filled with activity and meetings: new people, new images and experiences, new sites and smells and tastes and textures. To the delight of both women, the museums and galleries were of the highest standard and it was easy to forge new contacts. The people here were friendly – urbane, intelligent, and innovative, but also wonderfully down-to-earth – much friendlier and less pretentious than those in New York.

Sitting on her own for the first time since arriving down under, Yvetta relaxed in the hotel lounge, watching the magnificent view from the cool interior of the sleek and newly renovated hotel. She put her shapely legs up on a footstool and sipped a flat black that came with a nutty biscotti, which she bit into while flicking through her emails, an activity she generally avoided while away.

Still, she had to catch up with some important people back home, and to confirm upcoming arrangements with some of the contacts she had made in Australia. The biscotti fell into her coffee with shock as she began to read an email from Fritzi. The very person she least wanted to think about let alone hear from, the person whose actions had led to her brother being crippled and later taken from her all too soon, the person she had never felt so distant from … until now. Bad memories dredged up. The coffee tasting suddenly bitter. The cup in her hand shaking softly. She felt suddenly dizzy. The cool interior of the hotel lobby swam, a vague but beautiful blur.

Putting the cup down on the coffee table, she rushed over to the bathrooms to read the message in solitude. She didn't want anyone, least of all her wife, to find her so highly agitated. And yet the words in the letter were a blur, too, not immediately making any sense. Even her vision seemed to shake.

Putting her hand to her forehead, her hands still shaking somewhat, breathing deeply and trying to steady herself, she sat on the toilet to read the email once more.

The message was unemotional, to say the least. There was nothing of a personal nature about their relationship. only an apology for accidentally shooting Sasha, and an expression of her shame for any harm her actions might have caused in the past to Yvetta or anyone close to her.

What followed, in the second half of the email, was Fritzi recounting her story about what had happened to Erika, ending with Fritzi finding her friend safe after all these years, having reconnected recently. Fritzi explained how this reunion and the knowledge that Erika was still alive (and, in fact, a successful professional in America) had lifted a terrible burden of guilt off her shoulders.

Yvetta read all of this with total disbelief. It wasn't the story that was shocking, but hearing from Fritzi once more after so long brought back emotions she thought had died. And now her whole body was atremble, her mind a mess.

She sat on the toilet for a long time, too scared to face Gina, or, for that matter, anyone else – at least until she was able to calm down long enough to internalise how she felt or what, if any, action she needed to take.

A footnote in Fritzi's letter informed her that Safi and Mika had received similar letters too, but the most shocking revelation was that Fritzi was in Australia. Yvetta reeled with shock her mind numb at this information, after which she found it raced ahead, with scenarios. She wondered whether Safi had read her letter from Fritzi yet, or had she seen it and not said anything? No, Yvetta decided, it wasn't possible: Safi would have told her if Fritzi had sent her a message; she would not have kept it a secret from Yvetta, especially since the two women spent most of every day in Australia together.

She stood up slowly, flushing the toilet even though she had not used it. Her mind was now made up. She needed to be ready when she faced the others. But before she faced Safi or Mika or Gina, before they flew back to America, there was something she had to do. And that something was to speak to Fritzi.

She read the letter one last time. She had missed the telephone number at the bottom of the email: it sat there on the page blinking at her. how could she have missed it! Yvetta knew it had to be Fritzi's contact number.

Walking out of the ladies' restroom, looking left and right for any signs of Safi or Gina, she made her way out of the hotel to a side street, where she found a large brasserie. Walking to the back of the restaurant, she hid herself away from prying eyes and ears. The waitress brought her a menu and Yvetta made it clear that she had an important call to make, and would order after, all she needed was a bottle of sparkling water for now.

Feeling cold and shivery all of a sudden, even in the cool restaurant, her forehead prickled with moisture. She wiped her brow with a napkin and dialled the number on the email. The ring tone sounded like a time bomb in her ear, then a long crackle and a voice from the past invaded her senses.

'Fritzi, it's Yvetta,' she said, struggling to get the words out.

For a moment she thought she had lost the connection, then she heard an intake of breath and a soft voice say, 'Mein kleiner Schatz, how are you?'

'Fritzi, oh my God. It's really you. Where are you at the moment are you in Sydney?'

'I am not in Sydney, like you' Fritzi said.

Yvetta was aghast.

'But how do you know I am here?'

'Ah. it's a long story, never mind,' Fritzi said, her old bubbly, breathless energy and convivial, cheeky, restless charm reasserting itself. It was as if they had last spoken just a few minutes or a few days ago, as though there was not a distance between years and significant trauma between them. 'Tell me about you, all about you, don't leave anything out, I want to hear everything.'

Yvetta wasn't sure what to say or how to feel, so much had changed in the long, difficult, but also liberating years that they had been apart, and so much of the pain appeared to disappear when Yvetta heard that voice on the phone. She breathed, steadied herself again, and said, 'I am a very different person now than when we were together, Fritzi.'

'Me too,' Fritzi said.

'I met someone, you know.'

'Yes, I know,' Fritzi said. 'It does not matter now, as long as you are happy.'

Yvetta felt her heart thumping in her chest, but also felt relieved. She told her old lover all about her life, her marriage, her successful gallery, and how settled, centred, and content she was.

'Now it's your turn, Fritzi. Please, I want to know what has happened to you since New York.'

Fritzi tried to fill her in on all that had happened since that time, but more importantly she wanted Yvetta to know she had turned a corner, too. Erika had come into her life again, which had changed everything, including her whole perspective of the past – and hopefully she had a future in Australia.

Chapter 26

A decidedly cold chill had swept into their normally relaxed relationship. Darius didn't know what explained the change in Fritzi, but he knew something was up, and he was intent on getting to the bottom of it.

Relieved that Yvetta and Safi's trip had gone without a hitch, Darius had returned to Byron Bay. It had been playing on his mind for months, as had DuPont's visit weeks earlier. Keeping his involvement with Yvetta and Safi from Fritzi had not been easy. From experience he knew not too cross her, and how keenly she felt any perceived disloyalty or betrayal. She had cold-shouldered him once before, after he employed a friend to investigate her life. He did not blame her then, and he did not blame her now, still he wondered if Safi and Yvetta's visit had somehow come to her attention. He had not told Fritzi about their trip, but the timing certainly made sense.

Fritzi's treatment of him was not directly dismissive, instead he had become aware of her continuous jibes about his trip away from Byron Bay with his clients. 'So, these clients from America,' she had said sharply, 'where did you meet them, in the States?'

Or, 'They must be pretty important clients for you to spend so much time with them. Did you not go to Tasmania with one of the clients from the States?' Or, 'What kind of business were these people in – or was it mainly a tourist trip?'

After a while he became suspicious that she knew something. Did she? But how? The remarks continued over breakfast one day, lunch the next. The questions were never-ending. They weren't exactly abrasive, but they were insistent and interminable, and there was something odd about them. One thing was for sure: this was not the Fritzi he had left behind days ago. Back then she was soft and sympathetic, grateful and gracious – now she was … well, he couldn't figure out what she was, or, more importantly, why she was this way, the reason for her change in behaviour. Ever since he first met Fritzi, back in Bali all those months ago, she had been unpredictable and erratic. But this new mood was something else altogether and it concerned him deeply.

Darius had fielded her questions close to the truth, but he was tiring of the whole charade. 'Where did you meet them, New York?' He would answer some with a 'yup, that's right' or if that did not cut it and, the questions continued, 'I met them through a business contact and they needed a guide, just repaying a favour.' After all, she had shown little interest in his trip before he had left. He had never thought of her as an overtly jealous person, but his suspicions that she herself was suspicious of him were becoming more convincing by the day.

After a week of fielding her seemingly skewed, loaded questions, he decided to call Jared, who would perhaps be able to shed some light on Fritzi's behaviour. She had had moods in the past that he had found difficult to read, but for the first time since he had met Fritzi an uneasy atmosphere was settling over their relationship. But Darius only had so much patience, and could be quick-tempered and unpredictable himself. Before he lost his cool with her snide remarks and told her to spit out what the problem was – or just, for God's sake, move on – he needed to know whether his suspicions were correct that she somehow knew who he had met on his trip. But who could have told her? And why?

Perhaps she was waiting for him to come clean, but he wasn't prepared to jeopardize everything for nothing if he had it all wrong. Jared answered on the first ring.

'Hey Jared,' Darius began, 'anything happen while I was in Sydney that you haven't yet shared with me about Fritzi?'

'Why,' he said sharply, his usually calm voice, pitched slightly up an octave, 'what's going on?'

'Not sure, mate,' Darius said, 'but her behaviour towards me is off, that's for sure.'

'Right,' Jared said, and his voice sounded different now, 'well, she did not want me to tell you about her suspicions.'

'What the hell are you talking about?' Taken aback, Darius barked out, not expecting his response to be so sudden or so harsh.

Jared explained what Fritzi had heard while on a call with Darius, and added that she was absolutely positive about who the voices she heard in the background belonged to. He concluded by telling Darius that she had immediately called Jared to sound him out.

'What did you tell her?' Darius asked.

'Mostly to be very careful about what she chose to do if her suspicions were correct,' Jared said, sounding careful even now.

'So, does she know or not?'

'I guess she does, but not from me.'

'Shit,' Darius said.

'You could say that. I'm not sure how she's going to deal with your meddling this time, Darius,' Jared said softly. 'Perhaps you've overstepped some very personal boundaries. I know I would be pretty damn pissed if it were me. You can't blame her, can you?'

Silence followed Jared's response as Darius registered the truth: Fritzi was right to be angry; he had seriously crossed a line. But on some level, he had known this already. Now he sat with his infelicities and misjudgements, suffocating in them momentarily like a bad odour. He felt, not for the first time, like a naughty boy exiled to the corner of the class, suddenly and shockingly alone.

'You there, mate?' Jared finally said.

'Got some serious explaining to do if she'll give me the chance.'

'Good luck!' Jared said, hanging up.

Darius sat in the car for some time after the call, not sure how best to tackle the situation. There was no good way to explain his motives for invading her personal life and complicated past to the extent that he had. The only defences that came to mind were that he had been trying to fathom out how to help her, and for his own peace of mind. But all of these motivations felt hazy now, with the benefit of hindsight and the full knowledge that he had been in the wrong. It was too late to undo any of it. The damage was done. What remained was Fritzi's anger and pain and the rift that had caused between them.

The more he thought about his own duplicity towards Fritzi, the less confidence he had about coming clean. As he looked at the picture of the past few months, he became aware of the complexity and extent of his misdeeds, sins of omission and abuses of trust that he had not viewed as such at the time. And then the picture simply shattered and all he was left with was a sense of shame. Everything he had done was wrong, and from the very beginning. Travelling to America on a fact-finding mission about Fritzi, meeting

DuPont in a disingenuous manner, under manufactured circumstances, then forcing an introduction with Safi and Yvetta, not to mention attending Yvetta's wedding. He realised with a shock that Fritzi would never see it his way or forgive him and, he could not blame her. Realising there was no way he could face Fritzi without interrogating both his actions the past few months and himself, he put his car in gear and headed to the airport.

Sitting on the flight back to Sydney he at last admitted to himself that he was being a coward about it all.

After speaking with Jared, he had had every intention of going back to the apartment to tell Fritzi the truth. Yet as he rewound his investigation into her time in America from the beginning, he became painfully aware that he did not have a leg to stand on. He had entertained Yvetta, the love of Fritzi's life, and her sister-in-law in Sydney, while Fritzi remained behind in Byron Bay, none the wiser. This behaviour was, to say the least, out of order. Yes, Jared was right, he had by anyone's reckoning overstepped the boundaries of fair play towards someone he respected and loved.

Before the flight took off, he sent a text message to Fritzi: 'Had to return to Sydney. Something has come up I can't ignore. Speak soon.' He ended it with a kiss emoji. She would probably delete, delete, delete every single text he had ever sent, in disgust and anger. He did not want to dwell on his cowardly behaviour, he already felt worse than shit. Instead, he put his seat back, closed his eyes, and hoped that sleep would lighten the load.

Stepping into a cab at the airport, about to head home, he had the idea of speaking to Maggie about all of this. Maggie knew Fritzi perhaps better than anyone in Australia, and she always listened reliably to Darius' problems, and gave great advice, too. She would be honest and straight to the point, she always was. And if she gave him a rollicking – well, he deserved nothing less.

Calling up Maggie's address on his phone, he read it out to the driver and said, 'Can you take me to this address, please.'

Standing on her doorstep, he hesitated another moment before ringing the bell, it was pretty late to be visiting, Maggie would know something was up. Maggie opened the door with her cell phone in her hand. Her usually composed features and comforting gaze, changed to alarm and shock at seeing Darius on her doorstep after 9pm, she ended her call and showed him in.

'I think we both need a stiff drink,' she said hurriedly, 'yes?'

Acquiescing, sitting where he normally sat when he came around, he requested a whiskey on the rocks. Maggie poured them both a tumbler. Handing Darius his drink, she sat down in her armchair facing him and waited.

Twisting the tumbler in his hands, swirling the drink around anxiously, he drank the whole lot down. 'I think this is a mistake,' he said suddenly. 'Perhaps I should go?'

'As you wish,' Maggie said, sipping her drink contemplatively, 'but now that you're here why don't you just spit it out. Whatever it is, Darius, it's done. You obviously need to unburden yourself, and you are here now.' Sensing his renewed anxiety, her face softened with something close to a smile. 'Someone will have to mediate between you and Fritzi, and it may as well be me?'

His head shot up, 'Oh, you have spoken with her then.'

'That I have. And more than once. In fact, that was her on the phone a moment ago.'

'Did you tell her I was here?'

She shook her head.

'What did she say?' he inquired.

'I keep confidences,' Maggie said. 'That goes for you too. I want the best for Fritzi, true. And for you too, Darius. Even when I don't agree with what you may have done.'

Smiling ruefully, he could only imagine what Fritzi had told her. 'Never mind,' he said.

They sat in silence for a while, comfortable with each other in spite of the quiet and his growing unease. He was grateful for the company. He felt less alone now, more like himself. And he was thinking more clearly, too. But he wasn't yet ready to articulate his predicament. Maggie gave him a refill and waited.

'I deserve her anger, Maggie,' Darius said, leaning forward, nursing his second drink. 'I know I have overstepped the boundaries of Fritzi's personal life – and broken her trust in me, and in the process the bond that we had. Honestly, I have no excuse for what I did – none at all – apart from it all turning out favourably, I hope?'

'Yes, it has,' Maggie said quietly, 'more than you realise.'

Surprised to hear this and desperately wanting to feel better about this dire situation, Darius enquired, 'How?'

'Well,' Maggie said with a surprising sharpness, 'that is not for me to share with you, Darius. It's up to Fritzi.' She took a breath before continuing. 'But right now, I am afraid she has no intentions of seeing or speaking with you.' She gazed at Darius, who finished his drink and put his glass down. 'Not until she has had time to process why and how you managed to invade her life to such a degree without her permission.'

'Well, I completely understand,' he said, registering how helpless he sounded, 'it's the reason I am here. I desperately need someone to tell me why I was so obsessed with Fritzi's story. My reasons for delving so deeply and inappropriately into her past.'

'It was beyond the realms of decency, Darius.' He had never before heard Maggie sound so severe. She kept her gaze on him, nodding now. 'After all, you are not her boss, no one requested you to be an official arbiter of her character or her life.'

'No,' Darius replied, 'I set myself up as all of those that you said. Not to judge her, but to try and find a way through.'

'A way through?' Maggie asked, and finally, for a moment, she looked away from him. 'What does that mean?'

'I wanted to meet all the people in the drama that was Fritzi's life up until now,' Darius said, wishing he had another drink but not willing to ask for one (he was already being judged quite enough). 'At first my reasons were not a hundred percent clear to me. I was feeling my way through, trying to make sense out of it all. That French fellow DuPont was the only one who knew the truth about my fact--finding. I set about befriending them – DuPont, Safi, Yvetta, Mika – yes, one could say I was deceiving everyone about my true intentions, but I did not have a clue as to what those intentions were. Fate intervened, and everything that has happened, I am hoping will work out in Fritzi's favour. I said that I was obsessed with Fritzi's story, but maybe the truth is that it is Fritzi I am obsessed with, and her story is part of her, and also a key to understanding who she is, and what she means to me, I have no desire to harm her.'

Maggie listened as keenly as she had gazed at Darius moments before. It was a complicated situation for sure. He had meddled where he shouldn't have, taking advantage of those who trusted his stated intentions as sincere. Maggie felt sure that if Yvetta or Safi had known of his involvement with Fritzi, they would never have continued their association with him. He had sought them out and falsely ingratiated himself into their midst. And he had done it, as best Maggie could tell, for no reason other than to gamble with their lives for his own purposes. Whether for good or for bad, Maggie concluded, it was wrong.

'Darius,' Maggie said, gazing at him again, 'do you think you love Fritzi? Am I to understand that by going to all this trouble on her behalf it means that you do – or maybe you did it on your own behalf, for your own benefit?'

'Both,' he said softly.

'Well, I am not so sure it's both. I think it's more on your behalf.'

'Why do you say that?' Darius asked, trying to return her hard gaze.

'To my mind,' Maggie began, 'if you love someone you accept them for who they are.'

Darius had not expected Maggie to hit him with such a profound statement, and with such a stern demeanour. Now he felt less sure than when he had started to unravel his motives.

'I don't see it that way,' he said. 'I do love Fritzi – why else would I go to all this trouble, and put myself through this. I could just walk away! I am not going to beat myself up over what I did because I have not harmed anyone, apart from deceiving them of my intentions, that is. I believe I did what I did with the best of intentions.'

'Well, good luck!' Maggie said. 'It is not me you will have to convince of all of this, but Fritzi, and she is one tough customer.'

'I know, Maggie, and I am grateful to you for hearing me out. Whatever you may think my intentions were motivated by. I will take my chances.'

Back in his penthouse on Bondi Beach, he changed into his jogging gear. Going for a brisk run was a long-time habit that helped him clear his head. It was the best way he knew to deal with stress – and so much else.

The answer of how best to deal with the shit he had landed himself in with Fritzi would, he hoped, come to him during his run, or shortly thereafter, possibly in the shower. If not, he had no other choice but to confront her anger at his betrayal of her trust. But, after the run and even the shower, no such problems were mentally resolved. He was distracted by the telephone ringing, thinking for a moment it was Fritzi, telling him she forgave him, that she loved him, that all was well once again. But no, it was one of his friends, inviting him out. And instead of staying in and ruminating, torturing himself, going around in circles, he agreed to the invitation, and quickly dressed and headed back out. And that was the last he thought about Fritzi – for a while, at least.

After a night of drinking with friends he had neglected for the past few months, he woke to distant ringing – and his usual hangover. At first, he thought it was his cell phone that was ringing (a reasonable assumption, as this was often how he woke), but no, that was the sound of his buzzer, he quickly realised, wiping the drunken fog from his mind, steadying and sobering himself.

The clock in his bedroom told him that it was just after eight. He staggered to the intercom on his wall and peered at the screen to see who had their finger glued to his buzzer – who on earth would call round so early on a Sunday morning? What he saw instead was the name of a well-known Bondi Beach deli printed on a brown paper bag. 'Okay,' he said to the faceless stranger – or, more accurately, the machine on his wall – 'you got me, who's holding the grub attached to that deli bag?'

The brown paper bag was slowly lowered and three faces appeared on the screen: his brother and the two scrunched-up, toothless grins of his young boys.

'Hey, dude – as they say in the States – we haven't seen or heard from you since you've been entertaining all those American friends of yours,' his brother said cheerily.

The kids were a welcome diversion from the intense zone he had been inhabiting for the last two days. Of his three brothers, it was Matteo, older by three years, who was his closest sibling, they had similar interests. Darius and Matteo had spent many years hanging out together, playing soccer and chess and discussing everything from politics to women, until Matt found his soul mate and he, Darius, had thrown himself into making a success of his own business.

Quickly turning his penthouse into a playground, the boys polished off the bagels, orange juice and coffee they had brought with them in record time. It wasn't yet ten o'clock, still early enough to enjoy the beach before the heat of the day set in.

The boys were staring at the beach and the rolling surf from the window. He had forgotten how much fun it was to be surrounded by their energy, their enthusiasm, their vitality. And how refreshed he now felt. Some five minutes later, no longer able to resist the pull of the sea, they all set out for the surf with belly boards – until, some three hours later, the heat chased them indoors for some shade and more food.

Darius returned to his apartment well after noon, having had the best day in ages playing with his boisterous nephews in the surf and eating fast food. His mood considerably uplifted, feeling almost like a different (and much better) person, he showered, threw on a tracksuit, and, continuing the childlike, slightly lazy feel of the day, lay on his bed to watch a movie.

It suddenly dawned on him: his life had become ridiculously complicated of late – altogether too complicated for his liking – now all he wanted to do was to chill out on his own, spend time with his family and those who loved him simply, unconditionally, and watch whatever took his fancy, like some science fiction thriller, total escapism, perfect mindless garbage for a mindless day like today.

That was his intention, anyway. But the movie had just begun when his buzzer sounded. He paused the movie with a sigh, wondering who would be visiting him without calling first, and what other surprises today might bring. Looking at the screen again, he was shocked to see his mother's face staring back at him. 'Mom, what on earth are you doing here?' he asked. 'Everything okay?'

'Well,' his mother began, her soft voice creased in mock-severity, 'if the mountain won't come to Mohammad, as the saying goes … I better come and see for myself what's going on. Aren't you going to buzz me up? Or are you going to make an old woman stand here in this heat.'

'You are not old, Mom,' he said into the machine, buzzing her up. A moment later she was standing beside him.

'Hi Mom,' he said, hugging her, only to see that she too had come bearing gifts, the kind of goodies only she knew how to provide, in the form of a delicious—smelling, homemade lasagne and tiramisu for afters. It was the lasagne he had grown up eating and that was rivalled by no other (though Lord knows, on multiple trips abroad, he had tried to find a meal that equalled it).

She went about setting a place for two at his seldom-used dining table: with napkins, placemats, and using his best crockery and glasses. While the lasagne was being warmed in the oven, she decanted the dessert into glass dishes, decorating each with chocolate sprinkles she had brought with in a Tupperware container. Smiling at how homely she had, within a matter of minutes, managed to make his neglected flat feel, he indulged her by playing her favourite music by Andreas Bocelli.

'Okay now,' she announced from the kitchen, 'everything is ready. How about a little wine while we eat and catch up,' And that too was music to his ears.

They chatted into the night. He entertained her with stories about the Americans who had just visited and the great day he had spent with Matteo and the boys.

An artful observer (who better knew the moods and manners of Darius as well as his beloved mama), nothing escaped his mother's attention for very long. From years of experience, he knew that her custom was to patiently wait to be told – yet tonight, seemingly impatient or troubled by her son's distracted behaviour, she broke with that tradition and asked after Fritzi.

He never burdened his mother with his problems; those days were long over – he was an adult now, whatever that meant – yet here she sat, ready and waiting to hear the truth. She was, he realised suddenly, the closest he would ever come to having unconditional love and support. Could he confide his treachery to his mother? Would she believe he did what he did to Fritzi for the best intentions? Was he brave enough to find out?

Darius leaned forward at the table, and, recognising the signal, his mother leaned forward, too. Speaking slowly and avoiding eye contact at first, he said, 'I am going to tell you a story, mom: a very complicated one with some unasked-for interference from yours truly. I don't feel proud of what I have done, but I am convinced I did it with the best intentions.'

Over tiramisu and what was left of the bottle of wine, Darius laid out his affair with Fritzi, beginning in Bali and ending in Sydney. He included his visits to the States to further investigate her life, and ended with the dilemma he now found himself in, due to, as he described it, his selfish, thoughtless, relentless pursuit into her private life.

After he had finished speaking, he waited for what felt like a long time but was really only a few seconds for his mother to deliver her judgement. When she did she smiled and said simply, 'An idle mind is the devil's playground.'

But Darius did not smile. 'You used to say that to us as kids, Mum,' he said flatly, in a voice she recognised as being irritable, impatient, 'I am no longer a kid.'

But in many ways, he was (and would always be – at least in front of his mother) a child, he realised suddenly.

'Maybe, Darius,' his mother replied, still smiling, 'but it applies whatever age.'

'That's cruel, Mum,' he said. His face was downcast, sullen, almost angry. She gazed at him again, but he looked away.

'Nonetheless, it's not as cruel as you've been to Fritzi,' she said.

Freeing himself of his irritation at, what he now realised, was her honest perspective on his actions, he turned to her. 'Is that what you honestly think, Mum? That I did all of this to be cruel to Fritzi? But why would I do that?' He threw up his hands in renewed frustration. 'I'm in love with her.'

'No,' his mother said sternly, 'you think you are in love with her. If you were in love with her, you would not need to travel halfway around the world to investigate her private life before committing to the relationship.'

It was the second time he had been told this: Maggie had more or less voiced the same sentiment, and both women were older and wiser than him. It was a long while before either of them, spoke again.

'I honestly don't know what to say or do to fix this,' Darius finally said.

'Maybe you can't fix it, Darius.'

'Mom, you're not helping.'

'Perhaps I'm not,' she said, surprising him. It wasn't like his mother to concede defeat.

'Are you angry with me, too?' he asked, his anxiety painfully apparent in his suddenly shaking voice.

'I'm not angry, Darius – I'm disappointed. I thought you'd know better than to meddle in other people's lives without being asked.'

'Maybe you're right, Mother. I appreciate your honesty as always.' He put his empty wine glass, which he had gripped so tightly for the longest time, down on the table. Trying to relax both his body and his voice, he said, 'Now that you've scolded me, do you have any suggestions as to how – or even if – I can fix this?'

'Well, I can't speak for Fritzi,' his mother said, 'but I can speak for myself – and I think you should leave her alone. For now, at least. You know, not everything can – or should be – fixed. If she contacts you, then by all means explain or apologise or go down on your knees and ask her for forgiveness.' There was a twinkle in his mother's eyes now: she was enjoying this a little too much for his liking.

Trying again, but this time failing, to control his irritation, he said, 'So, you are saying I should not be upfront with her directly?'

'No,' she replied. 'It would be like a cheating lover or husband unloading his guilt, just to clear his conscience sometimes it's kinder and, less selfish to bear that guilt alone.'

Darius was shocked; he'd never heard his mom talk like this, she usually listened without judgement.

'Mom, really, that's a bit rich.'

'Well, I think you should take time out and let this stew a bit in your brain before you go making it worse. If you go and see her now, it won't wash. You need to give her time, too. After all, you have taken advantage of her vulnerability, and just when she needed your support the most.'

He was beginning to see it his mother's way. She had a point, even if he hated to admit it. The truth was, he had not shown Fritzi respect; he had taken advantage of her situation to satisfy his own curiosity.

'Well,' she said slowly, in an even, sympathetic voice, and her bright eyes were full of understanding, 'life is about learning from one's mistakes. This will be a learning curve for you, too. No relationship comes without risks of one kind or another. Perhaps you aren't yet ready to share your life with another person. If you were, you would not go looking for reasons not to have that person in your life.'

She had whacked him good with her words; they were hitting the spot, right in his solar plexus. Hearing this stuff from his mom wasn't easy; still, he respected her wisdom, which he obviously hadn't inherited.

'Mom,' he said, checking his watch and suppressing a yawn, eager now to have this conversation over with, 'I love you and I deserved every word you have hit me with tonight, but it's late. Let me drive you home.'

'No need,' she said, her voice still bright, standing up, 'I drove down here. My car is in your parking garage.'

'How?' he asked.

'The concierge recognised me. I'm not sure why – I hardly ever visit.'

'Perhaps we look like mother and son,' he said, but his words felt flat. For once, she did not smile. 'You sure you want to drive yourself? I thought you didn't like driving after dark.'

'Well, as I said, sometimes one just has to be brave, and go for it without too much forethought'

It was dark now and cool outside, but he could already tell it would be hot tomorrow again. The night air was sobering and refreshing. After talking so much for over an hour, they said little on the way to the car. After watching his mother drive off, Darius went out. His apartment contained too many memories of the conversation they had just had, and, indeed, of Fritzi. He was awake again, and full of self-doubt and an odd kind of sadness. Mostly he felt confused. He no longer wanted to be alone. The bars along the pier would be a welcome diversion from his thoughts.

All the way along the pier his mother's words rang loud and clear in his brain. He had to admit she had a point about idle hands. It was time he went back to work; it would be one way – perhaps the only way – to keep his mind off Fritzi. He had multiple projects waiting for his attention, and now was as good a time as any to immerse himself in work. His attention had been diverted for long enough on unrelated matters. In the back of his mind he knew that, left unattended, he'd be checking his cell for calls from Fritzi too often and thinking about her all the time; being immersed in work would take care of that, and hopefully push Fritzi to the back of his mind, at least for a little while.

Chapter 27

Her life was in turmoil, and her mind was in a worse state. Erika had gone over with Fritzi the details of Darius' scheming duplicity. She had to agree with Fritzi: the guy had overstepped boundaries, invading her past without as much as giving her warning or asking permission. It was beyond belief that he entertained DuPont, to say nothing of the Rubicovs, in Sydney. And all this while Fritzi was completely in the dark. That said, Erika had to remind Fritzi that if it had not been for Darius's involvement with Yvetta, Fritzi might never have heard from her former partner.

They went back and forth on the details of his duplicity, on all of the little information at their disposal, and on how and, if to respond to – or even ever forgive – him. Was it malice on his part? Mere ignorance? A misdeed? A mistake?

What if Darius' actions had been – oddly, perhaps even unintentionally – to Fritzi's benefit? The two women discussed this possibility up and down, too. But even here Fritzi did not want to give

Darius any credit. Erika had to accept that right now, for Fritzi (and not without reason), Darius could do absolutely no right. She was in full-on Darius blasting mode, and only just getting started. Erika reckoned she still had a long way to go before she began to forgive him, if she ever did. She was mortified about him befriending the Rubicovs and even DuPont.

Going over events of the recent past, events they were not even a party to, Erika felt they were caught in a seemingly endless loop. She felt the need to snap her out of her self-serving, self-pitying, circular reverie, to change the subject, to at least try and lift the mood.

'Have you had any replies to your recent correspondence with Mika and Safi?' she asked.

'No,' Fritzi replied sullenly, bluntly, as though suddenly – at long last – not in the mood to talk. 'Neither have come back to me yet.'

'Nothing?' Erika continued, pressing her point, hoping for something positive at least.

'The only thing,' Fritzi said slowly, still sounding notably aggrieved, 'Yvetta this morning sent me her private work email address, so we will be able to correspond from now on.'

Erika was surprised – she had not known about this development.

'How do you feel about that?' she said brightly.

'Happy, Erika,' Fritzi said, still sounding a little glum despite the exclamation, 'really happy. I suppose I am still processing everything,' and her soft voice became lighter now. She looked at her friend and now, for the first time in many hours, she smiled, albeit a little sadly. 'Having you back in my life has been so wonderful – different from Yvetta, but the same feeling of exhilarating disbelief, really. It has given me strength and security to know I have you both back in my life. At least I hope I do!'

'You do,' Erika said, 'of course you do. I will never leave you again – you know that.'

'And Yvetta?' Fritzi asked.

'Well, all you can do now is to build on your relationship with Yvetta – your new relationship, I mean. You realise you have been given that most rare and wonderful of things – a second chance. Have you written back to her?'

'I was attempting to when you called,' Fritzi said, a little bluntly (neither woman was exactly beholden to social niceties). 'In fact, I want to go through my thoughts with you before I send it. But what do I say

– or not say? Do I mention Darius and our relationship and how he has pulled the wool over everyone's eyes?'

'I would mention it,' Erika said firmly, 'definitely. It will be very interesting to hear what Yvetta has to say. Perhaps it will throw a different light on Darius' meddling, offer a new perspective.'

'Maybe,' Fritzi said, sounding decidedly brighter now, buoyed by the possibility of reconnecting with the person who (even more so than Erika even) was most important in her life, realising her good fortune at being granted a second chance, 'but I am sure they will feel as angry and let down by Darius' behaviour as I do.'

'I am not saying that what he did was to be applauded – far from it… But on the other hand, and on reflection, no one has come to any harm from what he did, and you have actually benefitted.'

But Fritzi was still not entirely at ease. She was simmering, albeit at a lesser level than before, that much was clear. Mostly she was angry with Darius, at being double-crossed by him, and not for the first time. She who had so often double-crossed others in the past, could not abide to be deceived herself.

'I know what you are saying,' Fritzi said slowly, 'yet it has not felt that way to me.' She sighed, but in an exaggerated, almost theatrical, manner. 'If he loved me, would he be running around the world behind my back, trying to investigate my life? No matter how rotten I've been, he wouldn't even think of doing any of that, if he loved me, would he? I mean, he had already had me investigated when I was in Bali. That was months ago now. So much happened between us since then – so much that was good, I thought. We developed a real bond, a deep bond, our relationship evolved – I thought. Maybe I was wrong. I don't know what he was thinking – or not thinking. Why fly all the way to America, right around the world, and start to snoop? What could he gain from meeting my antagonists? From digging into my past?'

Erika, who was rarely at a loss for words, paused, deciding how best to articulate her response. 'I think,' she finally said, 'Darius wanted to meet the actors in your drama – in order to be part of your life, to take part in your life.'

'But he is part of my life. He always has been. How could he not know that?'

'Maybe he wanted to be more involved. Maybe he felt insecure. Or something else… Maybe it didn't start out as all that much. Maybe it started small and sort of snowballed. When he met DuPont, he must have been given first-hand information – information which clarified the document he originally received from the investigator. Then one thing led to the next and he visited the galleries, as I did, to try and figure out how to help you…'

'So, you think that what he did was in my best interest? Not for his own benefit? You don't think it was the equivalent of getting an extra insurance policy in case he couldn't trust me?'

They went over it all again, and still Fritzi felt he had wronged her to such an extent there was no way she could ever trust him again. It would take time for her to see it any other way, if ever, Erika realised.

One thing was for sure: Darius was out of her life now, and she did not want him anywhere near her for a very long time. She had mistakenly taken him back into her life after the incident in Bali, when he had her investigated the first time, in the consequence putting her in danger of being caught by Mika's men. At the time she had been thankful he had sent her a warning about being exposed. But that seemed a long time ago. Now he had taken it upon himself to befriend her old enemies behind her back, to deceive her at every turn, to lie to her face, in fact. It was too much. She felt completely betrayed by Darius.

'Well, let me know what response you receive from Yvetta and the others?' Erika said.

For a long time after the call was over, Fritzi sat in thought. She was readjusting to her situation. She was used to changing, adapting, but this time felt different somehow. It was lonely without Darius in her life, but so be it. Darius wasn't the be-all and end-all of her life, he was merely a very small part of it – and now nothing at all.

She had other, more important things to consider. Other friends, other interests, a whole world of social obligations and new avenues of interest. The indefatigable, creative, flirtatious, ever-curious Missy would be good company while Fritzi remained in Byron Bay. Certainly, Fritzi had no plans to up and move right now; she was happy where she was. Maggie had invited her for Christmas, and Fritzi intended to take her up on the offer and head back to Sydney next month. Jared would want to coach her for her next important interview, if it went ahead.

She was open to anything – anything that had nothing to do with Darius, at least. Her life was hers to do with as she wished now. No interruption, no invasive behaviour, no snooping or double-crossing or deceit. She wanted only honest relationships going forward. This meant, of course, that she had to be scrupulously honest herself. This was her new life and she had every intention of enjoying it. Darius reminded her of everything in her past that she wanted to move on from. For that reason, she wanted to put him – and her past – behind her.

She was free from fear and she had gained two old friends back into her life. Both of them were in the States, where Fritzi was no longer welcome – but there were plenty of other places in the world they could reunite. Erika had already decided that she and Fritzi would meet up in Berlin in the new year – Berlin, where their lives had begun, and, in a way, also ended. Well, now was a time for new beginnings, and her life was looking up. Darius was just an unnecessary diversion she could quite happily live without. Fritzi decided that she might not deserve much, but she deserved honesty and a lover she could trust, someone who had her back, so to speak, Darius had proved he wasn't that person.

Still, Fritzi had some unfinished business to take care of, unpleasant, perhaps, but nonetheless important. Yvetta and Safi deserved to know the truth, which was that Darius had befriended them under false pretences. It would be their call if they wished to continue their relationship with him after learning how he had misled them.

With these thoughts in mind, she sent off an email to Yvetta. In the message she outlined her relationship with Darius and how he had represented himself to her. She went on to detail how Darius had flown to the States with the sole purpose of making the acquaintance of members of the Rubicov family and people from Fritzi's past, and how he had done so secretly, deceptively, without ever consulting her.

She wrote how she found out surreptitiously about Safi and Yvetta being in Sydney while speaking with Darius on a call – how she had heard their voices in the background and known almost instantly it was them. It was then that she had had an inkling of the extent of Darius' betrayal, something she was still coming to terms with. She mentioned that it was impossible not to recognise Yvetta's voice, and all of the emotions hearing that voice had set off in her. And who else could be called 'Safi,' or respond to her name in an unmistakeably English accent.

Ultimately, she felt that she was fated to find out about their encounter and Darius' ruse, and she stated that she no longer wanted to continue a relationship with someone she could not trust. Although some might find it hard to believe, given her criminal history, she believed in loyalty. Her whole life had been about being loyal to those she loved, and she wished only to be shown the same respect in return.

The letter went on to explain the events in her life after escaping from New York City – up until the present moment. She mentioned that she was still waiting for the hearing to decide the fate of her application for citizenship, which was, she felt sure, hanging by a thread. She was not sure whether she would be granted an Australian passport, and if not, she would have no choice but to leave with a heavy heart. She was not prepared to break the law any longer, to fly under the radar, to live in disguise, or to hide her true self.

She wrote about the friends she had in Australia, new, honest relationships that were, she stressed, affirmative and healthy for her. Maggie, who had been her rock through some very difficult times. Jared, the human rights lawyer who was championing her case. And the ever-resourceful, ever-generous Missy. She signed off the letter, which was already longer than she had intended, 'Forever your loyal friend.' And she underlined the word 'loyal.'

Pressing 'send' she stared at the computer screen. She hoped this would be the beginning of a new chapter in their relationship. Fritzi did not know when her obsession with Yvetta had changed from love to friendship, but it had, she no longer wanted to possess Yvetta. Erika's nightmare past, had become her salvation, when she appeared alive and resurrected into her life and, she believed that, was when she let go of her obsession with Yvetta.

She would have to wait and see if a reply was forthcoming from Mika and Safi; somehow, she doubted it, but maybe Yvetta would be able to fill her in on how her email to them was received. She looked forward to hearing back from Yvetta and renewing a relationship that was more vital to her than any other.

Fritzi had not been alone for some time – not long enough to enjoy her own company, at least. She needed alone time to reflect on what was happening in her life. The changes were significant; her life had without doubt taken an upward turn. Her confidence had wavered for a while, but through that period she had gained a sense of who she wanted to be, rather than what she had become.

Instead of people needing her, the tables had turned on her: she had become dependent on others. It was an awful realisation when she lost that independence at first. If not for Maggie and Jared she might have cut and run. The thought made her shiver – how many years had she been running? Probably since her childhood, certainly her entire adult life. It was time to stop; she had no reason to run any longer. She hoped to forge a new life in Australia: everything about this country felt right for her, including the people.

Her reverie was interrupted by the doorbell. She opened the door to find a young boy foisting a huge bouquet of mixed pink peonies and red tulips into her hands. She searched for a card, but found none. Cutting the packaging away, she cut the stems, then filled a glass vase and carried the flowers through to the sitting room. The florists' name was on the packaging and she picked up her cell to call them; they had to know who had ordered the flowers. The card may have fallen off, which made it impossible to thank anyone.

Mystified, she called the florists, only to be told they had no idea who the flowers were from. All they knew was that an email had come through for the order, and the payment was done by a bank in Byron Bay.

Darius! She was sure it had to be him. Who else? She felt a strong urge to throw the flowers out, it would be like throwing Darius out, by the scruff of his pants. Feeling a little disappointed but still oddly buoyant (flowers represented, if nothing else, opportunity and renewal), she determined to enjoy the flowers all the same. If it made him feel better, she did not care one way or another. That didn't mean she was going to forgive him anytime soon… But this thought was interrupted by the sound of the doorbell jingling again.

More flowers, she thought with a combination of amusement and mock-horror. He was being ridiculous, but then this whole situation seemed exactly that: ridiculous. But on opening the door she found a box on her doormat, and this time there was a card attached – but no one was there. The box was wrapped in plum-coloured paper and around it was wrapped a huge red satin bow. On the card was a huge koala bear hanging from a tree.

Slightly unnerved (the fun and sense of possibility of the moment was long gone), she carried the box through to her hub, where she sat behind the desk and stared at the box. Snipping off the ribbon, she tore open the paper to reveal a box full of brightly coloured jelly beans. She grabbed a handful of jelly beans and greedily stuffed them into her mouth, while opening the card.

> I have been a fan for a long time
> How about meeting me at the Bolt Hole tonight

I'll be at the bar by 8 pm.
Hope to see you soon
From a devoted friend xx

What the hell, she thought, closing the card with hands that were suddenly shaking. She wasn't sure she should like this invitation, or even know what to make of it. She would be crazy to go, right? Still, for some reason, perhaps because she was still the same reckless, impetuous, fly-by-the-seat-of-her-pants Fritzi she had always been, she was considering the invitation. She was intrigued all right. After all, if things didn't feel right, she could always leave.

She called Missy to sound her out.

'Should I go?' Fritzi asked.

'Sounds very romantic to me,' Missy said softly, her wry, sophisticated voice sounding even more amused than usual. 'It's a public space, so yes, go.'

By six-thirty that evening she had made up her mind to meet her mysterious fan. The Bolt Hole was a semi-smart restaurant, cement floors and, unpolished wood tables with mismatched chandeliers and antiqued mirrors added a rustic yet sophisticated atmosphere, not wanting to overdress she went through her wardrobe choices for the evening.

She eventually decided on skinny blue jeans, a dark-green ribbed silk cold-shoulder top with green tassel shoulder-sweepers in her ears for glamour, and backless heels. She carried a green Gucci drawstring bag, large enough to store sunglasses in, containing her credit card and lip gloss. When the sun dropped low over the sea, the inky black night felt such a contrast from the blinding glare of the day.

Missy had loaned Fritzi a jeep, which she had always loved driving when in Bali. She jumped in, put her foot down, and headed the four-wheel drive to meet her mystery date. Pulling up outside the restaurant, she checked her lipstick in her hand mirror, pulled her fingers through her windswept hair after the short drive, ready to strut her stuff down the long bar to meet Mr or maybe even Ms Secretive.

She arrived at eight on the dot, her Germanic timekeeping still very much part of her character. The long copper Bolt hole bar was already packed with people standing five deep. The summer attire of flip flops and skimpily dressed woman with bronzed midriffs, white teeth and sun-kissed blonde hair, a blur as she made her way through the din of chit chat flirting and pick up lines. Those seated were mostly women, their boyfriends hovering close by to ward off any unwanted attention, it was the same all over the world, a familiar scene she knew only too well.

She hoped her mystery date would recognise her through all these bodies standing about drinking. The noise level was pretty loud, not to mention the beer sloshing all over the place as the drinkers at the bar joked about rowdily. She made her way through to the outside, trying to avoid being drenched by trays of drinks being carried to outdoor tables. So, far she had not noticed anyone looking out for her – that's if they could see through the crowd.

Eventually finding a spot to stand where she could survey the crowd and people entering the bar, she felt herself being grabbed from the back by small, soft hands. Swinging round to see who it could be, she was surprised to see Missy, and, behind her, Jared. They were both laughing at her shock and surprise. 'You really had me going there for a moment,' Fritzi said, when she had recovered her composure. Now laughing with them, she followed the other two to a table on the outdoor decking, away from the noise and heat of the crowd.

'May I ask,' Fritzi said, 'why the flowers and jelly beans with such a strange message? Thank you, by the way: jelly beans are my favourite.'

'Did you notice the koala bear on the front of the card?' Jared enquired. Shaking her head, Fritzi said, 'Yes.'

'Well, congratulations,' Jared said, smiling warmly, his genuine delight only too apparent on his handsome face, 'your application has been approved. You no long have to go for an interview. You are soon to be a bona-fide Aussie.'

'What?' Fritzi spluttered, now beyond words, barely able to speak. Shocked tears began welling up.

'I see that, for once, you are lost for words,' Jared said, still smiling, registering her astonishment with no small amount of pleasure.

'But why have they all of a sudden decided to grant me citizenship?'

'Well,' Jared continued, the smile never leaving his face, 'not long after the Rubicovs left for the States, I received a letter from Yvetta, and signed by Safi and Mika.'

Fritzi was totally aghast. It was one surprise after another, and this moment felt like a dream.

'Really,' she said, her mouth wide open, 'that can't be; is it true?'

'Absolutely,' Jared said, grabbing her hand and staring into her eyes, wanting her to know that this was not a joke – or a dream. It was all, wonderfully, incredibly true. 'I sent the letter off to the people in immigration who are overseeing your case.'

Taking a long-delayed and much-needed breath, Fritzi said, 'May I know what the letter said?'

'I actually brought you a copy, Fritzi – for you to keep, if nothing else. The contents of the letter are pretty clear. I think you will be pleased.'

Fritzi unfolded the letter, while Missy and Jared watched her face change from doubt to delight and amazement. And their faces, too, were animated with happiness, having waited for this moment all day, after planning the mystery set-up and reveal.

'My God,' Fritzi said, her hand with the letter in it trembling, her mouth still wide open, 'they are forgiving me, absolving me from all charges that are pending on their behalf against me – charges which will now be dropped. That is truly incredible.' She flung herself around, still holding the letter, and embraced each of them in turn.

Jared looked at Fritzi.

'Now it's my turn to ask you,' Jared said, his smile thinner now, his voice a little sterner, but still evidently happy, 'do you know anything about this or how this has come about?'

Fritzi looked uncomfortable all of a sudden. She was not yet ready to break the news about her newfound relationship with Yvetta, but knew that she owed Jared and Missy, these two very special people, under these circumstances, after all their hard work on her behalf, the truth. They deserved to know.

'I wrote to all three to apologise,' Fritzi said bluntly. 'Not asking them for forgiveness, but just to let them know that I regretted everything. At the bottom of the email I wrote to Yvetta, I added my telephone number. Just before she flew back to the States, she called me.' Fritzi paused, smiling, taking in the expressions of her two friends. Now it was their turn to be surprised. 'We spoke for a very long time – reconnecting, explaining, opening up again.

Recently she sent me her work email, and I wrote her a long letter about my life since our time together in New York. Maybe when Safi and Yvetta returned from their trip, Yvetta had something to do with the Rubicov family sending that letter. I don't really know.'

She did not want to say too much more. What she knew for sure was that she had to be careful in this situation. After all, Missy did not know the full truth of Fritzi's previous life, to say nothing of the full extent of her criminal past. It was not fair to involve her now. Now was not the time for the naked truth.

Missy looked mystified, not following the conversation fully. There were obviously gaps in her knowledge about Fritzi's past, but she was nonetheless thrilled for her friend, who would now be a firm and frequent part of her life, living right here, safely, in Australia.

'Sorry, Missy,' Fritzi said softly, knowing some sort of explanation was in order, 'I know you are in the dark about some aspects of my past, and if you don't mind, I wish to keep it that way for now.'

Fixing Missy with her gaze, she continued, 'I have moved on, but the one thing I will share with you is that Yvetta and I were lovers for a very long time. She had problems, as did I, and together we were not what one would call 'suited.' The opposite, in fact,' and she looked away, at Jared, and then, for a long moment, at the sky. 'We caused her family much heartache, and, after we were separated, I continued to pursue her. It's all water under the bridge now. Yvetta is happily married, and the two of us have resumed our friendship. You understand that I will always love her, as I do Erika. They were an integral part of my childhood, of my growing up, of my journey, in one way or another.'

Missy did not look at all disturbed or any longer bemused. She wasn't stupid, she had lived herself, and she well understood that her friend had a very complicated life. In fact, this was one reason why she was so drawn to Fritzi – for her shrewdness, her knowingness (combined with a winning but very real naivete, a freshness), and her sense of mystery.

'I hope one day that you will share some of your stories with me. I would very much like to hear more about Erika and Yvetta; they sound like very special people.'

'That's kind of you, Missy,' Fritzi said, making eye contact with Missy once again. She touched her hand, warmly, softly. 'Yes, they are both very important to me, and they always will be. But unfortunately, they both live in America. Next year I hope to meet my childhood friend Erika in Berlin, the city in which we grew up.' She didn't quite know why she was telling Missy this, but suddenly she couldn't stop. 'We plan to reconnect and come to terms with some of the horrors we suffered there as kids, during the communist era in the DDR. In those days everyone belonged to the State, and the State could do as they wished with those, they deemed enemies of the State.' She stopped speaking and was surprised to see how horrified Missy looked.

Missy was dumbstruck; she did not know much about Fritzi's former life, only the snippets Fritzi had fed her from time to time. Now she finally understood the truth, or some tiny part of it: her friend had one hell of a past.

Jared was mortified about overstepping Fritzi's personal boundaries, especially in this strange location, after the initial shock of their news, when she was more vulnerable than usual. He and Missy had been so excited about her new immigration status (which even he had not expected); everything else – propriety, professionalism, discretion – had flown out of the window, he could see that.

Missy had always been his closest cousin, they had grown up together and remained good friends. They had shared many secrets over the years. But Fritzi's secrets were not his to share. He had put her in an awkward position, one that could have been avoided. For this he felt bad, but there was so much good news, and the moment, the evening, itself felt overwhelming and a little crazy, as though whatever was happening did so independently of the three of them.

Seeing Jared's discomfort and knowing him, at this point, only too well, Fritzi leant over and put her hand over Jared's. She knew that he was upset, of course, and also that it had been highly unprofessional on his part to open her up to scrutiny from someone who knew next-to-nothing about her past.

'Shit sorry, Fritzi,' he mumbled close to her ear, feeling almost as awkward as Fritzi had just moments ago.

'Really,' Fritzi said with a softness that surprised him, 'don't worry, it's all in the past, and I completely understand. You know, one day I may even write a book about my past life: it's pretty incredible, don't you think?'

'I do, and you should. I have many friends who work in journalism and publishing, and they would love to print your story. It's not a bad idea at all, Fritzi.'

'I am so incredibly grateful for everything you have done for me, Jared,' she said. 'Please, don't ever forget that. I wouldn't be here right now, free, in Australia, finally putting the pieces of my life together, in order, in the right direction, if it wasn't for you.'

But this time Jared did not reply.

Staying on the deck, the night sky stretched out endless before them, full of wonder and possibility, the three friends ordered dinner and remained chatting into the night. Darius' name was not mentioned once. Fritzi wondered whether he knew of her newfound immigration status, but she did not want to ask or bring up his name, not now, at least. It was not something she needed to discuss with Jared.

'I will be flying to Sydney for Christmas,' Fritzi said, feeling relaxed now and joyful, after all of the day's many surprises. 'Maggie has invited me to stay with her. I hope I will be seeing you too, Jared.'

'Absolutely,' he said, in between bites of steak and frittes a Bolt hole speciality 'my folks will be in Sydney. They usually throw a huge party, Missy flies up, too,' he said, gesturing with his free hand to his cousin, 'so we'll all be together.'

Sometimes life was hilarious, there was no other word for it. In fact, she often wondered if there was someone up there having a laugh. For so long she couldn't see any way through, but everything was different now. The sky was bright, and so was the next part of her journey. Here she sat, as if her life had only just begun.

Chapter 28

They flew down early one morning to discuss the letters they had all received from Fritzi; all wanted the matter cleared before Christmas.

Safi had opened her email on the return flight to New York, shocked to find a letter from Fritzi. She immediately informed Yvetta, giving her the letter to read. Yvetta scanned it quickly; it was a similar letter to the one she had received some days earlier, admitting her mistakes and apologising for any harm she had caused. Fritzi had stressed that she knew full well she did not deserve any forgiveness. Still, she needed to write this letter: her life had changed beyond belief, a tremendous burden of guilt had been lifted from her shoulders, a burden that she had carried since childhood. Learning her childhood friend had survived had set her free to examine her own past, bringing with it the promise of redemption and sins she needed to atone for.

Yvetta handed back the email to Safi, admitting she had received one, too. The two women discussed what – if any – ramifications there would be to Fritzi's letter, wondering whether they should respond. Yvetta did not want Safi to know she had already spoken with Fritzi.

When Safi and Yvetta were back in New York, and Mika had heard that they too had received similar letters, he contacted both, asking them to fly out to Miami at their earliest convenience, to discuss the course of action he had taken after his meeting with Erika and DuPont.

After much soul-searching by Safi not wanting to regurgitate her past and her painful separation from Sasha, all Fritzi's doing, not to mention Sasha being accidentally shot by Fritzi in an attempt to escape, she listened with a heavy heart as Yvetta pleaded Fritzi's case.

To her great surprise, Yvetta received support from Mika. Neither had met Erika, Fritzi's childhood friend, but both were shocked to the core by her story. Indeed, under these circumstances, now knowing the truth, it was impossible not to empathise with Fritzi, who had lived with the horrendous guilt for all those years. She appeared to have processed her childhood trauma by focussing her resilience to survive on Yvetta, by role playing, by becoming other people – or no one at all. True, Fritzi had engineered Yvetta's escape from every institution her family had locked her away in; but ultimately, symbolically, Fritzi was saving her childhood friend Erika repeatedly.

Safi and the Rubicovs agreed that Fritzi's early trauma, was the catalyst to her later behaviour. During her years in Moscow and New York, Fritzi had become obsessed with all of Yvetta's enemies, people she perceived (rightly or wrongly) were harming Yvetta intentionally. To Fritzi's mind, these people had to be punished, in order to avoid a repeat of the distant past, of the Erika trauma, and so the sabotage and attacks on the Rubicovs and others began to take place.

Visiting the past was painful but necessary for both Yvetta and Safi. Even Mika found Sasha's kidnapping hard to come to terms with, to say nothing of all the other trauma they had suffered due to (they now knew) Fritzi's survival skills relating to her childhood trauma.

Over lunch they discussed how best to reply to Fritzi's letter. That was when Yvetta suggested writing a letter to her lawyer absolving Fritzi from all grievances relating to the Rubicov family and past events.

At first Mika balked at this idea – to absolve Fritzi (of all people!) and of everything – but Yvetta went on to remind them of Fritzi's pending citizenship in Australia and explained the circumstances behind it.

'She is no longer a threat to anyone,' Yvetta told them, 'She won't ever be returning to the States, and is living on the other side of the world. It seems smallminded not to try to help her start with a clean slate.'

Yvetta drafted the letter; Mika and Safi made minor alterations, but on the whole agreed with its content. Safi signed it, apprehensively wondering whether their battle with Fritzi was truly at an end. Mika, on the other hand, wanted the matter closed and signed. The other two watched as Yvetta mailed the document to her legal counsel.

Fritzi sat cross-legged on the bed, watching the computer screen whilst speaking with Yvetta. They were now corresponding more intimately and more often. Fritzi could have listened to the story about the Rubicovs deciding to absolve her a million times, but she played it cool when the details of the letter to Jared was explained in detail. This letter, she quickly and gratefully realised, had been the turning point in her fortunes. As such, she would always owe the Rubicovs a great deal for her freedom, thanks to Erika and Yvetta.

In time, both Fritzi and Yvetta would confide in their partners and friends of their revived relationship; but, for now, they wanted to keep it under wraps. For Fritzi, being able to communicate with Yvetta, had become proof of her newfound ability to separate her past, enabling her to compartmentalize early and unhappy experience from her present reality, without anger or regret. She was happy that Yvetta was happy in her new life and love, remembering how troubled she had been for many years; her old lover had found her own peace. They were now happy to share their separate lives as friends.

She remained troubled about Darius, though. He had not contacted her since returning to Sydney, once he realised, she had found out about his duplicity. She found herself conflicted about whether she wanted him to crawl back on his knees for forgiveness or not. Three weeks had gone by without hearing a word. She found this more than a little irritating, could not believe it was that easy for him to shut the door on their relationship.

Maggie was the only person she could speak to about Darius – and perhaps Erika also, but she knew her friend's attitude would be more pragmatic than she would like right now.

After her chat with Maggie, Fritzi sat contemplating Maggie's suggestion about packing up and returning to Sydney for the festive season. She had to admit that her life in Byron Bay had not felt the same without Darius. Missy had been more than inclusive, involving Fritzi at all times in her ever-expanding circle, keeping her busy socially.

Their business venture, finding funding for charitable projects, could be planned from Sydney before any major event was arranged. Missy wanted to expand her base, and Fritzi was happy to help her find new funding. Now that Fritzi's future in Australia was secure, it was an ideal opportunity to put all her energy into the venture. She had been counting on Darius for introductions to the corporate and tech world, but now that that idea was no longer an option, she would have to find other avenues.

The festive season was fast approaching, there were tourists and holidaymakers everywhere, and Sydney was sweltering. Many schools and businesses had taken time off before the December chaos set in. Maggie had taken leave from her job at Jared's to concentrate on her own festive arrangements. He had staff she had trained who were quite capable of running his household, especially when everything in the city was slowing down in preparation for the holidays.

Maggie loved having her around to share shopping sprees with, and Fritzi, now carefree in spirit, no longer weighed down by impossible-seeming problems, enjoyed her time with her friend. The two women, very different in temperament but now as thick as thieves, visited museums and art galleries, and pottered around in shops and stores for whatever Maggie needed to enhance her festive seasonal table.

Maggie had invited all her unattached friends to share her table over the holidays with, especially those who had children on other continents, whose only real communication with their loved ones during the holiday was over FaceTime, after the celebrations were already over down under.

Maggie and Fritzi decorated the tree in the entrance hall as only Europeans could, complete with fake snowflakes, hanging snowballs, and green-and-red shimmering reindeer adorning every branch. It compensated for the hot weather at Christmas that Fritzi had never before experienced and, that felt so strange to her. She wondered if she would ever get used to Christmas in summer, few things seemed more unnatural. But then, she supposed, Australia was called 'down under' for good reason.

Many things seemed upside-down here, least of all her own sudden and unexpected good fortune, making this truly a memorable holiday for her. With Maggie, with Missy, with Erika on FaceTime, and even with Yvetta in her life again, never before had Fritzi felt so loved – and, better still, accepted, appreciated. From her tortured childhood onwards, she had never thought she would ever be understood, but now, at last, she was beginning to feel this way.

Maggie had mulled wine on offer, chestnut mince pies, and had baked a Christmas pudding filled with enough alcohol to knock anyone's socks off. The table had been extended to accommodate the extra guests arriving to share their celebrations. There were shiny crackers at every seat, and running along the centre were red poinsettias on a red tablecloth, gold-rimmed glass candleholders. White crockery was set on gold-rimmed chargers containing small red-and-gold gift-wrapped boxes for each guest. Maggie used her best wine glasses and tumblers with gold edging for each place setting. It set the atmosphere and the effect was sumptuously glamorous.

The whole experience had been overwhelming for Fritzi. A few days before the festivities she spent hours late into the night helping Maggie prepare each and every dish. The turkey was stuffed and ready for the oven, which was to be turned on in the early hours of the morning. They had prepared German stollen laced with chocolate, apple kuchen bars, German apple-flavoured almond cake, sweet potato pie, and thrice-cooked roast potatoes, crisp on the outside and crumbly on the inside. All the stops were pulled out and Maggie made no secret of her delight in having Fritzi share in the festivities, which she said would double as a celebration of her new Australian status.

Maggie's friends arrived on cue, laden with gifts to put under the white sparkling winter Christmas tree with its tufts of green poking through the shimmering snowflakes. No one indulged in extravagant gifts. Instead, it was a tradition here to give books. Some were rare, others old classics or coffee table books printed each season on various topics of interest. Fritzi had wracked her brain, not knowing what to give Maggie. It was then that a eureka moment occurred. But after the eureka came a new wave of indecision. She was nervous Maggie would reject her offer; Fritzi hoped instead that she would see it as an adventure. It wasn't entirely altruistic, either; Fritzi wanted Maggie to accompany her.

At three o'clock a toast was made to the slicing of the turkey by one of the male guests brave enough to take on the job. As each person opened their small red gift-wrapped box containing a question about how the festive season was celebrated around the globe, there was laughter and hooting and derision for not knowing most of the answers. Many toasts were made to the delicious food and the gifted cook.

Towards the end of the afternoon, as the guests were slowly leaving, other neighbours arrived to share a glass or two. Maggie left the door on the latch for easy entrance. Fritzi was in the kitchen, clearing the leftovers into black plastic bags that Maggie (in her most Maggie-like way, fastidious about mess) had lined up like soldiers. Between the clatter of plates and glasses, Fritzi thought she heard a familiar voice all the way across the house. Darius? It couldn't be. But she was as sure of the sound as she had been when she had heard Safi's voice on the line that time, she had telephoned Darius … which was when all the trouble had begun.

Leaning out of the kitchen door, Fritzi was shocked to see that standing among the new arrivals was Darius, chatting to Maggie's neighbours. Fritzi did a double take, shocked in spite of her intuition.

She wondered whether he had arrived uninvited, or whether Maggie had taken it upon herself to bring them together to sort out their impasse. The last person she had expected to see, she now felt awkward after his sudden flight from her life. But then she reminded herself of his invasive meddling. He had been neither open nor honest about the lengths he had gone in his strange quest to invade her world.

Yet she did want to see him – she had to admit. She had missed him; he had been a kind considerate lover and a friend and confidante to her. And, in his own way, all those months ago, back in Bali, he too had saved her life. His subsequent betrayal wasn't easy to forgive, but alcohol and the festive season was making her less judgemental.

Perhaps she should give him the benefit of the doubt; maybe he had done what he did for ultimately altruistic motives, his goal only to help her, to help her make amends, to set her free from her past. She thought about all of this while still looking at him from the kitchen. Still mingling with the neighbours, talking to them like old friends, as was his friendly manner, his eyes locked with hers. Fritzi had never felt a charge when seeing Darius, not the way she had felt when Jared was near her. But now her legs were weak, her heart was thumping in her chest, holding her back. She stood rooted to the spot, and watched in animated suspension as he made his way towards her.

Picking her up in his arms, he hugged her tightly, swung her around and nuzzled his head in her hair.

'I am so happy for you, Fritzi,' he murmured into her ear. 'Please forgive me. I hope my meddling went a little way to helping you become an Aussie! Happy Christmas, beautiful lady.' And then he placed a gift-wrapped box in her hand. 'With my love, always,' he said, standing back to see her reaction.

A hush had fallen over the few guests standing about. Slowly, she became aware of his words, her brain a little slow from the mulled wine and champagne, not to mention the alcohol-infused pudding. She had never been one for overt expressions of emotion, but feeling him so close, inhaling his spicy smell, was too much for her. Stepping closer, she threw her arms around his neck, kissing him full on the lips. The other guests clapped, encouraging them to make up; it was obviously a lovers' tiff they were watching. Only Maggie knew the significance of Fritzi's reaction; a part of her was pleased for Darius, but she was still holding out hope for Jared to win Fritzi's heart.

The ice had been broken between them. Darius was overcome to receive such a warm reception after the frosty one he had had in Byron Bay, which was the last time they were together.

Maggie tried to shoo them out of the door, but Fritzi insisted on helping her clear away what was left of the dessert plates and bowls, and put Darius to work carrying out the garbage bags for collection. They hung around helping Maggie until the place was, finally, to her satisfaction, at which point the older woman was exhausted and retired to bed. Faced with no distractions, Fritzi led Darius to her room, where they fell onto the bed and into each other's arms, fumbling to tear off their clothes and to make up for lost time the only way they knew how.

Encouraged to stay the night by Fritzi, Darius joined the two women for breakfast the following morning. Fritzi had not yet opened her gift from Darius and brought it to the table.

'Is this safe to open at the table?' she asked, smiling broadly.

Laughing, he encouraged her to open the box. Tearing off the ribbon, she opened the orange box gingerly, not having a clue what to expect. Lying under the Hermès tissue paper was a stunning traditional silk Hermès scarf, and beneath it, a calf leather passport holder.

Putting the scarf around her shoulders, she said, 'Thank you, it's beautiful,' she said, and touched the leather holder, 'and I can't wait to fill this cover with my new passport.' Turning to Maggie, she said, 'Maggie, did you open my gift, by the way? The passport cover reminded me to ask you.'

'I did, Fritzi,' Maggie said softly, still looking a little tired around the eyes from last night's festivities and their lengthy preparation. 'It's a very generous offer and I promise to think about it very seriously.'

'Anyone going to fill me in on this mysterious gift?' Darius said, after a moment, with mock consternation.

'I gave Maggie a ticket to join me on a trip to Berlin next year, where I hope to reunite with Erika,' Fritzi said with a smile.

'Wow!' Darius said, sounding genuinely thrilled. 'That's fantastic; both ideas are wonderful.'

'Well,' Maggie said, her still-cheerful voice a little harder now, 'I'm not sure Jared will be delighted to lose me for that long.'

'We will just have to persuade him that I need you, Maggie,' Fritzi said, reaching for her friend's hand. 'And, to be honest, I do.'

'Why on earth do you need me when you have Erika to meet?' Maggie asked, bemused.

'It's complicated,' Fritzi said, taking a step back, releasing Maggie's hand, as if to give the question some thought. 'Erika is not an emotional person – but I am sure that I will be. Which is why I will need you for emotional support. You will be doing me a favour by accompanying me. And the trip will also allow me the opportunity to give you something in return, the opportunity to visit Germany.'

But despite the enthusiasm in Fritzi's voice and body language, Maggie looked doubtful.

'It's a wonderful gesture,' Maggie said slowly, sounding almost uncomfortable, gazing not at Fritzi's eyes but at her new scarf, 'but I am going to have to give it serious thought before I agree to this trip.' As if noticing that her words had dampened the mood, she said, 'We'll see, Fritzi. There is time for me to stew over my insecurities about returning to Germany. My overriding desire, of course, is to be with you – so we may well do this important thing together.'

Fritzi was taken aback at Maggie's honesty. 'I understand, Maggie. I myself know the pain that Germany can inflict. But, for that reason, maybe we will both regret it if we don't do this?'

She got up to hug her friend who had become such an integral part of her life in Australia.

The three of them settled down to sort through all the Christmas gifts left by the guests and neighbours, which Maggie had been too exhausted to even think of opening last night. 'It's such a pleasure to have company,' Maggie said, relaxing on the couch, smiling warmly, her old self again. 'Usually, I am left on my own to open the gifts.'

Darius was expected for lunch at his mother, who had already heard the good news. She was delighted that Fritzi had made up with her son, and extended an invitation to her to join them.

Darius' family's Christmas celebrations always consisted of a ten-thirty brunch in their family home, since the family's restaurants were at their most busy over the festive period.

His mother had her traditional lunch for the grandchildren and their mothers the following day, in order to spoil them with her Italian home-baked pastas and pastries. Since Darius was the only unattached son not in the restaurant business, he always indulged his mother at these lunches, helping to entertain his rowdy nephews and nieces, who ran to and fro, often armed with fistfuls of chocolates and cakes.

Like most things in his mother's life, this day too had a sense of routine. The first order of the day was for the grandchildren to help her bake the Christmas biscuits. Each child was given prepared pastry, pyramid-shaped cookie cutters, and a small flat spatula to slice incisions into the pyramid. They watched their grandmother as she made the first Christmas tree biscuit of the day, then copied her as best they could. Each sliced incision was twisted until it resembled tree branches, a small flat trunk was added to the bottom, and – voila! – the tree was ready. The biscuits were all placed in her oven, to be taken out later for decorating.

Lunch was a noisy affair; everyone spoke at the same time, and Fritzi had difficulty keeping up with the conversations, or even hearing herself think.

Darius' mother had help, so after lunch the family all retired to the outdoor patio and pool area. But even here it was anything but quiet. The only person missing was Darius. The kids were obviously highly charged, waiting for something to happen. But where was Darius? Fritzi wondered. She didn't have to wonder for long, however. A minute or so later, among the considerable murmuring and even screams of pleasure of the children, face-painted like a Pierrot doll, wearing a harlequin costume and wig, Darius appeared with umpteen brightly coloured balloons to keep the kids entertained while clowning. He taught them how to make balloon shapes into animals.

For Fritzi it was an endearing scene, and a surprising one as well. Darius was so relaxed with his brother's children, and attendant and alive. It was then that Fritzi felt that, for her at least, a balloon had popped. She no longer had any illusions – she was not meant for this man. He would want a family with a homely wife, a brief she certainly did not fill.

His mother was warm and welcoming to her, while the sisters-in-law were polite if a little dismissive, not ignoring Fritzi but not exactly including her, either. After all, Fritzi was the stranger in their midst – and obviously not a keeper, as far as they were concerned. Fritzi couldn't agree more: They were quintessentially Italian Aussie wives, while she, well no more needed to be said, only Darius could not see what was so blatantly staring him in the face – they did not belong together.

Perhaps appropriately, given the distance she now felt, Fritzi was sitting in the corner, in the shade, with the Christmas-tree cookie Darius' mother had made lying in her lap, tied up in cellophane. Each branch was decorated with icing sugar and the trunk had a red ribbon tied around it. The cookie looked beautiful, but as with everything else about the family, about the lunch, she felt a remove from it.

It was close to four when, exhausted from lunch and entertaining the kids, Darius dropped her back at Maggie's place. Maggie had been invited to a Christmas dinner with an invitation extended to her house guest. Fritzi felt obligated to accompany Maggie, who had informed her of the invitation and the time they were expected.

Fritzi changed into her long lime-green silk wrap dress, open to her waist. She wore pointed gold sling backs, and tied her hair back in a knot with long tendrils hanging down, adding gold hoop earrings for a bit of glamour. Holding her favourite snakeskin Judith Lieber leather clutch and new Hermès scarf, she was ready.

To her surprise, Maggie wore a black sleeveless loose--fitting V-neck maxi-dress with strings of long pearls. Fritzi marvelled at her friend's style. She looked completely different than she had even hours before. The last few days had been full of surprises: first Darius chatting to Maggie's neighbours at the doorway, then Darius dressed as a clown – and now … this.

'Wow, Maggie,' Fritzi exclaimed, 'you are looking Chanel chic this evening.'

Maggie smiled, faux-shyly, and did a self-amused rotation, as if on the catwalk. The lines of fatigue around her eyes were gone, but that was the smallest of the changes that Fritzi noticed. Her hair, worn off her forehead and in a short bob, had a light grey steak. It suited her angular jaw and gave her a stylish contemporary look. 'You have been to the salon,' Fritzi said, still surprised. 'They have given you a perfect cut. I love the new you.'

Blushing, turning again, but this time out of embarrassment, Maggie said shyly, 'Well, it's almost the new year. I am about to turn seventy in a few days. I thought it was time to introduce a younger me – before Father Time beat me to it.'

Fritzi was shocked; she had no idea Maggie was turning seventy. In fact, she had always thought of Maggie as no age at all, as just Maggie. But, as it turned out, just plain Maggie was anything but plain.

'You don't look seventy at all,' Fritzi said.

'Well, not anymore I don't,' Maggie replied.

'Oh, you never did,' Fritzi said. 'But certainly not now.' But then she stopped and came closer to Maggie, gave her an oddly interrogative look.

'If you don't mind my asking,' Fritzi continued, her voice softer now, 'has there ever been someone special in your life?'

'You mean apart from my husband?'

'Yes.'

'Well,' Maggie said, and dropped her voice, though there was no one else in the house, 'I'm going to let you in on a little secret. Hubert, a neighbour, has been my companion for many years, but we prefer to keep it low-key. It suits us to live close, but apart.'

Fritzi hooped, then spoke in German: 'Du bist ein dunkles Pferd.'

They both laughed as they climbed into the Uber for a night out on the tiles (Fritzi hoped), with who she did not know, but Maggie had made a huge effort to look amazing and had succeeded shockingly well.

They were ushered through the restaurant to a private area, where a group of people were standing about drinking and chatting. Maggie, who obviously knew everyone present, had just started to introduce Fritzi when Jared appeared and took over.

'Let me introduce you to this amazing, beautiful woman who saved my life during the Christchurch earthquake,' Jared said with his characteristically boyish, breath-taking smile.

There was a buzz as everyone had something to say in response to this revelation, and the chatter seemed to increase tenfold. Fritzi was given a glass of bubbly, which she held aloft as they toasted her.

Jared introduced her to the team he worked with, who were a young and vibrant bunch, already tipsy as they took their places at the long table. She found herself seated between Jared and an older partner, while she noted that Maggie was placed next to a very attentive, tall, grey-haired gentleman at the other end of the table. She leaned over to Jared to ask who the man next to Maggie was.

'Hubert de Jong,' Jared replied. 'A retired partner, I think he has always had an eye for Maggie.'

Ah, that Hubert, Fritzi thought. She didn't say anything to Jared, but she was impressed with Maggie's taste: Hubert was, indeed, very distinguished. She wondered why he had not been invited to the Christmas lunch; she would ask Maggie later.

Sitting next to Jared, the same anxious, familiar and yet still somehow thrilling, almost dizzying sensation hit her. It was as though her stomach was full of butterflies, while her heart did somersaults. It was ridiculous to feel this way about him – he had absolutely zero interest in her – but how wonderful this feeling was!

He was always polite and attentive, and indeed he was all of that this evening, engaging her in light conversation, with a smattering of gentle humour. The older partner seated on her right was an overt flirt, and Fritzi enjoyed his attention, hoping it would make Jared jealous, if such a scenario were at all possible. If her plan had succeeded and Jared was jealous, Fritzi did not notice, as the woman on the other side of Jared was being loudly possessive of his attention. Finally, her curiosity overcame even her pride, and she found herself asking the partner, 'Do you know who that is sitting next to Jared?'

'Ah,' the flirt said, making even this exclamation sound a little naughty, 'that's Mary, the doctor, Jared's present squeeze. I think she's a bit put out by you, I don't blame her, you are quite a ravishing beauty.'

Pleased at his compliment but slightly depressed to learn that Jared had someone in his life, she turned up the charm with both Jared and the flirt seated on her right. Mary was going to have some serious competition for Jared's attention tonight.

By the end of the evening, Fritzi noticed Mary was quite embarrassingly drunk, swaying between the tables to the ladies' room. While she was away Jared ordered her a black coffee, apologising for his 'friend's' behaviour. Friend, Fritzi thought. Well, really, that said it all. Or did it? She wasn't sure anymore – about anything.

'I think she is a little jealous of you,' Jared said, leaning in again.

Fritzi laughed and said, 'To be honest, I have been trying to make her jealous.'

Jared, genuinely taken aback, looked at her. 'Really?'

Not sure why, Fritzi took Jared's hand and whispered, 'Perhaps that's because I am a little jealous of her.'

Mary returned to the table and smiled in a contrived manner. She had obviously freshened up and seemed more in control of herself. Drinking down the black coffee in front of her, she leaned over Jared to speak with Fritzi, having ignored her the entire evening. Smiling again, this time nastily, she said, 'I hear you're from shitty Deutschland uber alles?'

Fritzi decided that neither her manner nor question warranted a reply. Ignoring Mary, she turned to Jared and whispered in his ear, 'Oops, maybe the lady needs to go home and sleep it off?'

Jared turned to Mary and had a few sharp words. But Mary was evidently no longer playing nice. 'Why don't you just screw your little fraulein,' she said, with great energy but not quite loud enough for those at the other end of the table to hear (Maggie later confirmed). 'Everyone knows you have the hots for her.'

Not one to make a scene, Jared wasted no time in helping her stand. Expertly, as if he had done this at other establishments, with other girls, he held onto her elbow and marched her out of the restaurant. Everyone ignored the scene, apart from Fritzi and those close by.

'Good riddance,' the partner seated next to Fritzi remarked, not flirting for once. 'I hope that's the end of that. I never liked her much. Jared's much too good for the likes of her.' Fritzi did not join in when those around them lifted their glasses in agreement, but she smiled nonetheless (indeed, she couldn't help herself). Jared returned to the table without Mary and apologised. To Fritzi alone he said, 'Should we order desert? I need something sweet after that.'

On the drive home Maggie enquired where Mary had disappeared to halfway through the evening. After filling her friend in on the little drama, Fritzi was not surprised when Maggie, in a more polite way, shared the sentiments of those around her at the table.

'Now it's my turn to ask a question,' Fritzi said. 'Why have I not met Hubert before? He never joined our Christmas lunch.'

'He has his own family,' Maggie said flatly. 'While you were staying with me, Hubert was holidaying in Europe. He is a keen golfer, and often flies to watch major championships. He just got back home.'

'Well, he certainly is a very handsome, distinguished man,' Fritzi said, the admiration in her voice evident. 'I am proud of you, Maggie, and he is a very fortunate indeed.'

Maggie, a little more forthcoming after the champagne, confided in Fritzi. 'Well,' she said softly, 'since we are being honest, I will share one of my wishes for you.' Fritzi leaned in closer. 'I have always hoped you would get together with Jared.'

Fritzi smiled at her friend and squeezed her hand in hers. 'I think I share that wish, too.'

'Really?' Maggie said, surprised.

'We'll just have to wait and see what happens in the future.'

'But what about Darius?' Maggie inquired.

Fritzi sighed; she had not voiced her thoughts to anyone since her revelation at Darius' mother's lunch.

'To be honest, Maggie, today was a turning point for me. Darius has a wonderful, warm Italian family, but I am not the right person for him. Everyone knows it but Darius.'

Sighing herself, Maggie said, 'Yes, perhaps you're right about that.'

The two days before Jared's New Year's party were taken up with seeing Darius. And yet, after her revelation at Darius' mother's house, Fritzi felt she was stringing him along. It was time to be honest with him – but how? Fritzi tried to broach the subject as diplomatically as she could; she wanted Darius to see for himself what she had so blatantly felt at that Christmas lunch.

Then, one unseasonably warm afternoon, Fritzi was reading a magazine in Darius' penthouse apartment, and everything came out. Darius, who had returned from a run on the beach, came in and kissed her on the forehead. She gave him a long look and, apropos of nothing in particular except the thoughts that had been driving her crazy the last few days, she asked, 'You will want to have children when you find the right person?'

'Absolutely,' he said.

'You know I am not that person,' she said slowly, 'don't you?'

'Why do you say that,' he asked, gazing at her now, sensing something was up. 'Don't you want kids?'

'I have never given it much thought,' she began, trying hard to hold his gaze. 'At least until I saw you with your nephews and nieces the other day. And then it suddenly hit me: I am not right for you in that respect – not at all.'

Darius came to sit next to Fritzi at the breakfast bar where she had been reading. 'Fritzi, you are serious about this, aren't you?'

'I am, Darius,' she said, closing her magazine and pushing it across the counter. 'I believe we are the closest of friends, but I am not a 'keeper,' as they say. It was so clear to me, and to everyone of your family, I believe, including your mother.'

Dumbstruck he stared at Fritzi, then stood up and walked around the breakfast bar, up and down, until he returned to face her. His voice had not changed but the expression on his face was distraught.

'Tell me the honest truth,' he said, 'is it still about my meddling? Can't you get past it, Fritzi? I thought we had.'

'We have, Darius – at least, I have got past it.'

'Then why now,' he demanded, turning away from her again, 'when we have just got back together?'

'I don't actually know,' she began, stumbling, the words refusing to take shape, feeling truly helpless for the first time in a while. She gamely continued, but still the words did not come, '... but it seems wrong of me to lead you on when it's so obviously ... wrong.'

'Did any of my family say something to upset you?' He sounded almost angry.

'Oh, absolutely not,' she said hurriedly, again not really knowing how to continue 'they were all wonderful, especially your mom, but while you were playing so beautifully with the kids, it was blatantly obvious to all of us there ... I just knew, as did your mother seeing my expression, that it is never going to work.'

But this explanation seemed to anger him even more. He swung around and said, 'How would you or my mother ever know such a thing? I feel like you are using my mother as a cover for your own...' But now it was his turn to fail to form the words.

'My own what?' she said. Not waiting for him to respond, sensing his upset and anxiety, she continued, 'Darius, be serious, I am not the motherly type – or the homey type, for that matter, and that's exactly the type that will make you happy, the type you want and need. You must see that, surely?'

'What I see is that you are being very cold and calculating about this, Fritzi. I guess you don't feel the same way about me as I do about you.'

'Perhaps,' she said, 'but I don't think you would see it that way if you were to meet the right person. And I am not that person, no matter how much you think you love me.'

'So where do we stand now?' he asked.

'Nowhere. Why do we need to stand anywhere?' She was feeling increasingly exasperated and tried hard to keep her voice calm. 'I don't see relationships like that, Darius.'

'And how exactly do you see relationships?' Darius asked. 'I mean, our relationship?'

'We are what we are,' Fritzi said, 'but not for keeps. We love one another, but are free to see others, if they come along.'

'Oh, that's convenient,' Darius said, grimacing. 'Have you met someone?'

'Not exactly.'

'What does that mean, exactly?'

'I like Jared too, you know this. He is not free, but I like him – and I like you. But I may not be right for either of you, don't you see that?'

Darius stared at Fritzi. It was as if he had never set eyes on her before, or was seeing her for the first time in a long while. The second explanation was closer to the truth: he was seeing the old Fritzi slowly coming out of her shell once more. The sophisticated, decadent Berliner of old coming to the fore, the Fritzi he had not seen much of since her arrival in Australia. Her attitude to relationships had always bothered his more conservative mind.

'So let me get this straight,' he said incredulously, 'you are happy to have a relationship with both Jared and me?'

She smiled: he was right, she would consider that option if she had to, but of course it wouldn't sit well with either of them. They were not like her, had not grown up in her world, where such things were quite acceptable.

'Maybe I would,' she said, 'but I know full well that it wouldn't be acceptable to either of you. In any event, Jared has not shown any interest in me whatsoever. In fact, he has someone.'

He stared at her for perhaps twenty seconds, still in disbelief. Then, in a pained voice, he said, 'So where does this leave us, Fritzi?'

'Wherever you want to leave it, Darius. I am happy to continue as we are – as long as you accept that it's not going to end up in marriage. Maybe I'll never get married, who knows. It's not something I am that keen on.'

He stood again, walked away from her, then returned to the breakfast bar. Fritzi had not moved. 'Christ, I'm confused, Fritzi. I have never had a conversation like this with anyone before; it's doing my head in. I'm going to have to sleep on this, maybe even take a few days to think about what we've discussed. Right now I'm not in the mood for this. Let me take you back to Maggie.'

'No need,' she said, 'I can find my own way back. It's no problem, shatz, none at all.'

She picked up her bag, kissed him on both cheeks, and closed the front door behind her. At least he knew where he stood now, she thought. It wasn't an easy conversation, but if things happened with Jared, he would not feel she had cheated on him.

Her thoughts went back to her childhood in Communist Berlin. It was a young, decadent society in which people had all kinds of relationships. But here in Australia, an altogether different time and place, she did not think people were open to complicated affairs of the heart.

She had watched her older sister, Greta, experience alternative relationships on multiple occasions. Firstly, when Greta had a Cameroonian boyfriend in East Berlin. And then, several years later, when she married a German in the West who could not have children. They found a solution of sorts, one that pleased them both; they were Berliners, after all.

Greta had an affair with her best friend's husband, while his wife had an affair with Gunter, Greta's husband. Whenever Greta spent a weekend away with her lover, Gunter would move in with the other man's wife to help care for the children that he could not have and dearly wanted. Each happy to exist with the other's infidelity, the two couples were all cohabiting together – but separately. And Gunter, who loved kids, became a dad – at least for the time he was with his friend's wife and kids.

It was an adult, open relationship, and Fritzi knew of many similar affairs in Berlin. Things had always been that way; people preferred pragmatism over emotion when it came to love. Perhaps Berlin was not like the rest of Germany at all. For these reasons, her answer to Darius was from the heart: she legitimately did not see anything wrong with having two lovers – if they both agreed to such an arrangement, that was.

On the other hand, such arrangements did not always work out. Fritzi had heard of another love story that wasn't quite as neat and tidy as her sister's. For some reason, that particular story, and in particular its awful climax, made her think of the situation between her, Darius, and Jared – except that Fritzi wasn't the kind of woman who'd jump out of a window because her lovers were fighting over her.

That was exactly what had happened to Greta's best friend. The story had ended with the two men looking after the woman they loved, for, as it happened, she had not killed herself when she jumped out of that window. Instead, Gisela had ended up with a broken spine and had to spend the rest of her life in a wheelchair, with her two lovers seeing to her every need.

Fritzi's mind was all over the place, thoughts popping up that had been buried for years. As she sat in the back of the taxi, a feeling of empowerment suddenly shot through her: it was good to feel strong again, and not have to depend on others for her freedom once more. Instead, she was now free to be – and do – as she wanted, and that's exactly what she intended on doing.

She resolved then and there that neither Darius nor Jared were going to box her in. She had always been a free thinker and wasn't about to change now – or ever. She needed to find her own way once more in the world, and this time she would not mess up. She swore as much, to herself. Fritzi decided that it was time to look after Fritzi. After all, she had spent her entire life trying to look after others, and for the wrong reasons. Now she had to find out exactly who Fritzi was, and what she could achieve on her own. Yes, she was free; there were no limitations standing in her way any longer, only herself.

Maggie was puttering about in the kitchen baking was one of Maggie's many ways of relaxing, when Fritzi walked in. She could immediately tell by Fritzi's manner and sing song German dialect she used, when either excited, or worried that something was up. 'Everything alright?' she asked.

'I suppose,' Fritzi said slowly, looking around the room as though it was her first time there. 'Well, not really, actually … I just told Darius that I wasn't the marrying kind, not the right girl for him.' She repeated the words with a sense of disbelief.

Maggie felt she didn't need to ask, but did in any case. 'How did that go down?'

'Well, to be honest,' Fritzi said, 'I was a bit too strident in my delivery. With hindsight, I could have been less honest about my thoughts.' No matter how much soul-searching and self-analysis she had done in recent days, it still hurt to criticise herself so bluntly.

'What's done is done,' Maggie said firmly.

'I guess,' Fritzi said, less decisively.

'Jared called, by the way,' Maggie said while drying her hands on a dishtowel, the dough for her bread put aside to proof 'and left a message about the invitation to the New Year's party. We have to be at the Prime Minister's residence at 10 pm.'

The two friends sat in the kitchen chatting. Fritzi realised that it was going to be a long day until she saw Jared tonight. Now feeling less confident, she wondered whether Darius would be going to the party, too. Fritzi and Darius had a dinner arrangement with some of his friends beforehand – but those plans long predated their most recent conversation. Now she wondered whether he would keep their dinner date. She decided that she would just have to wait and see.

Maggie, on the other hand, was spending a quiet evening with Hubert at his home – at least until they departed for the party at the Prime Minister's residence. As a result of her uncertainty about tonight's plans, Fritzi did not know what to do before leaving for the party. To be on the safe side, she dressed for the evening. This way, if Darius called as arranged, she would be ready. Otherwise, she would make her own way to the party. After all, her name was on the list, she hoped, at least.

At seven-thirty, after what seemed like an interminable day, Maggie's doorbell rang its little tune. Fritzi was just putting the finishing touches to her makeup. Making her way to answer the door, she checked her outfit in the hall mirror before opening the door. Formal do's were never easy, she reflected as she fiddled with the door handle. She found long dresses restrictive at the best of times, and so opted for a palazzo black crepe catsuit, the front of which had a love V bandage over her chest that criss-crossed down to her waist at the back. It showed off her slim waist to perfection. She wore her hair in a messy updo, with large droop pearls hanging from her ears. To finish the look she chose her black Chanel evening bag with a pearl chain handle.

Peeping through the side window she was relieved to see Darius holding a bunch of flowers and looking dashing in a navy tux and waistcoat. His trousers, to her surprise, were dark navy slim-cut jeans, and instead of shoes he had on black patent leather cowboy boots, which gave him an extra few inches of height. He looked suddenly so elegant, he almost took her breath away.

Kissing him on the cheek, she said, 'Hi! You look incredibly handsome tonight. I like the dark navy jeans instead of the usual trousers – nice touch.'

'Pleased you approve,' he said, before taking a step backwards and admiring her in turn. 'What you're wearing is pretty daring.'

'Too daring?'

'On anyone else it would be,' he said softly, thoughtfully, 'but you have the height and the figure to carry it off demurely – so no, not on you.' Approaching her again, he said, still softly, gesturing to the flowers, 'These are for Maggie, by the way. Has she already left?'

'Yes,' she said, trying not to sound disappointed that the flowers were not for her, 'she is dining with Hubert de Jong before the party.' Gazing at him again, her voice as soft as his, she said, 'Darius, how are we now: still lovers or just friends?'

'Why don't we take some time and see how things pan out,' he said, 'give each other space before we make any fast decisions. That okay with you?'

'Yes, perfect,' she murmured, still struck by his handsomeness. 'As long as you know, Darius, that you are my dearest lover and friend. I want and need you in my life: as a friend, if not a lover.'

Darius did not like it, but he understood Fritzi: she did not hide her intentions; instead, she was always straight to the point, honest above all else when it came to her relationships. Germanic in her delivery, he guessed, which made everything sound, harsher than it was.

Feeling awkward for a moment, but mesmerised by her once again, Darius surprised himself by saying, 'Fritzi, I am at your service any way you want me – especially when you look as devastatingly beautiful as you do tonight.'

'Ag, that's your Aussie sense of humour again. Should we go?'

The Uber dropped them at the hotel where they were dining with Darius's friends. As they rode the lift to the revolving restaurant on the top floor, Darius stepped closer to her and put his hand over her breast. His thumb pressed her nipple as he leaned in to kiss her. It all happened very fast, his tongue finding the tip of hers, a hot shiver shooting through her.

'Just to remind you what a good lover I am,' he said slyly, in her ear.

Too weak to answer, she held onto his hand as they walked out of the lift to the sounds of loud thumping music and a buzzing crowd at the bar outside the restaurant that overlooked the city lights below. The receptionist in a short black bodicon dress caught her eye as her hips swung seductively as she stepped from behind the desk, the waiter a pretty blonde boy in his long back apron equally pleasing to the eye, showed them to their table, where several people were already seated, their party mood in full swing, with champagne glasses being refilled for jovial new year toasts, all Fritzi could think of was making love to Darius. He had completely taken her by surprise and it had done the trick; she was panting for him to finish what he had started.

Before the coffees arrived, she upped and made for the ladies' room, hoping Darius would follow. It would be like having mile-high sex up here on the top floor, looking down over the city below. If he did not follow her, she would just have to satisfy herself – or go mad until he gave into her needs.

She was fixing her lipstick in the mirror with one eye on the door of the unisex toilets when the door pushed open. She was exhilarated when Darius entered the room. The full-length wooden toilet doors behind her were mostly empty and she watched as Darius opened the door directly behind her. As he stood on the threshold he turned and they locked eyes in the mirror.

She did not waste time, locking the door behind them. Not a word passed between them. He unzipped her jumpsuit and it fell to the floor. She was buck naked apart from her thong. Both satisfied, they slumped onto the toilet seat: Fritzi on Darius's lap, her arms around his neck as she straddled him, kissing his ear softly.

'If we can do that again – and again and again – I will be yours forever,' she murmured. 'I love the naughty you, mein shatz.'

Sexual chemistry was one thing, but reality was another.

Back at the table they found everyone had left for the bar outside. Remaining to finish their coffee, they found they had a lot to talk about before leaving for the party. Things had changed between them once more. Darius felt he was back in charge, and he liked it. But he also knew that nothing lasted for long with Fritzi nothing; she always turned the tables. Maybe that's what he liked: she kept him on his toes, he was never bored. Still, he knew she was right: she was not the marrying kind, eventually they would both move on. He saw no other future for them.

Chapter 29

The car snaked up the long drive to the prime minister's Sydney residence. Valets dressed in khaki chinos and white T-shirts with sports logos were hired to park the cars, while the seemingly endless stream of taxis, were told to drop off and leave to keep the traffic flowing. It was a hot balmy night and the guests followed the fire torches round the property to the gardens at the back.

Festive tables were spread out on the lawns leading to the lake. A six-piece band playing popular ballads was set up on a stage with a circular dance floor close by. Fritzi and Darius stood on the perimeter, taking in the well-organised yet somehow simultaneously chaotic-seeming scene of guests numbering more than four hundred. The designated table numbers were printed on the invitations, as were instructions on how to find one's table. Everything had been carefully and meticulously coordinated; but not everything was ideal.

'It seems we have been separated?' Fritzi exclaimed, but felt a sense of excitement, she was always up for something that brought new possibilities and adventure. Darius checked his ticket to see his table number.

'Our tables must be very close to each other,' he said, 'this party has been worked out with military precision.'

Just then, as though she had been listening in on their conversation, a smartly dressed young hostess emerged beside them and said, 'Hi! May I guide you to your tables. I am here to help.'

Darius and Fritzi followed her to their respective festive tables, covered with floor length white table clothes, wine glasses and different coloured crackers, strewn amongst the baskets of bread rolls and central candle settings. Fritzi found she was seated with Missy and Jared, while Darius had been seated three tables away. From the way he greeted his tablemates, he obviously knew some of them. She was hoping he would return to her side, but noticed he was happily chatting to very pretty girls seated on either side to him, and thought of the old proverb 'what's good for the goose is good for the gander'

Missy did not waste any time in introducing Fritzi to those at her table: she was the only stranger amongst them; the others had been friends for years, some going back as far as school.

'Wow, Fritzi, you always wear something individual,' Missy said. 'I love your catsuit, it's divine. I am in a long dress as usual – so boring.' She gestured at her dress, which was anything but boring, and made a face. Fritzi was about to tell her that her dress was not boring at all, but Missy was talking. 'By, the way, even though Jared is at our table, I doubt whether we will be seeing much of him this evening.' She made another face, but this one was more, wry than the previous one. 'He usually socialises by table-hopping, to make sure everyone's being looked after – you know how attentive he is – so if Darius wants to take his seat, I am sure Jared won't mind.'

They both looked towards Darius's table and laughed.

'I guess he is otherwise occupied with those on either side of him,' Missy said. 'Do you know who they are, Fritzi?'

Fritzi shook her head, looking at one of them, a petite blonde with soft features and a wide smile. 'I don't have a clue. Why? Who are they?'

'Minor celebrities out there in the big wide world, I suppose, but here in Australia they are huge,' Missy said in a voice that was amused but nonetheless impressed.

Missy's husband, John, was in deep conversation with a woman seated next to him. Fritzi quickly realised that she, Fritzi, was the topic of conversation; the woman's eyes did not leave Fritzi for one moment while they were chatting.

'I guess everyone wants to know your back story,' Missy whispered to Fritzi in her urbane-yet-amused voice. 'Don't worry, John won't let you down. He's sure to paint a highly colourful Eurotrash celebrity status of you.'

Fritzi tried to get into the swing of Missy's mischief-making, but found her mood had darkened somewhat after seeing Darius so taken with the two women at his table; he hadn't even given her a second glance all evening.

Long buffet tables were groaning with food from all the different corners and cultures in Australia. She noticed sushi chefs, and Greek and Italian chefs, amongst others set round the perimeter.

Maggie and Hubert were moving along the desert table, standing so close together even someone unfamiliar with one or both of them could tell they were a couple. Fritzi went over to chat, fearing that, once they were seated amid the mass of people, she might not get to see them again that night. Fritzi, who had not formally met Hubert, was dying to talk to Maggie's beau, Hubert dressed for the party in a formal tux, did Maggie proud, he was Fritzi thought a perfect match her friend, tall, slim and elegant, age sat well on his rugged lined face, his white hair and closely shaved beard added to his masterful persona as he leaned in to speak in a surprisingly cultured British accent, that suited someone who was comfortable in their skin, charming in a quiet way.

'It's a pleasure to meet you in person, Fritzi,' Hubert said in a surprisingly soft, but earnest and educated voice, one that was nonetheless amiable and alive. 'I did not get the chance at the Christmas party.'

But it appeared that they would not get the chance now, for just then the band picked up its tempo and it became impossible to chat.

As Fritzi was about to give up on any pretence of a conversation and attempt to negotiate her way back to her table, Darius appeared at her side from out of nowhere and swept her off to the dance floor.

In no time at all what had started as a slow dance felt more like a nightclub shuffle, with bodies bumping up against one another, sometimes annoyingly, other times quite erotically and in a manner that was anything but unpleasant. But a little of this went a long way (Fritzi was no longer the youngster, craving excitement, full of energy and enthusiasm, that she had been back at the clubs in Berlin all those years ago; in fact, she was older than she was willing to admit, certainly not a spring chicken anymore), and after a couple of minutes or a couple of songs (she wasn't sure which), feeling claustrophobic and hot, she and Darius left for the lake, where others had begun to dance away from the main area, not far from the dance floor, fire torches were burning around the lake to ward off the mozzies. Shoes were kicked off to prevent tripping on the paving stones, a hazard with high heels. The party guests were a mixture of foreign dignitaries, politicians, and a healthy smattering of celebrities, all partying amongst friends and family, giving the evening a happy-go-lucky, relaxed atmosphere.

When the music eventually stopped, everyone took the hint and returned to their tables. The MC, an actor Fritzi did not know, made a short amusing welcome speech that went above her head, but she could tell by the laughter that whatever he said went down well when introducing a number of live acts. Jared returned to take his seat next to Fritzi, who was happy to have his attention – if only for a while. She noticed with relief that Mary, his date from the office party, was not amongst those at their table.

Smiling questioningly, mischievously, she asked, 'Mary otherwise engaged tonight?'

'Past tense,' he said in an equally amused manner, and then added, in a flatter tone, 'no longer an issue.'

She leaned to whisper in his ear, winking as she said, 'I can't say I'm sorry. Maybe there is a chance for me now that I am no longer your client.'

'Stop teasing, Fritzi,' Jared said, but you could hear from his tone that he was not sure that she was, in fact, teasing. Was she? In response she smiled warmly, but as their eyes met a fission passed between them; it was unmistakable, they both felt it.

'Where's Darius,' Jared said quickly. 'I thought you had made up?'

'Oh, we have,' she said, and he wondered if she was teasing still.

Jared was about to answer when the cabaret section of the evening started. The featured performer was none other than the nymph of the moment, the gorgeous Kylie Minogue, being at her most sexy, doing numbers from her 'Aphrodite' tour in an incredible skimpy feathered vaudeville costume, and with a full accompaniment of barely dressed male dancers.

That's when Fritzi realised the identity of the woman who had been seated next to Darius when Missy had been teasing her earlier in the evening. It was none other than Aphrodite herself, Australia's sweetheart, known countrywide by her first-name alone: Kylie!

Three more acts followed, wowing all the guests, and giving no opportunity for further conversation. Just as the dancing finally, breathlessly resumed, Jared was called away, leaving Fritzi feeling frustrated.

The other female who had been seated next to Darius, the one who had been at his left, a leggy brunette, was now – Fritzi noted with dismay and a surge of something akin to anger – wrapped around him, swaying to some slow music by Van Morrison's Brown Eyed Girl near the lake.

Fritzi took it all in: a dispiritingly romantic scene with the torches burning around the perimeter. Left alone at their table while everyone else headed back towards the lake to sway to some very hot blues music, and feeling for the first time in a long while like she was on the outside looking in, a not unfamiliar but nonetheless unwelcome feeling, Fritzi was relieved not have to wait long before, a lanky, blonde, hot young stranger swept her off to dance. Darius and Jared were dancing with the nymphs who had been seated at Darius's table; they were, Fritzi noted, giving their undivided attention to the girls.

Turnabout was fair play, and Fritzi could play this game as well as anyone, so she did the same with her new partner in crime on the dance floor, who appeared to already be completely infatuated by her. Indeed, she did not discourage him when he became a little too amorous. This tried-and-tested feint had its desired effect; ever since her partner and her began to dance in a more intimate manner, neither Darius nor Jared had taken their eyes off her for one second (no doubt to the increasing consternation of their dance partners). Still, neither man came to claim her as their partner; they were, it appeared, at an impasse. Then Darius turned his back on her manoeuvring, moving further away from her. Fritzi was not sure why he was ignoring her, but she was going to find out.

When the music stopped, her youthful, handsome dance partner was abducted by his approving, yet amused mates, and, others headed for the groaning desert table and drinks area, while the stage was, being prepared for the last act before the night's main event, the countdown to the new year, began. Fritzi did not want to be left without her friends when the new year came in and the festivities reached a crescendo.

She suddenly realised how important her Australian friends had become to her wellbeing – they had, after all, saved her life, perhaps literally, and some had done so more than once – without them she would be lost, alone, and in a much darker place. Ever resilient and quick on her feet, she was not averse to making new contacts; she understood her need to move forward, to be self-sufficient, in control of her own life – and yet she was not quite ready to do this, not yet. Interestingly, her newfound freedoms had brought with them certain insecurities she had never suffered from in the past. Having found warmth and friendship in Australia, she now understood that her past existence had been one of isolation. This had been mostly due to her instincts for survival, to seal both herself and those close to her off from the world, years of both flight and fight and, her need for personal safety.

Fritzi walked over to Darius's table, to spy on his advancement (or, hopefully, lack thereof) with, the brunette. Surprised (and, in fact, delighted) to find the seat next to him free, she sat down. But her elation was short-lived when she noted his downcast, almost hostile, expression. He was biting his lower lip, and when he saw her he looked down at the table, as though studying something on his plate, though his plate was in fact empty and his face was full of hurt. 'Darius, what's the matter?'

He turned in his seat towards her and his gaze slowly travelled up to her eyes. But the expression of hurt was still on his face, and his voice was grave when he said, 'I have realised I no longer want to be part of the games you like to play.'

She sat quietly for some time, shocked by his quiet outburst, fiddling with the unopened cracker at her table.

'I love you, Darius,' she said, 'you know this, but I am who I am.' Now it was Fritzi who found herself looking at the table, at the cracker, at the ground. 'It is hard to change the habits of a lifetime,' she said meekly. Then, realising that this explanation perhaps let herself off the hook a little too easily, she continued, 'All the same, I realise my previous lifestyle did not bring me happiness.' She made eye contact with him again. She felt stronger now, felt that this explanation was, in fact, the beginning of something solid, something altogether more helpful and constructive. 'In my previous life I was, above all, lonely – independent, fiercely so, but without love in my life. Now I have love and friendship, and I am altogether happier and more fulfilled. I do not want to lose either. I like this life much better.'

'Then don't abuse them, Fritzi.'

'Is that what you think I am doing?'

'Perhaps you see kindness as a form of weakness,' Darius said slowly. 'Friendship to you is perhaps something to take advantage of, and sex is a battle for superiority?'

'Are you talking like this because of what I suggested at your place, about my having two lovers?'

'Maybe yes,' he said and smiled, but in a flat, affectless manner. It was a cold, almost cruel, smile. 'I am, as you pointed out, conservative in that way.' He softened slightly and said, 'But neither of us may be at fault. After all, you are, as you also quite rightly pointed out, not the right girl for me.'

'But I would never give up on us as close friends, Darius. Never.'

'What happened tonight at the restaurant did not feel like friendship to me, Fritzi.'

'It was great sex,' Fritzi said, keeping her voice low, level, 'wonderful sex. Sometimes one has to play games to create the right climate for such sex.'

'And what comes next, Fritzi? You move on to do the same with Jared? The same games only with different people? Or different games only with the same result? And who gets hurt at the end of it all? Not you, Fritzi, but perhaps everyone else. And who benefits, really? In the long-term, I mean. You might think you do, but do you, really?'

Suddenly, finally, she saw it his way. She had been, and was continuing to be, utterly selfish, and to the very people who had been so selfless to her, who had put her, time and time again, above themselves. Was she not capable of treating them in kind?

Instead, she had abused his kindness and his feelings for her; she had taken him for granted, played with his emotions, walked all over him. And why? For what ends? Except for his excursion to New York, and his relationship with the Rubicovs, he had been nothing but loving to her. Was this why she had toyed with him, as a form of revenge for his indiscretions? No, she had mistreated him long before he ever travelled to New York. He had been looking into her life ever since they met in Bali, and perhaps he had been driven to do so because of her misdeeds, her manipulation, her multiple lies. And, also because – it could not be denied – he was enormously attracted to her. He loved her.

Seeing the whole picture all at once, she realised she deserved his scorn. Still, she wondered if there wasn't a double standard at work. After all, she was doing nothing a guy wouldn't do given half the chance. But she stopped herself, realising she was trying to let herself off the hook once again. She had to accept his charges and face up to his accusations head-on. She was long past shifting blame or changing the conversation.

'I am sorry, Darius, you are right, I will stop these games. I should know better.' She gave him a hard stare and said, 'Maybe we are even now?'

'Even how?'

'You took advantage of my vulnerability when you went poking around in my life, befriending the Rubicovs.'

Darius was about to challenge her when the band started up once more. Jared had returned to the table to claim her for the next dance before the New Year's countdown began. For a moment Fritzi was at a complete loss, it was a tense moment after her discussion with Darius and, she did not want to add to his already bruised ego. She reached out her hand for Darius. 'Let's all see the New Year in together' she suggested. 'It would mean the world to me.'

Darius hesitated, clearly uneasy. Then he smiled thinly and managed to overcome his initial reluctance, as Missy and Maggie beckoned for the two of them to join their group of revellers near the lake to see in the new year together. Relieved, she held all her friends close as they gathered in a circle to see the year out; indeed – for Fritzi, at least – it had been one hell of a year. And it was a year she would never have got through if it wasn't for these precious people with whom she was at this very moment singing Auld Lange Syne.

They partied well into the early hours. Fritzi felt put out at Darius calling out her bohemian behaviour earlier in their discussion, after all isn't that what had attracted him in the first place and, she was determined not to let his prudish hurt spoil their relationship, now was the opportunity to get him to forgive her, loosen up a bit, before their friendship became strained and, beyond repair, the magical atmosphere and affect the arrival of the new year had on everyone around them brought a light-heartedness and enjoyment no one could ignore.

And so, Fritzi and Darius kissed and made up once more; this kind of thing, rinse-repeat-rinse, was fast becoming a pattern in their relationship, and one she didn't much care for, she hoped with time he would accept the Fritzi he wanted, without having to possess her exclusively.

New Year's wishes over with to all of his friends in attendance, Jared had disappeared into the distance to wish his parents. Heading home, Maggie and Hubert offered her a ride – which Fritzi welcomed, wanting to avoid any further awkwardness with Darius. She had had enough of their games for a while – perhaps their new year's resolution could be to stop playing games altogether. She needn't have worried, though, for Darius was strolling off towards the dance floor, arm-in-arm with the blonde nymph and her sister, who were making their way to the mic to serenade the stragglers still partying into the small hours.

Fritzi woke to the sound of her cell phone buzzing on her side table. Opening the phone, she heard a familiar voice on the other end of the line. 'Happy New Year again,' the voice said warmly, 'and welcome to your new country and home. How about we celebrate just the two of us today, on my boat? Do you fancy that – or are you otherwise occupied?'

'Jared hi!' Fritzi said, and her happiness at hearing his voice, this wonderful surprise to wake up to, was evident in her tone. 'No, I have no arrangements as yet, so that would be perfect.'

'Can you get to me for noon?' he asked.

Choosing a pair of skinny white ripped jeans a navy and white stiped T-shirt, white canvas boating shoes, she threw a hat and one-piece bathing suit into her straw bag and closed the door behind her. Maggie had not come home from Hubert, so Fritzi left a note on the entrance table for her.

The taxi stopped on the street below Jared's driveway, and she made her way to his front door; finding it on the latch, she walked inside, announcing herself loudly. But no answer came back. Dropping her bag on the entrance table, she did a tour of the house. She knew the house well, of course, but today, the first day in a new year, felt fresh and full of possibility. A day to encounter new adventures in old places. Standing at the library window with the view onto the terraces below, she saw Jared pulling himself out of his swimming pool. She had never seen him in a bathing suit, and was admiring his broad-shouldered, narrow-waisted physique when he caught sight of her at the window. Waving, he made his way up the steps towards the house, the towel draped around his neck.

Fritzi suddenly felt like an awkward young girl, all nerves, not knowing how to treat Jared now that she was no longer his client. She found it easy to tease and flirt with him in the company of others, but now they were on their own; no one else was around. He walked through the side door, his hair still damp from his swim. They stood staring at one another for a few seconds, then moved towards each other at the same time. There was no need for words; both knew what would come next.

In bed, Jared was everything that she had hoped. He was not afraid of letting go, and Fritzi enjoyed his teasing. In fact, she willingly encouraged his devious sexual games with a few of her own, for good measure. They were well matched. He tied her hands to the bedpost as he stood above her, squirting whipped cream all over her body. Then he began licking from her toes to her tongue, with which she licked him in turn. As he untied the ribbons they found their rhythm, completely lost in their desire for one another.

The day flew by as they ate, made love, and ate some more. The boat remained moored at the jetty – it would have to wait for another time.

'Well, I know who will be overjoyed about us.' Fritzi murmured to Jared, one arm around his waist, as they lay together in bed.

'Who?' he asked, his voice teasing, probing, as he traced his fingers across her back, ready to write a name with an invisible pencil.

'Maggie.'

'I know who won't be overjoyed about us,' he said, still teasing, but his voice slightly graver than it had been a moment before. He turned and kissed her on the mouth before she could speak.

Neither needed to say 'Darius,' however; they both knew who Jared was referring to.

'Maybe yes and maybe no,' Fritzi said softly, slowly, surprising him with her response.

'What do you mean?' he asked.

'Well, I am not for Darius,' she said, and kissed him tenderly, too. 'I do love him, Jared, but we would be so wrong for one another.'

'How could you know that?' he asked.

She told him about the Christmas lunch at Darius' mother's house, and how she realised his family were everything to him, and, by extension, she could not, would not, be a part of a large portion of his life. The wives of Darius' brothers were all Italian: they belonged in the family circle; Fritzi did not. The wives knew this implicitly at that moment at the party, as did she; 'It was so obvious to all of us what – or who – Darius needed,' Fritzi told Jared, 'But he could not see it.'

'Wow, that's pretty profound,' Jared said. 'Did you tell any of this to Darius?'

'I tried, but it came out all wrong, of course, and he wasn't having it. He asked me to leave – which I did. Then we made up again, on New Year's Eve. But by the end of the evening, we weren't on the best of terms any longer. I have no idea how this will play out. It worries me; he means so much to me, but we are not meant for each other.'

Jared's face had a serious expression, but he smoothed down her hair, kissed her cheek, breathed deeply, then checked his watch and said, 'It's after six o'clock – let's get some fresh air.' Before she knew he was on his feet and gazing out of his bedroom window, still stark naked. She admired his body once again and the ease with which he moved. 'It's a stunning evening, the boat's ready to take out; we can laze along the bay until we find a place to stop off for dinner. And before you ask you look great in anything – and nothing,' he said, glancing down at her.

Fritzi laughed; she felt happier than she had in a very long time. Things felt so right with Jared; she hoped he felt it, too.

Maggie could tell Fritzi was displaying characteristics that Maggie had not seen in Fritzi – or at least had not seen in Fritzi for a very long time. She was light-hearted, even humming to the music on the radio as she helped Maggie tidy up after breakfast.

It was Maggie's first day back at work, and Fritzi was flying down to Byron Bay to tie up some loose ends as she had decided to make a permanent move back to Sydney. Byron Bay was too small for her now that she could live the life she intended. She had every intention of finding her way back into some kind of work relating to her past experience with the arts and, Sydney and, her contacts here would go a long way in her achieving that goal.

Erika had suggested they book for their trip to Berlin towards the end of winter, when the German weather improved and she had a spring break. To Fritzi's surprise (and delight), Maggie had decided to spend a couple of days with them in Berlin, after which she would join Hubert in Paris for a romantic long weekend.

While down in Byron Bay, packing her belongings and cleaning her soon-to-be ex-apartment, Fritzi received a message from Darius on her cell phone. The two of them had not spoken since that fateful New Year's party, and she found herself wondering whether he had got wind about her and Jared – not that there was any major change in their fledgling (but, right now, very special, blissful, and also, right now, wholly uncertain) relationship. When she left for Byron Bay, she and Jared had left what they had – whatever it was – hanging.

They both wanted, and felt they needed, some space to recharge their batteries, and to get a clearer perspective on how exactly (if at all) they were going to carry this forward. For those reasons, if she was honest with herself, she doubted Darius knew any more about her and Jared than she did. Still, opening his text, her apartment in a disarray of empty boxes, clothing, kitchen implements, and brown paper bags from various shops, she was surprised to find he wasn't in the country at all. The message read:

'Hi! Just in case you were wondering why you have not heard from me, I am in Hong Kong. Something has come up at work that needed my attention – not sure how long for, but will be in touch.'

This was followed by a kiss emoji, the significance of which she couldn't quite work out and wasn't sure whether to even bother trying. Instead, she responded,

'Oh okay. I am in Byron Bay, tying up some loose ends before I make a permanent move back to Sydney. We'll catch up when you get back.' She keyed in the hug emoji and concluded with 'F xx'.

After she sent the message, she shuddered suddenly, dreading Darius' reaction when he heard that her relationship with Jared had moved to a different level. Indeed, her relationship with Darius seemed to consist of one step forward and two steps back, over and over, month after month. And she had grown tired of it. Had he? She imagined the answer was yes.

Besides, in many ways, as a person, she had grown. For example, never before in an about-to-end relationship had she had second thoughts about moving on. In the past, she had simply done what pleased her, and if anyone had instructed her otherwise, she would have disregarded their advice – or worse, tell them to shove it.

The one exception was her relationship with Yvetta, which had ended in a kind of devastating (and, for at least one person close to them, near-fatal) roller coaster ride, a cataclysmic moment from which it had been very difficult to come back. The whole sordid, tragic escapade had resulted in many humiliating, tough experiences – and serious consequences – for them both. She knew she would never forget any of this; or, really, live it down. That was why moving to Australia, and a complete change of climate, temperament, character even, had been not just advisable but absolutely necessary if she was to continue to feel free.

She had spent her time here, mending bridges with her past but that past was with her, was who she was, the new Fritzi was because of her past and, she wanted to remember the old as well as the new, they were not exclusive to who she would become and, a future without her past she knew would never work they had to exist side by side. She was lucky to have escaped with her life: not once, but twice. Mika had allowed her to go free. Interpol, which was a lot less forgiving than Mika, had eventually caught up with her smuggling activities.

Her five years in jail had been anything but a walk in the park. If it had not been for the underground contacts she had forged during her smuggling years, she would still be rotting in a Russian gulag. Money and who you knew were everything in a corrupt society like Russia – and Fritzi had both. On the other hand, her two years in an American jail hadn't been so bad; even then her contacts had come through for her. Her American contacts were interconnected with the same international criminal syndicate, beyond reach in its layers of complexity to authorities.

Not even the insurance fraud law enforcement agencies had been able to crack their codes.

With her back against the wall, and the threat of a life in prison looming, Fritzi had given the agencies information; The Antiquities smuggling ring had existed through the ages longer than anyone could imagine. She doubted anyone would scratch the surface; the secrets were deeply embedded into its history like some ancient religion, that moved with each era it lived through. They activated minor players like her through many different contacts, codes and layers. She had been wiped from their database and was no longer involved in their organisation in any way.

She was dead to them – or, rather, she had never existed at all. She was a ghost, invisible, free to start fresh, which was exactly the way she wanted it. It had been her first escape from certain death. To whom she owed her life to in the syndicate she would never know. Mika calling off his men had been her second escape from certain death. His Russian contacts would have tracked her down eventually, eliminating her.

Luck had been kind to her, if 'luck' was the right word. She had found people who believed in her – in Bali, in Australia, and elsewhere – the strange thing was that she no longer found those people useful. On the contrary, she found they had saved her from herself, enabling her to come to terms with her past. Finding Erika, and re-establishing ties with her oldest friend, had released her from her dark side into the light. Because of the empathy of these people, she had found her own cynicism in human nature fading.

When she seduced Darius in Bali, her purpose had been to use him to get to Australia – but he had turned the tables on her. When she found he had copied her passport, and would find out some of her past: things she wanted no one, least of all him to know, but Darius's kindness, empathy, and altruism after discovering the truth about her past had saved her – and had set her on the road to freedom.

She owed him a great deal, more than he realised. Involving Jared, was a stroke of genius and luck but Darius had played into her hands when she had seen him at that restaurant on Bondi Beach, shortly after her arrival in Australia; she knew he would follow her, and was prepared to take that chance. And so, this time, she turned the tables on him. It had paid off handsomely. After discovering Darius had sent that messenger to warn her off remaining in Bali, she knew he was a safe bet, a decent person, he would not purposely harm her.

Nor would it, take Darius long to figure out she had saved Jared in Christchurch during the earthquake. After reading about the rescue in the papers, he would put two and two together. It turned out that saving Jared's life had been a stroke of good luck; it was a safe bet that both Jared and Darius, with a little extra push in the right direction, could move mountains to help her get what she needed.

They had fallen into her lap, so to speak, and thus her ability to manipulate matters to advance her cause had been relatively easy. They were amateurs in her world of duplicity and deception; she had many years of experience in strategic planning, but it was time to throw in the towel. She had achieved a great deal and a chance at a new life, one that would bring with it, power and, acceptance. Jared would be a useful person to cultivate to achieve what she wanted, she knew that now. Above all else, she was loyal to those she loved and respected; they would all be beneficiaries when her plans for the future materialised.

Yvonne Spektor was born in South Africa but moved to the UK in the 1970s. The Royal Academy of Arts named her Woman Artist of the Year in 2002. She lives in London with her husband Ken and cockapoo Shandy.

Printed in Great Britain
by Amazon

26122689R00205